Mistaken Magic

AN ACCIDENTAL FAIRY TALE
BOOK ONE

A.H. HADLEY

SPOTTED HORSE PRODUCTIONS

Mistaken Magic is a work of fiction. Names, characters, places, brands, media, and incidents are either the product of the author's imagination or are used fictitiously. Any resemblance to actual events, locales, or persons, living or dead, is entirely coincidental.

Copyright © 2024 by A.H. Hadley

All Rights Reserved. In accordance with the U.S. Copyright Act of 1976, the scanning, uploading, and electronic sharing of any part of this book without the permission of the publisher and the copyright owner constitute unlawful piracy and theft of the author's intellectual property. Thank you for your support of the author's rights.

ISBN-13: 978-1-956455-79-3

Cover Art by DAZED designs (www.dazed-designs.com)

Edited by Sarah Williams

Dedication

There are many bad things out there in the dark. There are more hiding in the light. The "rules" try to tell us which are which, but don't listen.

Make up your own mind. Break a few rules. Learn how to be bad, because sometimes, that's the only way to be good.

Chapter One

There was a strange creaking coming from the back wheel. It didn't quite sound like it was going to fall off, but it fit the rest of this car, some twenty-year-old luxury thing that was so far past its prime, it had become a joke. I'd gotten pretty good at figuring out my latest foster family by the type of vehicle they drove to pick me up. In this case, it wasn't good.

The interior was covered in cracked and brittle leather. The headliner was loose and looked like someone had tried to glue it back up. Yet even though it was the middle of winter, the outside had been washed and waxed. I hadn't seen a single scratch before I got in, so I'd expected some kind of lovingly maintained classic car. What I got instead was pretty on the outside, rotten in the middle.

Everything about this car said the owners wanted to make a good impression without doing all the hard work. If they'd put half the effort on the inside of the car or the mechanics, it could've been a decent vehicle. Instead, it might look good, but the thing was ready to fall apart. I could only assume they treated everything else like this, including their foster kids.

But that was how it went, wasn't it? All people cared about were how things looked. Appearances, impressions, and opinions were the real currency this world ran on, and I'd learned that the hard way. With my history, if I wanted a chance, then I'd have to make sure I didn't make a single mistake this time - and I desperately wanted that chance.

So I sat there with my hands clasped in my lap, watching the patchwork of snow-dusted farmland pass outside the window. In the front seat, Mr. and Mrs. Sparks talked softly. I couldn't quite hear their words over the squeaking of the back wheel, but I had a feeling that was intentional. Mrs. Sparks was reassuring the mister about something - which was probably me. Not many people wanted a seventeen-year-old foster kid. That was how I'd ended up with them.

The Sparks' place wasn't exactly a group home, but it wasn't far off. My previous advocate had told me they had seven other foster kids: three boys and four girls. All of them were older, getting close to aging out. This was the last, desperate place for kids like me who didn't fit anywhere else. If I couldn't make it here, then I wouldn't be able to make it anywhere.

So right now, I was on my best behavior. Hopefully, it would be good enough to make these people happy, but I honestly had no clue what I was doing. According to my file, I just couldn't settle. I self-sabotaged. Yeah, and there were a few other phrases like that in there that all basically translated to me pissing off the people willing to take in a kid no one else wanted. It wasn't intentional, though!

But that was how I'd become the foster child who got bounced around every few months. With November just starting, I had a little under a year left of high school, and this move meant I hadn't spent a whole year at the same place since I'd been in the eighth grade. I was officially a rubber bouncy ball. Throw me at something, and I'd ping off it with miraculous agility, only to end up lost in the dust bunnies under the sofa.

God, I hated my life.

Yet, when the car pulled off the highway, I started to pay attention. Plainsboro, Iowa, was a new town for me. Google said it had a population of just under thirty thousand people, one high school, and one private college well outside town. No malls, no movie theaters, and the largest industry was agriculture. Go figure. Although, what I saw as we drove through it made me dare to hope.

The streets were quaint, but the square had some real businesses, including an old-fashioned ice cream parlor. At least two stores sold clothes. I saw one restaurant and a game store. Ok, so I hadn't jumped back into the dark ages; I'd just landed in podunk-middle-of-nowhere's-ville.

A few blocks further on, Mrs. Sparks tapped her window, raising her voice to me. "That's the high school you'll be attending next week, Lorraine. I'm friends with the principal, so we can get you into some good extracurricular activities. Sports, or maybe band?"

"I never learned how to play an instrument," I admitted, "and I'm pretty sure they require me to have been in a sport at my last school to get into one here."

"Then maybe debate," she said. "Kids your age need clubs to keep you engaged and out of trouble. You *will* participate in something, Lorraine. Either you can choose, or I will. We won't allow you to simply be a delinquent."

Yeah, and I'd always wanted to do those sorts of things, but I'd never had the chance. Every time I'd tried, I'd been told I should've started sooner. Since I had no experience, it was too late to join now. Because I wasn't part of the team, or group, or club, I couldn't simply jump in halfway through the semester. Rejection. Always rejection, and it sucked. But if this woman thought she could make it happen, then I sure wasn't going to stop her.

"I'm sure I can find something once I look at the options, ma'am," I said politely.

She turned in her seat to look at me. A frown flicked over her face before she turned back, but her tone was a warning. "Believe it or not, we know what we're doing, child. And we've got some more appropriate clothes for you, too."

Uh, there was something more appropriate than a blue cable-knit sweater and jeans? I thought I'd found something pretty unobtrusive. The first day with a new family, it was always a good idea to be boring. How much more boring could I get? Then again, my record made my choice of clothing moot.

So my only good option was to say nothing. Because while I was willing to bust my ass to prove myself, I still had limits. Too many times, I'd seen kids screw themselves over. Some were people pleasers, willing to do anything to make their latest foster parents happy. Unfortunately, enough foster parents were creeps, which made that a *bad* idea. The other half went the other way, fighting so hard against everything they ended up causing their own problems.

It was basically a no-win situation for us. Ok, and maybe I was bitter about it. I was also a realist. If I wanted to succeed in life, then I had to play the game. I needed to be a perfect little addendum to this family I'd been assigned. I had to get it *right* this time.

While I was silently feeling sorry for myself in the back seat, we pulled into my new "home." The house was an old two-story farmhouse sort of thing. It could've been adorable if it was kept up, but just like the car, it had been shined instead of loved. The exterior was painted a shocking shade of baby blue, yet the cracked and peeling paint from the last coat was visible. The handmade sign by the door that declared it as "home sweet home" leaned precariously, as if it had long ago been forgotten.

This place seemed to be on its last leg, but the paint was definitely fresh. Maybe last year's attempt to hide the decay? Never mind the obvious lack of cars either in the drive or parked by the curb. With so many kids my age or older, there should have been at least someone who could drive, right? The lack of vehicles made this place feel a bit like a prison.

At least it wasn't isolated. The entire street was filled with older homes like this. Most of them had vintage cars or trucks with obvious rust around the wheels. It looked like the sort of neighborhood a grandparent would live in, where time had done its best to stand still while the rest of the world continued to move on. I hated it on sight, knew that wasn't fair, and still couldn't stop myself.

Maybe that was just my resentment at my lot in life? I didn't know. What I did know was that over and over, I'd tried as hard as I could, and yet somehow, I still couldn't manage to be what people wanted. But this time, things were going to be different. I'd make sure of it.

Thankfully, it didn't take long to shuffle my things inside. My entire life consisted of a black suitcase - one wheel chipped so it didn't even roll properly anymore - and a nylon bag. I'd given up on anything cool. Something always got lost, usually whatever I loved the most, and the next family would have rules against anything I found fun. No laptop, no tablet, and not even a cell phone. All I had were a couple of old books no one could complain about and two weeks' worth of clothing. Then there was my bear.

Theo had been with me through all of this. I'd been five when the cop - also named Theo - had given him to me to keep me entertained while they waited for Child Protective Services. The bear had been cute enough I didn't remember a thing about them carrying out my dad's body. He'd caught my tears when they took my mom away to jail. Now, he was a little threadbare and worn, but that stuffed animal was the one thing I'd keep with me forever. He was basically the only family I had left, since my mom would be in prison for the rest of her life.

"Let's show you the room," Mrs. Sparks said, turning me to the stairs.

Her husband simply dropped my suitcase on the couch. When he started to unzip it, I turned back, but the wife kept tugging. Damn, I hated the first day in a new place. I never knew what was expected, but if I wanted to start off on the right foot, I'd follow.

With one last glance back, I let her lead me up the stairs and into what was little more than a storage closet plastered with store-bought art. Everything was a pale, sickly yellow. Piss yellow, if I had to name it. Not buttercup or even vanilla, just gross, like puke, but not even that pretty.

"Thanks," I said softly, trying my hardest to appreciate what I'd been given.

Mrs. Sparks beamed at me, bobbing her head like I'd just performed some sort of trick. "And in the closet, we have nice slacks and proper shirts for you."

When she pulled open the door, I wanted to cry. Pastel plaid - which should have been ok, and yet somehow wasn't. The tan khakis were worse, caught between mom pants and something just a little too business-casual. Then there were three pairs of canvas shoes. Not the cool kind, but the cheap white ones from Walmart.

These clothes were exactly the sort of thing that made bullies target kids! The last thing I needed was to get myself in trouble yet again, so I swallowed, trying to think before I said anything. That was what my favorite foster mom had taught me. Think first. Respect that people were trying. Damn, but it was easier said than done.

"I appreciate this, Mrs. Sparks," I tried, "but I have some clothes, and this isn't really my style. Maybe you can return them? It's a really nice gesture."

The woman's eyes narrowed slightly, but her plastic smile didn't falter. "Oh, no, honey. This is what you're going to wear to school. John and I believe kids like you need structure, and your generation doesn't understand that word. You *will* learn to dress modestly. You will make good grades at school. If you don't, the only place left for you is the state-run home, and none of us want that, right? So learn to follow the rules, young lady, and fast."

I nodded quickly. "I'll do my best, ma'am."

"Good. We attend church as a family on Sundays. You'll go to youth group on Wednesday evenings unless it conflicts with your extracurricular activity. Once a month, you'll volunteer to do some kind of community service. Every evening, you'll help with the household chores. Tonight, I'll put you on the schedule, which means you won't need to start that until tomorrow."

Again, I nodded. What else was I supposed to do? Thankfully, my easy acceptance seemed to mollify this woman. Smiling at me like I was simple, Mrs. Sparks took me back downstairs and into the living room. I followed, dying to see what the man of the house was doing with my things. Yet when I walked into the living room, I decided this whole "being nice" plan was over. The bastard was looking through all my clothes and putting most of them into a garbage bag!

"What the hell?" I snapped. "That's my stuff!"

He sighed before looking up. "These clothes are not suitable for a girl your age. You'll have to keep the underthings until Nancy can replace them." Then he held up a boring black long-sleeve. "But this? Are you trying to convince the boys you're easy? We will not be raising a child having a child here!"

"It's a shirt! It's not even low-cut. Are you insane?" But the shirt went into the bag. Before he could discard anything else, I reached past him and snagged Theo. "Let me guess, the bear's a problem, too, right?"

"That? No. Girls your age need comfort." His tone was dismissive instead of understanding.

My fingers dug into the matted fur, and I clung to my only friend while I seethed. "Then, while you decide if my slut-wear needs to go, I'll make sure I'm neither seen nor heard. So you know, I was *trying* to be nice!"

I turned back for my room and heard Mr. Sparks as I climbed up the stairs. "You see, Nancy? Rude and temperamental. No wonder no one else wanted her."

"John, we already agreed to this. Besides, she can't be as bad as those boys."

Great. Throwing myself onto the bed, I stared at the ceiling. I hadn't even done anything wrong yet and I was already in trouble? Four hours ago, my life had sucked. Now? Yeah, there was no love and understanding in this house. There was no feeling of welcome. All I'd gotten from these people was a list of rules and threats of punishment!

Mr. Sparks wanted to give me stability by changing everything I'd ever known. Mrs. Sparks wanted me to smile sweetly and prove to the world that she was such a good woman for taking in this hard-luck case. Neither of them were the kind of person I'd even bother to spit on, but I hadn't been given an option. I was here. I had nowhere else to go. I'd run out of options, so this was going to be my new life.

And if I wanted something better after I aged out of the system, then I needed to suck it up and deal with this. I had to find a way to be what they wanted. I *had* to get my shit together, because I could not fuck things up again. This was my last chance.

Was it so wrong to want a home? Friends? To be loved by someone? I didn't think so, but it sure felt like everyone else did. I was trying! Couldn't they see that? But before the tears could start flowing, I shut myself in my room, deciding I was done for the night. I'd reached my limit. Day one, and I already couldn't take any more.

For my entire life, I'd been judged by my mom's record and my bad luck. I'd been screwed over by coincidence and horrible timing. It was as if the harder I tried to succeed, the bigger I managed to fail. One day, I wanted to write my own damned story. One with a happy fucking ending.

Sadly, today was not going to be that day.

Chapter Two

That night, I heard the voices of the other kids as they tromped up and down the hall. No one spoke loudly, though. There was this hushed feeling that drove me crazy, as if the entire household was scared to laugh out loud. I didn't think much of it at first, but the next morning was the same way.

With seven kids in the house, there should've been a ruckus. Instead, the loudest noise was the hurrying of feet. I woke up, but since I didn't have to start school until next week, I didn't want to get in anyone's way - so I stayed in my room. Going through my things, I found a pair of jeans that hadn't been thrown out and a light sweater. There wasn't much left of what I'd brought with me, but I refused to wear the stuff in the closet. Partly because it was hideous. Mostly, it was just on principle.

Once I heard the bus stop outside the house, I knew it was safe to get up. Sure, it was early, but it wasn't like I'd be able to go back to sleep. Plus, since I'd missed dinner last night, my stomach was currently demanding breakfast. Making my way downstairs, I was thinking about checking out the neighborhood after I ate. Well, until I was spotted.

"I didn't expect to see you up so soon, Lorraine," Mrs. Sparks said. "The others just went to school."

"I heard, ma'am," I told her. "I'm a pretty light sleeper."

She simply pursed her lips as if that was something disgusting. "Well, I guess this means I can start showing you your daily responsibilities. Every evening, one of you kids is expected to make dinner. Someone else will set the table. Another will do dishes. There's also vacuuming, laundry, cleaning the bathrooms, and straightening the living areas. You're all responsible for keeping your own rooms clean, and yes, we will check."

I nodded. This was pretty standard stuff. "I understand, ma'am."

"With eight of you in the house now, we rotate, so you will get one day off from chores," she went on. "You will be expected to keep track of your duties, since the day of the week will change. Now, let me show you where the laundry room is, hm?"

"Actually," I tried, jerking my thumb to the back door, "I was kinda hoping I could see the neighborhood? I mean, to get an idea of where I live now? I thought I saw a park on our way in."

The expression on the woman's face changed. "No. You will not go to that park, nor will you socialize with the delinquents who frequent the place. They sell drugs, Lorraine. The last thing *you* need is another mark on your record, so I suggest you dedicate yourself to changing your attitude."

"What?" I gasped. "I don't have an attitude!"

She stabbed a finger in my direction. "That one. Oh, we were warned about you, young lady. You're a thief, a miscreant, and a bully. The only reason you weren't arrested for punching that boy is because you were leaving, so you wouldn't be a problem."

That boy? The one who'd grabbed my ass? The guy I'd told to keep his hands off me, and yet he'd still ignored me? All I'd done was stand up for myself!

"He assaulted me," I mumbled under my breath. "I'd warned him. I'd told the teachers. That 'boy' put his hands on me even after I said no!"

"That doesn't mean you had to hit him," she shot back. "There will be no fighting in this house. Try it once, and we will send you to the state."

I just dropped my head and sighed, knowing there was no way to win this. "I understand."

Then I allowed her to teach me all about my chores. So much for a week off from school. Instead, I was being made into slave labor. It wasn't so much that I hated the chores, but being locked inside? That felt off. It was almost as if this woman felt the less freedom we had, the more likely we'd give up, give in, and become meek little robots to do her bidding. Like she was trying to break us down or something.

I hated it. I wasn't being given a chance; I was being punished, and over the course of the morning, Mrs. Sparks made that very clear. Every little dig, jab, or reminder of my record came with another warning, and there were far too many. Not once did she ask my opinion - about anything. She simply told me how it would be. From laundry to my free time, it was all put on a schedule, and if I didn't stick to it, she made it clear I would go back to the state.

I pushed down my anger. I smothered my frustration. I could do this. I *had* to do this. I wasn't sure how, but it wasn't like I had any other option.

Eventually, the others came home from school, and I was given a little break to meet them. A list of names was thrown at me too fast for me to keep track of. People were pointed out. Then I was ordered to head upstairs and clean the main bathroom because that was my chore for the day.

I was on my knees, scrubbing the toilet, when Mr. Sparks stepped into the doorway. He didn't say a thing at first. The man simply loomed in the entrance, looking me over as if he was judging me. I glanced up and tried to smile, but that made his harsh face turn into a scowl.

"What are you doing?" he demanded.

"My chores," I replied.

"On your knees?"

I looked at the toilet, then back to him. "Yeah? She said I had to clean the base too."

"You look like you're vomiting. Stand up, girl. If you want to seem presentable, then you must act like it!"

He waited until I got to my feet, then stormed out. Weird. The whole thing was amazingly weird, and it was not helping my feelings about this house at all! Even worse, trying to bend over while scrubbing the outside of a toilet was murder on my legs. I had a feeling my ass would be sore tomorrow, and that was probably breaking another stupid rule: no aches and pains where they might inconvenience one of the Sparks.

When I was done, I put the cleaning supplies back under the sink. The cabinet banged as I closed it, making me wince. When feet moved toward the bathroom, I was braced for Mr. Sparks to come yell at me again. Instead, an older girl appeared in the doorway.

"Lorraine, right?" she asked.

I nodded. "Yeah, and I'm sorry, but I forgot your name."

"Stephanie," she said. "Word of advice, Mr. Sparks hates banging."

"Yeah," I breathed. "I didn't know it would do that."

She quickly waved me down. "The kitchen cabinets do the same. So does the washing machine. Any of them will get you a lecture."

"So, walk softly around here, huh?" I asked.

She nodded. "Very. I guess they had a few wild fosters who convinced them being strict is the only way to be. It sucks, but at least we know what to expect." Her smile made it clear that wasn't much consolation. "Oh, and I highly recommend sleeping in pants."

Alarm bells sounded in my head. "Why?" I asked.

"They come check on us in the middle of the night. No locks on the doors, no knocking to announce them. Gets real awkward at times, if you know what I mean. So, change by your closet and sleep with everything covered."

"Is he a creep?" I whispered.

She shrugged. "I think they both are. No clue what they're looking for, but they will check every night to make sure we're still in our rooms. The front door has a squeaky hinge, so it's not like we can just sneak out, but who knows what they think we're doing."

"Going out the window?" I suggested.

Stephanie scoffed. "There are bars on the windows. No going out that way either. Kinda why it's weird."

"Yeah." I leaned against the sink. "Anything else I need to know?"

"No kissing boys. At all," she said. "The guys are all on the first floor, but it doesn't matter. They're our brothers now, and that means off-limits. No cussing. No yelling. No running in the house. You know, the kind of rules a five-year-old should have. Right, and don't be late to dinner. Mrs. Sparks was pissed when you didn't come down last night. She was going to make you go without, except you kinda did that on your own."

"I fell asleep," I admitted.

"They don't care," she said, turning around and walking away. "The only thing that matters here are the rules. *Their* rules."

From the direction she turned, I could only guess she was going to her room. I hurried to follow, and sure enough, her door was the one on the other side of the bathroom. I assumed I'd eventually work out who went where, since neither of the Sparks had felt the need to tell me.

Even worse, I had no idea when dinnertime was. The best I could do was leave my door open, so when I heard everyone else head downstairs, I followed. I made it to the table, but when I grabbed the first chair, a boy shook his head at me. Then he pointed to one at the end. Evidently, that was my place.

Naturally, the ordeal was antiquated. There was a prayer, led by Stephanie. I got the impression we took turns with that too. Once she was done, the main dish was passed to Mr. Sparks. When he had enough, it made its way around the table, ending with me. Surprisingly, there was plenty left.

While we ate, Mr. Sparks talked to his wife about his day. No one else spoke. Mrs. Sparks nodded and asked questions, but we kids were clearly only here to be props. Still, kids will be kids, and the girls beside me were gesturing in their laps. Not sign language or anything, but it clearly meant something to them.

A few smiles were traded, but they were soft and subtle things, designed to not draw attention. Needless to say, more alarm bells were going off. This place had creepy written all over it in capital letters. So, when I went to bed that night, I took Stephanie's advice to heart. I put on a pair of sweats and a tank with a sports bra. If Mr. Sparks tried to put his hands on me, I'd be out the door and running for the state-run home as fast as possible.

The house got quiet. The others fell asleep. I was tense, my mind spinning, waiting for the worst, but sleep came first. I didn't even know when I drifted off, but the sound of my doorknob turning woke me up completely. I didn't jump. I made no move to sit up. In the darkness, I barely opened my eyes enough to see a shadowy form step into my room.

That was definitely Mr. Sparks. The man made his way in and walked a lap of the room. A few times he touched things on my dresser or shelves, then he paused to stand over me. I closed my eyes again, pretending to sleep, but I could still hear him. For a little too long, he watched me. I was about to pretend like I'd stirred when he finally turned around, his feet soft on the rug beside my bed, and headed back out.

I waited until the door closed before opening my eyes all the way and scanning my room. I tried to figure out what he'd touched. Over there was a picture frame with some cheap print of a sunset. I was pretty sure he'd checked it. On my shelf was a bookend, which looked homemade. Then, on the nightstand beside my bed, I found something new.

It was a little figurine made of metal. Curious, I reached over to pick it up, wondering if there was a nanny cam in it or something. Nothing. No cord, no hole for a camera. It was just a little statue of a dog, maybe a Scottish terrier, and small enough to fit in the palm of my hand.

Was this supposed to be some kind of gift? Talk about creepy! I had no idea what the man was doing, or why he'd think it was ok to just walk into my room in the middle of the night, but I wanted none of it.

Sadly, I didn't have any other options. This was my new life. Lucky me.

Chapter Three

The next morning was a repeat of the one before, mostly. The little dog was still on the table beside my bed. In the light, I could see it was black, like cast iron or something. Actually, it kinda reminded me of a Monopoly piece. Then there was the sound of birds outside, and the things were *loud*, cawing like they weren't happy.

Curious, I knelt on my bed to look out the window. Cheap blinds covered it, so I raised those, not shocked to see the metal bars screwed onto the outside. Maybe this was a high-crime area? Not really a comforting thought, but they didn't obstruct the view of the leafless trees in the backyard.

Black birds covered them, and not just any black birds. I was pretty sure they were crows. A whole murder of them, from the looks of it. Unable to help myself, I found one of the many silly trinkets in the room - a ribbon with a charm on the end that may have been a bookmark - then headed back to the window.

Cracking it open, I slipped the gift out so it hung on the bars. The ribbon should flutter enough so one of them would notice it, right? Maybe it was the morbid part of me, but I'd always thought crows were pretty cool birds. I'd once read an article about a girl who'd befriended them, and they were known to remember people who were kind to them. In one of my last homes, I'd actually made friends with a few.

Besides, if they crapped all over the Sparks' car, then even better.

Smiling to myself, I headed downstairs to start my daily list of chores. Stupid as it was, the crows had made the day a little better. Some foster kids dreamed they were really a long-lost fairy princess. Others hoped for a rich relative to appear out of the woodwork. I just liked the idea of not being alone in the world.

The crows were quickly forgotten when Mrs. Sparks went on her first tirade. Evidently Maria hadn't brought down her laundry yet. I was sent upstairs to get it. When I asked which room was hers - because I honestly could not put a face with that name - I got a lecture about paying more attention.

God, I already hated this place. A part of me wanted to call my caseworker and complain, but I knew it wouldn't get me anywhere. I hadn't been abused. I wasn't being molested. Thinking these people were weird was *not* a good enough reason to get moved out of here. In other words, I had to tough it out.

Eventually, Mrs. Sparks told me to make a sandwich for lunch. I took that as permission to take a break from the drudgery of cleaning, and slipped out back. The weather was cold, but the space from that woman made it worthwhile. Sitting on the back steps, I looked around, trying to get some idea of what kind of neighborhood this was.

I could hear a dog barking in the distance and a few cars on the roads around here, but that was pretty much it. Well, besides the crows. They cawed with all they had. Then one bravely flew down to land about ten feet away from me. It tilted its little black head, inspecting the newcomer.

"Hey, you," I said softly, peeling off a bit of my crust. "Hungry?"

Then I tossed the crumb halfway between us. The crow fluttered up, but didn't leave. Landing again, it hopped closer to inspect the crumb. The first time it pecked was a test, turning the scrap of bread over. Then it took the bite and flew off. Just to see if they were paying attention, I tossed out another bit of bread.

Sure enough, another crow came down to do the same thing. Well, I assumed it was another because it came from the opposite direction, but they all kinda looked the same. Then a second joined it, so I picked off one more piece. The moment I threw it toward them, the rest of the flock realized I was handing out food.

A dozen or more began to caw, and probably five flew down to beg. I kept pinching off little pieces and tossing them onto the ground, and they kept getting closer. Considering I didn't have a phone to distract me, and I was pretty sure I wasn't allowed to watch TV here, this was the best entertainment I'd had since I'd arrived. One more piece got swallowed, so I went to throw another.

Caw!

The crow was loud and looking right at me just as the back door opened. "Lorraine Brooks!" Mrs. Sparks screamed, sending the entire group of crows into the air. "What do you think you're doing?!"

"Uh, feeding bread to the birds?" Because I'd thought it was pretty obvious.

The woman's eyes narrowed, then she stormed over to grab my arm, yanking me onto my feet. "I told you to stay inside!"

"No, you didn't," I insisted. "I was just having lunch, and I've done all the stuff you told me to."

"Inside!" she snapped, pushing me that way like the boogeyman was about to get us both. "First vines and now crows? What is wrong with you kids?"

I had no idea what she was talking about, but I wasn't dumb enough to ask. I simply headed back in, finishing my sandwich in two bites. If today was going to be like yesterday, this was all I'd get until dinner, so I wanted to make it count. But once I was in the kitchen, the woman grabbed my arm, spinning me around to face her.

"I don't know what kind of tricks you think you're playing, but you should be grateful we're putting a roof over your head!"

I nodded, because my mouth was full of my sandwich.

So she stabbed a finger toward my face. "It's always the ones who can't stay in one place. No one wants you, Lorraine, so I'm your last hope. You stay away from the birds. You don't mess with the trees. You definitely don't bring any of it inside my house, do you hear me?"

"Mhm," I mumbled, nodding quickly.

But I was convinced this woman was wacko. Completely off the deep end type of mental problems. Clearly, she hadn't taken her meds this morning. Maybe that was what Mr. Sparks had been looking for in my room? Was someone getting high on her prescription drugs? If so, it wasn't me. I was doing my best to be a good girl, thank you very much.

Unfortunately, my little "mistake" with the birds meant I had to do extra chores as punishment. Armed with a bucket and a sponge, I was told to wash all the baseboards in the house until I either finished or dinner was served. The worst part was that it wasn't a small house. With at least nine bedrooms and two floors, I knew exactly which of those things would happen first.

I was sitting on my rump in the first-floor hallway when the others got home from school. Hearing the front door open made me realize the previous sound must have been the bus, because no, we weren't allowed to drive while living here. But when the first boy stepped in talking to someone behind him, he had my complete attention.

"I've never seen that many in my life, and they're all in *our* backyard!"

The guy was maybe a year younger than me, and a junior. I thought his name was Markus, but could've been wrong. I got him and Dominik confused. One was Hispanic, the other was Black, and the names could've gone either way. Since they'd never talked directly to me, I supposed it didn't matter.

Stephanie came in next. "I hope they shit all over John's car."

That made me chuckle, which made her notice me. "What *are* you doing?" she asked.

"Day three, and I'm already feeling like Cinderella," I said. "I tossed a piece of bread to a crow, now I get to scrub baseboards. Is there, like, a manual for the rules around here?"

The guy chuckled. "Good luck with that. They're usually pretty hard on you for the first month or so. After that, if you keep the volume down, it's like they don't notice."

"Breaking me in or something?" I asked.

He shrugged. "According to Mr. Sparks, it's the only way to keep discipline, because you never know what kind of heathens we might be."

Stephanie nudged his arm. "You're scaring her, Markus."

He pushed her back playfully, but his smile was a little too fond. "I am not." He paused as the door opened again and the next group began to pile into the house. "Sooner we get chores done, the sooner we get to bed, right?"

The group of them all headed for the stairs, but I kept scrubbing. On the upside, I'd guessed his name right. On the downside, going to bed early was a good thing? Wasn't that what normal parents used as punishment? How the hell was I going to last a whole year in this place?

Then again, I'd probably get moved in a few months. I'd make another non-mistake like feeding some stupid birds and get punted again. The frustration was almost overpowering, so I pushed it all into the scrubbing. The rhythm of the brush against the wall was cathartic, almost hypnotic. Mind-numbing was a better word, but it didn't matter.

Of all the horror stories I'd heard about foster homes, this hadn't been on the list. We were basically the Sparks' maids! I woke up, started cleaning, and that was about it. Prisoners had more rights than this! Granted, I was probably just being selfish. We were fed. We had our own rooms, so we didn't even have to share. From the sounds of it, the Sparks didn't beat us, and I hadn't heard a whisper of anything worse.

They were just strict. Super strict. Like evil-stepmother kind of strict. Sadly, I didn't have a fairy godmother to make the birds help out, and if there were any mice in this house, I hadn't seen them. I was too worried about getting extra chores to do anything as frivolous as whistle, never mind that the songs I liked were probably scandalous or something.

But I hated it. I hated them. I hated feeling like a prisoner here when I hadn't done a single thing wrong! I'd promised myself I would try harder at this place, and I was. I hadn't mouthed off without a good reason. I'd been careful not to cuss. I didn't have any friends, so it wasn't like they were the wrong crowd or anything.

I merely woke up and cleaned this stupid house from the time I got up until when I finally was allowed to take a shower and head to bed. I owned two books, and I'd read both of them a dozen times or more. I didn't have a phone; I had no laptop to get online for anything and not even a deck of cards to play solitaire. I was miserable, and it was only day three!

Just when I thought things couldn't get any worse, Mr. Sparks came home. First, the crows went off. Their cawing was so loud Mrs. Sparks looked up in worry. It was almost enough to drown out the sound of his car, but the clunking noise from the bad wheel was hard to miss. Then I heard Mr. Sparks yell at something.

His feet thundered up the stairs, onto the rickety porch, and it sounded like he was hurrying. When the front door burst open, the man of the house rushed inside, but he wasn't fast enough. Something black streaked in with him, swooping around the man's head. Shit, a crow had followed him in!

Mr. Sparks flailed his arms to keep it away from him, but the bird didn't seem to care. It cawed again, making the kids come see what was happening. In the living room, Mrs. Sparks squeaked in what sounded like real fear. Putting aside my cleaning supplies, I hurried up the hall to see what was going on just as Mrs. Sparks threw a pillow at the thing.

"Get it out!" she yelled. "John, make it go away."

"Iron!" he barked.

Like this had happened a million times before, Mrs. Sparks bolted into the kitchen to get the cast iron skillet. Wielding it like a weapon, she swung at the panicked bird, but either it was too fast or she was too slow. The bird easily evaded her attempts to hit it like a softball.

"Wait!" I begged, hurrying into the room. "It's just a bird! If you stop moving - "

I didn't get the chance to finish because the crow saw me. As if it knew me, the thing changed directions and flew straight at me. Naturally, I did the only thing I could. I threw my arms up before my face and tried not to move, hoping it wouldn't hit me. The rush of air from its wings made my eyes close - and then I felt its feet close on one of my arms.

Caw!

My breath stopped, but my eyes opened. Sure enough, the large black bird had decided my arm was a safe place to rest. "Ok," I breathed, easing my arm down to a more comfortable angle. "I think you're supposed to be outside, birdy. So, like, don't freak out or anything..." And I started moving toward the door.

But Mrs. Sparks was having none of it. "John!" she screamed. "It's happening again!"

"Out!" Mr. Sparks yelled, storming over to grab my other arm.

"No, it'll fly again - " I tried, but I was wrong.

Mr. Sparks shoved me forward, right toward the front door, and then out. The whole time, the bird just sat there like some properly trained parrot or something. I couldn't take my eyes off it, not even caring where we were going. The crow tilted its head, and I watched its funny eyelids blink. When I tripped over the door jamb, it flared its wings, but still it didn't leave. Not until Mr. Sparks pushed me all the way to the edge of the porch.

"I don't care if you're royalty," Mr. Sparks snapped at me. "I don't give a shit what excuse you have. The bird goes and the tricks stay out of my house, or you will be gone so fast your head will spin!"

The crow ruffled its feathers as if offended and then took off. I just stood there stunned, too confused to know what the hell I was supposed to say to make this better.

"I'm sorry, Mr. Sparks." It was all wrong, but it was the only thing I had.

"You're one of them, aren't you?" he demanded.

I shook my head in confusion because I had no idea what the hell he was talking about, but the man didn't care. Still holding my arm, he pulled me back into the house almost as roughly as he'd shoved me and that bird out.

Chapter Four

"She has to go!" Mrs. Sparks was yelling as Mr. Sparks hauled me upstairs to my room.

"I just tried to get it out," I said, hoping he'd give me the chance to explain.

But Mr. Sparks wanted none of it. When we reached my door, he yanked it open and then all but threw me inside. "Stay here. A meal will be brought to you."

Huffing out a breath, I wandered the rest of the way to my bed and flopped down on it. I'd left the tub of water and sponge downstairs. Granted, the baseboards in the hall were mostly done, but fuck it. They could clean it up. These people were crazy enough that staying in my room sounded like a great idea.

Then I heard voices in the hall. "You call him and get this sorted out," Mrs. Sparks was saying. "He promised that if it happened again, he'd handle it. Well, it's happening again, and I want it handled *now*."

"Nancy," Mr. Sparks said, "she'll be fine in the room. There's nothing she can do in there."

"Except turn it into a jungle!" Mrs. Sparks wailed. "You call him right now, John, or I will. And he won't like what I have to say!"

"Fine," Mr. Sparks agreed. "Now calm down before the other kids get worried. I'll handle it."

I heard her feet thump toward the stairs. A moment later, Mr. Spark's voice came back. "Hi, Liam. Yeah, I think we have a problem. Just had a flock of crows move in and one broke into the house. Yep, the new one. Mhm. Well, Nancy's not willing to take any chances. You know what those other boys did to her." There was a long pause. "I think I can convince her to wait until tomorrow, but she'd prefer tonight. I understand, Liam, but can you blame us? These *things* have no place in our home! So, if you won't deal with her, I'll drive her back to the state home myself." Another pause. "Sounds good. She'll stay in her room until then."

Until when? I wanted to ask. Never mind this Liam guy. Who the hell was he? I didn't have to wait long to find out. By the time I'd kicked my shoes off, Mr. Sparks was back. My bedroom door burst open without even a polite tap, and the man was just there, glaring at me as if I was some kind of monster.

"I thought I was trying to help," I said, doing my best to explain.

"Your kind don't know how," he grumbled, turning back to my door.

That was when I realized he was holding something. Two somethings, because one was a screwdriver. Mr. Sparks used that to begin working on my door knob. The thing came apart rather quickly, which was when I realized the other thing was another knob. Was the asshole going to lock me in here? I hadn't done anything *wrong*!

"Do I at least get to know how long I'm grounded?" I asked.

He turned to glare at me. "Grounded? Do you think this is a joke? You will stay in this room until you see your caseworker!"

Ok, so Liam was my caseworker? Good to know. I hadn't met the guy for this area yet. Maybe he'd even listen to me, because this? Very much not ok.

"What if I have to pee?" I asked.

"Then you can knock on the door and hope someone hears you," he snapped.

"I was just trying to get the bird outside," I groaned, flopping back onto the bed. "We had a sparrow in the house once, and the foster mom I had at the time tossed a towel over it, but we all had to be still so it would land. That's it! I didn't bring it in. *You* did!"

"Don't play coy with me," he grumbled.

Yep, insane. Complete basket cases. Maybe it was best that I'd get to talk to my caseworker. Clearly, the state home would be better than this! How the hell was a wild bird my fault? Besides, it was a crow. They were supposed to be very smart and could hold grudges. I'd read about that too.

But it wasn't worth arguing, I'd figured that much out. So, while Mr. Sparks worked on my door, I found my suitcase and rummaged in it until I had my book. One of my previous families had given me copies of *The Outsiders* and *Pride and Prejudice*. Classics, I'd been told. Right now, I went for *Pride and Prejudice,* just because it was bigger.

By the time I was settled on my bed with the book on my lap, Mr. Sparks was done. He closed the door - hard - to test it, then opened it again. The slamming made me look over, to find him simply waiting.

"The doorknob is iron. Think hard before you grab it." Then he left, slamming it one more time.

Strangely, I didn't hear a lock click. I was dying to test it, but I wasn't stupid. Mr. Sparks was probably waiting on the other side, hoping I would do something wrong so he could beat the shit out of me. Instead, I lost myself in the story. It was Wednesday night. That meant I had four more days before I could escape to school - unless I managed to get myself moved.

The irony of that made me chuckle. I'd never imagined I'd think of going to school as an escape. Then again, this was a pretty good incentive to make sure we made good grades. The more extracurricular stuff we did, the more time we could spend out of the house, and the less time the Sparks had to deal with us.

The whole thing sucked, though. It wasn't my fault my mother had killed my father. In truth, it wasn't her fault either. The man had left her no other choice. I had a feeling the seven other kids here would say just about the same thing. It felt like we were paying for the sins of our parents, and nothing we could do would change that.

I couldn't remember the last time I'd had a place that felt like home. The idea of stability was foreign to me. I'd mastered the art of packing my things quickly and moving without complaint. Unfortunately, that wasn't a skill I could make look good on a resume.

Never mind my options once I aged out of this place. If I was lucky, I'd get accepted to college, live on grants and student loans until I got my degree, and then be able to get a good job. If I couldn't manage that, I might get a stipend to help cover my housing while I found a job.

The more likely option was I'd have to figure it out on my own, but I would. I'd been a foster kid long enough that I knew how to plan ahead, work hard, and ignore the shit that sucked. Mostly, it was because *everything* sucked in the foster system. At school, I'd get picked on for being a foster kid. At home, it appeared I was going to be slave labor.

The hours ticked by, and no one said a thing. There was no lecture, no threats, and thankfully, no beatings. Finally, someone knocked on the door, waiting until I said they could come in to open it. On the other side stood Stephanie, holding out a plate of food.

"I'll bring breakfast up in the morning too," she said.

I got up to take it. "Thanks. Do I get a hint of what's going on?"

"They're a little superstitious," she whispered. "I'm sorry. I didn't even think to say anything!"

"All I did was get the stupid bird out of the house," I insisted.

She nodded, taking a step back to make it clear she couldn't stay. "I know. Sounds like you have to talk to your caseworker after Mr. Sparks gets home tomorrow." Then she grimaced. "I really am sorry."

But that was all I got. The door closed before I could ask anything else, leaving me standing there with a plate of cold leftovers from the "family" dinner. I wanted to throw it against the wall, have a tantrum, and scream until someone came and told me what was going on.

I didn't. The smell of it made my stomach growl, reminding me I'd only had a peanut butter and jelly sandwich today. I was too hungry to waste this on making a point. I also had a feeling the Sparks wouldn't give me a second plate. Instead, I sat down on my bed and ate, reading while I shoveled the tepid food into my mouth.

When I was done, I pushed the stupid trinkets out of the way and set the plate on my bedside table. I wanted to get out of here, but how? There were bars on the window, and I was sure the door was locked. Why else would the man change the knob? Still, if I told the caseworker about this, it should get me out of here, right? Who knew, it might even get the Sparks in enough trouble they wouldn't be allowed to keep any other kids.

So I went back to reading. At some point, I fell asleep. Once again, I woke to the sound of the door opening. Like before, I barely parted my eyes, hoping the darkness would hide the fact that I wasn't sleeping. This time, it was Mrs. Sparks who walked in. The woman stepped lightly, heading straight to my closet. There, she carefully checked that door, and finding nothing out of the ordinary, she turned to inspect me.

I closed my eyes again. Her steps came closer. I could hear the soft swish of her skirt, and then the fork clanked on the plate when she picked up my dirty dishes, but she didn't immediately leave. Instead, the woman let out a soft sigh. For a little too long, she watched over me. It was almost long enough for me to drift back to sleep, but my anxiety prevented me from relaxing that much.

Eventually, she left again, taking my plate with her. I heard one of the stairs creak when she made her way back down, yet there was one big problem. I had to pee now, and kinda badly. So, crawling out of bed, I made my way to the door and looked for a hole to release the lock. Not finding one, I decided it was worth giving it a try, just out of sheer desperation.

The knob turned and the latch released. Confused, I carefully opened the door, listening for any hint that someone else was awake. The house was completely dark, only the light from a streetlight out front making it possible to see at all. Stepping as lightly as I could, I hurried up the hall and into the bathroom. There, I locked the door behind me, but I didn't bother turning on the light.

Once I relieved myself, I did the whole thing in reverse. My door wasn't locked, but I was being kept prisoner? What the actual fuck? This place just kept getting weirder and weirder! Would it be worth it to make a break for it? If I tried, where the hell would I go?

But no, I had a meeting with my caseworker tomorrow. I'd at least give him a chance to do something about this. Then, if that didn't work, I'd risk whatever charm, curse, or insanity these people thought was keeping me in my room. Obedience? Ha! I doubted that. No, there had to be some kind of trap somewhere, and I had a feeling it would be safer to just deal with my caseworker.

Granted, it would mean another mark on my record, and I was definitely going to the state home. The problem was that once I went in there, getting out would be next to impossible. I'd heard a million horror stories about those places - because there wasn't just one. Things ranging from older boys molesting the younger girls to the bullying and criminal activity that ran rampant without enough parental oversight.

I wanted to be a good kid. I had plans to get my act together, make something out of myself, and grow up to have a decent life. I wasn't foolish enough to think I'd be either rich or famous. I just wanted a job that paid more than minimum wage, so one day I could have a home of my own, and maybe stay in the same place long enough to think about a real boyfriend.

I wanted friends. I wanted consistency. I wanted a little normalcy in my life, and yet here I was, shut in a room with a heavy metal doorknob and bars on the window, being treated like I was some servant for the lord and lady of the house! I hadn't asked for any of this. I'd simply been trying to *help!*

Then again, maybe that was my problem. Maybe I needed to stop trying and accept that all of this shit sucked. I'd give it one last chance, but if my caseworker couldn't do anything, then I was done. I clearly couldn't get it right. I couldn't figure out how to be the kid someone wanted to care about, so fuck it. I'd learn how to be the best loner. I'd show everyone *I* wasn't the problem. They were.

Chapter Five

I woke up to someone knocking on my door the next morning. Cracking my eyes open, I hurried over to open it, finding Stephanie on the other side. She held out a plate of eggs and toast. It wasn't anything spectacular, but I thanked her anyway. She didn't need to carry it up to me, but she still had. Then, after telling me she was still sorry, the oldest girl in the house hurried downstairs so she didn't miss the bus.

I set the food on my bedside table, then went to use the bathroom, brush my teeth, and take a quick shower. When I got back, the eggs were cold, but I no longer cared. I was done with caring. I hated my entire life right now. On the upside, I didn't need to spend the day cleaning. Instead, I read. It actually made the time fly.

Eventually, I heard the other kids get home, but no one came to check on me. I didn't really blame them. Guilt by association and all that. A couple of hours later, Mr. Sparks came back from work. The man made a ruckus when he walked in, but I couldn't make out his words. I did hear Mrs. Sparks making a fuss over him.

Their voices faded, but that didn't last long. Soon enough, Mr. Sparks shoved open my door and told me I had five minutes to get ready to go. Clearly, I was expected to change and look presentable on his schedule, not mine. I was merely the prisoner, an inconvenience for him to dump on someone else now.

I took the time to put on the same thing I'd worn that first day, and then I packed. If I was getting bounced again, I didn't want to lose anything. My bear and book went on top of my suitcase. My nylon bag went beside it, and I was glad I hadn't bothered to hang anything up yet. I was done with this joint - or at least I hoped I was.

But since he'd left my door open, I took that to mean I should come downstairs when I was ready. Mr. Sparks was waiting there with his keys in his hand. I barely even got a grunt before he walked out the front door, clearly expecting me to follow. Together, we headed to his dilapidated luxury car knock-off, and he didn't even wait for me to buckle my seatbelt before he backed out of the drive without a word.

To be honest, the entire situation was a little terrifying. He didn't tell me where we were going. He didn't explain what was going on. I could only guess because of the talk he'd had with me yesterday about my caseworker, but I didn't know who or where we were meeting. Needless to say, I was almost relieved when Mr. Sparks pulled the car into the massive parking lot of some church.

Seriously, this guy was flying a whole arsenal of red flags. Mrs. Sparks was almost psychotically lost in some age gone by, but the mister? He gave off this vibe like he had a cruel streak. He was the kind of person who, when the cops finally caught him, everyone would nod and say they'd always known he wasn't quite right. And I was now stuck with him, alone, in a darkening parking lot? My heart was racing in the worst way.

The bastard still didn't say a word, just got out and gestured for me to follow. Across the asphalt, into the building, then we turned right, wandered up a white-on-white hall, and into a large room. In here, the carpet was dark blue, the walls had been painted in crude murals, and a lone man waited with a briefcase on the table before him. Mr. Sparks headed right to this guy, who probably was in his mid-thirties.

"Liam, this is the kid I told you about, Lorraine Brooks," Mr. Sparks said, making some weak gesture in my general direction.

The guy had a round face, the kind which seemed easy to talk to, and he turned it on me with a bright smile. "Lorraine?"

"That's me." I shrugged.

"My name's Liam, and I wanted to talk to you a bit, if that's ok?" He waited until I nodded, then turned back to Mr. Sparks. "We'll be done by 8:30, if you want to pick her up then."

"That works. Just figure out what to do with her." Mr. Sparks didn't bother to smile before he stormed out of the room.

Liam, however, wasn't as rude. With a kind look in his eye, he gestured for me to have a seat across from him. A sinking sensation of dread tightened my gut as I eased myself onto the chair, ready for just about anything. This had the feeling of "bad." Like, the seriously bad kind of crap I'd spent my life trying to avoid.

"So, are you liking Plainsboro?" he asked out of the blue.

Not the question I expected. I'd already braced myself for a lecture on my behavior. "I guess it's ok. Probably the smallest town I've lived in so far, but kinda seems modern. I guess it's cool."

"Yeah. The City Council is hoping to attract new businesses and help the place grow. We can't all be farmers, but it's a nice, quiet place. So, where are you from?"

I gave him an incredulous look. "Iowa. Pretty sure I haven't lived in the same place for more than a year since I was five."

"Sounds rough. Guess that means you've pretty much seen it all, huh?"

And there it was. He'd eased into it nicely, but I knew how this game was played. Now was when I'd either get a lecture on being grateful for what I had or informed I was being moved to a group home. There were never enough foster homes for all the kids in the system, and I'd been given far too many chances. I had a feeling there'd also be a lecture about burning bridges.

So I sighed. "I was honestly trying to do the right thing. It was a stupid bird that got into the house. I guess Mrs. Sparks is scared of them or something, because she freaked when I fed bread to some earlier. I know you won't believe me, but I'm not trying to make problems. I just have the crappiest luck."

With a single chuckle, he lifted a finger and then stood. Walking over to the fridge, Liam opened the door, grabbed a can of Coke, and offered it to me. When I nodded in agreement, he got another for himself, then returned. The whole time, my words hung between us.

"So, besides that, how do you like living with the Sparks?" He passed me one of the cans as he reclaimed his seat.

I opened the soda and took a drink, but he refused to let me out of the question so easily. The silence started to stretch on for a little too long. Even worse, he wouldn't look away.

I gave in. "I'm sure they're really nice people."

"Mm." He mimicked my tactic with the soda before sighing. "I'm sure they are too - deep down."

I looked up at him. "That didn't sound very professional."

He laughed, lifting his hands in admission. "It's the best I could do on short notice. Thing is, Lorraine, I'm a social worker. My job is to take care of kids who've had every other adult fail them, and well, you're in that group now. I'm not about to pretend the foster system is either fair or wonderful."

"Well, that's refreshing," I mumbled. "I just don't know what I did to make them so mad at me, you know? I keep trying, and well, I'm sure you've seen my record."

Liam patted his briefcase. "I have. Your mom is in jail for killing your father. You've been bounced through homes in every county of this region. Lorraine, do you really expect me to believe you're just a normal teenage girl?" He lifted a hand before I could smart off. "That's what they'll say to anyone who'll listen. I think you seem nice. I think you've been through a lot. I also know stereotypes hurt more people than they help, and your foster parents have made sure everyone in town knows your backstory."

I let out a heavy groan, because I wasn't actually surprised. "So, what am I supposed to do?"

He lifted his can and took a small drink before continuing. "What happened with the crows?"

I mimicked him, taking a drink to cover the tightness in my throat. This whole thing shouldn't have mattered so much. "I promised myself I'd do better this time. Mrs. Sparks wanted me to help clean the house, so I got up when the other kids headed to school and did. I thought I was doing everything right, but I dunno. I fed some bread to the birds in the backyard. Then, when Mr. Sparks got home, one flew inside and I tried to get it out. That's it. I swear."

"And your file says you've done that before," he pointed out.

Groaning, I flopped forward to press my forehead against the table. "I know I should've thought about it, but I didn't, ok? I mean, they're cool birds. Crows can learn to talk, and they bring presents to people they like. It's stupid, but I figured it was kinda like having a friend or something. Not like anyone else in the house was talking to me."

"So, it was the crows who stole the trinkets from Ms..." He paused, trying to recall that foster mom's name.

"Ellis," I supplied. "She said she'd lost the earring outside. It appeared on my windowsill. She said I must've stolen it because it had diamonds. Little ones, Liam! Like, I thought they were just rhinestones, but she made a big deal about it. And I guess there was some other stuff missing too."

"Keys," he told me. "Including a key to the garden shed where a few dangerous power tools were kept."

"And?" Because what difference did that make?

He lifted a brow. "You've watched horror films, I'm sure. Use your imagination, because she did."

I groaned. "This is so not fair. I'm not one of those bad foster kids! I'm not selling drugs or joining gangs. I'm just... I'm *trying*, ok? I just can't seem to get it right!"

"Because maybe you don't really fit in?" he asked.

A sigh fell from my lips and I nodded. "Sometimes it seems that way. I just feel like I didn't get the rules everyone else plays by, you know? Like, I keep trying so hard, and the more effort I put in, the faster it all blows up."

Slowly, Liam slid the Coke between his hands in a pool of its own condensation. "What if I could get you into a dorm situation for school?"

"What?" I couldn't even wrap my mind around that, let alone have an opinion. Not at all what I'd expected!

He nodded. "Full disclosure here, Lorraine. John Sparks is my older brother. That kinda makes you my foster niece, right? Well, I'm well aware of what my brother's like. We may both be involved in social services, but our versions aren't the same."

"Ok..." So I could see how Mr. Sparks had gotten a meeting so fast, but it just didn't seem like enough for this guy to do something so big. "How would you get me into a boarding school? I don't have the grades to get a scholarship."

"No, not a boarding school. Well, not exactly. But if you're my foster niece, that makes you 'family,' and because I work there, I get a few benefits. Lorraine, I'm the on-site counselor at Silver Oaks Institute. Have you heard of it?"

"Is that the college in town?" I asked.

He nodded. "It is, and Silver Oaks offers an Advanced Placement program. Think of it like taking college courses for a combination of high school and college credit. If you're interested, I'd be happy to suggest it to John and Nancy. I just want to make sure you realize this is college. That means dorms, curfews - because you're still a minor - plus, you'll have to keep your grades up, and acting out will get you sent back to the public school. To live with *them*, Lorraine."

Holy fucking shit. What he'd listed off was basically a dream come true for me. College? That was my best-case scenario! To get a chance to start early? Wait.

"But I can't afford it," I reminded him. "I'm kinda not working, and college is stupid expensive, right?"

"Family discount," he countered. "I'm allowed to send one family member to the college per semester. Since I don't have children of my own, it's a perk I'm not using, and it sounds like this might be useful for you - but only if you intend to take this seriously."

I was already nodding my head. "I can do that. I already told you, I'm not one of those punks who gets off on breaking the rules or anything."

He smiled. "Yeah, I had a feeling you'd be on board. Now tell me, what grade are you in?"

"Twelfth." I bit my lip, hoping that wouldn't be a problem.

Liam murmured approvingly. "So a senior. That makes it even easier."

There was just one thing I couldn't wrap my mind around. "Why? You don't know me. I could be some thug, and yet you just throw this out like it's no big deal?"

"Lorraine, my big brother learned how to care for kids from our father. Mrs. Sparks has her own story, but she was never able to have children. Believe it or not, they honestly want to help. They've had good success with plenty of problem children, but I can't say I condone their methods. So, I'm just going to circumvent this entire dilemma. They want you out. You want to be out. According to your file, your options are limited, but your grades aren't too bad. You've shown an interest in secondary education, so this seems like a solution that works for everyone. I guess you can just think of this as my way of helping those who don't fit in with the system, ok?"

"Yeah, sure," I agreed, deciding it really didn't matter so long as I could be anywhere else. Looking a gift horse in the mouth and all that. "So, is there anything I need to know about this school, or am I just supposed to leave myself at your mercy?"

That made him chuckle. "Silver Oaks is a small, privately owned college with a unique education system. The state classifies it as a trade school, because the courses offered are focused on future jobs, yet we offer associate, bachelor's, and even master's degrees. Our goal is to take students who may not excel elsewhere and create an environment that will put them on a path to excellence in our modern world. Because you'd be attending as an Advanced Placement student, there is a placement test. It will let us know *if* you would be able to handle the program, and exactly where you would do best."

"Right." Because I could read between the lines. "In other words, I'm not guaranteed to get in. But if I do, am I going to end up as the diversity or pity case to round out the books?"

He canted his head with a sly look. "Something like that. Still interested?"

"You have no idea," I told him. "Right about now, I will do *anything* to get out of the prison your sister-in-law calls a home."

Liam smiled slyly. "I had a feeling you'd say that. So, the downside is, you'll have to pass the entrance testing. The upside is I can arrange it for tomorrow. But, if you do this, then I have one requirement. While you're in school, I'm going to be your academic advisor and counselor, ok? Is that a deal you can make?"

I nodded to make sure he didn't misunderstand. "Can do, Uncle Liam. For the chance to actually get ahead for once? Yeah. I have no problem with reporting to you."

"Kinda what I thought," he told me.

Chapter Six

Mr. Sparks was ten minutes late to pick me up. Liam waited with me. Not that I needed him to, but rather because he wanted to deal with this school issue right away. When Mr. Sparks showed up and saw his brother beside me, he wrenched open his door and surged out, the expression on his face filled with rage.

"What did she do!" he demanded. "What kind of freak is she?!"

Liam merely lifted a hand. "She's not a freak, John, and you didn't answer my text offering to give her a ride home. I wanted to talk to you and Nancy about a school option."

Mr. Sparks narrowed his eyes. "Why?"

"Let's talk about that with your wife, ok?" Liam gripped my shoulder in that supportive way adults had. "I'll be five minutes behind you."

My foster father didn't respond, so I slipped into the passenger seat silently, buckled myself in, and folded my hands into my lap. All I had to do was be meek and mild for a little longer and I could get out of this hell. I had this.

That didn't mean I missed the rage coming from Mr. Sparks,

though. I wanted to ask him about Liam, just to make sure this guy wasn't some kind of pedophile or something. Well, I wanted to ask *someone*, and my options were kinda limited. I couldn't really rule anything out, could I? The Sparks had turned out to be freaks, so what were the chances Liam was actually as cool as he seemed? Unfortunately, the older brother didn't seem like he was in the mood to talk.

When we pulled into the driveway, Mr. Sparks got out, slammed his door behind him, and simply stormed toward the house. He didn't even look at me. His reaction was so strange, so completely over the top, that I felt nervous. Not the new family kind, either. Everything about this man made me wonder if he was going to show up in my bedroom again, and I couldn't decide if he'd be naked or carrying a hatchet. I also wasn't sure which would be worse.

The truth was, this family just wasn't right. Maybe they could fool everyone else, but some of their issues were completely out there. Then again, Liam was a part of the family, or so he said, and he seemed pretty normal. Plus, he was a caseworker, so he had to be safe. They went through some kind of background checks, didn't they?

Still, I decided to wait there for Liam instead of going up to the house. Mostly because they hadn't given me a key, they'd made no move to tell me I was welcome to come back in, and I honestly didn't know if walking in would make things worse, so I did nothing. The passenger seat was fine, and it gave me a little time to try to wrap my mind around what had just happened.

Liam was offering to basically pay my way through some college courses? Just because he wasn't using the perk of his job? But why me? And why now? Was it because his brother was screwing me over and he felt guilty?

That was the option I liked the most. Granted, it could also be because Liam was some kind of sick pervert, but he wasn't really giving me that vibe. Or maybe my luck was finally turning around? Because college? Really? That was my *dream!* And starting early? There was no way this could be so easy.

The flash of headlights announced Liam's arrival even before his car was parked. I hopped out of the rotting land-barge and did my best to look calm. Evidently, I failed.

"You ok?" Liam asked.

I nodded vigorously. "I think Mr. Sparks might be upset, though."

Liam blew that off. "John's always upset. It's his default emotion." Then he gently rested a hand between my shoulders and turned me to the door. Yep, he knocked.

So I stood beside him, waiting. It didn't take long for Mrs. Sparks to answer, and the look she gave me could've frozen Hell. When she stepped back to let us in, I tried really hard to keep my eyes on the carpet. Liam, however, turned to give her a hug. That made my foster mom titter. Ok, so maybe there was hope for her yet?

"What school option?" Mr. Sparks asked before we were really all the way in.

Liam clasped my shoulder and expertly steered me to the loveseat, then sat down. Mr. Sparks sat across from us in the recliner, and Mrs. Sparks took her place on the couch as close to her husband as she could get. I'd been in enough family discussions to recognize the placement as us against them.

"Where are the other kids?" Liam asked.

Mrs. Sparks pointed up. "I gave them the evening off from chores. Why is *that girl* back here?"

"Nancy," Mr. Sparks chided. "You knew she wouldn't get moved immediately. Liam seems to think we need to talk about options or something."

"I think Lorraine should go to Silver Oaks Institute," Liam told them.

"Can't afford it," Mr. Sparks said, his tone sounding like that should end the discussion. "Send her to the group home."

Liam just lifted a hand. "Hear me out, John. I've got family placement credits for working there, and I can spend them on any member of my family. A niece counts. It'll get her a year of education, and since she's a senior, that's all she needs. She'll be housed on campus, fed on campus, and would only need to come back here for the winter holidays at worst. It's the kind of opportunity that not a lot of foster kids get. It would also look very good on your record."

Wait, a year? At the church, he'd made it sound like I could get more, but still, a year was a lot. Hell, a year of college was a head start. Worst-case scenario, I'd get ahead. Best case, I'd get even more, right? I also kinda didn't want to ask right now. Now with the Sparks looking so pissed.

Mrs. Sparks was starting to look interested. "But isn't Silver Oaks Institute a college? Liam, she's in high school."

"She'd be in a special program," he explained. "It's like those Advanced Placement classes they offer at the public school, but more intense. She would be earning both her high school diploma and a few college credits at the same time."

"Ok," Mrs. Sparks said, "but doesn't that place require a uniform?"

Liam hummed a thoughtful noise. "There is a dress code, yes. The uniforms are supplied by the school, though." He waved that off as if it was inconsequential. "Until we see if she can even be accepted, the rest doesn't really matter, does it?"

Mr. Sparks was now leaning forward just the slightest amount. "So, if she gets into this school, she won't be back here until December?"

"Correct," Liam agreed. "There's also the chance that she could winter on campus."

"Is this an all-girl's school?" Mrs. Sparks asked.

"No, Nancy," Liam said. "Silver Oaks is co-ed, but the male and female dorms are divided and chaperoned. The classes are intermixed, though." He lowered his voice to a conspiratorial level. "But I happen to be one of those chaperones. Plus, most of our AP students tend to stick with their education and receive a bachelor's degree or better. Like I said, it would look *very* good on your record."

"Oh!" The woman reached over and patted her husband's hand. "This would be a great opportunity for her, John."

"What's the catch?" Mr. Sparks asked - which was ironic, because I was wondering the same thing.

Liam sighed. "I'll have to make sure there's a place open tomorrow, and it's always possible she won't qualify. Her records make me think she has a good chance, though. *If* she's accepted, it'll take a few days to get her a dorm, which means she'd be staying here through the weekend. Usually, the first week is a sort of trial period, both for the school and the parents, but I'll try to shorten that as much as possible. Unfortunately, this means one of you will need to drive her to class on Monday... or I could come pick her up."

Mr. Sparks sighed. "Well, I have work, and Nancy doesn't drive. So, if you want this for her, you'll need to take her."

"I can do that," Liam promised. "John, this is a great opportunity for all of us. Silver Oaks is an elite private college, and getting one of your foster kids to graduate from there?"

He didn't need to add in the last part, that it would impress everyone. That it would be something they could brag about and not even need to pay for. No, Liam seemed to know exactly which buttons to push and when to simply plant the seed of an idea.

I knew he was doing this for me, but I had no clue why. It was also strange to see two brothers who were such complete opposites. Liam seemed to always have a smile on his face. He looked like the kind of person someone simply knew they could trust. Most importantly, he acted like he cared.

John? He was bitter about something. No, make that about everything. I wasn't completely sure what he did for a living, but I knew he wore one of those uniforms where his shirt had his name on a patch. Janitor, mechanic, or something. Not like it was anything to be ashamed of - since I figured I'd be lucky to get a job like that - but it also wasn't exactly bragging material either, and John Sparks seemed like the kind of man who really needed to brag.

Then there was Nancy. She supposedly wanted children, but she sure didn't act like it. Maybe she'd wanted a doll? Servants? Because that was how she treated the kids here. Or maybe these two were just inherently nasty people. Those did exist. After all, I had a few memories of my dad, and he'd definitely been one.

Nothing had ever been his fault, Mom should've fixed it all, and a beer would solve everything. Mr. Sparks reminded me of him a bit, but without the beer. He had the same smug look in his eyes, the same arrogance that clung to him, and the same ability to make everyone around him feel like they would be better off in any other room. And to think, I'd only been living here for about four days.

But would this college be any different from a group home? Well, first off, it was a chance to get started on a degree, and if I wanted to set myself up for the future, I would definitely need one of those. Secondly, it meant I'd be away from these people, so at least I could actually sleep at night. Third? The idea of breathing without being wrong sounded like heaven.

Then there was the thought of going to the same school for more than a few months. If I wasn't underfoot, there was a chance I might not have to move again! Which meant friends. It meant doing normal things, hanging out, and maybe even a boyfriend. In other words, it meant I could actually have the freedom to be a normal seventeen-year-old girl. Oh, I knew some things were just out of the question. A driver's license, as an example. I had to wait until I was eighteen, because there was no way I'd manage to pay for driver's ed. A cell phone was another. Still, I could manage.

"Fine," Mr. Sparks said, pulling me out of my daydreams. "She can go to this Institute of yours, but I don't want it to come back on me. We've already had to live through the hell those others put us through. Nancy couldn't survive that again. So, either she gets in and does well, or you get her out of this house."

Liam licked his lips almost carefully. "That's exactly why I thought we should send Lorraine to Silver Oaks. Those boys were bored in public school, John."

Mr. Sparks narrowed his eyes. "Yeah, but didn't one end up at your place?"

Liam slowly nodded. "He did. I also don't think you'd even recognize him anymore."

Nancy patted her husband's hand. The gesture seemed almost excited - or possibly distressed. It was hard to tell with her. "If this school can fix *that* boy, then we have to. Besides," she said, dropping her voice, "think how good this will look on our record."

Yeah, their *record*. The one that allowed them to keep fostering kids, and who knew if Liam would have any more credits to help the next one out - but I didn't want to think about it. Right here, right now, I was getting the kind of break that didn't come along very often. I had to make the most of it, because no matter what people thought, I really wasn't a bad kid.

I wasn't exactly a good one, either. I wasn't some brainiac to get myself a full ride to college. I wasn't an artist or good at sports. I was simply the girl who knew how to pack her entire life into one suitcase, blend into whatever situation was thrown at her, and make it out alive. I'd survived my father, a few dozen foster homes, and the horrors of the other kids in the system. So far, I'd made it to seventeen in one piece, without a record, and with the very real hope of a future I could be proud of.

"So," I asked, keeping my voice nice and calm, "when do I start?"

"I will get you an appointment to be tested tomorrow," Liam assured me.

"But she doesn't have a uniform yet," Nancy warned him.

Liam waved her down. "It's fine. This is just a test. Put her in slacks and a nice shirt. I can call you in the morning to let you know what time, then I'll come pick her up and bring her back. Will that work?"

"Sounds good," Mr. Sparks decided, which meant Mrs. Sparks wouldn't contradict him. "But William, since this is your idea, you're in charge of her. Nancy and I can't be running all the way over to that place."

"Then you'll have to sign a paper giving me power of guardianship," Liam told him.

John didn't even think about it, he simply nodded. "Sure, since I do *not* want to be woken up in the middle of the night because she got caught having relations with some boy."

Right on cue, Nancy gasped in horror. I wanted to roll my eyes, but I didn't. Nope, I was smart enough to see what Liam - which evidently was short for William - had just done. He'd effectively become my foster father, at least while I was in school. I wasn't sure if John was that stupid, lazy, or simply cared so little, but it didn't matter.

Tomorrow, I was going to be on my best behavior. I'd also be looking for this boy who'd managed to survive the Sparks.

Chapter Seven

The next morning, Liam called to say he had an appointment for me to take the entrance exam just after lunch. It seemed there were still a few spots in the Advanced Placement program, although they wouldn't have a dorm ready until Sunday afternoon. That meant I was definitely spending the weekend with the Sparks, sadly. Nancy - who I still called Mrs. Sparks to her face - said we could all go to church as a family on Sunday morning. Joy.

When Liam showed up, I was dressed in the horrendous plaid shirt from the closet, complete with puff sleeves, shoulder pads, and fake pearl buttons. It wasn't even a cool retro look. No, it was like some knockoff of a good idea, twisted until it was embarrassing. This thing was just horrible, and the khaki pants that went with it had the necessary tummy pleats, which made me look at least three months pregnant. Of course, makeup was *not* allowed, so I was really hoping I wouldn't meet any students today.

Riding there with Liam was pretty nice, though. He talked to me and let me pick the radio station, but our conversation was all shallow and polite stuff. Local weather, mostly. Soon enough, we were there. Silver Oaks Institute was located just outside the city limits on a rolling stretch of beautiful land. The drive curved up from the main road, winding between massive, perfectly cultivated trees. I had no idea if they were oaks since the branches were bare, but it didn't really matter. The whole thing screamed posh.

Then the main building of the school came into view. Most of it was made from a dark red brick. The trim around all the windows and the columns by the entry were white stone. The style was very colonial, and this place was massive. I counted four stories, plus the wings of the building that swept back. At least I hoped they were wings, because if this was one very large, square building, well, I'd seen malls smaller.

Just like I'd expected, there was a fancy curved drive at the front, then a set of stairs that led to one of those typical fountains. The kind they put in front of museums, with the layers of tiered basins in the middle. In some ways, it felt like those buildings in Washington, D.C., what with all the stiff, straight lines and powerful architecture. Not that I'd ever been to Washington, D.C., but I'd seen pictures.

The moment Liam parked the car, I climbed out of the front seat. He followed only a moment later, moving to my side. As we crossed the wide drive, he began to tell me about this place I might be attending.

"Silver Oaks Institute was founded in 1972," he began. "The college was created to give an elite education to special students from southern Iowa. Now, we have students from all across the country and affiliates in places like Ireland and Greece." He paused as we reached the main doors. "Classes are restricted to twenty students per class so everyone can get a little more individual attention. It's more personal than what you're probably used to from the public schools you've been attending. Plus, tutoring programs are offered for free, along with mentorship programs."

"So, I'm not expected to just know everything?" I asked.

He shook his head and held open the door for me to go first.

"Not even close, Lorraine. Promise. We simply need to make sure you're a fit with our special program."

Inside, the lighting was dimmer than outside, but still bright because of all the windows. The hallways were large, and on the back wall, I could see nothing but green. Yes, it was winter, but the back wall of this area led to what seemed to be a courtyard, kinda, but this wasn't like any courtyard I'd seen before.

"Is that *inside?*" I asked.

Liam laughed. "It's actually a greenhouse of sorts. They call it the atrium. There's a glass roof on the fourth story, which keeps it warm enough for the trees and flowers to grow, but it's almost an acre of natural space that's comfortable all year." He flashed me a devious smile. "Except right at midnight, when the sprinklers go off. You can thank me for the tip later."

"Nice," I breathed, deciding he was definitely the cooler of the Sparks brothers.

He was already moving, guiding me to wherever I was supposed to be, but the path took us right beside the windows. I couldn't help myself. I looked up, surprised to see large metal beams at the top, and yes, that was definitely a glass ceiling. Probably plexiglass or something, but still rather amazing. The idea of a whole yard that big, suitable for all seasons and weather? I couldn't explain it, but it made me excited about living here.

I didn't get to do more than steal a glance, though. We turned up a hall, and I found myself gawking at the rest of this massive building. To my immediate left, there were halls filled with classrooms. Further down, there seemed to be more, but on my right side was a large glass window. Behind that was nothing but a long counter and plenty of adults. It looked like an office, so when Liam opened one of the double glass doors and waved me inside, I wasn't surprised.

"Liam," a woman said, moving to the spot across the counter from us. "Your niece, I suppose?"

"She is," he agreed. "Lorraine, this is Ivy Rhodes, the dean here at Silver Oaks. She will be giving you the entrance exam."

This lady did not look nearly old enough to be the dean of a college. A student, maybe? Because, if I had to guess, she wasn't more than thirty - and probably younger. She was also gorgeous. Not just the normal kind of pretty, like cheerleaders I'd known. Nope, this woman was the jaw-dropping sort of stunning. Combined with her elegant brown suit, she looked more like a model than any sort of dean.

"Pleasure to meet you," I said politely.

"Same," she said with a hint of a smile.

Liam chuckled, reaching up to clasp my shoulder. "I think Lorraine's a bit nervous. She's fostering with my brother, you see."

That made Ms. Rhodes' eyes widen slightly. "I see. Well, I promise I'll be kind, Liam." Then she smiled at me. "Ms. Brooks, is it?" The woman made her way around the counter, carrying nothing but a pencil and a folder. "There's a room up the hall we can use for this."

"Please tell me it's not college-level stuff?" I begged.

"It's more psychological," she assured me. "I've already set everything up for you." When she gestured for me to leave the office before her, Ms. Rhodes looked back to Liam. "I'll let you know when we're done. You can meet her in the atrium, if that works?"

"Perfect," Liam agreed. "Thanks, Ivy."

For some reason, I liked how Liam sounded worried about me. Then again, I didn't like that he wasn't completely confident I could pass this. I'd kinda hinted around on the drive here, hoping for some idea of what was on this test, but he said he didn't know. He'd never taken one, and they changed based on each person. As if that was any help!

Ms. Rhodes led me to the last door before the atrium. It was technically across from the glass-walled office, but the door opened to face the indoor greenhouse. I wanted to pause and look at the plants again, just because seeing something like that in a school meant this place had to be super fancy, but Ms. Rhodes didn't give me the chance.

Inside, the room was merely a small classroom. Nothing too far out of the ordinary. It was just better than what I was used to. The teacher's desk was made from real wood and looked like it belonged in some CEO's office. The other desks weren't the cheap pieces of crap I was used to either. They still had the side desk attached to a chair, but the seat was shaped to be comfortable, and the top was larger, made of plexiglass, and there was a USB plug in the corner. Clearly, this school was tech-friendly.

The woman gestured for me to take one of the chairs, the sweep of her arm making it my choice. I looked across the empty room, then sat down in the center of the front row. She moved to claim her spot behind the desk, taking her time about it. My guts were in a knot, and I was more nervous than I'd been before, because I *really* wanted this. It would solve so many of my problems.

"Lorraine, right?" she finally asked, opening up her folder.

"Yes, ma'am," I said.

"The first part of this test is going to be a simple examination of your preferences. The choices may not make much difference to you, but please try to be honest, since it will allow us to place you correctly." She paused to flip past a few pages. "If you could live anywhere, what would your dream home look like?"

Ok, not at all what I'd expected. "Small," I decided. "Lots of windows to let in light, um, but with bright colors."

"And outside?" she asked. "Where would it be? City, country, beach, mountains, or something else?"

"I want to say someplace like this, but it's unrealistic," I admitted.

"What do you mean, 'like this?'" she pressed.

"The rolling hills, so much open space, but lots of trees," I explained. "Like, not a wild forest, but not an open meadow. Like, um, kinda in the middle? Granted, I've lived in southern Iowa my entire life."

"There's nothing wrong with that," she assured me. "If you could have any pet in the world - with no worries about practicality - what animal would you choose?"

Ok, that one was easy. "I think a crow. Maybe a raven, but I've only ever met crows."

"Good," she told me, making a mark. "If you could have any magical ability in the world, what type would you want? Anything you've ever heard of," she explained.

Yeah, I had to stop and think about that one. "Um, immortality, I think."

"Ok, now this one is harder. My middle name is Dawn. My middle name is Hazel. Which one is a lie?" She smiled, her eyes hanging on me.

"Can you say them again?" I asked.

She nodded. "My middle name is Dawn." Then she paused, but her face was completely expressionless. "My middle name is Hazel."

"Hazel is the right one," I guessed, simply because it sounded better in my opinion. I honestly had no clue.

"Pick the one that sounds the most interesting," she went on. "Earth, air, fire, or water."

"Fire," I said without hesitation.

Then she changed tactics. "Is there anything about this room that surprised you?"

"The desks are clear with USB plugs."

That got another mark on the page. "Ok. Now, we get to do a few more preferences, but these will be tactile."

Ms. Rhodes set down the papers and opened a drawer in the desk. Pulling out a box, she carried it around the front. The thing was bigger than a shoe box, but shaped more upright. I watched while she removed the top and reached inside. Lifting out two things wrapped in cloth, she set them on the desk before me.

"You can unwrap those and look at each as much as you want. Which one do you like more?" she asked.

I pulled back the black cloth to reveal a simple hunk of metal. There was a bit of rust on the smooth surface, clinging to the edges, but that was the most exciting thing about it. Then I moved to the other. When the cloth fell back, it revealed a piece about the same size and shape, but it was a very different metal.

I lifted both, surprised to find the rusty one was definitely heavier. The shiny one, however, seemed almost iridescent in the light. Curious, I tilted it, watching hints of colors play on its surface. It was almost like anodized aluminum or something, but the colors were reflections, not a part of the actual metal.

"This one," I told her. "The other just looks like iron."

"Now wrap those back up," she told me, "and I will get you the next."

After that came flowers, then liquids. She asked me to pick whichever I liked most, regardless of why. Then there were a pair of broaches. Next came knives, then pieces of wood. When I made my choice between the last two, she put everything back in the box and moved it into the drawer once more.

"And that's it," she told me. "I'll have to analyze the results, but you can wait for your uncle in the atrium if you want."

"Really?" I asked. "No math or English stuff?"

"None," she promised. "We want to see how you think, not what you've been taught. You see, we can't help every student, so we've focused our attention on those who would excel with a slightly different type of instruction. It will probably take about half an hour for me to go through this, so feel free to explore the plants. We have a few that are unique, and nothing is poisonous."

I eased myself out of the chair, knowing a dismissal when I heard one. "Just out the door and to the right, yeah?"

"Exactly," she agreed, smiling at me until I walked out of the room.

But as the door closed, I saw her let out a sigh and drop her head. That didn't look good. Had I failed a test on my opinion? Was that even possible? And what would I do if I couldn't go to school here? For a split second, I wanted to rush back in and beg her to give me another chance, but I knew it was pointless.

Liam had said this place was elite, prestigious, and special. With that many posh words, the chances of me actually getting in had to be impossible. Never mind that college was my dream. For me, this was a chance that could give me a solid head start on the rest of my life - but my luck didn't work that way. In other words, I now had half an hour to figure out what the hell I was going to do with the rest of my life.

It didn't seem like nearly enough time.

Chapter Eight

Just down the hall was a pair of spotless glass doors. I headed straight for them, and since they opened easily, I stepped through. The air in the atrium was thick and humid, but not cold. It also wasn't warm, although considering it was nearly freezing outside, I was impressed. This felt like spring, and the plants clearly agreed. I slowly made my way around the area, letting my fingers trail across some of the tropical-looking and unique leaves.

There were flowers everywhere - of all different colors. Some of the trees were impressively tall, but the roof was just a little taller. And right in the center of it all was a tree I could only describe as silver. The bark was pale like a poplar, and the top sides of the leaves were green, but the undersides - which was pretty much all I could see from down here - looked like they were shiny. Silver was the best word for them.

Clearly, this was the silver oak the school was named for. The base of the tree was large. Big enough I couldn't reach all the way around it. Not that I tried, because this thing was massive. Likely, that meant it was very old. I had a feeling the school had been built around it instead of the reverse. Large roots broke from the ground around the base, making spaces that looked like inviting places to sit.

I loved it. Something about this felt like a fantasy come to life. Maybe I'd seen too many pictures on Pinterest or something, but it reminded me of the kind of place a girl in some fancy dress would sit to read a book. Making my way out from there, I paused at a collection of unique flowers. One set was blue, and the royal kind. Not baby, not pastel, but a bright, vivid blue. The most shocking thing to me was that no one had picked them all.

But one acre of garden was a lot more space than I expected. At a glance, it seemed to be about four times the size of the Spark's yard. Like, their entire yard, house included. Then there were all the flowers, shrubs, and even a little pond with some fat fish. Every time I turned around, I ended up bumping into another plant - even though I swore I should have enough room.

What I loved most were the trees, though. There had to be at least twenty different types in here, and I was pretty sure no two were the same. Evergreens, normal trees, and strange ones that looked like they were from somewhere far away. It was like a damned tree zoo! I was looking up at a massive weeping willow when someone appeared beside me.

"Hey."

I squeaked and jumped back, feeling one of those exotic flowers brush my leg. The girl was lean and willowy, but also beautiful. Her hair was so pale it was almost silver, complete with the darker streaks through it, and her porcelain skin looked like she'd used a filter to get her stunning glow.

The smile on her lips, however, was warm and welcoming, which made me feel stupid for jumping like that. Impishly, she held out a paper straw of some kind - oh, a Pixy Stix - like a sign she was sorry. I laughed off my fright and accepted the paper tube of colored sugar.

"You startled me," I told her. "Kinda thought I was out here alone."

"Sorry about that." She shifted from one foot to the other, her eyes jumping down beside my legs. "So are you starting here?"

Talking to her made me feel a little self-conscious. "Yeah, um, I want to. I just took the exam for the Advanced Placement program, but I think I failed it."

For a long moment, she merely looked at me. Standing so close, I couldn't help but notice her eyes were the coldest shade of blue I'd ever seen. They weren't pastel. More like electric ice. Like everything else about her, she was vivid in her lack of pigment.

"Um, I'm Lorraine," I said, trying to break the awkwardness.

"Yep, Rain Brooks," she said, her gaze just a bit too intense. It was almost as if she could see straight through me. Then she blinked and shook her head. "Oh! Sorry. I'm Aspen. Aspen Fox."

"Pretty name," I said.

She shrugged that off. "My guardian chose it. Who chose yours?"

"I honestly have no idea," I admitted. "I haven't talked to my mom since I was like five, and my dad's dead. Kinda how I ended up in the foster system."

"Mm," she said, tapping her straw of sugar against her fingers. "Based on the shirt you're wearing, you're one of the Sparks' foster kids."

"Wait, does everyone know about the Sparks?" I asked.

"I do," she said with a little shrug. Then she turned to walk beside me, slowly ambling us both toward the trunk of the willow. "Rain, you don't want to be there."

"Which is why I want to be here," I agreed. "Never mind the chance to earn some college credits."

That earned me a little smile, the kind that made my lips want to match. Then she broke off the top of her own Pixy Stix tube and poured a little onto her tongue. "So, the room that shares with mine is open. I think they just finished cleaning it. When are you moving in?"

"I wish I could." I opened my own straw and poured some into my mouth. "From the way Ms. Rhodes looked, I have a feeling I'm not the kind of student they want here."

With an almost childish giggle, she flopped her back against the trunk of the willow. "I can help with that."

"How?" I asked.

But Aspen changed the subject. "Tell me, Rain, what kind of girl do you really want to be? Do you look at the rich kids in your school and long for their money? Do you watch the student council types and dream of futures like theirs? Where would you fit into your school if you could?"

"Truthfully? I never worried about those things," I told her. "I can't get the chance to be *anything* because I keep having to move. It's like I have the worst luck."

"I'll make you a deal..." she said, that devious smile coming back to her lips.

Liam's voice interrupted before she could finish her thought. "Aspen!" he barked, making her head snap around with wide eyes. "What are you doing?" he demanded, not even all the way into the atrium.

"I'm helping Rain," she said innocently.

"How?" he demanded, slowly walking toward us. "She doesn't know about your tricks."

Aspen laughed again. "No *bad* tricks, Liam. I just asked what kind of girl she wants to be." Then she looked at me. "Well?"

Something about those strange blue eyes held me, making me want to answer honestly. "The kind who isn't always alone," I told her. "I don't care if I'm popular or not. I'll never be rich. I just want to find someplace where I can actually be myself."

For a long moment, Aspen stared at me, almost like she was judging my words, but she didn't respond. Instead, she turned to look up at Liam. The strangest thing was how he was waiting, acting like her opinion actually meant something.

"I want her," she finally said.

"Aspen..." Liam tried.

But the jovial girl's attitude changed to pure rage in an instant. "I said I *want* her! You will make it happen. This is not a request, do you understand me? She is special, and none of you can see it. This is exactly where she belongs. Tell Ivy I said so!"

Liam dipped his head. "I'll handle it."

"She can't wear those clothes."

He nodded. "I have a feeling that's not a problem."

"And I'll be nice to her." She paused, doing a little half-shrug. "As much as I can."

"What about *him?*" Liam asked, not saying which "him" he meant.

Aspen's smile grew a little more. "He'll like her. She's interesting."

"So is she safe here?"

"For now," Aspen agreed. "And when she's not, I'll tell you. Is that a fair trade?"

"I'll accept it," he said softly. "I'm even hoping you two can be friends - since it seems you don't know her."

"I don't," Aspen admitted, "but I think I'd like to. She seems a little... lost."

"So were you once," he said.

"Not the same way," Aspen said, rolling her eyes. "No, Rain is interesting. I just don't know why yet, but I intend to find out."

"Um, it's actually Lorraine," I tried.

"Was," she told me. "Now it's Rain."

"Just go with it," Liam said before looking back at the girl who'd taken an intense interest in me. "And if you're done, I'm going to take her back and make arrangements for her to transfer here. Be nice, Aspen, and not your version, but mine."

She nodded emphatically. "I can do that."

And then, without another word to me, the manic little pixie girl just skipped away from the willow, aiming for the door on the opposite wall. She was almost too cute to be real, and oddly beautiful at the same time. I liked her, though. Granted, girls like her didn't usually care at all about girls like me.

All I could do was shake my head. I had no clue why she'd even noticed me, let alone cared at all. Maybe she was a little special? This wasn't a school for troubled kids, was it? Liam had described it as a college trade school.

"She's a little different," Liam explained, almost mimicking my thoughts.

"Is she..." I made a circle around my ear in the universal symbol of crazy.

"No," he insisted. "She plays by her own rules, but she's the furthest thing from insane I can imagine. She's just had a very hard life, so she values different things than most other kids. I'm betting that sounds familiar?"

"It does," I agreed. "So, do I really get to stay?"

He just nodded, slowly lifting his arm to invite me over. When I was beside him, he moved his hand to my shoulder, his arm lightly around my back. It was a very paternal gesture, but I liked it. It felt... homey. Then he steered me to the atrium exit, up the hall, and back toward the administrative area.

Ms. Rhodes was in her office to the side, but she stepped out as soon as we entered. "Liam?" she asked.

"Rain, wait here, would you?" he asked, gesturing to a chair. "I'm going to take care of a few things."

"Ok?" Because now I was very confused, but I sat obediently.

The office was calm and orderly. It was the type of place where people worked instead of chatted. Not that there were a lot of people in here, though. I could hear papers being churned out from a printer in someone's office. Then I heard Liam's voice in a side room.

"Aspen is adamant she attends."

"Liam," Ms. Rhodes sighed, "she has no affinity of any kind. I tried all the tests. There's nothing special about her."

"What about the crows?" he asked.

"I honestly don't know," she admitted. "The girl likes birds. Maybe she should consider becoming a zoo keeper or something."

"But isn't that an affinity?" he asked.

Ms. Rhodes made a murmuring sound. "It could be, in some cases, but without something to support it? I'm sorry. She might be lost, but she's not our kind of lost."

"Aspen is *adamant*," Liam told her. "She says she's interesting."

"When?" Ms. Rhodes asked.

"Minutes ago," Liam explained. "They met in the atrium while Rain was waiting."

"Rain..." There was an obvious and unspoken question in the woman's tone.

"Aspen says that's her name. Rain Brooks."

"It's just a name," Ms. Rhodes countered. "Plenty of people have them. It doesn't mean anything."

"Seems to mean something to Aspen, and from the way she talked, I have a feeling she won't be the only one. If she wants something this bad, you know he'll demand it, and you'd have to listen to that. Wouldn't it just be easier to not offend her?"

"Fine," Ms. Rhodes said. "But you get to explain it all."

"I've already agreed to handle it," Liam said. "It was a fair trade."

"Shit," Ms. Rhodes grumbled. "Ok. Arrange for her transcripts to be sent over. I'll get her enrolled. Just..." The woman huffed in frustration. "We do not need any more trouble from your brother."

"Kinda what I'm thinking," Liam agreed. "Think you can get her dorm ready by Sunday?"

"I will make sure of it," Ms. Rhodes promised. "I do not envy you this. They have you caught right in the middle, and the only one who's going to pay is you. You do know that, right?"

"Unlike you, I happen to believe they've been polished by the hardships. I think they're kind - in their own way. I also think they're only merciless when they need to be. Just get me the room and I'll deal with everything else."

"You're a braver soul than me," she said even as Liam stepped back into the main room.

"Ready?" he asked.

I was, surprisingly. I also had a million and one questions, but right now, I wasn't dumb enough to ask. Evidently, sharing a Pixy Stix with a crazy girl was all it took to get out of the Sparks' place and into a school like this? I was completely on board with that. Which meant I definitely needed to make sure to tell that crazy girl thank you!

Chapter Nine

Liam led me out of the office and back the way we came. We both headed for his car at the edge of the fancy circle drive, but neither of us spoke. I got the feeling he was just as confused about what had happened in there as I was. He was simply better at faking it. Once we were both inside, we fussed with our seatbelts, but the tension was growing. I couldn't take it anymore, so I broke first.

"Ok, what's the deal with Aspen?" I asked.

He just hung his head. "It's complicated."

"Well, I got the strong impression I wasn't getting in until she decided I was 'interesting.'" I lifted a brow and looked at him. "Don't you think I at least deserve to know what I'm getting myself into?"

He nodded slowly, but it still took him a little too long to answer. Liam delayed by starting his car. Then he had to turn down the radio. What he didn't do was put it in gear. I watched as his fingers tapped the top of the wheel, proving he was thinking, and then he simply turned to face me.

"Aspen is related to some very influential people. You might say she's royalty. Here's the thing..." He paused, biting his lips together. "Rain..."

"And what's with the name change?" I asked.

"Do you hate it?" he asked back.

"No, it's actually a lot better than my real name. I'm just feeling like I missed something in there, and I don't know what's going on. Liam, what do I need to know?"

He put the car in gear and slowly eased it forward. "Some of this won't make complete sense until you go through orientation," he warned. "Please, just give me that, and trust that I'll explain it all once we have you moved into the school, ok?"

"Ok..." But I was not going to let him out of telling me *something*.

"You tested as completely normal," he explained. "Nothing about your placement exam showed an aptitude that would benefit from Advanced Placement. So, they said you weren't a candidate. I was coming out to give you the bad news and to talk about your next options, but you were talking to Aspen Fox."

"Is she the dean's sister or something?" I asked, because Ms. Rhodes didn't look old enough to have a daughter, but there had to be something between them.

"Bigger than the dean," he told me. "But they send you to the atrium as one final test. It's a way to see how you operate without pressure. The fact that Aspen, of all people, found you interesting? Think of it like a Hail Mary. A long shot. It kinda works out, though, because she's going to be your suitemate."

"So, because some rich chick thought I was cool and decided she doesn't want to risk living with some freak, I get in?" Nope, saying it out loud didn't make that sound any better than it had in my head. "How the hell does that have anything to do with college admissions? Like..." I groaned. "I'm so confused."

"It's complicated," he explained. "But, regardless of the school politics, you're in. You're registered. Call it a lucky break if you want. The end result is that you're the one getting the benefits here. I'll request your transcripts this evening, and we'll get you moved in on Sunday afternoon, ok?"

I huffed. "You mean I really have to spend all weekend there? Liam, he's going to keep me locked in that room!"

"I'll convince him to at least let you eat with the family," he said.

I turned and looked at him as if he'd completely lost his mind. "Oh, because *that's* so much better. Really? I just finished Pride and Prejudice. I don't have a phone, a tablet, or even another book. Well, one, but I've already read it like twenty times."

"Then I'll get you a book," he said. "Rain, it's one day. Well, a day and two halves - and don't try to do that math. John will be happy you got accepted. Nancy will relax. I'll make it clear you're not some demon child, and maybe grab a set of Harry Potter books from the library?"

"Anne McCaffrey's Dragon Riders of Pern," I countered. "Like, all of them. Harper Hall, and the whole bit."

"It's one day," he reminded me. "Let's go with three books, and if you blow through those, I'll get you more."

"Deal," I said, grinning at him. "And I'll save all the other questions until I've moved into this super-secret not-dodgy-at-all school."

He chuckled. "I give you my word, I'll explain it all. It's just too much for a car ride, and neither of us want to do this in front of my brother."

"Yeah," I agreed. "It's not that I don't like the Sparks..."

"Rain," he said, "I know. Trust me, I know. John has never been an easy person to deal with. He's so angry about the way his life turned out. Nancy thinks that if she can be a better wife, then her husband will be happy. They took in the kids thinking that if they could just have a family, then they'd figure it out, but it's not something a few foster kids can fix for them. The problem is *they* don't even know what they want." He groaned. "And I'm not trying to dump my family's issues on you. Sorry."

"It's ok," I promised. "I just can't help but wonder what happened to them."

"Well," he said, his eyes locked on the road. "My father was abusive, and you know how children of abuse sometimes don't learn how to love any other way? That's my big brother. He doesn't hit, but he expects results." He laughed once. "He wanted our father's approval so badly, he gave up his own dreams to make Dad happy, and it never worked."

"So John got stuck?" I asked.

Liam nodded. "Very. That our dad said it was because John was worthless made it worse." He paused, pressing his lips together. "Nancy was the only good thing John ever did. They bonded over their negligent parents, but Nancy's family had nothing. John helped her out, they fell in love, and got married before they were twenty. Now, well, I think they're mutually miserable."

"That's sad," I mumbled, unsure how I was supposed to react.

Liam nodded his head at the road. "Yeah, it also explains why they have no clue how to relate to kids, but I think they are honestly trying. Neither of them could risk stepping out of line, Rain. My father loved to use his belt. Nancy's used his fists. Sounds to me like you know a little something about that?"

"My father only hit my mother," I explained. "Well, at least from what I remember. He was a cold man who never really talked to me or anything. I was five years old when she shot him."

"Yeah." He sighed. "Believe it or not, there actually are some very good parents out there."

"Like you?" I asked.

He paused for just a little too long. "No, I'm never going to be a parent. Sorry, kiddo."

"Why not?" I asked. "You're, what, early thirties? Never know, might find Miss Right and change your mind."

He licked his lips. "Rain, that's not going to happen." He paused, and the silence after it was a little too intense, but he refused to look at me. "I've been in a serious relationship for years. It's actually how I ended up working at Silver Oaks. You see, he was a student when we met. Now he's one of the instructors."

"So, you're gay?"

He grumbled, but it wasn't an angry sound. More like he didn't quite know how to respond. "My family thinks I'm devoted to my career. At work, I'm more open with my life. Yeah, I'm gay, but I'd prefer you not use that word with my brother. He might take it out on you."

"Understood," I assured him. "I kinda wondered what was wrong with you. Least being gay isn't wrong."

"It is in my family." He tapped his thumb on the steering wheel. "I'm also not brave enough to have that fight."

I slid down in the seat, stretching my legs out before me. "I think it wouldn't be worth it." Then I giggled. "Are you one of those gay guys who knows all about fashion?"

"What?" he asked. "No. Don't stereotype."

"Wasn't. I was actually hoping. I mean..." And I waved at the ugly clothes I was wearing. "This is pretty bad."

"I know enough to agree," he promised. "So, that doesn't bother you? Me being gay?"

"Nope." This time, I was the one flashing him the smile. I hoped it looked supportive. "I'm also not going to say anything. I'm willing to bet that living in a boy's dorm kinda makes things weird, right?"

"Not as much as you'd think," he admitted. "The faculty knows. Most of the students are aware. It's not being hidden, but I don't exactly offer up the information, if you know what I mean."

"Because kids are cruel and parents aren't any better?" I bobbed my head in understanding. "Believe me, I've had enough experience with foster families to have first-hand experience. We're cool, Uncle Liam. Thanks for telling me."

"I want kids, you know."

He just dropped that out there. The way he said it made it clear he didn't expect an answer, but this was me. I couldn't help myself. "You'd make a kick-ass dad. Single, with this boyfriend of yours, or whatever. Wait, do you live with him?"

He actually laughed. "Yes, we share the apartment."

"Wait, we get apartments?" Because that sounded even better than I expected.

"You have a dorm," he assured me. "I have an apartment. Benefits of being faculty."

Not long after that, we made it back into the actual town of Plainsboro. I expected we'd go straight back to the Sparks' house. Instead, Liam made a turn onto Main Street, then pulled up in front of a little shop with some cute clothes in the window. When he turned off the car, I gave him a confused look.

"I'm bribing you," he said. "Rain, I told the Sparks the uniforms are provided, but that's only partly true. Silver Oaks will assign you two blazers and four ties. The white shirts and appropriate skirts can be checked out from the school uniform office or purchased, but they aren't flattering." He sighed. "I'd planned to make sure you have something, which is why I told my brother the school would handle it. So, how about two skirts in exchange for pretending like our chat a minute ago never happened?"

"Liam," I groaned, "I'm not going to out you."

"And I'm not going to make you keep wearing that mess," he teased. "We both know that if Nancy bought you clothes, they wouldn't be any better. Consider this your seventeenth birthday present or something."

"That was back in May," I told him.

"So I'm a little late. I didn't know you then. Rain, don't make this harder than it has to be. You need a few things for school, the Sparks aren't about to get them, and I need to not have all the teachers laughing about my niece."

"Fine!" I huffed, but it was hard when I was smiling.

"Fine," he mocked, getting out to shut his door playfully hard.

When he stomped his feet as he made his way to the front of the car, I had to roll my eyes. "You really should've been a dad. You've got the perfect sense of humor for it."

"So you're saying I'm funny?" He pulled open the door and gestured for me to go first.

"No," I fake-whispered as I passed him, but damned if I didn't like this guy more than I'd expected to.

The moment we were both inside, a salesgirl showed up to help - most likely to get the commission. "Can I show you anything specific today?" she asked. Her voice had that overly-chipper fake thing salespeople did.

"Two skirts for the Silver Oaks Institute uniform," Liam told her. "Pleated or straight, whatever she likes most. Two shirts to go with it."

"All right," the girl agreed, leading the way toward the back.

We made a guess at my size, got one black pleated skirt and one stretchy black mini, then I was shuffled into the changing room to try them on. After each one, I had to come out and show Liam. He shook his head at the pleated one, saying I needed a different size and maybe style. The mini, though, he nodded emphatically.

The salesgirl traded out the pleated one for three more similar styles. It was the second I liked most, but Liam had vanished to look at something else. Still, he told me to pick, and the skirt I liked cost less than the one he'd picked, so I felt safe saying yes to it. Shirts were easier. I simply found two that were fitted. When that was done, I got dressed again, handed the salesgirl the stuff I didn't want, then wandered around to find Liam.

He was back by the shoes, looking over the options. In his hands he held a black pump. The heel was about two and a half inches tall, but with a blocky shape that wouldn't make it miserable to wear all day. More like a Mary Jane, I realized when he turned it a bit. In other words, super cute.

"What size?" he asked as soon as I walked up.

"Liam," I tried.

He just lifted a brow. "Humor me, ok?"

"Eight."

So he passed over the shoe in his hands. "Try it on?"

I sat down on the little vinyl bench, pulled off the canvas sneaker with a hooked finger, and then put on the heel. It was a little tight, so

I traded out for the next size up, then stood to show it off. Liam just nodded in approval.

"Ok, two skirts, two shirts, and a pair of shoes. Think of this as your welcome to my school present." When I pulled the heel off, I turned it over, hoping to check the price, but Liam snagged it out of my hand. "And none of that," he insisted.

"Fine," I teased.

He just grinned back. "Fine!"

Chapter Ten

Needless to say, when we made it back to the Sparks', neither of us mentioned the shopping trip. Liam apologized for running late, then promised them I'd behaved perfectly. Mr. Sparks had just gotten home from work and kept staring as if waiting for something. There was a new dimple on the side of Liam's face, though. I had a funny feeling he was picking on his brother intentionally.

"So?" Mr. Sparks finally asked. "Did she pass the exam, or do we need to send her back?"

Liam turned to me. "Lorraine, would you take your uniform upstairs and put it with the rest of your things?"

I gaped at him in astonishment. I was being sent away. They were going to start talking about me, and I was being sent upstairs to miss all of it? I managed to take the bag, but when I still didn't move, Liam tilted his head, giving me a look that begged me to trust him. I rolled my eyes in response. He'd bought me clothes that wouldn't make me look completely out of touch, so I figured I owed him this.

"Fine," I grumbled.

That dimple got a little deeper, proving my theory right. And while I definitely wanted to huff and trounce my way to my room, I resisted. A little good news was not enough to make me forget about the hell I'd lived through all week long. Never mind the fact that all the other kids were missing. Clearly, they'd planned for this to be a drama-fest.

Naturally, I paused just out of sight so I could listen in. "She will be attending," Liam said. "I also want you to know they did the tests. She's fine. She's a completely normal teenage girl. The birds were nothing more than a fluke."

"It landed on her arm," Mr. Sparks grumbled.

"The crow may have been possessed, but the girl isn't. She's completely fine. Also, your iron door knob isn't stopping her." Liam paused. "John, she's just a typical kid. The girl fed some crows at a previous home and they brought her things. She thought it was cool. Kinda like how some kids wear black. It's not magic, it's not evil, and it's nothing to worry about."

"But those boys..." Mrs. Sparks said.

"Very different," Liam assured her. "Those boys had serious psychological issues. They're getting help."

"It was more than that!" Mrs. Sparks hissed.

Liam murmured something that almost sounded like agreement. "The bad news, though, is she'll stay here through the weekend. I'll pick her up Sunday afternoon and move her into the dorms. After that, she'll be completely taken care of. Oh!" There was some rustling. "I have a paper for you both to sign. This gives me the authorization to act as her legal guardian while she's enrolled at Silver Oaks. Now, the checks will still come here, but just put that to the other kids, ok?"

"Really?" Mrs. Sparks asked.

"It's a full ride. All her meals, clothes, and supplies will be provided. I know things are tight with seven kids, so you can use it," Liam said.

"I still don't want her around the others," Mr. Sparks told his brother. "We got these kids behaving well, and the last thing we need is for them to all start acting up."

"John, she's fine," Liam said again. "You've already taken all the precautions. The only thing you need to worry about is typical teen drama."

"The crows are still out there," Mr. Sparks hissed. "Didn't you see them?"

"I wasn't paying attention," Liam assured him. "Look, some of these kids have mental issues. Some of them have delusions. Lorraine doesn't. She's just a bored girl who is sick and tired of being on lockdown. Give her a little space and I have a feeling she'll be good. I had a nice talk with her on the way back, and I can get her some books to keep her occupied, but you can't jail her in that room."

"What do you want us to do," Mrs. Sparks asked, "let her destroy all the order we've made?"

"Let her eat dinner with the family," Liam said. "Let her sit outside and throw some bread to a few stupid birds. Let her read a fantasy novel, Nancy. She's leaving on Sunday. Treat her like she's a guest."

"I'm not changing the doorknob," Mr. Sparks warned.

"Fine," Liam said. "Don't. Like I said, she's staying in her room because she was trying to be good. Go check if you don't believe me."

"I think I shall," Mr. Sparks said.

"Then I'm going to get a few books from the library for her," Liam said. "Thirty minutes. Do not harass her between now and then. I'm warning you, John, this kid would pass a psych eval, and you do not want a complaint of abuse against you. Not after the boys."

"Get her the damned books," Mr. Sparks conceded, "but I'm going to check if that knob works. Kept her in so far."

Which was my cue to get my ass in my room. Hurrying while stepping lightly, I made it around the corner and then put the bag with my new clothes on top of my suitcase. Desperate to look busy, I decided to pull out The Outsiders, then opened it to a random page and plopped down on my belly with it just as Mr. Sparks walked into my room.

"What are you doing?" he asked.

I turned the cover toward him. "Reading. One of my last moms gave this to me. She said it's a classic, but it's still pretty good."

He grunted, sounding like he wasn't sure what to say to that. "My brother says you got into this school. Is this really what you want?"

Setting the book aside, I sat up and crossed my legs to face him. "I need to go to college, Mr. Sparks. Once I age out, I will have no one to rely on but myself, so I want to have a degree that will make enough for me to pay any student loans I rack up and maybe buy a house. This? It's like a head start, so yes. I'm even excited for it."

"I see." He stood there nodding at me for a moment like he was analyzing my every movement. "So what are you thinking about doing with your life?"

The terrifying thing was that this man had never been this nice to me. I kinda wanted to get up, walk over there, and grab the doorknob so he'd leave already. At the same time, I wondered if maybe I hadn't given him enough of a chance.

"I've been trying to keep an eye on the jobs that are needed," I explained. "I mean, at my last home I had access to a laptop, so it was easy. I was thinking about being a professor. A lot of times, there's student loan forgiveness, and it pays more than a teacher, but it's hard to get into. Maybe translations? That seems to do well, and only requires a four-year degree."

"So you don't know," he said, making it sound like that was a bad thing.

"Not yet," I admitted. "I guess that's why I'm so excited about Silver Oaks. If I can finish high school while earning college credits for the basics, I'll be able to see what it's really like. You know, to test it out and figure out what I like and hate. Plus, I'm getting a scholarship, so the debt won't ruin me."

"Well," he said, "since you'll only be with us tomorrow and part of Sunday, I suppose you can read your books instead of doing chores. Just don't make problems for the other kids, and you can even have an extra piece of bread for the birds."

"Are you sure?" I asked. "I figured Mrs. Sparks was so mad because they make a mess."

"Where did you learn about birds anyway?" he asked.

"The internet," I admitted. "Same with tigers, but I'm not about to feed one of *those*." I almost left it there, but I couldn't help myself. "Mr. Sparks? Liam said something about a problem boy that stayed here. Did he feed the birds or something?"

The man's jaw clenched. "No. He did a lot of other things, but the birds weren't one. That boy caused enough damage, we're still paying off the loans to fix it."

"I promise I'll try not to cause problems all weekend," I said softly. "I just really want to go to this school."

"Sure, but I need you to do something for me," he countered. "I'm going to close this door, and I need you to open it from the inside so I can see if the lock's working."

"Ok." I climbed off the bed, struggling not to smile at the foolishness of his cover story.

Mr. Sparks stepped back and closed the door, then said through the wood, "Ok, can you open it?"

I turned the knob and pulled it wide. "Yeah. I think your latch might be broken? It doesn't even click."

"I see. Well, then there's no sense in changing it back until you're gone. Liam is out getting you a few books to entertain you for the next day or so. He should be back shortly."

Then Mr. Sparks simply turned and hurried toward the stairs. He looked like he was retreating, and doing everything in his power not to run to his wife and tell her the iron knob was pointless. The man was clearly insane. What did he think, that I was some kind of monster or something? The funniest part was how he assumed *I* was the crazy one.

This time, when I went back to my things, it was to pack up the new stuff I'd brought home. My uniforms went on the bottom. The box with my new shoes went in the nylon bag. Since Mr. Sparks had cleaned me out, there was plenty of room for all of it. I still wanted to wring the man's neck for that. One week, and I'd probably just lost half of my belongings.

None of this was fair. Not a single bit made sense.

I'd just turned to the closet to check for anything else I might've missed when a soft rap sounded at my door. I leaned back to see Liam standing there, holding a set of three books. From the pictures on the covers, I knew he'd gotten me exactly what I'd asked for. This was the original trilogy, which I loved more than anything else. It should keep me from going insane before I left here.

"Thank you, Uncle Liam," I said.

He jerked his chin at my room. "Can I come in?"

I scoffed. "You're the first person to actually ask since I came here. Sure."

Liam stepped in and pushed the door closed behind him. "Three books." He came around the corner, then paused. "What are you doing in the closet?"

"Uh, making sure I didn't miss anything I need to pack. I mean, if I do it now, then, you know, if something opens up sooner..."

"In the closet?" he asked again.

"What the hell, Liam? It's a closet!" I waved at the still open door. "I was kinda hoping your brother had stuffed the bag of my 'inappropriate' clothes in here instead of throwing them out. He didn't, but that was my thought."

"What inappropriate clothes?" Liam asked.

"A black long-sleeve," I said, ticking it off on my fingers. "There was also a pink tank that said 'Pretty Girl' on it. Um, I know there were a couple pairs of jeans with holes. You know, the distressed kind."

Liam reached up to scrub his face. "Yeah. In other words, nothing inappropriate. Fair enough." Then he set the books on the table beside my bed, pausing again. "Is this yours?"

It was the little metal dog. "Nope. The first night I was here, Mr. Sparks came in while I was supposed to be sleeping and left that. He checked the picture frame over there and something else too."

So Liam went to look. The moment he touched the frame, he let out a heavy sigh. "Some superstitions say iron wards off evil spirits," he explained. "Messes with the magnetic attraction of them or something. I guess he thought he was giving you good luck charms."

"Right." Because I got the impression Liam didn't believe that any more than I did.

The weak laugh he offered proved I was right. "Rain, I know all of this seems crazy. I promise it will make sense, but I want you to do something for me."

"Ok..." That sounded ominous.

"Take the weekend and think about this. Ask yourself if you truly want to go to this school. If you're ready to have everything you know turned upside down - and your education will likely be twice as hard."

"I don't care how hard it is," I insisted. "Liam, I just want out of here. Maybe most kids want to be lazy, but I've always known that the only person who can give me a future is myself. College? Really? You're offering me the one thing I've always wanted."

"Rain, this is going to be more difficult than you think."

"Don't care," I assured him. "I promise I'll work hard."

"And you'll be sharing a suite with the girl by the trees," he reminded me. "The one with enough power to make or break your future. Are you sure you're not trading one type of restriction for another?" He lifted a hand before I could answer. "Just think about it, Rain? Think hard, because when things seem crazy, I don't want you to say you didn't have the chance."

"I will," I assured him. "My answer will still be the same, but I promise I will think about it."

"Then enjoy the books," he said. "I'll be back Sunday afternoon to pick you up." He turned for the door, but paused. "They'll know you aren't like them. You'll get picked on for it. This isn't going to be easy, Rain."

"Still the same answer, Liam," I said. "See you Sunday."

"Yes, you will," he mumbled as he left. "I made a deal."

Chapter Eleven

After Liam left, I lost myself in dragons. Around seven, Stephanie tapped at my door, letting me know it was dinnertime. I hurried to put my things away and made it to the table just before Mrs. Sparks put the main dish in the middle. The woman gave me a dirty look, pulling in a deep breath like she was forcing herself not to say anything.

"Sorry," I mumbled as I took my chair. "I wasn't sure if I was allowed to eat down here today."

"Tone," Mr. Sparks snapped.

"She's only eaten with us once this week," the girl beside me pointed out. "I wasn't sure it was allowed either."

I smiled at her, but she refused to meet my eyes. Clearly, I was still a pariah in the house. Oh well. I could deal with that a little longer. Just like the first time, the whole family got to take their serving before it made it to me. Tonight, it looked like some hamburger helper thing. Regardless, it smelled good.

But the moment I put the bowl back where it belonged, Mr. Sparks cleared his throat, making everyone look at him. "Most of you haven't heard yet, but Lorraine here has been given a scholarship to Silver Oaks Institute. It's a unique situation, so she won't be going to school with the rest of you. Sunday, she will be picked up by your caseworker, Liam, so she can move into her dorm."

"Really?" one of the boys asked. Dominik, I was pretty sure, since he wasn't Markus. "I thought that was a college."

"Like I said," Mr. Sparks told him, "it's a unique situation. At any rate, we will be keeping her room, and we will not get another foster so long as she's in attendance. Lorraine may come back for some holidays, but with the rigorous schedule, I expect it will be infrequent."

I nodded, hoping it looked excited instead of annoyed. I couldn't believe the gall of this man. He was ready to kick me out of the house, and now Mr. Sparks was acting like he'd somehow done me a favor. Whatever. Liam had said he wanted me to honestly think about this, and so far, all signs were pointing not just to "yes," but to "run fast."

When the meal was done, I decided to help with dishes. Supposedly, I didn't have to do any chores, but I felt bad about it. I ended up with the girl who'd spoken up for me. Her name was Esperanza, and she was in the tenth grade, but almost sixteen. When both of the Sparks left the room, she even admitted they'd all thought I was going to be sent back after the incident with the crow.

But no one knew what the big deal was with that. Esperanza said the Sparks were weird about some things. No plants were allowed inside, not even a cactus. No symbols either. Evidently Dominik had gotten into trouble for a game logo on one of his book covers. Mrs. Sparks had ripped it off and stuck the thing in the garbage disposal. Then there was the whole church requirement.

Because if a kid was possessed, they clearly couldn't go into a church? I was too scared to ask, afraid that would start an entire discussion on the rules around religion in this house. Yep, I had a day and a half, and I'd keep reminding myself of it any time I got curious about things.

That night, I went upstairs and lost myself in my book again. I read until late in the night, so engrossed in the story I completely lost track of time. When the door to my room opened, I jumped, letting out a little squeak. Mrs. Sparks stood in the opening, glaring at me.

"Why aren't you asleep?" she asked.

"Uh..." I looked over at the clock. "I kinda had no idea what time it was. Sorry. Do we have set bedtimes?"

Her stare could've frozen hell over. "Not that it matters now, but don't think you'll get to sleep in tomorrow."

"Yes, ma'am," I said.

Then, just to be a smartass, I leaned over and shoved the little metal dog out of the way and set my book where it had been. Yeah, that woman watched me like someone trying to figure out a magic trick. Superstitious didn't begin to explain this family. A bunch of other words jumped to mind, though. Whack-jobs, lunatics, and psychopaths, just to start.

Thankfully, when I turned out the light, she left. Clearly, I'd passed the midnight inspection. Although, the next morning, no one woke me. I slept until just after ten. Even then, it wasn't the people in the house who woke me up. It was a small tapping on the window. I debated going back to sleep, and then I heard it again.

I got up and raised the blinds. Startled, the bird flew off, but it came back only a moment later. On the window sill, right about where I'd left the ribbon trinket, there was a collection of pretty little pebbles. The crow dropped another while I watched, then tapped its beak on the glass again.

"Well, aren't you kind?" I asked, carefully cracking the window.

Caw!

Damn it, I didn't have anything to give it, but Mr. Sparks had said I could have an extra piece of bread for them. Deciding this was worth tempting my luck, I hurried to get dressed and headed downstairs. The TV was on in the living room, and everyone was sitting around it, watching some movie. Well, at least there was a little relaxation in this house, but I was more interested in the bird.

Making sure to not get in their way, I made it into the kitchen, got the bread, and then almost made it back upstairs before Mrs. Sparks had to speak up.

"Where are you going, Lorraine?" she asked.

"To read," I said. "I just wanted a little snack, and Mr. Sparks said I could have this."

The woman flipped her hand, dismissing me, and I didn't waste any time getting out of sight. The hardest part was not thundering up the stairs, because I had a feeling that would make her call me back down. Thankfully, once I made it to my room, I saw the crow was still there. So was another little present. This one was an old, rusted bolt someone had clearly lost.

Opening the window just a few inches - so the bird wouldn't accidentally come in - I took a rock and traded it for a piece of bread the size of my pinky nail. Hopefully, this crow would realize I preferred rocks, so maybe it wouldn't steal any diamond earrings!

The crow ate the bread quickly, then cawed again. I gave him another, but I was pretty sure they shouldn't eat too much at a time. Still, he was gorgeous, with his nearly iridescent black feathers. And smart. Definitely smart enough to have started up a hoard of gifts.

"Don't be greedy," I told him. "And please stick to pebbles? Yeah, those will be nice and safe." I watched as he nudged one of the rocks towards me. Or she. I didn't really know. "You're a pretty bird, aren't you?"

"Jack," he croaked.

I wasn't sure if he actually said a word or if his caw just sounded like it. "Is that your name, bud?" Because Jack was a boy's name, so I'd use those pronouns.

"Jack," he croaked again.

Well, screw it. That was cute enough he got one more piece of bread. "Now go fly or something. I don't want to make you sick, Jack. You're too cool of a bird."

Caw!

And with that, he was gone. Soon enough, another took his

place. This one was smaller, but otherwise just as black. Like I had with the first one, I offered the new bird a little piece of bread. It took it and flew off. Another quickly landed for its turn. I had no idea how many crows I managed to feed, but none of the others croaked a sound like Jack had.

It made me wonder if he'd been trained to talk, or maybe he'd just picked it up? No, it clearly had to be a normal sound. Still, it kinda made my day. When I finally ran out of bread, I closed the window again, then the blinds, and went right back to reading my book.

Somewhere in my isolation, the silence finally began to get to me. My mind started going, and I immediately thought of the strange girl in the atrium. Aspen was beautiful in a way that made her impossible to forget. She'd also seemed nice. There was something about how she'd casually offered me some of her candy that had completely lowered all of my defenses.

Yet none of that erased how quickly she'd lost her temper - and at Liam! Maybe being a counselor wasn't as impressive in college? Then again, she looked to be about my age, so maybe she was an Advanced Placement student too? And maybe her daddy owned everything, so she was just that much of a brat? I didn't have a clue, but I had a feeling living in the same suite would be a little challenging.

Liam had told me to think about this, and I tried. I sat there with my book open in my lap, doing my best to find a reason why I'd rather stay here than go there, and I came up with exactly nothing. The other students might pick on me for being a foster kid. Here, my foster parents were already doing that. I'd be the laughingstock. Would that be any different if I went to school in the outfits Mrs. Sparks made the girls in this house wear?

Plus, I'd never been one of the cool girls, so why would college be any different? It wasn't as if I'd be losing something or dropped down a notch. I'd been the invisible girl at my last school. I'd had a few friends I'd hung out with. There'd been a few boys I'd had crushes on. I also never stayed in the same place long enough to do more than decide a guy was kinda cute before my life was upended again.

I just wanted a little stability. I didn't even need comfortable stability! I simply wanted to have the same enemies for more than a handful of months. Maybe the same parental figures. Possibly the same teachers. Hell, I couldn't even remember the name of the man who'd taught my tenth-grade English class. Or the woman.

And what was the worst-case scenario? If I didn't do good enough, they'd kick me out, and the Sparks would lose it and send me to the state-run group home. That was pretty much where I was already at, so at least this way I had a chance. I'd put up with some pretty wacky stuff if it meant I had the smallest sliver of control over my life.

In reality, the only thing I'd actually lose if I tried this was a friendship with a bunch of wild birds who'd only just realized I was here. The funny thing was I'd read they were supposed to be bad omens. It didn't really work that way for me. Every time the crows came around, things were pretty good for a while. Well, until they weren't.

But I couldn't blame the bad stuff on them. Not really. In truth, it all came back down to humans. The birds did what birds always do. They picked up shiny things, ate other things, and flew around crapping where they wanted. It was the people who tried to read something into it.

Ms. Ellis had lost it because of her earring being outside my window. Didn't take a genius to realize that if I'd stolen it, the thing would've been inside. Probably hidden in a much better place than a window sill on the second floor.

Now, the Sparks were going nuts with metal door knobs and figurines in my room because one had flown into the house. If those birds were trying to tell me anything, it was that I was better off away from the nutjobs. So, there - I'd thought about it. I'd promised Liam I would, and I just had.

I was going to Silver Oaks Institute. I would learn how to stay out of trouble, get a degree, and figure out how to make this opportunity work for me. It had to. The law of averages said I deserved to get a lucky break at least once in my life, right?

Hopefully, this would be it.

Chapter Twelve

The next day, I went to church with the family. I got dressed up in one of those plaid shirts and a khaki skirt that fell to the middle of my shins. The fact that it was paired with some white canvas shoes made the whole thing look even more stupid, but the other girls in the house matched me. Our shirts were different versions of pastel, but that was about it.

I wasn't surprised when we all sat together. The three boys got to share the same pew as Mr. and Mrs. Sparks. We girls ended up in the row behind them. For the most part, it was pretty painless. So long as we mumbled something in the general tune of the songs and bowed our heads at the right times, the Sparks only gave us a few warning looks.

It took two trips to move us all from home to church, then from church back home. Evidently, the Sparks did this every weekend. It was insane, and I couldn't be happier to leave it all behind. So, the moment I was home, I hurried to change into something normal, then waited.

And waited.

Eventually, Liam arrived. No, he wasn't late, but every second felt like an eternity. I was picking at the split ends of my hair when the sound of knuckles rapping against my open door made me look up. When my eyes landed on Liam, I smiled. He merely glanced over to where my things were still packed from the last time I saw him.

"I'm getting the strangest impression you still want to do this," he teased.

"I promised I'd think about it," I assured him, "and I did. A lot. All signs point to yes."

"Rain..." he tried.

"Liam," I broke in, "if I don't do this, I'm going to the state home. If I fail at this or decide I hate it, then I'm going to the state home. The worst-case scenario here is that I try something which could work out. If it doesn't, I'm not really losing anything."

"Yeah." He moved to grab my suitcase. "I want you to remember that, ok? When I get you settled in and start laying out the rules, just keep in mind that I gave you a chance to back out."

"Promise," I said, hooking the strap of my nylon bag over my shoulder. "Lead the way, Uncle Liam."

He grunted at that, but carried my suitcase downstairs to where the entire family was waiting. Most of the kids looked like they'd rather be anywhere else. I didn't blame them. It wasn't like we knew each other. Stephanie offered me a smile, which I returned. Mr. Sparks warned me to behave myself. Then Mrs. Sparks had to give me a big, mushy hug, acting like she'd been the sweetest mother ever.

I somehow made it through all of that without my fake smile slipping. Outside, Liam had me put my things in the backseat of his car, then I moved to the passenger door. Just as I reached for the handle, a crow landed on the roof. The thing couldn't be more than a foot away.

"Jack," it croaked.

"Gonna miss you, Jack," I told him even as I opened the car door. "No more bread, bud. I'm going to college and won't be back."

"Jack!" it chirruped even louder.

"Go on." I made a subtle shooing gesture, not wanting to scare him, yet knowing he had to move.

He cawed normally, then flapped away, his wings almost hitting my head when the large bird took off. I groaned, then dropped into the passenger seat. While I was buckling my seatbelt, Liam stared at me.

"You know that isn't really normal, right?" he asked.

"For most birds, sure," I agreed. "Crows are very social, though. If one's imprinted on humans, they'll be friendly with almost any human. I watched a documentary about it. That's how SeaWorld got one that talks."

"Uh huh." And with that, he backed out of the drive, and I was officially out of that hellhole.

On the way over, I decided I really liked Liam. Not just tolerated or was willing to take his offer. I *liked* this guy. He wasn't ashamed to sing when a song he liked played on the radio. He could hold an actual conversation between those good songs. Then, he told me we'd have to get me a few supplies from the main office before he could take me up to my dorm. Basically, the man acted like he actually cared.

The drive from the Sparks' to Silver Oaks took almost half an hour, but it blew past this time. Yet when we pulled into the drive, the gate was closed. Liam had a little transmitter stuck to the corner of the window that made it open, the silver tree in the middle of the fancy metal gate splitting so half went one way and half went the other. When it stopped moving, he eased his car forward.

I gawked, turning in my seat to see the property around us. Friday, I'd been entranced with the trees. Today, I looked past them, at the land beyond. It was all perfectly manicured, with trees, shrubs, and flowers set up like some fancy European place. Everything was asleep for the winter, though. Snow clung under the lines of bushes, the grass was yellow, and most of the leaves were gone, and yet it looked so well-maintained.

Where last time we'd stopped in front of the main entrance, this time Liam drove around to the side. Tucked behind another line of bushes - which were taller than I was - a parking lot was hidden. All the cars had the same transmitter in the window, and most of them had a black sticker with a silver tree in the middle: teachers' cars.

"Do students get to bring their cars?" I asked.

"Yes, but they're only allowed off-property on the weekends," he explained. "There's another lot on the other side for them. They also get a transmitter, and it records every time they go in and out the gates. Means we know when someone sneaks off campus."

"Even for the actual college students? Not just the Advanced Placement ones?"

"Even them," Liam said. "Because of the structure at Silver Oaks, some things are more restrictive than the average university. We have specific benefits to make up for it, though. That's why our student body is small, but dedicated."

"Cool."

Because what else was I supposed to say? I didn't have a car, so it didn't really matter, but if the students could leave, then the place would be pretty barren today, wouldn't it? It was Sunday, so no reason to stick around campus. It also meant fewer people to see me moving in, which was kinda nice.

Once he was parked, we both got out. Liam grabbed my suitcase, I got my nylon bag again, then I followed him to a side entrance. The halls were empty, so Liam led me the back way to the office. The moment we stepped inside, a woman looked up with a smile. Clearly, there was always someone in here. It also seemed we were expected.

Without needing to be asked, the lady passed across a stack of papers for him. "Her enrollment forms, her class schedule, and a welcome packet," she said.

He took the stack, pulled a few pages out, then passed the rest to me. "I'll pick up any supplies you need this evening, if that's ok?"

All I could do was shrug. "Dunno, is it?"

That made the woman chuckle. "If you give me a minute, I'll find a tablet for you. Liam, her uniforms are in your office."

"I get a tablet?" I looked at Liam to make sure I wasn't dreaming.

"Don't get too excited," he warned. "It's wifi only, and your access to certain apps is limited due to your age. It's just for school, and maybe for talking to other people in school."

"It's better than I have now," I pointed out. "I'm going to guess all social media is completely locked out?"

"Oh yeah." He rubbed my shoulder, the gesture almost playful. "We want our students to study, remember. That includes you now."

"So, if I don't make straight A's, I get grounded?"

He rolled his eyes. "No, but let's work for As and Bs, ok? And if you need help with any of your classes, I'm here." He pointed to an office on the opposite side from the one Ms. Rhodes had been in on Friday. Then he steered me that way. "So, the official uniform is either a black or a green-plaid skirt, a white button-down shirt, and a tie. You can wear a black sweater or blazer with it, and you're expected to pick one or the other. Black shoes, your socks can be white or black, and tights are allowed under your skirts."

He finished just as he opened the door to his office. Sitting right in the middle of his desk was a rather large box. The cardboard kind. From the top, plastic-wrapped clothes peeked out. New ones, and from the green plaid, I could only imagine this was one of the skirts he'd mentioned.

"So, not only do I get the clothes you already bought, but these too?"

"I may have ordered a few things," he admitted. "The skirts are yours. The shirts too. The blazers and ties will be returned at the end of the year. You will be issued a new set each year you're here. If you outgrow anything - or undergrow - just let me know."

"Ok..."

I moved to grab the box, but Liam offered me the handle to my suitcase instead. Picking the box up took both of his arms, because it wasn't a small amount of clothes. I just heaved my suitcase against my hip and followed. When we were back in the main part of the office, we stopped again. The woman working there handed me a tablet and instruction booklet, then had me sign for it. Once all that was done, Liam led me back out of the office and towards the atrium.

When we passed, I couldn't help but look at the trees again. A split second later, I noticed the students. The space was clearly popular, and groups hung out among the vegetation. They weren't in uniforms, though. Most people out there were just wearing jeans and t-shirts or long-sleeves. I supposed that meant the uniform was for class only?

Liam didn't even slow. Not until he made it all the way around the other side and pressed a button for an elevator. The lights at the top began moving, and I wanted to steal another look at my new fellow students. I also didn't dare. If I looked desperate, they'd smell it. Sense it. Whatever. No matter what I called it, I knew how this went. I'd been the new girl enough times to be a pro at it.

When the elevator finally arrived, we got on, Liam pressed the button for the fourth floor, and up we went. The motion was what finally made me start feeling anxious. I was actually doing this! I was enrolled in college. I was moving into my own dorm. I honestly had no idea what to expect, but this was real. It was happening!

And then the doors opened. Liam just kept leading, although the trip wasn't far. Immediately to my right was one door. To the left was a set of double doors, which had been thrown open. Beyond those was a very long hall that stretched the length of this massive wing. Dozens of doors were visible along it, and most had signs or whiteboards on them.

Liam aimed for the second door on the left. Juggling the box, he managed to pull out a key, then opened it, tilting his head for me to step through first. I did, and then stopped hard. I'd seen pictures of dorms, and I'd watched enough movies to get the basic idea. This? It was not like that.

This was *amazing*.

The room was big. On the far side was a full-sized bed. An entire set of built-in drawers and shelves took up the rest of that wall. Straight across from the door was a window, and the big kind. Four people could easily stand shoulder-to-shoulder in front of it. There was a desk to my right, another door to the left, and a pretty green-and-silver rug in the middle. The place looked like a luxury suite!

"Whoa," I breathed, setting my things down in the first open spot I found.

"I need a spot for this," Liam said as he shuffled in behind me. "Ok." He set the box down on the desk, then dusted off his hands. "This is your room, Rain. That door..." He pointed to the one to my left. "...leads to the bathroom you share with Aspen." He walked over and knocked on it. Getting no response, he opened it to show me what was inside. "Double sink."

I stepped in behind him to see this was a lot more private than I'd expected. The sinks were in full view, but there was a door for the toilet, making it almost like a stall but built more like a tiny room. Then there was a set of cabinets, and behind them I could make out a shower nook. A big shower, not the institutionalized type found in most locker rooms. One that wasn't immediately visible to someone at the sink.

"This is really nice," I breathed.

"Yep." Liam headed back to my room. "So, now is when we get to talk about all the not-fun stuff. Sit down, Rain. It'll be easier that way."

I moved to my bed and sat, but something about it felt ominous. Evidently, this was when the other shoe dropped.

Chapter Thirteen

Liam pulled out the chair from my desk, then turned it around to face me. Everything about his mannerisms had changed. The smile was gone and the man looked tense. I pulled my legs up, crossing them under me on the pretty mint-green comforter, and just waited.

"So..." he tried before blowing out a heavy breath. "Yeah, I'd hoped that practicing this would make it easier, but it's not really helping. Rain, this isn't a normal school."

"You already warned me about that," I assured him. "Elite private college and all that."

"No, even less normal than you think," he insisted. "The entrance exam was to place you in one of five learning programs. I sorta explained that, but I didn't tell you what they are. You see, this school was designed for a very special, and very secret, subset of people." He stopped again. "No, I'm making a mess of this. Let me try a different way. You know how the Sparks had all those things in your room?"

"Like the metal dog?" I asked.

He nodded. "The *iron* dog, Rain. An iron doorknob. An iron picture frame. What have you heard of that has problems with iron?"

"Uh, demons?" I guessed. "So, you think I'm actually possessed?"

"No!" he groaned. "Demons have nothing to do with iron. Fairies do!"

He just blurted that out, sounding almost frustrated that I didn't know the lore. But that was the thing. He didn't say it like it was a lie or a joke. More like he couldn't believe this wasn't public knowledge.

"Ok? What do fairies have to do with this?" I was very careful not to let him hear how crazy I thought he sounded. "Are you a fairy, Liam?"

"Wrong kind of fairy," he assured me. "Rain, the fae folk are real. Most of the students at this school are children of a fae who took a human lover. Half-fairies, although they don't use that term. They are fae or fae folk. Faelings is a common term for the half-bloods."

"Yeah, I don't even want to know how that works," I joked, trying to imagine Tinkerbell with Peter Pan.

He huffed, squeezing his eyes closed, and tried one more time. "Not like Disney. I'm talking the old-school type of fae. No butterfly wings, Rain. These are magical beings who have a completely different society and morality. This school was built to help the children they left behind learn how to control their magical powers. The testing was to sort you into a class style: Enticement, Glamour, Enchantment, Conjuration, or Legacy. Those are the trades we teach here."

I lifted my head, about to nod at him, but paused when I realized he wasn't joking. "You're serious about this?"

"Very," he admitted. "A few of us here are completely human. I'm one. In truth, I encouraged my brother to become a foster parent so we could funnel kids here. You see, with the current situation, a lot of refugee children are being slipped into the world, and the foster system has replaced the need for changelings."

"Yeah..." This was not getting any less insane.

"Just hear me out?" he begged. "There's a war in Faerie. The doorways have been locked, but every so often, a few make it through. One, maybe two a year, and spread all across the world.

Most of the fae on Earth right now came when the war started. They made lives for themselves, fell in love, had children, and all the usual things. Those children, however, were born with magic. Half-bloods, quarter, and sometimes even less. After all, the fae have been entertaining themselves here long enough to have become folklore."

"Right," I agreed, deciding that was safest.

"But abilities can crop up through the generations. The more fae blood, the more likely someone is to have magical abilities."

"And I'm supposed to be one of these?" I asked. "You're trying to say I'm magic."

"Yeah, that's the thing…" He reached up to shove his hand across his mouth, his eyes locked on my rug. "You tested as normal, Rain. You can touch iron, and even the smallest hint of fae blood tends to make someone uncomfortable with that. The more a person has, the greater the reaction, up to burns and severe pain."

"So, you've actually seen this?" I asked.

"I have," he assured me. "Rain, I was coming to the atrium to let you know you hadn't been accepted. After the ordeal with the crows, and the number of times you've been moved through different homes, I assumed you had to be accidentally casting magic, causing your foster families to move you on instead of trying to explain something they don't believe in. All the signs were there, but it seems you're completely normal. They've agreed to put you in the Legacy class, though."

"Because that girl said so?" Yep, even weirder.

"Aspen," Liam said softly. "She's a very powerful girl. When she says you're interesting, we tend to believe her."

"Liam!" I finally snapped. "Magic isn't real. This is stupid. You can't expect me to sit here, smile, nod, and pretend like any of this is supposed to make sense! If this is supposed to be some kind of hazing for my first day or something, give up already!"

"No, it's real," he insisted. "You will have classes about the normal things like English and math. You will also have classes about the history of the fae, the powers they can wield, and so on."

"Right." I rolled my eyes.

Then the door on the far side of the bathroom opened and Aspen stormed in, carrying something. "You're messing it up," she snarled at Liam. Then those electric blue eyes turned on me. "You want magic? Here."

One little flick of her fingers was all it took for my entire world to change. One second, I was on a bed in a dorm room. The next, I was in the middle of what looked like a London street. Well, the double-decker buses made me think London, at any rate. I jumped up, tripped on something, and fell right across the road. Scrambling, I pulled myself back to the safety of the median in the middle just a split second before a car ran me over.

I spun, trying to figure out how to get out of here! The sounds were loud. The smell of car exhaust and the city was almost overwhelming. Finally, I saw a gap between the oncoming traffic, so I ran, hoping to get to the sidewalk before someone took me out. I was almost to the curb when an arm grabbed me around the waist and the vision simply faded out, returning me to my room.

It was Liam who held me, my face mere inches from the wall. "It's real," he said. But as his grip relaxed, he turned back to Aspen. "What did you do?"

"Glamour. London." She turned her attention back to me, then pointed toward the table next to my bed. "I got you a housewarming gift." Then she spun right back around, her short skirt flaring with the motion, and marched back to her side of the suite.

The shutting of the door was like a slap to the face, pulling me from the shock of what had just happened. I was still breathing too fast, the terror of being trapped on a busy street a bit too real. My mind was trying to reject the truth of me being in my room. Liam just watched me, a worried look on his face, so I gave up. Making my way back to my bed, I sat down and looked at the "housewarming gift" Aspen had brought.

It was a plant. A strange one, to be sure. It almost looked like an orchid and a Venus flytrap had been mixed together. There were large leaves that grew from the bottom. They were a deep, almost blue-green color. The "flowers" that reached up were what reminded me of the Venus flytrap, though. They looked like little mouths clamped down around something. It was actually a pretty cool little plant, even if I would most likely end up killing it.

"Is gardening a magic skill?" I asked, unsure what else to say.

"Can be," Liam admitted. "It falls under enchantment, mostly. The stronger a fae's magic, the more control they have over nature, and that includes circumstances. Acts of God, if you will. There are also potions, spells, and all the things you'd expect. The problem is you *will* see it in the halls of this school. You will be expected to understand and identify all types of magic. You will also be trained in defending against them and avoiding them."

"Because I'm not magic?" I asked.

"You are not," he admitted. "You seem to be completely human. No fae ancestry anywhere." Then he murmured a noise, stopping himself. "I should also explain that a person is a fae, F-A-E. Their world is Faerie, F-A-E-R-I-E. We usually see the A-I-R-Y version in books, but to them, that kind of fairy means gay. Believe it or not, some can hear the difference."

"Great," I breathed. "So, I guess I get to learn a second language too?"

"It's an option," he said. "Unless you're ready to go back, call all this off, and take the group home option?"

No, I didn't want that. I also wasn't completely convinced I believed Liam, but I couldn't doubt it either. My quick trip to London had left a lasting impression I was trying very hard to ignore. Right now, I was just completely and totally confused. My mind was spinning, the smell of London still so fresh in my memories, yet I'd never been there.

I didn't know what I was supposed to do or what was expected of me. I had no clue how I was supposed to pass my classes in a magic school if I didn't have magic. I also couldn't quite accept this magic thing wasn't just a big joke. I wanted to check the walls for a projector. I tried to think of anything I may have ingested that could've been drugged. There was nothing. This had to be real, yet my brain wanted to reject it as impossible.

But London had been real. So terrifyingly real.

The bigger question was if I could do this. Granted, that put me right back to where I'd been this morning. It also made me realize why Liam had told me to think about this. I already had my arguments for and against fleshed out. This? It really changed nothing. Either I could figure it out and muddle through, or I could go back, go to the state home, and grow up to have some minimum-wage job that wouldn't even cover my bills.

"I'm not going to get very good grades," I warned him.

Liam's shoulders relaxed and the man breathed a sigh of relief. "So you're staying?"

"Might as well try, right? Worst case, I'm no worse off than I was a few hours ago." I shrugged. "But this isn't some kind of joke, right?"

"I'm sorry, but it's not," he told me.

"And Aspen?" I gestured in the direction of her door. "Is she... safe?"

"She likes you," he said. "That's not going to mean the same with her as it does with most people, though."

"Why?"

Liam's mouth opened, paused, closed, and then he tried again. "She's a purebred, Rain. There are five pure-fae students in this entire school, and she's one of the strongest." He tipped his head at the plant she'd left for me. "That? It's a fae flower. No one else can get them to grow on our world. When Aspen plants them, no one can make them die. Very powerful. Very different set of standards. Be nice to her, stay interesting, and you should be just fine."

"I don't even know *how* I'm interesting," I pointed out.

"Me either," he admitted, standing up to head for the box of my stuff. "And one last thing? Your tie marks your class type." He dug in the box and pulled one out. "Diagonal stripes are for Legacies. Anyone else with this pattern has no magic."

"And the rest?" I asked.

"Enticers wear plaid. Glamours have vertical stripes. Up and down. Enchanters wear horizontal stripes. Side to side. Then there's the Conjurers. Theirs will be solid black. It's the most versatile type here. They're the ones who can actually throw spells."

"And kiss all their asses if they're not in diagonal stripes," I said. "Got it."

"Don't," he told me. "Instead, find a subject in your course type that makes you just as good as them. Even Legacies can make a name for themselves here. Not having magic isn't the same as being worthless, Rain. It just means you can handle some things the others can't. Like touching iron, for instance."

I finally felt like I could smile a bit. "Yeah, I guess that's a good point."

He walked over, then gave me an unexpected hug. "From one human to another, trust me when I say it's worth it to live in this world."

"How'd you get involved anyway?" I asked.

He leaned back, a smile on his face. "When I was in high school, I went to a party. There was a cute boy there, and I had an instant crush. Imagine my surprise when he felt the same way. He was fae, and I figured out pretty quickly that there was something special about him. Somewhere along the way, I learned about all of this, and then I started helping. I find the lost ones, Rain. I have abilities they don't, even though I'm only human. It makes me an equal in their eyes. Well, most of them."

"Social worker just got added to my list of potential career paths," I teased.

"That's my niece," he praised. "But hold off on that until you're here a bit longer. Never know, you might find something else you're good at."

Chapter Fourteen

It was still relatively early in the afternoon. According to the clock on the wall, just after four. Because of that, Liam offered to introduce me to my mentor, a girl who'd explain my course options to me. Evidently, I had one week to decide which electives I wanted to take. Everyone in the high school program was required to have math, English, a science, and Fae History. That left three other classes for us to tailor our studies to our personal interests. College-level courses, and ones we'd be able to use towards an eventual degree.

Sure, we'd get something for the required ones too. It seemed that the way this worked out, we earned both high school and college credit in a way that would make us immediate college sophomores when we reached the equivalent of our high school diploma. And yes, we would get those diplomas, but they'd be issued from Silver Oaks Institute, not a normal school, like the one in town.

Liam explained all of this, taking the time to answer my questions about credits, rules, and so on. But as he stood to leave, Liam seemed to remember something else.

"Let me give you my phone number," he said, turning back

MISTAKEN MAGIC

"Won't matter," I told him. "No phone. My last one was on the family plan, and the Sparks aren't really into things like that."

"My idiot brother," Liam grumbled. "Ok. Well, if you need me, I'm on the opposite side of the atrium, fourth floor, the room outside the double doors." He sighed. "And I'll handle the phone problem. Let me go find your mentor. Unpack or something."

I figured that was as good of an idea as anything else, so once he left, I started putting my stuff away. My personal clothes went in a few of the drawers beside my bed. Uniform stuff went in others. All combined, I had enough options for seven days before I'd be forced to do laundry. Thankfully, the Institute handled that for me as well.

But now that word made a lot more sense. Institute. This wasn't a university, and while they called it a private college or a trade school, that seemed to be a front of sorts. This was a school for supernatural things that weren't supposed to exist. It was a school for learning magic. Fucking magic! So yeah, maybe "Institute" was a better choice, all things considered.

I was thinking about that when I reached the blazers. Those would need to be hung up; the question was where? Searching the massive amount of built-in storage, I opened a cabinet and found it was actually a wardrobe. Well, that changed things a bit. The blazers went in there, along with anything else I didn't want someone to accidentally rummage through - like underwear.

Putting Theo on my bed was the last thing, and it gave a little "homey" feel to the room. This was my space. Mine. All mine, and I wouldn't have to worry about upsetting anyone if I left a book out or a light on. It was also a lot easier to focus on that than the weirdness.

Because, seriously, London? Magic? Faeries? There had to be some catch, but I didn't want to rock the boat. I certainly did not want to lose the chance to live in a place where Mr. Sparks couldn't stare at me while I was sleeping. If they wanted me to go with the magical thing, then I would. Hell, I could remake my personality in two point five seconds to keep from getting in trouble. I'd done it when I'd moved in with the Sparks, so this was the same thing.

And if I had to, I'd buy into this magic stuff. There was certainly a trick to it, and yet London had felt so real. That had happened. I'd been here, then there, then here again. No cameras, no drugs, and no explanation. No. I wasn't going to think about it too hard. I was just going to go with it - mostly because I was not going to risk the best break I'd ever had in my life.

I was coming to terms with this and "surveying my realm" when Liam returned, knocking at the door before he stepped in. "Rain?" he asked with the door only open a crack.

"Come in," I called to him.

He opened the door all the way, then invited a girl to follow him. Unlike Aspen, this girl looked completely normal. Her hair was brown and straight. She wore glasses. There were freckles on her cheeks, and while she was cute, she wasn't unnaturally stunning like my suitemate.

"Rain, this is Lynn. She's with the student welcoming committee, and she'll explain to you how the course options work."

Since she was wearing jeans and a typical tee, there was no tie for me to judge by, so I just asked, "Are you normal like me?"

She laughed, sounding almost embarrassed. "Um..."

"I explained about Faerie," Liam assured her.

"Yeah, my mom's a refugee," Lynn explained. "Dad's human. I'm half, and actually an enchanter, but I do more potions and salves."

"Horizontal stripes," I said, looking at Liam to make sure I had it right.

He nodded. "I think you've got this." Then he stepped back. "Believe it or not, I have things to do, but if you need me, Rain, I'm just across the atrium. Oh, and Lynn will meet you before your first class to help you find where to go."

"I'll be fine," I assured him. "Not my first time to be the new girl."

"But possibly the weirdest," Liam pointed out. As he turned, he paused to clasp Lynn's shoulder. "Thanks for this. I take it as a personal favor, and I'm in your debt."

"No debt needed," she assured him. "Just put it on my transcripts."

"Will do," he said before lifting his hand at us both and leaving.

Like that was some sign, Lynn relaxed and walked further in. "Wow, you already organized everything, huh?"

"Not much stuff to worry about," I admitted. "Just the basics."

"Probably for the best," she said. "Guess having an uncle working here makes it a little easier, since you know what to expect and all. We're not supposed to talk about this stuff with pure humans, you see, but I guess he got approval since you were accepted."

She was rambling. Granted, there was a lot of interesting stuff in there, like the fact she thought Liam was actually my real uncle. I decided to just go with it. One less thing to get bullied about later.

"So you can't talk about this with your dad?" I asked.

"Oh, not like that," she said. "He's a *caradil*. Uh, a human in the know, I guess you'd say. Like Liam. I guess you're one too."

"Right." I just nodded, because I wasn't sure what else I could say to that. *Caradil* was a word to add to my vocabulary, though.

"Anyway," Lynn said, reaching over to pluck something from the far side of the box on my desk. "I'm guessing this is your room key? If you want, I can give you a tour so you can find your way around a little easier?"

"That would be perfect," I agreed.

She passed me the key, then warned me the doors could sometimes be tricky. I got a demonstration on how to make sure they were secure - which was pretty standard stuff, considering the houses I'd lived in - and then we were off. Lynn led me all the way down the hall, showing me how some of the girls had signs or whiteboards posted so someone could see if they were in, studying, or leave a message.

It was a good idea. The problem was I had exactly no money, and no parent to ask for it. I just nodded, making it clear I was keeping up. Then, at the far end, she turned right. This was the hall at the front of the building.

"Over there," Lynn said, gesturing to her left, "is the study area for fourth-floor girls. And around this corner is our common area for this floor." She turned for a set of double doors in the space between two wings of the building, then paused. "The boys have the same setup on the other side. We're allowed to use each other's spaces during the day, but not after curfew. Well, not for those of us who are still minors. Once we're over eighteen, we don't have to worry about it. The rules relax a lot after we're out of the AP program."

"Nice," I said, thinking that was only a year away.

"Oh, and don't try to use the doors between our side and theirs after-hours. They're enchanted and locked against minors." She took another step, unaware of how surreal that entire phrase was. "Sometimes, we have movie nights, and the hall is a mixture of AP and college students, but it's pretty cool. Just sucks when they're allowed to do more than we can, you know?"

"Don't I ever," I mumbled.

I wasn't sure if she even heard me, though. Lynn simply pulled open one of the doors and stepped in. I followed her, unsure what else I was expected to do. Inside, both guys and girls lounged on couches and loveseats set up to make multiple conversation areas. On the far side was a massive TV, and a movie played on it that a group of girls was watching. It actually seemed almost normal.

But these weren't high school kids. Ok, some were, but the age range looked to be a lot broader than I'd expected. From a bit younger than me to a guy with a beer over by the corner. That meant twenty-one, didn't it? Otherwise, wouldn't he be hiding it?

Ok, and I was sorta gawking. Then again, quite a few of the students in here looked back. When their eyes landed on me, some tapped a friend or pointed, making the others look too. It didn't take long before at least a dozen people were inspecting me, and I wasn't sure if they were passing judgment.

"New girl," Lynn explained. "This is Rain, Liam's niece."

"What proficiency?" someone asked, and I didn't see who, but it was a guy.

"Legacy," Lynn said, gesturing for me to head back out. "Doing the full tour."

"Didn't think Liam had any fae in his family," a girl called after us.

"Ignore it," Lynn told me. "Legacies get a lot of flak because the magic users think they're *so* important."

I made it back to the hall and waited to see which way we were going next. "Yeah. Not overly shocked. I mean, someone always has to be the cool kid, which means someone else is the not cool one."

"Some Legacies are pretty cool," she assured me. "Anyways, this is the study area."

This time, she just opened the door so I could peek my head in. Library would've been a better description, if there'd been more books in the room. Instead, everything was digital. There were a few computers against the walls, maybe six or seven, and the group of people in there all had tablets. It was also very, very quiet.

"Then, if you go this way," Lynn said, continuing on her tour, "we get to the A wing. See, they're labeled from left to right, if you're standing at the main entrance. A and B wings are for girls. The atrium is in the middle, then C and D wings are for the boys. The first two floors are classrooms, and the upper two are dorms."

"Cool," I said, letting her know I was keeping up. "And we're just all mixed in together? High schoolers and college students? No structure to keep us apart? No rules about things like the beer I saw that guy holding?"

"Magic," Lynn explained. "Ms. Hawthorne, one of the pure fae instructors, spells all the dorm room doors. Minors are not allowed in a boy's room after curfew. Well, and same thing the other way around too. But the spell prevents us from entering after-hours, and if we're inside when curfew hits, the floor monitor is notified." She made a face. "Which is not fun. Parents get called if you have them, compulsions are placed, and so on."

"Compulsions?" I asked.

Lynn nodded. "Yeah, like Enticers can do. They give you a

compulsion to leave the other side before curfew. Both parties get one, and it lasts for months. Sucks." She flashed me a smile. "I happen to know that personally. I was two minutes late and Ms. Hawthorne busted me."

"Haven't met her," I admitted. "Is she the chaperone for our floor?"

"No," Lynn assured me. "She's the A wing, third floor. Pearl Hawthorne left Faerie back in the sixties, they say. Doesn't look a day over thirty, either. Fucking pure-bloods."

"What?" I gasped, because that shocked me more than anything else.

Lynn turned me toward a set of stairs in the corner beside the study hall. "Yeah, pure-bloods grow up like we do, but they stop aging somewhere in their twenties. Mom says the average fae lives for about a thousand years. They're not immortal, but pretty damned close. And they only start aging about a decade before they die. Just not fair."

"Whoa," I breathed. "And how many pure-bloods are here?"

"Um, five students," she said as we made our way down, "the weapons instructor, the heads of Enticers and Conjurers, and the dean, plus about six other teachers, like Ms. Hawthorne."

"Ms. Rhodes?" I asked, thinking about the woman who'd given me my entrance exam.

Lynn nodded just as we reached the bottom. "Ivy Rhodes is the dean. She's our wing's chaperone too, actually." Then she pushed through the door and into the main part of the school. "I'm sure you noticed the atrium, right?"

"Oh, yeah," I said, looking that way. "It's amazing."

"Half the stuff in there was brought as seeds from Faerie. The big silver oak in the middle? Stories say it was stolen from the Queen's orchard on the day she declared war. They're made of magic, you see - well, breathe it out - so it makes it easier to learn being so close to one. If you take the elevators to the basement level, you'll come out in the Never."

Did I hear her right? "The what?"

"The Never," she repeated. "It's a natural basement made by the silver oak. The spaces work as ley lines, kinda. Um, like underground rivers of magic that double as hallways, since magic is intangible." She pointed away from the atrium, then started walking. "If a student messes up some big spell, the tree eats the excess. It also gives it off, which is a really complicated thing I failed on my last test." She waved that off. "Just know there's a lot more under the school, but as a Legacy, you'll probably never go down there."

"Gotcha." It sounded like this place was even crazier than I'd first imagined.

Then she turned into the space between the A and B wings, directly under our common area but on the first floor. "And this is the library."

A pair of large wooden doors marked the entrance. Lynn opened one just enough to slip through, and I followed her, only to stall out just inside. Yes, this was definitely a library. Elegant wooden bookshelves were packed with spines of all colors and sizes. There were freestanding bookcases in the middle of the room, making rows in a space that was almost the size of the atrium. Along the sides, they kept going up to the ceiling. It appeared to take up two stories.

A walkway spanned the room about halfway up, making it easy to reach the books at the top. Signs marked the sections. I saw one for reference materials and another for romance, which meant this wasn't all learning materials. Lynn kept walking, not nearly as impressed as I was, but she'd also been going here for a while. Long enough to take this miracle for granted.

It was like the most amazing public library I'd ever seen, but just a few floors down from where I'd be living. I was so enamored I didn't realize we'd walked straight through the whole thing until we reached a door on the back side. Then, like all the others, Lynn went through, expecting me to follow.

On the other side was outside. It was brisk, so I hugged my arms against myself, and she stretched her legs a little. We both hurried away from the building, with her in the lead. Then, as we rounded the back side of what must be the B wing, she pointed out across the dormant lawn.

"You can see a building out there? That's the training ground for sentinel courses. Self-defense, practical application of magic, and a few other things are taught there as well. Everyone calls it the 'gym.' And around the corner, just out of sight is the Forge."

The whole time she talked, she never stopped, making a straight line down toward the D-wing side of the building. It wasn't a short walk. Thankfully, the school blocked most of the wind, and as fast as we were moving, I wasn't freezing out here. We passed the atrium, letting me see the back side was also glass, and kept going. Soon enough, we reached the next section, and there was a door.

When we got inside, I realized this was a dining area. It was also wonderfully warm. We both paused and chaffed our arms for a moment, then Lynn started pointing again.

"There's a buffet over here. Drinks are over there. Meal times are posted on the doors over on the other side, but it's an hour later on the weekends than weekdays. In between, there's always snacks like sandwiches and such for us. Food's included with tuition, so there's no checking out or anything, and this place never closes. Lunchroom duty is one of their favorite punishments for breaking the rules, so be sure to read your handbook. No one wants to spend the evening washing dishes!"

She kept talking about all the foods and what to do if I had any allergies - I didn't - as we crossed the room. A few people were sitting around either eating or studying, but it was mostly empty. We came out the opposite side, having almost made a square through the building, then Lynn led me past the front of the atrium and back to the same elevator Liam had used to show me to my room.

"Over on the other side of the atrium is one just like this," she explained while we waited for the car to come down. "During communal hours, you can visit the boys, but at nine on weeknights and ten on weekends, we have to be back on our sides. If there's a boy in your room, you're supposed to leave your door open, but no one ever does. Just expect a lecture if you're caught."

The elevator showed up, and I stepped onto it. Lynn didn't. "Coming?" I asked.

She jerked her thumb back behind her. "I was going to hang with my friends. I'll be at your door at eight sharp tomorrow, though. Fourth floor, Rain." Then she waved and backed up.

I just reached over and punched the button for the fourth floor. At least I still had one more book to finish. I also wanted to try on my uniform to make sure I didn't look like an idiot.

But when I unlocked my door and stepped into my room, I found a bag sitting on my bed. The gift type. It was lime green with neon daisy-like flowers on the outside, drawn in a childish manner. Inside was tissue paper in a silver color. When I looked at the tag on the handle, it simply said, "Welcome to Silver Oaks."

Pulling out the paper, I found an entire collection of makeup. Confused, I turned back to see if someone was watching me. Had Liam done this? He didn't seem like the kind to purchase makeup, but he was the only person I'd talked to about it, and even then, it had just been a passing comment.

The strangest thing was I honestly needed this. Sure, I could start my first day at a new school with the fresh-face look, but I happened to like eyeliner and lipstick. Then, when I dug a little deeper, I found some sample-sized bottles of hair product, shampoo, and conditioner. Even soap!

Maybe this had been a gift from the school? No, not with that much makeup. Then again, this place was pretty amazing, even with the weirdness of magic - which I still had some doubts about. Was this like a fantasy novel type of thing, or more of a Criss Angel illusions situation? A little smoke and mirrors, maybe?

Either way, it was better than a group home. No matter what else was true, I was going to hang onto that, because it made all the rest easier to deal with.

Chapter Fifteen

The next morning, the alarm on my tablet woke me at six-thirty. I had enough time to get up, put on the version of my uniform I wanted, then make my face all pretty. I wasn't exactly a knockout, but the tight skirt Liam had bought for me, a fitted shirt, one diagonally striped tie, and a waist-length blazer worked for me. I went easy with the makeup, not sure what the trends were yet.

I had my hair in a ponytail, a pair of white socks that went to just over the knee - which Mr. Sparks had somehow missed in his slut-wear purge - and my cute new Mary Janes. With one tablet, two pens, and no clue what else I was missing, I was ready just as Lynn knocked at my door.

"Rain?" she called from the other side.

I opened it. "Is there anything else I need for classes besides this tablet and a pen?" I asked desperately.

"You're fine," she assured me. "There should be an app on there with your schedule and the building map. Everything else you'll get in your classes. Now c'mon."

I quickly locked up my room and followed her. Not surprisingly, there was a crowd at the elevator. Looking back down the hall, I saw even more people heading the other way. When the car opened the first time, a herd of girls pushed into it, filling the thing up completely. The next time was a little better. On the third time, Lynn and I finally managed to squeeze in.

"This is why you want to leave early," Lynn whispered as the car made its way down, stopping on the third floor so a few more students could push in. "You know your first class?"

"It's in A127," I said, reciting it from memory.

"Then the first floor," she told me. "Wait, Literature?"

"Says English," I admitted.

We had to shuffle around a bit when the students made their way off for the second floor. Then, the car began moving again. When we reached the first floor, everyone else got off, and I could only assume the car would head all the way back up. Lynn grabbed my arm and towed me forward, straight toward the entrance to the school. It was the one landmark I knew in this place - well, besides the atrium we were walking the length of.

"Ok," Lynn said when we reached the cross hall. Then she pointed to the right, away from the atrium. "That's the A wing. All of your classes with an A before the number will be there. B is the same wing we live on. Then C, then D. The first number is the floor, so all one hundred rooms are first floor, two hundreds are second floor, and anything else is probably a mistake. Even numbers are on the right. Odd numbers are on the left." She gently patted my shoulder. "Good luck, and I'll meet you right here when you get out of fourth period to show you how lunch works."

I found my head bobbing in acknowledgement, but it sure sounded like she was leaving me on my own. When the girl turned and jogged for the stairwell, I was sure of it. Granted, mentor and welcoming committee didn't really sound the same as babysitter. I'd also done this enough I was pretty sure I knew what was expected. Heading toward the western-most wing of the building, I checked the number plates beside each door.

When I found the right room, all my anxiety hit at once. I'd been trying hard to ignore it, but that didn't mean it didn't exist. Now, I was about to open this door and seal my fate. College-level courses. Magic school for fairies. This was all real. I was a nobody, so no one should really care about me, but that didn't mean they wouldn't notice.

Taking a deep breath, I looked down, wondering if my uniform was ok. I should've checked the other girls on the elevator to see what they'd been wearing. I hadn't. I'd been so overwhelmed, I'd completely flaked on that. Now, I was standing outside a door to a class that was already mostly full.

Waiting wouldn't make it any better, so I turned the knob and forced myself to open the door. The moment I was inside, everything paused. All the students turned to stare at me. The teacher noticed the change and looked over. Like I had so many times before, I put on my best smile and tried to make the most of this incredibly awkward situation.

"I'm new," I explained.

The guy nodded, but his eyes were on his own tablet. Flipping at something, his expression changed, and then he looked up. "Ok. I'll have a copy of the textbook sent to your tablet. You can take a seat at the back." He pointed. "Class, I'd like you all to welcome Lorraine Brooks, a new Legacy."

I didn't bother saying hi. I just went where the teacher had pointed, walking sideways between the aisles to avoid the bags and blazers piled beside chairs. Heads turned to follow. Around the room, voices were murmuring.

One, in particular, stood out. "Fresh meat."

I turned to the sound and saw brilliant green eyes. Not emerald, not forest, but the bright almost-lime color of new leaves, which made them *really* stand out. He smiled from the chair right beside and behind the one I'd been assigned, although it didn't look kind. Yep, he was hot. Of course, he was; this was a faerie school, after all.

Fae were supposed to be beautiful, weren't they? Trying to be nice, I smiled back weakly.

"Don't even think it," the girl in front of me whispered.

"Huh?"

She turned in her chair and tilted her head to Sexy-Green-Eyes. "Torian Hunt. Don't even dream of him unless you want half the school to come down on your head for one reason, or the other half to come down for the opposite. He's not really the kind you want to get involved with." Then she smiled. "I'm Amber."

"Lorraine."

Her brow lifted. "Like from Back to the Future?"

"No idea. I didn't get the chance to ask."

She laughed once, then turned back around, but I wasn't offended. In fact, this hadn't been too bad so far. In truth, it was incredibly normal, and after Liam's whole magic speech and Aspen's little psychotic demonstration, I was braced for just about anything. So far, it was like a typical school, but with preppy-looking clothes. I might actually be able to do this!

It didn't take long before the teacher, who my schedule said was Mr. Connors, cleared his throat. "Alright, excitement's over. Like I was saying at the end of class Friday, Tam Lin explains some aspects of the Wild Hunt. Even though it's portrayed as an offering to Hell, the medieval authors tended to put a religious slant on any literature at the time to prevent it from being dismissed as heresy..."

Yeah, we'd covered that poem in my last school, with a slightly different twist, so I felt safe to let my mind wander. Around the room was nothing but a sea of black, white, and green. Still, there were subtle differences. Most of the girls wore fitted shirts, tailored to show off their curves. Some were a bit heavier, so had gone with a more relaxed style. Socks, tights, and shoes were the major fashion statement, though. I saw plenty of heels, ranging from kitten to impressive. The guys tended to have boots or dress shoes, but all of them were shined. One guy had on a pair of Chucks. Another wore Crocs. Then there was the jewelry.

That seemed to be how the social classes were divided. Some wore leather and rubber. The pretty girls wore real gems and gold. The rest of us either went without or some mixture of the two. Evidently, no matter what the rules said, students would still find a way to mark ourselves, declaring our tribe. The problem was I didn't know the categories for this school yet.

I had a feeling they wouldn't be the typical stuff I was used to. Jocks wouldn't fit, since there was no athletics program. I wasn't sure if all Enchanters would dress alike, but I seriously doubted it. Still, teenagers would find a way, and it seemed the signs were there for anyone who cared to look. Unable to help myself, I turned to check the cute boy again, wondering where he belonged.

Torian had the sleeves of his white shirt rolled up to his elbows and dark bracelets lined his wrists. One side was a cluster of rubber, like the cheap 90s things. The other was a leather cuff on his left wrist. His hair was long enough to almost reach his shoulders, and slightly wavy. His pants weren't crisp and pressed, but they somehow didn't look wrinkled either, and he wore boots, but the combat kind.

This guy had the same perfect skin as Aspen, though. The freakishly amazing kind. Torian Hunt was beautiful in a way I'd never expected a man to be. Guys like him walked down runways, not school halls - but this place was definitely different. I was so distracted trying to figure him out that it took a moment to notice he was looking back at me. Then the corner of his mouth curled.

I wasn't exactly the kind of girl to turn away, but I wanted to. My instincts said to look down, smile, then glance back, but I wasn't here to flirt. Instead, I met his eyes. Long lashes made him look almost like he wore eyeliner, and the green was *piercing*. Only then did I realize I couldn't put a finger on his race. His skin was neither pale nor brown, but rather caught in the middle. Olive, maybe? His hair was dark, but he wasn't Hispanic or Middle Eastern, not with the teardrop shape of his eyes. Granted, I wasn't really sure how races worked with mythical creatures. Still, whatever he was, it looked good on him.

"So," Mr. Connors said, but only half my mind was listening, "who knows how Tam Lin was freed?"

"Fell off his horse?" guessed a guy near the front.

"Only if you consider his wife pulling him off as falling," Mr. Connors corrected. "Next time, try at least reading the assignment, Cliff."

"True love?" This from a girl in the middle.

Then Torian pulled his eyes away from mine. "Trust." Even his voice was amazing.

My head snapped to the front of the class in time to see Mr. Connors nodding enthusiastically. "Exactly."

"Wait." A guy at the side was rubbing his head. "How do you figure that? She held on to him until the cycle was done."

Torian didn't give the teacher a chance to answer. "The guy was turned into a whole list of monsters, but he'd promised his wife he wouldn't harm her. She had to hold on to him as the Queen went through her powers. Tam Lin was changed into some pretty terrifying things, but his wife believed he wouldn't hurt her - that the things she held were all still him."

"Exactly," Mr. Connors said again. "And while we don't know if this story is historical or allegory, the lesson from it is the same. Magic has limitations -"

The digital bell chimed, cutting him off, so I looked over to the clock. I hadn't realized how quickly time had flown. Crap. I had ten minutes to get to my next class, and no clue where it was. I should have been looking into that instead of those green eyes beside me. Pulling up the student app on my tablet, I tried to figure out the layout of my schedule. My next class was in room D117. That meant the first floor, but where? On the map, that should be the other side of the building, right?

"I like the skirt."

My head snapped up. The room was mostly empty, students rushing out before the teacher could assign homework, but Torian stood there, leaning right over my shoulder. Close enough I could smell him, and all I could think was summer grass.

Hoping I didn't look desperate, I turned my attention back to my map. "Thanks, my uncle picked it out."

He laughed once. "Looks like you're lost, Rain. Your next class is here." He tapped the map with a long and perfectly manicured finger.

"No, I'm looking for room D117."

He chuckled softly. "Yeah, look again. Your next class is here, though."

Room B210. It wasn't even on the same floor, let alone the same side of the building as I'd thought. I pulled up my schedule to prove him wrong, but paused. He was right. I thought I had History, but that was third period. Next, I had math in room B210.

"How'd you know that?"

"Welcome to Silver Oaks." He blinked slowly and turned for the door, striding out like he didn't give a damn that he'd just blown off my question.

Chapter Sixteen

Ok, that guy was seriously hot, but I was starting to realize quite a few people in this school had a pretty problem. Not that *they'd* see it as a problem, but damn! At least half my class were drop-dead gorgeous - boys and girls. Then again, fairies, so it made sense. I was going to have to remind myself of that a few times, because it still felt strange to think of it as anything but a lame joke.

Except this was real. My entire Literature class had just talked about the fae application of history to a poem. If this was some kind of gag, someone had put in way too much effort. All signs pointed to real. Yeah, and maybe it was kinda boring so far, but at least the view was nice, right? Besides, I had a feeling I'd get to see some magic eventually.

Trying to get my head back in the game, I picked up my tablet and hurried out of class. At least math was closer to where I was now. I just had to figure out how to get there. First, I needed the stairs, and the stream of people made it clear where those were. Heading up, I realized I was probably going to be late, but they usually forgave that on the first day, didn't they? I simply had to figure out where I was on the second floor, then find the wing I wanted, and start counting again.

I probably looked like some nerdy tourist with my tablet held up in front of me like a homing beacon. Staggering through the press of bodies, I finally figured out where I was. I could see windows over there, which meant that was the A wing, so if I turned around, it would put me heading back in the direction I needed, because my hall should be right...

Lifting my eyes, I saw him again. Torian leaned against the wall by the corner, his arm wrapped around Aspen, of all people. Of course they were together. Granted, of all the amazingly pretty people in this school, she definitely had on the sexiest version of this uniform I'd seen yet, complete with a body-hugging mini-skirt and the most adorable heeled boots. Two more "models" stood beside them, both guys. Beautiful, *delicious*-looking guys. It was like a designer ad filled with perfect people. The three boys were fit, the girl was lithe, and none of them had a spare ounce of fat anywhere, as if they'd been airbrushed.

Even better, they looked like a rainbow of skin colors, but their features weren't quite right. The Black guy had almost Asian eyes, as an example. It was like their creator had picked pieces of all the nationalities in the world and thrown them together in new and exciting ways. Ways I liked very, very much. I could almost feel my cheeks getting warmer as I tried not to gawk.

Which was how I ended up walking straight into the shoulder of some guy heading the other way. Bouncing off him, I staggered, clutching at my tablet so I didn't break the thing. My heel slipped on the slick floor, and I turned, completely disoriented, only to have a hand grab my arm.

I looked up to find Torian's grip steadying me and Aspen with an arm out like she'd been ready to do the same. Great, now I looked like a complete moron. Not really the best first impression I'd ever made in my life.

"Sorry," I said, hugging my tablet to my chest. "Guess I should've looked where I was going."

The Black guy chuckled. "New girl, huh? Guess you don't know the rules around here yet. You're supposed to bow to the king."

"Be nice, Wilder," Torian said.

The olive-skinned guy with them - maybe Hispanic? - jerked his head at the apparent leader of their little clique. "Seriously, Tor? She's obviously a burner."

That was when Aspen spoke up, shoving her finger into the guy's face. "Shut it, Hawke. Tor says to be nice, then you're real fuckin' nice. Besides, she's my suitemate."

"Right," I muttered before trying again. "And an embarrassing moment is only getting worse."

"You're fine," Aspen promised, tossing a warning look at Wilder and Hawke. "Isn't she?"

"Clearly," Wilder agreed.

Without moving his arm from Aspen's neck, Torian pulled her closer to his side, then whispered something in her ear. She smiled, turning her head just enough to see him, then pulled away. The couple traded an intense look, but Aspen's smile was only getting bigger. I wanted to walk past and head to class, but with the way they were standing, I'd have to push through someone, and I had a feeling my luck was already at its limit.

"Um, if it isn't any problem, can I slip between you guys?" I asked the darker-skinned boys.

Hawke lifted a brow as if that question was somehow obscene. "In a hurry?"

"First day, so I'm trying to figure out where everything is," I admitted. "In all honesty, I'm so lost and confused, and I'm pretty sure I'm making this worse somehow." My eyes shifted to the Black guy. "Unless you just scowl at people all the time? I hear it gives wrinkles."

As if that was some magic trick, Wilder huffed out a laugh. "Ok, Aspen, you're right. Interesting."

"Do I want to know what that means?" I asked.

Hawke simply grunted, the sound making it clear he wasn't impressed. "Tor? Class?"

"Yeah," Torian agreed.

Leaning toward Aspen's ear again, he whispered something else. I couldn't hear, but evidently, the other two guys could. They all nodded, the boys breaking off, and Aspen held up her fist to bump against Torian's. He grinned at her, tapped it with his own, then fell into the last scraps of high school traffic. Aspen, however, leaned back against the wall like she had all the time in the world. Never mind that the halls were starting to empty out, which usually meant seconds until we were late.

"Tor says you're going to math? Room B210?"

I nodded. "Yeah."

She reached into her bag and pulled out a cluster of tubes. No, more of those Pixy Stix she'd been eating the other day. "Cool. Let's go."

I was not keeping up with her at all. "Excuse me?"

She winked. "I'm in there too, hun."

"Oh. Then maybe you can show me where I belong."

She grinned impishly. "Follow me, meat."

Looked like that one little phrase was going to haunt the next few months of my life. Rain wasn't bad, but meat? It wouldn't bother me at all if they forgot that joke as fast as Torian had made it. Still, I followed her down the hall, looking at numbers as we passed. The bell rang while we were still walking, but Aspen turned into a classroom like she didn't care at all.

I followed, feeling a bit like a lost puppy, but while she moved toward the desks, I headed to the teacher. Out of the corner of my eye, I saw her gesture, and some kid got up and moved. Clearly, Aspen was the queen of Silver Oaks Institute, and she'd just evicted someone from the chair I had a feeling would become mine. The one right beside her.

That didn't mean she talked to me. After I was checked into the class, I sat down beside her. Aspen held out a Pixy Stix. With a smile, I took one. The paper called it orange, but they all tasted like sugar. It was the last attention she gave me, but I'd done this enough to know everyone else around us had noticed. I could almost feel their eyes on me. She'd just made me "interesting."

That was math, and when it was finally over, I braced myself to deal with the stairs again. This was the class in room D117, but it was on the far side of the school. I was scanning the map, trying to figure out the most effective way to get from here to there without getting turned around again, when the smell of honeysuckle drifted to me.

"Hawke and Wilder are in History with you," Aspen said, leaning over my shoulder from behind me.

Her voice was soft, right beside my ear. Shivers ran up my spine at the lyrical perfection of it. Ducking my head, I tapped my tablet. "You happen to know the best way for a newbie to get all the way over there without running into anyone else?"

"Yep." Stepping around, she offered me her hand like she was going to help me up. "I owe you for London, right? I'll show you."

"No, I..." When a crease appeared on her perfect brow, I paused. "You don't have to do that. Liam was trying to explain, and you kinda proved his point. I'm just trying not to ruin my first day."

Those pale blue eyes of hers watched me intently, almost like a falcon about to swoop. "You mean that. So why didn't you touch the flowers?"

"The plant you gave me?" I almost slapped my head, because what else would she be talking about? "Um, I was a little overwhelmed - *am* a little. A lot."

So she looped her arm in the one holding my tablet and tugged, all but forcing me up. I got out of the chair and let her tow me back into those halls. Strangely, people didn't jostle her. They moved, like a tide parting ahead of her sheer presence.

"If you pet the plant, it will like you," she said as if there hadn't been a pause. "They're good ones. Also, don't let Hawke call you a burner. I don't think you are."

"Why am I interesting?" I asked.

She just shrugged like that wasn't important. "Dunno. They didn't want to let you come, huh? Said you were too normal? They're wrong, but I'm not sure why yet." Then she turned, angling for a set of stairs on the other side of the atrium. "Wilder will be nicer to you now. If he's not, tell me, ok?"

"Yeah, sure," I agreed as we began heading down, Aspen still linked with my arm. "And so you know, I really owe you one. Well, a few."

"No debt," she assured me. "It's not a deal. You just make me happy."

"Is there any way I can pay you back?" I asked.

The smile this girl gave me could've lit up the entire atrium. It was so bright, like I'd just saved her puppy or something. "*That's* why you're interesting, Rain. They say you're normal, but I don't think so. You're definitely not a burner, but you aren't quite *caradil* either. You're..."

"Interesting," I finished for her just as we came out on the first floor. "Well, I'll do my best to keep doing whatever it is I'm doing naturally, then."

"Please," she said softly. "You make everything shine a bit better." Before I could ask what that even meant, she pointed. "That's where you belong. Oh! Give this to Wilder, would you?" And she passed me another Pixy Stix.

"Promise," I assured her, lifting my hand as she turned and headed the other way.

Yet as soon as she was looking away from me, everything about her changed. Her shoulders lifted, and her posture became almost aggressive. A couple of students jumped out of her path with worried looks. Maybe I'd misjudged her, or maybe she was putting on an act, but either way, I was glad I seemed to be on her good side.

Then, just like with my first two classes, when I stepped into History of Faerie, I made sure my teacher knew I was there. The woman who looked up at me this time, however, had a face I recognized. Ms. Rhodes dropped her eyes to the candy I was holding, then looked back at my face.

"Find an empty seat, Rain."

"Yes, ma'am," I said, heading to one on the same side of the room as Wilder. When I passed him, I offered the purple straw. "Aspen said to give this to you."

"A well-trained puppet," he teased.

I just sighed and kept going to the first empty chair in that row. Ms. Rhodes watched me the whole way, but the moment my rump hit the seat, she moved to the front of the class.

"For those who haven't met her yet, we have a new Legacy here at Silver Oaks Institute. This is Rain Brooks. Rain, you will need to catch up on your own time, because I'm sure most of *this* history will be completely new to you."

I nodded, doing my best not to draw any attention to myself whatsoever. It didn't really work, but so long as I didn't look each time someone turned to stare at me, I could pretend like it did. I could almost pretend I was just another typical girl in a Fae History class.

Chapter Seventeen

Somehow, when history let out, I made it to my next class - biology - all on my own. I even beat not only the bell, but also the teacher. Proud of myself, I was standing at the large desk, my tablet in my hand, when *he* walked in. Torian glided past me without a word and snapped his fingers once. Obediently, I looked at him, but the command wasn't for me. A lean, dorky-looking guy grabbed his things and vacated the table.

"That's kind of you, Jeff," Torian told him, flashing the kid a smile.

He beamed in response. "Sure, Torian."

Then the arrogant-but-beautiful guy crooked his finger, looking up at me. My mouth opened to protest, and the finger bent again. "Ms. Stewart is always late," he assured me. "I saved you a chair."

"More like evicted the previous owner," I countered.

His mouth twitched. "You make it sound like a bad thing."

Huffing out a breath, I obeyed his command, dropping my things beside him before sitting on the rickety stool. "You make it sound like you deserve it."

"I do. It's what happens when everyone calls me the king."

I was about to snap something else at him, but the complete confidence in his voice made me shut my mouth. It wasn't sarcasm, at least it didn't sound like it. The arrogant bastard actually thought he had the right to push people around? Well, that made him *a lot* less attractive. It didn't matter how pretty it was on the outside, when it was rotten in the middle, the best idea was to stay as far away as possible.

"Wow," I drawled, turning to glare at him. "Does it hurt to be such an ass?"

A moment of surprise flashed across his face before he stopped it. "Only a little. Don't worry, I'm used to it, so you don't need to kiss me and make it better."

"Keep dreaming."

I turned back to the front, but from the looks being tossed at us, everyone had heard the exchange. Torian drummed his fingers on the polished surface of the table, and while I tried to ignore him, a giggle slipped out. This guy was completely baffled by my lack of hero-worship. The sound made a few more heads turn. I let my eyes close and reminded myself I'd survived things so much worse than this. I wasn't trying to be cool, just normal. No, *invisible*. My goal was to not get in trouble for long enough to prove I belonged here.

"You know that's my line, right?" Torian asked softly, leaning closer.

"Which?"

"About dreaming. I'm supposed to tell *you* that, not the other way around."

"Yeah?" I finally turned to look at him, then leaned back when I found his face closer than I expected. "You do realize I'm not here to impress anyone, right? Especially not people who'll be little more than memories in a few years. Certainly not people who don't give a shit about me. See, I may not know a lot of things, but there's one thing I'm sure of." I flicked my eyes over him. "None of this actually matters to people like you. It kinda does for me."

"And that's where you're wrong," he told me, those strange green eyes almost as intense as Aspen's blue ones. "You see, the whole time you thought you had the world figured out, you were so very wrong. You think this place is about an education? It's so much more than that, and it does matter to me. It's going to change everything."

"Mhm," I mumbled. "I guess even 'fairy' boys have ego problems."

Ms. Stewart finally walked into the class right after I said that. Unfortunately, Torian managed to get the last word. Leaning right up to my ear, he breathed, "I don't rule the school, Rain, and I'm not here to impress these people either. Oh, and the word you wanted is 'fae.' I'm not gay."

I rolled my eyes and pushed out of my chair, heading for the front desk. For once, I had no problem standing before everyone while they gaped at the new girl, because it meant I wasn't sitting beside him. It would've been nicer if the biology teacher had taken a little longer to add me to her roll, but at this point, I'd take what I could get. Eventually, I had to go back, but I dawdled as much as I could without being obvious.

"Nice eyeliner," Torian said when I reclaimed my stool.

I didn't even bother replying. After all, what could I say that wouldn't make me sound desperate? Pretty much nothing. The simple fact this guy had called me "fresh meat" in first period was just a little too recent. It was a big mark against him. That his girlfriend was my suitemate was a second one. Well, since I was pretty sure this was his version of flirting, it was. The arrogance a minute ago? Yep, the best idea was to accept he was gorgeous, and then forget all about him.

The self-proclaimed king wasn't used to being ignored, though. The moment Ms. Stewart was done talking, he turned his attention right back to me. "Answer one thing for me?"

I didn't have a good reason not to, and I kinda didn't want him to tell Aspen I was a complete bitch, so I gave in. "Ok?"

"How did a very human foster kid end up at an elite trade school for the fae folk?" he asked.

Now that was easy. "I have a really cool foster uncle."

"Liam," he breathed. "Well, well. Seems like the little brother is still playing by the rules. Good to know."

That was odd enough to capture my attention. "How so?"

"It's not your deal," he told me. "It also sounds like Nancy Sparks hasn't changed a bit. Oddly, the uniform Silver Oaks makes us wear is a *whole* lot better than the plaid and khaki getup Nancy Sparks puts on her fosters."

Yep, I caved. "Has she been doing that for a while?" I kept my voice low so the teacher wouldn't hear.

"Oh yeah. Aspen said you were wearing it on Friday. I think you should ask Hawke about his time there." He smiled, well aware he'd just thrown me a bone. "You may not believe me, but I'm actually trying to help."

"Why?" There had to be a catch. This guy didn't seem like the type to do anything because he was kind.

"Because I owe that bitch." His tone was deadly serious and sounded like a serial killer. "I'll make sure she pays over and over. We don't take kindly to people trying to take advantage of us."

"Wait, what bitch, and who is 'we?'"

His lips closed and his eyes flicked away as if he'd just realized what he'd said. "Nancy Sparks."

"And 'we?'" I insisted.

Those lips curled in a forced smile. "My court, of course, since you've just convinced yourself I'm a narcissist."

"And you aren't?"

"No, Rain. There are a lot of things I love more than my own reflection, although it is a nice one. Wouldn't you agree?" He pushed one finger across his bottom lip as if he was thinking, but I had a funny feeling he was trying to distract me with his perfect man-pout.

"No." I wrenched my eyes away.

Torian chuckled. "Then I guess I might be losing my bet with Aspen after all. Lesbian?"

"Fuck you."

"I'll take that as a real big no. Interesting how you aren't scared of me, though." He leaned even closer. "What I want to know is why not."

I huffed. "Maybe I just have nothing left to lose."

"Everyone has something to lose. Everyone. The bigger question is what you have to gain. Most burners prefer to wallow in their safe little ruts, and will fight with all they have to stay there." Then he leaned back to his side of the desk. The evil little curl was back on his lips. "What will you do, human girl with a fae name?"

"It's not fae," I assured him just as Ms. Stewart looked over.

"I'm assuming you're helping Lorraine catch up," she said, her attention on Torian.

"Rain," he corrected.

The woman turned to me. "Do you prefer to be called that, or would you rather I use Lorraine?"

"Rain's fine," I assured her.

She nodded. "Then I'll mark it on the records. Torian, assist her at least a little. She's coming here from a public school, and I'm sure you understand how drastic the change can be for some." Then she turned back to the class. "And for the rest of you, we're going to examine the effect of clay on fae plants. At the back of the room, you can collect a sprig of midnight grass and a vial of red clay."

Torian immediately turned to me. "Which means you're mine for the next thirty minutes."

"Would you like to actually help me with some of this?" I huffed. "She's right, you know. Saturday, I had no idea about any of this. The only reason I'm here is because Aspen thinks I'm interesting. I don't even know what that means!"

He reached over to trail a finger down my forearm. "We don't either, but it's still true."

"Biology, Torian," I grumbled.

Removing his hand, he flicked a finger toward where the students were gathering their things. "The answer to that is iron. It's always iron. The more fae blood we have, the more iron hurts us.

Some with a quarter fae ancestry or less will never realize they're being affected, but they still are."

"Then how can you call it affected?" I asked.

His lips curled in the most sensual yet diabolical smile. "Go get some of that clay."

"Fine," I said, sliding off my stool to pick up one of the little vials.

They were no bigger than my pinky, and the dirt inside looked incredibly common. It was the sort of thing you could dig up just about anywhere. The top was sealed with a pretty typical cork pushed about halfway in. When I made it back to our desk, I offered it to him, but Torian waved it off.

"Open it and take a little pinch," he said. "Little, Rain."

"Ok..."

I did, holding it between my index finger and thumb, then he did the last thing I expected. Pressing both hands together, Torian created light. Not a blinding one, but a soft undulating rainbow. As he spread his palms further apart, the glow stretched, making an arc that shimmered like a ribbon in a breeze.

"Now sprinkle the smallest amount of that into the light," he told me.

Easy enough. Reaching over, I rubbed my fingers together and a few grains broke free. They naturally fell through the band of light, shorting out gaps in the effect. Curious, I moved to dribble a little more, spreading it straight across the entire band. Sure enough, the light fizzled out, fading completely.

"Why?" I asked, gesturing to it. "How does that work?"

"Magnetic fields," he explained. "Magic is carried along them, just like birds following migration paths. Things that require magic to survive? They starve or suffocate magically in the presence of iron. All iron, Rain. Steel, other alloys. Doesn't matter, but the more pure, the faster and more painful it is."

"And there's iron in clay?" Because to me, that was the second most shocking thing about this. The first, naturally, being the rainbow he'd just made so easily.

Torian nodded slowly. "Yep. It's all about the fields of my will fighting against those of the substance outside my will."

Feeling a little silly, I pointed at his hands and made a circular gesture. "Is there any way you can do that again?"

"The light?" He looked confused.

"Yeah, um, it's kinda the first magic I've actually seen. Not experienced, but actually, you know, got to appreciate."

Something about his expression softened. "Yeah, I heard Aspen sent you to London."

"Did I really go there?" I asked.

"No," he scoffed. "It was a glamour. Perfectly safe, just impossible to identify on the inside without training."

"Why London?" I asked.

"She likes the taxis." He pressed his hands together again. "And if you put down the clay, I'll even let you touch it."

"Kinky," I teased.

He chuckled. "You have absolutely no idea."

When he spread his hands again, there was definitely light. This time, however, the colors were even more vivid, swirling with a little more intensity. I dusted my hands on my thighs, not wanting any clay dust to mess it up, and then I reached under his arm to poke a finger right into the light.

I couldn't feel a thing, but I could see it. It was like playing with the dust motes in a sunbeam. My movement made everything swirl and shift, so I drew a little circle, then I made zig zags. For every movement, his magic reacted, and it was absolutely beautiful.

"That's amazing," I breathed. "What's it good for?"

He tilted his hands, shutting off the light. "That? Nothing. It's a training exercise, just like humming a note. Harmless magic, Rain."

Which reminded me of another thing. "And what did you mean about my name being fae?"

"Think about it," he said. "Ivy Rhodes. Holly Glenn, Aspen Fox. All nature names. Rain Brooks."

"Torian," I countered.

"A watch point over a dale, also a title for the one who watches that dale. A nature name," he assured me.

"So, it's a cultural thing?" I asked, completely fascinated.

"It's a careful thing," he explained. "But you don't get to ask all the questions without answering a few in return."

"Fair enough," I agreed.

"What do you think of Aspen?" he asked.

I had to pause to really consider that. "She's really nice to me, but I get the impression she's not really a nice person. Like..." That sounded so bad. "I mean she's the kind of person who treats people the way they treat her, but exponentially more. I want to like her, but I don't really know her that well."

"And do you like the flower she gave you?" he asked.

I just ducked my head. "Yeah, it's cool. I mean, I think it's a pretty plant and all, but yesterday was a little crazy for me, and I'm terrified I'll kill it. I can't imagine how bad that will piss her off."

"You won't kill it," he promised. "Just be kind to it."

"To a plant?" Because that sounded a little insane.

"To a plant," he agreed. "It's a pretty universal rule for all things fae. Do unto them how you hope they would do unto you."

I smiled, looking up to meet his eyes. "Which, I have a feeling, is the second important lesson you've taught me today, and probably the most important, huh?"

"Second most important," he assured me. "The iron trumps that. It's also the one place where you can excel and we will always fail."

My eyes narrowed as I tried to read his bland expression. "That almost makes it sound like you're rooting for the weird human girl."

"Kinda am," he assured me. "After all, you're interesting."

Chapter Eighteen

When biology let out, I headed to meet up with Lynn in front of the school's main entrance. Never mind that I had to walk past the cafeteria to get there. She also wasn't alone. A few girls were standing around, talking to her. I didn't want to interrupt, but I also didn't want to make her wait, so I moved where she could see me, then waved.

"Rain!" she called to me, pushing through the group to hurry over. "The cafeteria's right over here."

"Friends of yours?" I asked. "Because you didn't need to rush off. Pretty sure I can tackle a cafeteria on my own."

"Not friends," she assured me. "So, how was your morning of core classes?" She was clearly changing the subject.

"Nothing like the core classes I'm used to," I admitted. "I have a feeling I'll be reading my textbooks for the next week just to catch up. At least math was pretty normal."

"It's universal," she agreed, turning to grab the cafeteria door for me. "And, here we are. So, over there is the line for the buffet. Just go get whatever you want, and while it may not be the biggest serving, you can always have seconds, or even thirds, so go crazy."

When I finally got to it, the food smelled good and looked better. It was served up by a trio of people on the other side of a glass partition. It kinda reminded me of the Subway line, actually. Once I had a meal picked out, I looked over the mass of bodies at all the round tables, hoping for someplace that had enough space for me to not interrupt. It didn't exist, and all the tables seemed to be taken, so I started walking toward the back, maybe even outside.

At least there I wouldn't have to ask if someone minded if I joined them, and I wasn't sure I could do any more groveling today. Lynn wasn't exactly going out of her way to be friendly. Sure, she was nice, but it felt a bit like an obligation, and I really didn't want to be *that* girl, the one people only talked to because they felt sorry for me. I almost made it to the far side of the dining hall when a voice called my name. Following the sound, I saw Lynn waving. Well, if she was calling me, then maybe I really was welcome? Not wanting to pass up my good fortune, I changed course, weaving through the student body for her table.

"Hey," I said, tipping my head at the empty chair across from her. "You mind?"

"Sit!" she said, making it clear I was expected to. "So, any horror stories yet? Ready to go back to a safe and normal school?"

"No, it's actually more interesting this way. School used to bore me," I admitted. "This feels more like reading a good book."

"I can see that." She gave me an understanding nod. "I started here last year, so I kinda felt the same way." Then she pointed around the table. "Ok, that's Matt, Chris, Amy, and Charlotte."

The group all looked up with a smile, but none of them stopped eating. "Lorraine," I said, since Lynn hadn't offered my name.

"We know," Amy teased. "Trust me, everyone knows who you are. Silver Oaks isn't that big. We also know we're supposed to call you Rain."

I opened my bottle of Coke. "Yeah. I guess that was my suitemate's idea. So, how bad is my life about to be?"

Matt shrugged. "Second period said you were a complete burner, but by third you were deemed tolerable. Something about Aspen passing you her crack?"

"What?! It was a Pixy Stix."

"That's what the bitch lives on," Charlotte grumbled. "Looks like she was airbrushed and survives on sugar. It's not fair."

Ok, so Charlotte was plump enough I could understand her frustration. Lynn was pretty, but generic and boring. Amy looked a bit bookish, and the guys were all safely in the easy to forget category. These were normal people, the kind I was used to being around. Not a single one of them had the unnatural beauty that was so common at Silver Oaks, and there was something a little comforting about their normalness.

"So, are they the center of the popular crowd at Silver Oaks?" I turned to scan the room for those four examples of perfection.

Lynn pointed in the other direction. Following her finger, I found them. The notorious foursome had claimed a table near the wall. Torian leaned back as if he was surveying his realm, one arm draped across the chair beside him. In it was Aspen, her pixie-cut silver hair a stark contrast to his burnished beauty. Wilder and Hawke completed the half-circle, flanking the couple. All of them looked highly amused, as if they knew something the rest of the world didn't. Oddly, they weren't smiling or laughing, just smug, exactly like nobility would be in the presence of those so far beneath them.

That was exactly how they made me feel. They were perfect. From their mannerisms to their clothes to the way they'd been nice to me so far. It was almost painful to look at them, reminding me of every flaw I was showing the world. There was a zit on my jaw, and I was hyper-aware of the clay I'd wiped on my skirt in my last class. With those four in the room, even the always-popular types looked like mangy children.

"We call them the king and his court," Lynn said. "Purebreds, the lot of them. Rumor has it they were smuggled out of Faerie as kids, so they were even born there. Now, you should probably know that title? Well, the Queen of the Fae would kill someone for even joking about it. So, yeah. I guess that should tell you something."

"You're all basically saying they should die?" I asked.

Amy leaned forward to see me. "Only because we're all so jealous. I mean, *look* at them. Four black ties. All can work in other areas of magic, too. They're so perfect, it makes the rest of us look bad, even when we're doing our best!"

"Yeah, I can kinda see that," I agreed.

"Thing is," Lynn pointed at the other side of the room. "Those are the jesters."

This time she showed me a completely different crowd. Anywhere else, they'd all be the standard popular types. A broad-shouldered guy was grinning with some busty blonde on his lap. Beside him, another was kissing on a redhead. That was more what I expected for the reigning clique at most high schools. Then again, this wasn't exactly a *normal* school. It was supposed to be college, where things like popularity shouldn't be as important.

But clearly that wasn't quite how it worked here. Sure, there were older students - the normal college-age crowd - scattered through the room. Plenty of them, but most were studying while shoving food in their faces, talking to friends, or generally not making a scene.

Never mind how most people in the room fell somewhere in the middle. Granted, being eighteen kinda went either way. Some would be seniors in high school while others would be college freshmen, but at Silver Oaks, we all got smooshed together it seemed. I was also getting the impression that was because this place was more about "fae" than "college," but no one had confirmed it yet.

Of their own volition, my eyes drifted back to the court. They didn't act like typical kids, not like the rest of us. Oh, they were having fun, but the quiet conversation type, not the groping, embarrassing, handsy type that was so common for teenagers. Those four were simply talking, watching over the peons before them, more like the older students here.

"So what am I missing?" I asked Lynn.

"Huh?"

I gestured between the two groups. "What's the social status between them, and where do the rest of us fit in? How do the people who aren't in this Advanced Placement program fit in? I mean, if this was a normal school, I could make a few guesses. Here? I'm completely and totally lost."

Charlotte leaned forward, catching my eye. "You know Silver Oaks is really for training us to control magic, right?"

I had to fight my urge to smile, because that confirmed my suspicions. "No, but it makes sense."

"Yeah," she said. "So, because of that, the age range was made to make sure it caught all of us. See, some faelings - "

"What-lings?" I asked.

"Faelings," Charlotte said. "Those of us who are part-fae. Well, the human side screws with our magical maturity. We might get nothing, hardly anything, or bust out with a surprising amount of power early on."

"But early," Lynn broke in, "is around sixteen. The normal age for a faeling to get magic is around eighteen to twenty - so college. But since it's not *uncommon* for it to start around sixteen, they made the Advanced Placement program. This way, it sorta explains all of us being here."

"Gotcha," I agreed.

Because that actually did make sense. It was also pretty subtle, so no one outside this place would even bat an eye. Add calling it a trade school on top of that? Yep, talk about blending in easily with the real world. Mundane world? I didn't even know the right terms yet.

But Lynn kept going. "Also, at Silver Oaks, there are two kinds of people. Those born here, and those born there. That's always been the dividing line. Most of us are part fae. Just enough to get magic, you know?"

"And they're pure-bloods from Faerie," I realized. "So, why'd they come here?"

"War," Chris told me. "The Fae Queen went mad. A long time

ago, she used to be the Queen of the Summer Court. Then, she got power-hungry and decided to take over the Winter Court too."

"Like, are we talking Seelie and Unseelie here?" I asked. I was a fantasy reader, after all.

Lynn groaned. "No one uses those terms. I guess it was some bastardized version of some Welsh or Old English. Something like that. The courts were named for the seasons, and their power waned when the other season was taking over, keeping balance in a way."

"Here or there?" I asked.

"Both are the same," Amy explained. "I mean, it sounds like there's not a lot of land in the southern hemisphere there, and there's not a lot of magic here, but the court's weather is pretty close to England's."

"Cool," I said, because that was not at all what I'd expected. "So, if those four are Faerie born, then I'm guessing all of you are from here?"

"We're all faelings," Lynn said. "I'm half fae, Matt is too, but both of his parents are half, instead of one of each like me. Um, Amy, you're a quarter, right?"

"Yep," Amy said. "Supposedly, my grandmother worked in the Summer Court at one point, so my parents always say I'm descended from royalty. She was a cook, so I'm not."

"But a lot of people like to claim more prestige than they really had," Lynn explained. "You know, like making themselves sound more important. I think that's mostly because old habits die hard, and a lot of our parents still judge each other based on their former titles. But how fae are you, Chris?"

He shrugged meekly. "No clue. I'm a foundling, Rain, plucked from the foster system."

Charlotte sighed. "I'm an eighth, and I have just enough magic to make people hallucinate around me. Glamours suck when they're out of control, which is how I ended up here. Surprise, you've got some fae blood sort of a thing."

"Glamours kinda suck when in-control too," I said. "Having

someone make you think you're somewhere else and it's so real it feels like teleportation? Kinda shocking."

"I can't do that," Charlotte admitted. "I'm more of the pink elephant dancing at the edge of your vision." Then her eyes narrowed. "Wait. Did someone do that to you?"

I waved her off, because the way her tone had changed made me think it wasn't a good thing. Whatever Aspen had done had been meant to help explain, but Liam was right, she didn't understand things the same way we did. Knowing those four were all purebloods, however, kinda made a few things make more sense.

Then Lynn subtly flicked her finger to another corner of the room. "Now, if you're talking about social circles, see the group who all look like they're a little too stiff? Yeah, children of the Exodus. Their parents want to rebuild the courts here on Earth, and those kids are expected to make it happen. Well, I mean, they're the kids who actually agree with their parents. Most of us don't."

"But most fae want the courts back?" I asked. "Or, um, here? Whatever the right term is?"

"Either," Charlotte said. "See, they were so used to the whole queen and duke type of setup that they're lost with this whole free-for-all thing humans do. Granted, when you spend a few centuries wishing you were a baroness or something, I guess it gets to be a habit?"

"Right." Never mind that feudalism sucked, and most people were peasants, but whatever. I could only guess that the hope was that when rebuilding the courts here, they'd move up? No clue - yet I couldn't look away from Torian, Aspen, and their friends. "I still don't get how they fit in with all of that. Socially, I mean."

"The court?" Lynn asked. "Yeah, just pretend like they don't exist. The four of them are powerful enough to make you disappear with a snap of their fingers. They also keep to themselves."

"They're the real deal, Rain," Charlotte added.

"So everyone looks up to them?" I asked. "Like, am I supposed to kiss their asses or something?"

"No!" Lynn assured me. "Rain, they might as well not even exist for most of us. I mean, they rarely date, and they barely talk to anyone in school, but every girl has to try for one of those boys. It never ends well. If it even looks like the court is going to be friendly to someone, the jesters quickly put them back in their place. The half-bloods don't want the pure-bloods to assume their pedigrees mean anything, I guess? No clue, but considering there's only the five pure-bloods here? Well, besides the teachers, I mean. It's kinda not a fair fight."

"Ok, so who's the fifth?" I asked.

"He's around somewhere," Charlotte explained. "He doesn't fit with the court, though, because he's Earth-born. His parents were already together when they left Faerie, but he's never seen it. Kinda like most of us."

Matt groaned. "More like sick and tired of hearing about it. My parents idolize the place, which is ironic since they've never been there either."

"So, only a few of our teachers and those four have?" I asked.

Lynn nodded. "As far as we know. Thing is, the court will *not* talk about it. If you try to ask, you get shut down fast, if not chased off. Like I said, they don't mingle."

Chris, who seemed to be the quiet one, added, "And those four latched on to each other the moment they arrived. First Torian, last year, and Hawke. They came together. Then Wilder got here. Took a few weeks before he was in their crowd, though. But Aspen? They pulled her right in."

"Keep in mind," Lynn said, looking at me pointedly. "Most AP students here were enrolled by their parents. Real fae parents who want their kid to understand their ancestry. Tends to make an impact when one shows up in the middle of the year."

She meant me. I knew she did, but I wasn't special. No matter how much the circumstances might seem like it, I'd tested as being completely boring. I'd only been allowed in because Aspen had demanded it. Then again, if purity of blood mattered so much to these people, then Aspen was basically the queen of Earth.

Yet that whole idea only made me even more confused. Was it possible the "interesting" thing about me was simply that I was so human? If pure-blood trumped half-blood, and Lynn's friends were acting like that was merely a fact of life, then didn't it stand to reason that a no-blood human was the lowest of them all?

Yeah, this was going to take a little more social dancing than I was used to. Normally, making a few friends was all it took to get ignored, and I was pretty fond of sliding under the radar. It meant fewer questions about my past and less poking into stuff I didn't want to talk about. Here, it seemed such mundane crap didn't matter, but ties to Faerie did. Ties that I had exactly none of.

The rest of lunch was spent being told about the school. Well, everyone else called it the Institute. They asked how I got in, fawned over Liam when I said he was my uncle, and never thought anything of it. Evidently, Liam was universally popular. Unlike the other teachers, he didn't go by "Mr. Sparks" - yes, he had the same last name as his brother. Instead, he asked the kids to use his first name. Then again, he was the counselor, not an instructor, so it kinda made sense.

Soon enough, yet another bell rang, signaling it was time to move on. My new friends all stood, leaving their trays on the table. Around the room, everyone else did the same. Unable to help myself, I looked back to the king's table one last time.

Green eyes were waiting. Torian smiled at me like he was deciding how to start peeling my flesh off. He held my eyes for a few seconds, freezing me in my tracks, then turned to kiss Aspen's temple and stood. The entire table climbed to their feet a second later, exactly like the court they were called, and began to disperse. That was when I realized I was standing there like a voyeur.

"Get your head on straight, Lorraine," I muttered, turning for my next class.

"What was that?" Lynn asked.

"Nothing," I assured her.

"Oh, good," she said, "because I'm supposed to show you the elective options this afternoon. Kinda gets me out of my own classes, so let's make sure to use all the time, ok?"

"Deal," I told her, but when her eyes widened, I realized that might be something else I needed to learn about.

Chapter Nineteen

"So," Lynn said as she led me toward the atrium, "because you're a Legacy, there are less courses open to you. The AP program says we're required to have three classes after lunch. I figure we can get the boring ones out of the way first."

"Ok..." I was following along. AP was short for Advanced Placement, which meant us high schoolers, but I wasn't quite sure where all of this was going.

Then she turned toward the elevator that led to the boy's wing. "First up is Home Economics."

"Faerie style?" I asked.

She flashed me a smile as we joined the cluster of people waiting to go up. "A bit. Sewing in enchantments and cooking with elixirs is included."

"You don't want Home Ec," a guy in front of me said, turning around just to make a point of looking me over. "Rain, right?"

"Yep," I agreed. "Seems everyone knows me."

"It's not really a big place," he explained. "Heard you got stuck with the freak."

"What?"

Lynn leaned closer. "He means Aspen."

"Oh." Because she *was* a bit of a freak. Still, I kinda felt the need to stick up for her. "She's actually pretty nice. Gave me a plant for my room."

The guy's eyebrows shot up. "Seriously? Be careful it doesn't eat you."

"Fuck off, Jayden," Lynn snapped. "You know she's not allowed to grow those inside."

Which made it sound like human-eating plants were a real thing. Noted. Then it was our turn. Lynn led me into the elevator with a group of boys, and she pressed the button for the second floor. One of the guys groaned about that, but everyone else ignored it.

The elevator went up, and when the doors opened again, Lynn led me out. The crowds in the halls were already getting thinner, but we still had plenty of time before the next class. Confused, I looked around, trying to figure out where all the students had disappeared to.

"A good chunk of the student body has classes outside or in the Never after lunch," Lynn explained when she caught me looking. "That's the whole trade part of the Institute thing. The classrooms are used for the college courses now, but the emphasis here really is on teaching fae folk how to fit into life on Earth." She giggled. "Which sounds so sci-fi like that. All it means is it's not as crowded in the halls after lunch."

"Ah, ok."

When we reached the far end, she turned left, going towards the D wing. I followed along placidly, but as we turned the corner, I realized that over the dining hall, the space had been built out to house even more classrooms. Lynn headed that way. Unlike all the rest of this building, on the second floor, between the C and D wings, there were halls which went the other way. Short ones. When we turned down one of those halls, I noticed there was only one door on each side. These rooms were clearly *much* bigger.

"This area is for the occupational stuff," Lynn explained, pausing at a room. "More space for all the sewing machines and ovens."

"There are ovens in there?" Because I hadn't expected that.

"Small ones," she assured me, turning the knob to step inside.

Immediately, the conversation in the room ground to a halt and everyone looked up to see who'd walked in - even the teacher. Lynn headed straight for him, so I followed meekly. I had a feeling that by the end of the day, everyone would get their chance to gawk at me. This whole system was almost designed to make sure of it.

"Mr. Greene," Lynn said, gesturing to me. "This is Rain Brooks, and I'm supposed to help her choose her electives."

"Liam's niece," Mr. Greene said. "Well, I have plenty of Legacies in here. You see, after the Exodus, we quickly learned normal shops won't sew clothes with enchanted thread or dye them with distilled potions. Seems such things are considered pointless."

"Magic," I realized.

He nodded, a cherubic smile on his happy face. "Exactly. So in most fae communities, there are jobs for people trained to handle some often expensive enchantments. Of course, baking with love potions is always in high demand. Not that we'd use anything so dangerous in here, but giggle potions have almost the same qualities. Then there's the simple reality that working with magic means someone will have to clean up the magic. The residues and stains left behind can require a specialist. Those are a few things you'll learn in my class."

"Ok, that sounds a lot more interesting than what I expected," I told him.

"Go, have a look around. If you have any questions, even if they come up later, feel free to ask me." Mr. Greene gestured to the rest of the room, basically turning us loose.

Lynn led me around the edge, allowing me to gawk at the minor differences I didn't notice at first glance. The sewing machines were pretty standard. The metal cage around the unused spools of thread weren't. The ovens were at the back, but the oven mitts hanging on the fronts had a very interesting looking fabric.

And while all of this was unique and different, I still didn't want to take Home Ec again. I'd had that course as a freshman, and I'd hated it. I didn't think adding magic would necessarily make sitting at a sewing machine more "my thing."

When we left there, we passed another class with the door open. Inside, it looked like a brewery with all the glass lines swirling around. My feet slowed so I could figure it out, but Lynn just caught my arm and kept going.

"That's an enchantment class," she explained. "Distilling and brewing with fae plants to make potions. Now, over here is something you might like."

She led me to a classroom straight ahead of us. Just like before, Lynn towed me inside, then moved to whisper a few words to the teacher. He pointed to a spot at the side, making it clear we could stand against the wall, and then kept going.

"So, where was I? Right, weapons." The man clasped his hands behind his back and meandered across the front of the classroom. "I'm sure you've all experienced iron sensitivity by now. Well, for those of pure fae blood, it's even worse. Naturally, that means swords, knives, and even armor can't be made from the metal. The problem is there are few other options here. The same is not true in Faerie."

Ok, he had my attention. When the teacher picked up a small rectangle of an almost iridescent metal, I recognized it. At least, I was pretty sure it was the second option I'd looked at in my entrance exam. The one with the rainbow reflections.

"This is *eltam*," he explained. "Unlike iron, it is not a magnetic metal. In many ways, the properties are similar to that of aluminum. The difference is *eltam* is stronger. It's harder to forge. It can also hold an enchantment much easier. Many fae swords or daggers had protections or additional damage properties built into them as they were forged. Flaming swords are just one example."

He went on to explain how the fae courts had been dazzling places, not only because of the pale silver color of the metal, but also due to the refractive qualities of its surface. Lighting for events was often chosen to bring out warm or cool shades, thus making guards appear dazzling to the nobility of the courts. In Faerie, beauty was as much a spell as any other magic the fae could perform, it seemed.

After about fifteen minutes, Lynn gestured for me to head to the door. The teacher looked over at us and nodded, but he didn't stop what he was talking about. I kinda wanted to stay and listen a little longer, but Lynn was clearly done with it.

Still, the moment we were in the hall, I made her pause. "Which class was that?"

"Oh, History of Magic," she said, all but blowing it off. "It's one of your options, but I hear the tests are killer."

"It sounds kinda cool."

She rolled her eyes. "Only if you're trying to pad your resume or something. They list it as a specialty history course. Seriously, what difference does it make? I mean, all that stuff happened in Faerie, and we're not exactly *in* Faerie. We're here, and there's no more *eltam* except what the refugees brought with them. Those weapons are hoarded. The things are priceless! All the rest of it? We may do it a little differently here because we don't have as much magic, but again, we're *here*."

"Yeah, I can see that," I mumbled.

Yet I didn't agree with her at all. Knowing the how of things often explained the why. It was something I'd learned the hard way as a foster kid. History had a way of coming back to bite us when we least expected it. Never mind that all of this was amazing! I wanted to know everything they were willing to share.

Maybe it was because I was merely human. I shouldn't even *be* at this school, but I'd gotten in, so I wanted to make sure I appreciated it. Hopefully, the harder I tried, the less likely they'd be to kick me out. Liam was a human. I was a human. There was no reason I couldn't figure out a way to make myself useful to the fae and eventually earn that title: *caradil*.

From there, we headed to another classroom on the far side of the building. This time, I didn't understand a single word. Considering the class was the introduction course to the fae language, that made sense. Still, listening to it was nice. The words were melodic and soothing. They lilted and flowed in ways which reminded me of a song, and I kinda liked it.

Somewhere along the way, the bell rang, and students once again shuffled through the halls to their next class. Lynn kept me moving, aiming for yet another classroom. A few people turned to look at me. A couple of guys smiled in a way that felt like an offer. Plenty of girls sneered as if I was something they didn't want to get close to.

Those were the jesters, I was pretty sure. They all had on too much jewelry, all of it was gold, and much of it had expensive gems. Golden blonde hair, reds, and warm shades of brown seemed to be the most popular in that group, and they traveled in small packs. Clearly, popularity worked the same way with fae as with humans. The prettier ones always rose to the top, and the more they were adored, it seemed the uglier their expressions became.

When the next class started, Lynn took me into another room. This time, it was called Taxonomy of Faerie. The instructor talked about the plants and beasts of Faerie, how they differed from those on Earth, and compared many to folklore. From the little I was able to hear, it seemed trolls were real. A few had escaped to Earth long ago and were gone now, but they were prevalent in Faerie.

Lynn was bored with the lectures, though, so she decided we could hit one more and then we'd call it good. Considering *she'd* been the one to say we needed to take the whole afternoon, I was a little confused, but not willing to contradict her. Once again, we walked the entire length of the hall, back towards those large rooms where we'd first started, and she picked a door almost at random.

The moment she opened it, I smelled fresh dirt. Pulling in a breath, I paused to enjoy it, thinking it smelled like it was about to rain. That earthy, rich scent was one of my favorite things. Lynn didn't even care that I'd stopped. She just headed to the teacher and did her thing again.

But this time, I was spotted. "Rain?" The voice belonged to Aspen.

"Hey," I greeted her.

"What are you doing in here?" she asked, leaving her place at a long table to come closer.

"I don't actually know where here is," I admitted. "Lynn's showing me the options for my electives. I guess that as a Legacy, I don't get to pick a lot of fun things."

Aspen's blue eyes narrowed. "There are a few. This is Botany. We grow a lot of the plants for distilling and to use in the atrium. Come."

"Rain," Lynn called out.

"*I* will show her," Aspen said, but there was a hint of warning in her tone.

Lynn visibly swallowed. "Sure. Um, I'll just wait in the hall then? Or if you're going to be a while..."

"I'll handle it," Aspen assured her. "You can go do whatever you want."

"Cool," Lynn said, backing toward the door. "Thanks, Ms. Linden."

"Aspen really is the one to show her," the teacher - Ms. Linden - said. "Enjoy the break, Lynn."

My mentor didn't need to be told again. The moment Lynn left the room, Aspen reached for my arm, but paused. Her hands were covered in dark dirt, the kind that did not mix well with my clothes. Pointing for her to lead, I followed her back to her desk. There, Aspen began showing me everything spread before her.

"So, these are seeds from a fae plant," she said. "They were grown here, though. Some things are easy, like the midnight grass. Others, like silver oaks, refuse to grow in dirt with any iron in it."

"And that's all you do in here?" I asked. "Just grow the plants?"

"Just?" She grinned at me. "These are all fae plants, Rain. They aren't like what you're used to. We have to give them attention, make sure they're eating, and things like that. Some are more like a cat than a fern."

"Whoa," I breathed, moving closer. "Really?"

My chest was right against her shoulder as I looked at the one before her. Aspen glanced back, and for a moment our eyes met. There was no malice in her gaze. No judgment or animosity, and yet a zing still shot up my spine. She smelled like flowers. She was the most beautiful girl I'd ever seen - even in ads or movies. This close, she still looked like she couldn't be real, and yet she was.

"Sorry," I mumbled, leaning back. "Personal space."

"It's ok," she assured me. "You can't see from over there, and I love plants."

"Is that your magic talent or something?" I asked.

This time, the smile curling her lips was softer. "No. When I was a baby, I was raised in a garden. I left Faerie when I was three, almost four, but I can still remember that garden. All the plants. All the flowers singing to me. My mother's voice would join them. She gardened, you see."

"I guess you miss her, huh?"

The smile faded. "I heard the Queen had her killed. I do miss my mom, Rain, and the flowers remind me of her. This? It's my passion, not my proficiency. I can show you if you want."

"That actually sounds pretty cool," I decided. "Maybe you can help me take care of my flower too? I'm kinda worried I'm going to kill it."

"I won't let you," she promised. "And tomorrow, I'll show you the rest of the electives. Lynn isn't doing it right."

"She's trying," I assured my suitemate.

Aspen grumbled like she didn't agree. "No. She's trying to impress the teachers and make herself look good. She doesn't care about you. She thinks you're just some burner who's a waste of her time." Those eyes returned, holding my complete attention. "I don't."

Chapter Twenty

I spent the rest of that class with Aspen, watching while she started seeds, replanted a few things, and took time to pet and talk to the other plants. She whispered her words in the fae language, so I couldn't understand them, but I could actually see the plants responding. A few moved, slowly reaching out for her hand. Others swayed. Some curled leaves or straightened them.

It was magical. Maybe not in the literal sense, but all of this was so almost-normal that it felt even more amazing. When the class was over - and since Lynn was nowhere to be found - I figured that meant I was done. It felt too soon - something I'd never expected to say about school - because I'd actually enjoyed myself, but I had nowhere else I was expected to be. Giving in, I headed back upstairs to change clothes and check out my text books. I clearly had a *lot* of catching up to do.

Just before six that evening, someone stopped to knock on my door. Hopping up, I answered it, surprised to see Liam on the other side. He held a box of pizza before him and had a plastic bag dangling from his arm. Before he had the chance to say a word, I stepped back, opening the door wider to invite him in.

"How bad was it?" he asked, setting the pizza down on my desk. "I brought sympathy food and a willing ear."

"I'll take the food," I assured him, "but it wasn't bad."

Liam just reached for the bag, then pulled out a stack of paper plates. "Some for pizza, and the rest are to keep in here in case you need them later."

Taking one, I picked out two large slices, then moved to sit on my bed. Liam turned the chair at my desk so he was mostly facing me, then grabbed a few for himself. Evidently, my "uncle" intended to stay for a bit. It was actually kinda nice.

"So?" he asked. "Don't I even get your first thoughts? Rain, I just dropped you into a magical school of faeries. I'm kinda waiting for the freakout to start."

"No freaking out," I promised. "I mean, in English, we talked about how a poem was related to fae history. Sure, math sucks, but that's because it's just math. I have History of Faerie for third period, and that was amazing. Like, the feudalism of the society was today's subject, and how humans did have a part in fae culture. Morrigans, I think they were called? Um, then there's biology, and while I expected some normal science, we learned how iron in clay makes it hard to grow fae plants. Torian kinda showed me how it messes with magic, too."

"Torian?" Liam asked.

I nodded. "Yeah, I sat beside him in biology today. Lynn gave me the rundown, though. Sounds kinda like more fae blood means more cool here. Which sucks, because that also implies I'm doomed to be a loser. Thankfully, as a foster kid, I'm used to it."

"It's not that simple," he assured me. "You also have to consider the power of the parents. Some were nobility in the courts. Their kids will have been raised to think they're more important than those of peasants. Then there's where they were born."

"Faerie or Earth, yep. Got that lesson," I assured him. "So, am I the only human at Silver Oaks?"

"No," he said. "There's a boy who's the stepson of a renowned fae soldier. There's a girl who was adopted by a pair of fae half-bloods. They're family of fae, but completely human. Like you, they're Legacies."

"Cool," I said, feeling a little better about being human. "I also got a tour of some of the available electives. I'm kinda shocked they let me pick, though."

"It's because normal schools don't have comparable courses," Liam explained. "If you're taking Spanish in your last school, it doesn't help much with learning Faeril. That's the official name of the fae language, so you know. But taking auto mechanics doesn't mean you'll do well in weapons crafting."

"There's a weapons-crafting course?" Ok, that hadn't been one I saw today.

Liam leaned back with a chuckle. "There is. There are also combat courses, because faeries aren't the only things that came to Earth in the Exodus. Well, that's not entirely true. The good fae you see here aren't the only things. Technically, these are the Sidhe." He pronounced it like *Shee*. "There are other fae things that do not look like normal people. Some fae communities need a police force to defend against the bad things which want to remove them from this world and haul them back to Faerie. Self-defense, combat options, and some survival skills are offered."

"What wants to take them back?" I asked, because he'd skipped over it a little too easily. "And how would that happen if the gates are closed like everyone keeps saying?"

Liam just sighed. "Ok, so I'm sure you've heard of the Wild Hunt?"

I nodded. "Possessed people on horseback. That was in the poem this morning, although the teacher said they aren't really being offered to Hell."

"They're not," he agreed. "Rain, the Wild Hunt is real. It's limited here on Earth because of the magic. It's also been trapped here since the Exodus, which was in 1971. Originally, the Hunt were enchanted warriors who were compelled to find criminals and return them for punishment. Here's the catch. If they can't take them to the ruling monarch, they are to execute the convicted. Yeah, they're convicted before the Hunt is turned loose, but it's not a trial like you're thinking. The defendant isn't allowed to be there. It's all about the accusations."

"That sucks."

Liam nodded. "So, in the Exodus, the Queen sent the Hunt here to bring back *all* the defectors. No one knows what happened, but she closed the gates - or someone else did - and now they're locked here. Any fae or fae descendant they can catch, they haul to the gates, find them still locked, and then they execute the captives. It's a death sentence. Over the last fifty years, the community has managed to break the Hunt into smaller groups, which makes them easier to escape, but they still exist. Unfortunately, they can't be killed."

"Yeah, not good news," I said.

"It's really not," Liam agreed. "A few times a year, they come to the Institute. We do have protections, but we also have lockdown procedures. You'll be safe, though. I am too, but that means we have more responsibilities when the fae have to shelter in place."

I nodded. "Ok. I'm sure I'll freak out, but it can't be any worse than going to London without warning, right?"

"It can," he said. "But that reminds me. I have a present for you." He turned and dug into the plastic bag again. This time, what he pulled out was a box. The front of it had a picture of a phone. "Hope you like Androids," he teased as he tossed it over.

"A phone?" I asked.

"Yours," he assured me. "I put it on my plan, but I figured this way you can check social media, look things up, and act like a normal teenager. Just don't use it in class, because the teachers will confiscate it. Silenced in your pocket or bag is fine. Checking your messages isn't."

"Understood," I assured him.

"And you have until the end of this week to pick your electives," he went on. "You can try a few classes, sit through them or join in, and that's fine. What you cannot do is come hide in here while everyone else is still learning. If you aren't sure what you should be doing, my office is downstairs, in the same place we went for your entrance exams."

"The glass office," I said, showing I was keeping up.

"Exactly," he agreed. "And now for the bad news. I have to tell John and Nancy how you're doing."

I groaned. "Really?"

"Mostly because they're worried about you coming back, I think." He let out a weary sigh. "I'm sure that's not what you want to hear, but you have to understand their point of view."

"Magic is scary," I mumbled, assuming that was where he was going.

"Terrifying," Liam said. "They had some fosters who went out of their way to destroy the house. Since you've now seen a few glimpses of what's possible, just imagine what John and Nancy went through. Believe it or not, the room you were living in was filled with briars. You couldn't even see the walls - and that was nothing. Glamours of Hell instead of London, compulsions to sleep for days, poisoned coffee that made John sick enough to go to the hospital, and more. The boys thought they were under attack because of all the iron in the house, so they fought back. It wasn't good."

"And the Sparks don't know about the fae?" I honestly couldn't tell one way or the other, but I figured Liam would know.

He bit his lips together, looking like he was choosing his words. "They suspect. They aren't sure if it's fae or demon possession, but they are convinced it was supernatural. I've laughed it off as much as I can. Now, I have to accept that the kids were 'strange' and that the fear was real. My usual excuse is mental illness. It's not right, but it's easier than getting my brother to believe in anything but what he knows."

"Yeah, I can see that," I agreed. "I guess I got lucky when the crow flew in the house, huh?"

"I happen to think so, but I like the fae," Liam said. "I also think you deserve more than the system could give. So in my opinion, this works out for both of us. And if you do well enough here, there's a chance you could settle down in a fae community."

Which no one had really explained to me yet. "Like, are there hidden towns or something?"

"Something like that," he admitted. "You know how there's a Chinatown in some big cities? Well, it's a similar idea, but a lot more secretive. Typically, fae don't like big cities, so they settle in small towns, creating those subdivisions of ranchettes you hear about. Sometimes, they move into the same apartment building. There are a few fae towns, but they're small things. Couple hundred people at most, and often not even big enough to actually be a real town."

"So, like Plainsboro?" I asked.

"No," he said. "Plainsboro is pretty normal. However, to the north of here is a settlement. There are about twenty-five families in a homeowners' association. There just aren't enough fae to really stand out. Their magic would, but they just look like very pretty people."

"I know," I breathed. "There are so many cute boys and beautiful girls in this school. Talk about having to work for it!"

He just laughed. "How about you don't make me sign for birth control quite yet? Although, if you need it, you can see the nurse. She will need your guardian's approval, and that is me, so I *will* know. I will also sign, Rain. I'm not condoning you sleeping with boys, but I'd much rather you didn't end up raising a fae child at seventeen either."

I lifted both hands, holding him off. "I've had 'the talk' in almost every home I've lived in," I assured him. "Condoms, birth control, abstinence, and more. I promise, I'm a pro."

"Then I'll trust you," he said. "Just don't forget that while the fae are beautiful, they're also not like us. They don't value the same things. They do not understand a lot of the morals we simply take for granted because they weren't raised with Christianity anywhere in their world. Murder, theft, marriage, and all of those things are seen a little differently. The closer they are to a relative from Faerie, the more different they'll seem."

"Like Aspen," I realized. "She was telling me how she remembers the garden where she grew up."

Liam's eyes narrowed. "Is that all?"

"Should there be more?" I countered.

"There's plenty more," he said, "but she doesn't usually talk about it. That she told you even that much means she must trust you. I have no idea what you've done, but earning their trust is not an easy thing. It's why those four keep to themselves. They're from Faerie, Rain. They all remember it. They saw the war firsthand, and that sort of trauma isn't easy to deal with. Much less when your new home is nothing like the old and you've lost everything you held dear. Be careful with them."

"Because they'll kill me or something?" I asked, not quite sure how dire his warning was.

"Probably not kill," he assured me. "Although, I'm not sure if being locked in a glamour no one else can break would be any better. They are *true* fae. The type the old stories talk about. On top of all that, Aspen thinks you're interesting."

Yep, I was starting to get nervous again. "Why does that now sound like a bad thing?"

"Doesn't have to be," he promised. "Think of it more like walking down the street with a hundred grand in cash. It could be a good thing if you make it home safely. It could be a bad thing if someone was willing to hurt you to take it. That's how the fae work. Either it's a very good thing or a very bad one. Rarely is it something in the middle."

Chapter Twenty-One

The next day started out as a repeat of the first. Well, without all the drama. I didn't get called meat. I didn't crash into anyone. I did get a Pixy Stix from Aspen in second period. She didn't walk me to third period this time, though. Wilder smiled at me in that class, but Hawke glared the same way as before. Then, in biology, Torian helped me do the class assignment.

It actually worked out. He knew what was going on, and I could grab the things when he hesitated. Evidently, there was more iron around than I expected. I'd just assumed that since this was a fae school, it would've all been removed. Still, things like pens, the microscope, and more were clearly a metal he didn't like. Each time I saw him pause for too long, I offered to do it instead, letting him know I needed to catch up. The guy almost seemed appreciative. Well, in his arrogant way.

Lunch was a little less exciting than it had been yesterday. Lynn and her friends let me sit with them again. This time, they talked about their own things. Some of it was about their classes. Others were about fellow students I didn't know yet. Evidently, someone named Nevaeh had a run in the back of her tights and no one was willing to tell her.

Then there was the fact that Danni and Layla - whoever they were - had broken up just before third period. The girls had the kind of dramatic falling out that made everyone stop to watch the drama. Layla had tried to put a compulsion on Danni, but Danni had resisted, only to enchant Layla's tablet to shut off randomly.

Not that I knew any of those people, but it made me realize the social squabbles had just been taken to a whole new level. But while they talked, I read. My tablet had all of my textbooks, and History of Faerie was the best place to start. It felt less like a school assignment and more like a documentary, and I seriously needed to know what I had gotten myself into.

When the bell rang to announce the end of lunch, Lynn finally seemed to acknowledge me. "So, you ready for day two of your elective observations?"

A pair of hands dropped onto the end of our table hard enough to make both of us look over. Aspen stood there, leaning on them. She raked her eyes across the entire group, convincing a few to leave - and quickly. Then she turned her icy gaze on Lynn.

"I'll show her the rest. You can have the credit. I don't even care," Aspen said.

Lynn jiggled her head, clearly intimidated by my suitemate. "Ok. I was just trying to help, because Liam asked."

"He should've asked me."

"Ok," Lynn said again. "I didn't mean to offend, Aspen."

"You can't see enough," Aspen told her. "You look for magic, and finding nothing, you make a decision. It's never that easy. The Queen values only power. We should value people."

"Sure," Lynn agreed. "I can do that."

Then Aspen turned to me. "Done with lunch?" Her nose wrinkled like something about the whole thing was disgusting.

"Ready to go when you are," I assured her, pushing back my chair.

The moment I was standing, Aspen looped her arm in mine again, then turned for the back of the building, not the doors I'd used to come in. I looked back, completely confused now, but Aspen didn't even slow. Like me, she held her tablet in one arm, resting the bottom on her hip. She also had a cluster of Pixy Stix in her hand. As we reached the back of the dining hall, she offered me one.

"Everything else is in another building, which means we'll need to walk over there. Take a straw. It'll keep you warm."

Sugar would keep me warm? If she said so. I accepted one, opened the top, then poured a bit into my mouth. It tasted like pure sugar, but it made Aspen smile. Once I swallowed, she reached for the door that led outside, then opened it so we could both pass through.

Immediately, the wind hit me, but it was... tropical? Warm, definitely. Shocked, I looked over at Aspen, who was grinning a bit too much. She tilted up her own straw, pouring the whole thing into her mouth, and kept walking, towing me along with her.

"It's just a glamour," she explained. "The wind is actually cold, and if we stay out too long, we will pay for it later, but it's a lot better than going to get coats, trying to deal with the coats, and all of that. Besides, I like the skirt you're wearing."

It was one of the green plaid ones with the pleats. A pretty typical school uniform thing, but I had on black tights under it. Still, if this was what a glamour could do, I was perfectly fine with her using magic on me. However, that didn't mean I didn't have questions.

"So, you can glamour yourself?"

"Yep," she agreed. "Not everyone can, though. Glamouring yourself is harder because you already know it's a lie."

"And you get cold like I do?" Which sounded stupid once it was out of my mouth.

Aspen just leaned her head back and laughed. "Of course I do. They may call me the ice princess, but I promise I'm not really made out of ice."

"I actually haven't heard that one," I admitted.

Which made her eyes snap over and lock on mine. "What have you heard, Rain?" Her tone was suddenly completely serious.

"That you four are all pure-bloods, born in Faerie, and that I need to be careful around you," I said. "I know people call you the court, and Torian's called the king, but I hadn't heard any other titles except the jesters."

She made a humming sound. "Summer court idolizers. Half-bloods at best. Never mind that their parents left the court. No, they prefer to ignore that part because it doesn't make them sound as impressive."

"Considering I'm a no-blood, I figure I have no room to talk," I pointed out.

"You're a pure-blood," she corrected. "Pure human. Do not let some mixed-blood bitch make it sound bad."

"So, being mixed is a problem?" I asked. "Aspen, I'm just trying to keep up with all this stuff. I'm sure my questions are stupid, but you seem to be the only one willing to answer them without making a big deal out of it."

She paused, turning to face me. "It's not the blood, but the attitude. We came here, not the other way around. When we were desperate, some of you offered to help, and the fae do not forget favors. That is what we should be proud of, not how pure we are or how noble our parents were. They haven't seen what Faerie is like now. They don't know what the Mad Queen..." She paused. "They only think of the magic there. Not the pain we ran away from."

"I'm sorry," I told her, reaching out to clasp her arm. "I didn't mean to bring up bad memories."

"You deserve to know," she assured me, this time offering her arm.

I took it, and we began walking again. Our destination was a small grey building mostly hidden by trees. When we got closer, I heard banging. Aspen's feet slowed, and she took a deep breath, then pushed on. I couldn't help but notice, but I didn't want to ask anything else that might upset her. I was already feeling like an idiot for reminding her of her dead mother.

But when we walked through the door, I suddenly understood the hesitation. This was the weapons-crafting class, and metal was everywhere. Gone were the blazers and uniforms, replaced with coveralls and leather aprons. At one side was a real, actual forge. In the middle were anvils. Along the sides were grinding wheels and other power tools.

No, they weren't all smithing weapons or anything. One girl was grinding down glass to make a triangle of some type. Another table had a group around it and what looked like a sheet of carbon fiber laid out between them. They were working together to place a curved object in the middle.

"I..." Aspen pulled her arm back. "I need to go outside."

"Go," I insisted. "You didn't need to come in here."

But her retreat made the instructor look over. Concern filled her face for a moment, and then the woman turned to march toward me. She was tall, muscular, and had hair even shorter than Aspen's. Her face was smudged with something dark, like soot, but I couldn't rule out dirt either.

"Can I help you?" she asked when she was close enough.

"Um, I'm Rain Brooks, and I'm supposed to check out the options for my elective classes," I explained. "Aspen was showing me..."

"She should know better than to come in here," the woman said, peeling off a thick leather glove to offer her hand. "I'm Anita Taggart. Most of the students call me Tag." Then she paused. "Wait, you're Liam's niece, right?"

"I am," I said.

"Full human, right?"

"Yes, ma'am."

"Welcome to the club," she said. "Most of the students in here are of lower fae ancestry, so a quarter or less. Makes it easier because of the metals. Sadly, we just don't have the means to work most of this stuff without iron in the power tools or hammers hard enough to hold their shape. It's one of the places Legacies often excel, and the fae are desperate for people who can make what they need without suffering while doing so."

"Sounds like a good place for me," I agreed.

"Could be," Tag agreed. "Our classes here in the Forge are mixed between the AP students and the older ones. This course is college level, so many consider it challenging. However, it also will set you up for many career opportunities in the real world."

Which sounded perfect, so I asked, "What is all of this stuff anyways?"

"The students make ceramic knives for the kitchen, glass ones for botany, and for the sentinels, we do some carbon fiber swords. Kinda the best of both worlds, there. We can use bronze or other metals, reinforce it with carbon fiber for strength, and get a usable weapon that doesn't harm the fae wielding it. Our more advanced students make armor, like the group working on the carbon fiber breastplate there."

"But why?" I asked. "I mean, swords? Why not some 3D-printed guns?"

She laughed. "First, because this is a school, and there are laws about having you all make guns. Secondly, because there are some things a bullet wouldn't stop. Lead is not a problem for them, and iron is too hard to cause enough damage. More splinter, less wounding."

Then Tag showed me around, explaining how the items made in here taught a bigger skill. Plastic molding was included in the instruction, which was used for all sorts of industries in the real world. Metal forging was the same. Carbon fiber wraps could be used for cars, planes, and so much more. I listened, completely and totally fascinated.

Knowing Aspen was waiting outside in the cold, I didn't stay as long as I wanted. Liam had said I could come back to learn more, so I told Tag I probably would. She made it clear I was definitely welcome, then I hurried to find my friend. I was halfway through the door when I realized what I'd just thought: friend. Aspen Fox sure felt like my friend. I wasn't sure she'd agree, but I kinda hoped so.

"Aspen?" I called when I didn't see her.

"Over here!" she yelled back, waving from a cluster of trees about a half a football field away.

I hurried that way, thankful her warmth glamour seemed to still be working. She met me part way, pointing over to yet another building behind the school. This one was bigger, and the clanking and yelling of people was hard to miss. It kinda sounded like an athletics room or something. At least from the cheers.

This time, Aspen didn't hesitate. She walked in without any problems, her heels clicking on the wooden floor. Trailing behind her, I followed her into a large, open space. There were mirrors on all sides, mats on the floor, and plenty of students all dressed in some green-and-black workout clothes. I spotted a kickboxing bag at one side. There was a pair dueling with wooden swords in the middle. They looked like they were fencing. Some were wrestling, some were boxing, and so much more.

Then someone let out a wolf whistle. "Nice legs!"

Aspen huffed, turning around like she wasn't surprised at all. "Shut it, Hawke!"

"I meant hers," he teased, making his way over. "Hey, Bracken? I think the new girl needs the tour."

The moment the instructor walked up, I knew he was a pureblood fae. His hair was icy pale, even more than Aspen's. His skin was burnished to a gold color that didn't seem to match, and his eyes were as green as Torian's. Then there was his stunning beauty. Holy crap, but this guy was sexy. From his muscular arms down to his impressive thighs! I tried to smile, aware my cheeks were probably a little too pink.

They did not make men like that where I came from. You know, Iowa.

"Liam's prodigy," the man greeted me. "I'm Bracken, the combat and defense instructor for Silver Oaks. This is my domain." He held out his arms and gestured to the space around us. "Hawke, would you keep Aspen out of trouble while I show Rain around?"

"Can do," Hawke agreed, his bad attitude completely gone.

Bracken just dropped a hand on my shoulder and turned me away, leading me on a lap around the outside of the massive building. "After lunch, we have a few courses offered out here. Survival skills is one. That's where we teach you how to spot signs of fae, track animals and people, identify warning signs of the Hunt - which Liam said he already explained?"

"He did," I agreed.

"The point of the survival class is to help a fae learn to not only blend into the society here on Earth, but also to hide, find more of our kind, and avoid the Hunt. Sadly, it's a necessary thing for most of us."

"Sounds kinda interesting, actually," I said.

Bracken nodded, thrusting his lip out like he was impressed. "Ok. Then we have self-defense courses. Those include weapons and magic. Naturally, you'd be in the introductory section. I also offer a combat course. Again, you'd be in the introductory class, but next year you could move into a weapon specialization, a training style, or a few other options. It's a lot of hard, physical work, though."

"I kinda always wanted to do a sport," I told him.

"And how do you feel about fighting?" he asked.

I winced. "Um, it's how I ended up getting moved to Plainsboro, actually. I punched a guy for grabbing me after I said no."

Bracken chuckled. "Well, you can't do much in that skirt, but we have different uniforms for these classes. If you're actually interested, just tell Liam, and I'll have something in your size so you can get an idea of what we do. How does that sound?"

"It sounds amazing," I told him.

Because seeing the people in there bashing at each other with swords? Yeah, I wanted to do that. It made the dorky fantasy nerd inside me a little too excited. Bracken turned to see what I was looking at, and the man chuckled again.

"Tomorrow," he decided. "Just change into some jeans and a tee, and I'll let you at least try. How's that sound?"

"Perfect," I breathed. "I thought the History of Magic sounded cool, but this?"

"You know, if you ask Liam, he can get you copies of those textbooks," Bracken said. "Rain, you don't always have to take the class to get the knowledge. We actually want our students to understand all of this."

"The problem is going to be picking," I admitted.

"And you still have next year," he pointed out. "Pretty sure there will be a few more after that too. So, let me show you the rest of the facilities while you daydream about slaying dragons. And no, there aren't any dragons here, but I can make sure no thug will mug you without paying for it dearly."

I looked up to smile at him. "I'm thinking that sounds just as good. I will definitely be here tomorrow. Promise."

Chapter Twenty-Two

The next day, I went to the "gym" to check out some more of Bracken's classes. I was pretty sure that wasn't the official name of the building, but it was what everyone called it. When I got there, Bracken was going through his survival course, demonstrating something to the students. I'd changed into a long-sleeve and jeans, plus I'd grabbed a jacket for the walk over. After sitting on a bench for half an hour watching his class, I was glad I had the extra layer.

The wind wasn't too bad today, but the trees were still swaying every so often. At one point, I looked up to see a bird land in the branches. It was black, making me think back to the insanity that had started all of this. If it wasn't for some crow flying into the house, I would be in a public school right now, probably wearing pastel plaid and khaki pants. I owed that bird a lot.

Finally, Bracken turned the class loose to follow a set of animal prints around the gym. I'd tried to listen in as much as I could, but sitting over here - to stay out of his way - meant I missed a lot of it. When the instructor walked his very beautiful ass over to sit next to me, I was hoping I hadn't done anything wrong.

"So," Bracken said, leaning over his knees to look at the ground between us. "I talked to Liam. Sounds like you're a little overwhelmed with your class options, huh?"

"I am," I admitted. "I always thought fencing was the sort of thing offered..." I paused, then actually giggled at myself. "In some fancy school, which I guess this kinda is."

"It sorta is," he agreed. "I also don't teach 'fencing.' I teach offense and defense." He pulled in a breath. "Can I be honest with you, Rain?"

"Please?" I begged, deciding I liked this instructor.

"Of the three courses I'm offering this semester, I think defense will be the most useful for you. You have no magic of your own. That means you'll need a way to protect yourself against it. I can also teach you how to defend against physical attacks, and it's something that every fae woman - " He paused. "Every *woman*, I mean, can use in this world." Then he gestured to the wilderness on the other side of the trees. "Out there is the real world. Men assault women. People steal. There are so many reasons why self-defense is useful, but if you plan to stay with the fae, then knowing how to protect yourself against both intentional and unintentional magic will be vital."

I heard him. I also agreed with him. The problem was this sinking feeling in the pit of my stomach. I'd actually dreamed about slaying a dragon last night. Granted, I'd also looked like a dark elf, and I'd been wearing the same clothes as a character from a book I liked, but that was beside the point. Sword fighting was just cool. I knew it wasn't all he taught in his class, but it was the thing that put it at the top of my list.

"So, I can't learn how to fence?" I asked.

"You can learn sword fighting and other combat skills," he corrected. "It's an elective, and you're actually allowed to choose any three of the courses offered to you. Legacies are welcome in my class. If you want, you could pick survival, defense, and offense." He made a noise and paused. "Basics of Survival Skills, Introduction to Self Defense, and Introduction to Weapons and

Combat. Those are the course names. However, it sounds like you also want to learn the fae language, History of Magic, Botany, and maybe a few more."

"Weapons-crafting," I said. "I mean, I kinda like how it's something I can do that others can't. Immune to iron, and all that."

"Tag will also teach you skills which are useful in the real world, so that's a good one," he agreed. "The problem is you only get three."

"But I don't have to pick until Friday, right?"

Bracken nodded. "Correct. I just want you to keep that in mind. Now go inside the gym and look around. It's cold out here, you aren't tracking my cat like the rest of the class, and I have a feeling you'll want to at least try a few things before you decide."

He was right, so I went in. I spent a little too long checking out everything. The mirrors were a little distracting, but I had a feeling there was a reason for them. Soon enough, Bracken's class came back in. Most of the students went into the changing area to get ready for their next class. A few took a spot on the mats and started stretching.

Then came his defense course. I sat at the side, listening as he taught his class a new move, then observing as he helped each one. Bracken eventually came over and had me join in. I got a little more special attention, but it was pretty cool. After that came his offensive course. The man allowed me to swing a stick at him for a good fifteen minutes, stopping me to teach me the proper angle and grip for a real sword.

I was exhausted when I got home that night, but I'd actually had fun. The next day, I went to Tag's weapons-crafting course. The woman was thrilled to see me back. She put me in a pair of coveralls which were only a little too big, then had me smash a hammer into a hot piece of metal. Granted, the guy in charge of heating it and telling me where to hit was about twenty, and seemed to know what he was doing, but he thought it was cool I was trying.

When that class let out, I headed back to the building to check out the Taxonomy of Faerie class Lynn had blown past. The instructor was willing to let me sit in the corner and listen for the entire hour. When that was done, I headed back outside for Bracken's offensive course again.

I knew self-defense would be a better option, but I'd never been allowed to do anything competitive before. No soccer, baseball, or even basketball. Not even debate! I was the girl who moved too often to get involved with clubs and teams, which had only made me want it more.

At the end of the day, I had a list of classes to pick from, and only a very small list of ones I didn't want. Needless to say, Home Ec was at the top of the "nopes." Desperate for a little advice, I knew there was only one person to ask. Instead of heading up to my room to mull it over a little more, I turned my feet to the office.

The moment I stepped through the glass door, a younger woman looked up and smiled at me. "Hi, can I help you?" she asked.

"Um, I need to talk to Liam Sparks," I said.

"Let me see if he's available for a student." She smiled, looked me over like I surprised her, and then turned for an office at the side.

I could hear her say something, but I couldn't make out the words. A second later, Liam poked his head out. "Rain? Come on back. Felia, this is my niece. If I'm not with anyone, she's always allowed in."

"Got it," the woman said.

I moved past her into Liam's office. The place was nice. It probably shouldn't be surprising, considering the rest of the school, but I still looked around with open curiosity. He had flowers on the shelves, some very fancy books - including two written in swirls I could only assume was the Faerie language - and a cute little nameplate on his desk. The kind that was made of brass and looked very fancy.

"Why does everyone call you Liam instead of Mr. Sparks?" I asked.

He chuckled. "Well, I'm not an instructor. Also, I find the students are more willing to talk to me if I keep the expectations casual. Plus, being human, if I try to force the fae to give me a title? It would cause more friction than it would prevent. A few other teachers do as well."

"Like Tag?" I asked.

He chuckled. "Yeah, she's a very good example. Tag answers to Master Taggart or Tag. She actually apprenticed as a blacksmith with a renaissance faire, and she knows her stuff. Now, I'm pretty sure my name isn't why you're here. What's going on, Rain?"

"I have to pick my electives," I groaned, flopping back in the chair. "I only get three!"

"So, what's out?" he asked.

"Home Ec."

"And?" he pressed.

I shrugged. "Taxonomy of Faerie is kinda low on the list because half the stuff will never be here, and I'll never go there. It still sounded cool, though."

"Ok, and what's in?" he tried instead.

I just sighed. "Bracken says I should take self-defense if I have to choose just one of his courses, but survival skills and combat are *really* interesting. I really want to do the offensive one. I mean, it'd be like the sport I was never allowed to do, but he's right. Self-defense - especially against magic - makes the most sense."

"And why can't you do defense and offense?" Liam asked.

"I kinda want to take Botany with Aspen," I admitted. "She's my only real friend here, and I'm not even sure it's more than an acquaintance, but she made it sound cool. The plants are more like pets. I also want to learn how to speak the fae language, though. And History of Magic is just cool. All the stuff from fairy tales that's actually real?"

"Some of these courses you can take next year - or the one after," he assured me. "A lot of the electives are open to anyone, at any time. History of Magic is one. So is the basic Botany class. Survival Skills, too. Other things have a chain, so you'll have to start at the bottom. Introduction to Self Defense, as an example. Faeril Two would require you to take Faeril One this year, and you're already behind."

I groaned. "So what do I do?" I asked.

He leaned forward to brace his forearms on the edge of the desk. "What will you use later, Rain? After that, what will give you the best foundation for your future both in and out of the fae communities? And then, you need to consider how excited you are for the class. Not just today, but how you'll feel about it in a month, two, or even six down the road."

"Faeril's probably out then," I admitted. "It sounds like a lot of tests, and I'm already going to be struggling with what I have."

"I think that's fair," Liam agreed. "Plus, no one really uses the language anymore. Even those who grew up speaking it are now all fluent in English. Well, here. Other groups use the language of the land they live in."

"Bracken said you might be able to get me the History of Magic textbook, and then I wouldn't need the class," I said, trying to think through this. "I mean, I think it's interesting, but again, tests."

"I'll have it added to your Institute book library," Liam promised. "So what does that leave?"

"Botany, Weapons-Crafting, Survival Skills, Self-Defense, and Offense," I said.

"Can you really do three physical classes back-to-back, every day, all week long?" he asked.

I sighed. "Probably not."

"Ok, so which one do you prefer, Botany or Weapons-Crafting?" Liam tilted his head just a bit. "Which will you use more? Which one will you like in six months?"

When he put it like that, the answer was a lot more clear. It didn't necessarily mean I had to like it, though. "Probably Weapons-Crafting, since it has real world stuff, and I kinda like that I could actually be useful with something. I mean, the plants are cool, but I kill plants. Even succulents!"

"Ok." Liam turned for his keyboard, then began typing. I watched as his eyes narrowed. "The beginner class for Weapons-

Crafting is right after lunch. It's the same time as Survival Skills. You'd have to pick one or the other."

"Weapons-Crafting," I decided, since I'd already committed this much.

He nodded and clicked a button. "Ok. So, for the next hour, you can take Self-Defense, Faeril One, Taxonomy, or Home Ec."

"Self-Defense," I said.

Liam clicked another button. "And for the third hour, you get Intro to Offensive Combat, Botany I - which Aspen isn't in - and History of Magic."

Well, that made it an easy choice! "Offensive Combat," I said, feeling a little rush.

"Ok, I've got you enrolled in those. You have one more day to change your mind, though. I'll talk to Bracken and make sure you have the necessary gear for his courses, because it sounds like you'll be taking at least one."

"No, I like that," I decided. "Weapons-Crafting, Self-Defense, and Offensive Combat. Kinda makes me sound tough, and it feels like something I should take at a magic school."

"Just know you can change your mind for one more day," he said again. "Now, get out of here and go be a teenager. School's over, young lady. I still have work to do."

I hopped up and headed to the door, but paused before leaving. "Hey?"

"Hm?" he asked, looking over.

"Thanks, Uncle Liam. I think this is now my favorite home I've ever been in."

The man smiled and looked down at his desk. "Good. I'm glad you like it here, Rain. I really am."

Chapter Twenty-Three

I ended up not changing my mind. With my schedule set, Liam took me out over the weekend to pick up a few supplies I wouldn't be able to get through the school. We went to Walmart for the most basic. Things like socks - which gave me the chance to get a couple more pairs for my uniform - and sports bras. Then we hit a sporting goods store for gloves. They were the leather kind, but not work gloves. These were more like baseball gloves, and Liam said I'd need them to keep from getting blisters when I gripped the weapon hilts.

I tried to ask him who was paying for this, but the man avoided the question twice without me even noticing. I had a feeling I knew the answer, though. When Liam had agreed to take me under his wing, he'd meant it. Just like he'd bought me clothes, he was now buying my accessories. I wasn't sure how much a student counselor made, but all I'd heard, all my life, was how expensive we kids were. I kinda felt guilty, so decided the best way I could pay him back was to make the best grades I could.

For the rest of the weekend, I spent my time reading my textbooks and playing on my new phone. I only had Liam's number in there, but the wifi access worked all over campus - and wasn't limited by school rules - which meant I had internet and social media. I may have stalked a few people from my old life, but I told myself I was just gloating. My ex from Des Moines was dating a freshman. The guy I'd punched had recently been dumped by his latest girlfriend, and she was posting pictures on Instagram to make it clear she was just fine. Unfortunately, no one seemed to miss me.

It was like I was a ghost. Even at Silver Oaks, it wasn't that much better. No one really knew me, so no one invited me to do anything. On Saturday, I heard people down in the atrium. Looking out my window, I saw an entire group of kids running around having fun. Couples were poorly hidden in the nooks between bushes, kissing like they were all alone. Others sat in groups laughing about whatever they were talking about. Me? I studied, hoping that when I went back to my classes, I wouldn't be quite so lost.

Then, on Monday, Lynn and her friends started pulling away. They weren't quite ignoring me, but close. At first, it was subtle. The gap between our chairs at lunch got bigger and they spent more time talking about their other friends than acknowledging me. The next day, no one even said hi, and on Wednesday, my chair wasn't really *at* the table, but more in the general area. Oddly, the more everyone else ignored me, the nicer the court became.

It wasn't much, but at least once a day I got a Pixy Stix from Aspen. By Wednesday, she was saving all her orange ones for me. Not that we talked much otherwise. If we bumped into each other in the bathroom of our suite, we were nice. If she saw me in the halls, she smiled. Mostly, she kinda just did her thing, but the sugar bribe kept me from going completely insane.

Then there was Torian. After his arrogance on the first day, he knew I wasn't impressed with his attitude. I basically ignored him, and he pretty much returned the favor. Tuesday, I took to sitting beside the nerdy guy in biology, Jeff, who'd been evicted for me the first day. That put the pair of us together at the back of the room, and left Torian sitting alone.

Harper, one of the jester girls, quickly tried to move in. Her butt didn't even touch the seat before Torian's glare had her changing her mind. A few words were exchanged, but they were soft enough I couldn't hear them. When electricity began to crackle around his fingers, Harper was done. She turned around and went back to where she usually sat. From the look on Torian's face, he wasn't impressed. Unfortunately, from the way he turned around to glare at me, I was the one getting the blame. Poor Jeff looked like he was worried about getting caught in the crossfire.

Even worse was that the entire student body heard all about that little ordeal. Harper told Katrina, another of the jesters, and she told pretty much everyone else. The king of Silver Oaks hated the "mudblood." I didn't know how to break it to them that they were mixing up their fantasy terms, but whatever. Those two were the most popular girls at the Institute, and when they got excited about something, so did everyone else. Except for the court, of course.

From what gossip said, both Katrina and Harper wanted to be with Torian. He wasn't interested, and was basically inseparable from Aspen. Aspen liked me, which meant I was allowed to talk to the three most beautiful guys our age. Aspen hated Harper and Katrina, so they couldn't. Thus, the vengeance quickly turned on me.

It didn't take long before the jesters decided it was time to do something about it. The first time I tripped in the hall, I thought little of it. My foot bashed into someone's leg, and I went down to one knee. Embarrassed, I quickly picked myself up and kept going. Obviously I didn't get the message they were trying to send, because they tried again at lunch. This time, they planned better.

With my plate full of food, I was winding through the packed tables when everyone started to giggle at the jesters' table. I blew it off. It wasn't the first time I'd been laughed at, and I had a feeling it wouldn't be the last. Plus, being fae didn't really make them much different from any other popular group. If I reacted to their tormenting, they'd simply torment a little more. Pretending to be oblivious was my best defense.

But I heard something. It was like a sizzle or a crackle. I sniffed, hoping that wasn't my hair, but I *refused* to turn around. Nope, the sniffing was bad enough. Then, just a few steps later, my ankle collided with someone's chair. Hard.

I staggered and stumbled for two steps, trying to keep my balance. I actually managed to catch myself, but to do so, my arms tilted. The plate of food did too, and everything began to slide. In slow motion, I watched as my entire lunch choice took to the air, and there wasn't a single thing I could do to stop it. The clatter as my fork and food hit the floor was deafening. The mess from my beef taco lunch looked like roadkill. The burning feeling in my face was unbearable.

"Guess you're lacking a little grace," Harper giggled from behind me. "Typical for your kind."

The dining room was completely silent and everyone was staring at me. That was when I knew it hadn't been an accident. Not the first time in the halls, and definitely not now. Standing there, with every eye on me, I wished I could just die. Was I supposed to find a janitor now? Did I try to clean it up myself? Should I go get another lunch? Frozen in horror, I closed my eyes and did nothing. When I finally opened them again, the first thing I saw was Lynn's table, devoid of any extra chairs for me to sit at.

I'd been banished.

Leaving everything on the floor, I simply left, using both hands to shove open the doors so I could escape. I didn't stop at the office to tell Liam. I didn't pause to ask permission, I just walked right out the front door of the Institute and kept going until my mind finally kicked back in. Shame hit first, but rage was right on the heels of that. They'd known I didn't have any magic to save my pride. I couldn't keep my food from hitting the ground or clean it up with a flick of my finger.

Those girls had done this because they wanted to show the rest of the school they were winning against someone. Aspen's friendship had lifted me up more than the jesters were willing to tolerate. Me, a stupid human girl with absolutely no magic, was getting the one thing those half-bloods wanted most. Even worse, they hadn't used magic to do it, almost like they were making a point. They just didn't realize I *wasn't* friends with the court! I was more like their pity case, or maybe even their personal amusement. After all, I was only going here because Aspen found me "interesting."

So I couldn't run from this. First because I lived here, which meant I had nowhere else to go. Second, because it wasn't right that those girls had decided my lack of magic was going to become their latest entertainment. They expected me to tuck my tail between my legs and get the fuck out of their way, but they didn't know me at all.

I hadn't done a single thing to them. Not after their sneers, not when they started gossiping, and not even this time. Clearly, they thought that meant I was an easy target. So far, I'd been working hard to learn about all the things I'd thought were myths. I'd kept to myself, hadn't caused problems, and I'd actually been *good!* My teachers had given me lesson plans to help me figure out what I'd missed - which took most of my free time - and my nose was usually in a book. In all of my classes, I was behind, getting individual attention to get caught up, and doing the regular coursework in my dorm. I hadn't done a single thing to deserve being their enemy - I didn't have the damned time to - so *fuck* them!

Dropping onto a powder-coated metal bench in front of the school, I stared out at the landscaped acreage of the Institute's "lawn." I hadn't brought my coat and the blazer for my uniform wasn't quite warm enough for the weather, but I was not going back inside. Tears burned in my eyes, the frustrated and humiliated kind, and nothing was going to make them stop. The last thing I was willing to do was let those amazingly beautiful people in there see me like this, but I was so *tired* of it all.

Time after time, I got singled out and bullied. This crap wasn't anything new. I was the foster kid no one wanted and had a psycho mom who'd killed my dad. I was poor. Now, I didn't even have magic to show off. This always happened at every school I'd ever been to, so I had two choices. I could take it and learn to hate myself, or I could fight back and ruin every good thing that had happened since Liam brought me here.

I didn't want to be popular. I just wanted to be normal. I wanted to be like everyone else, able to laugh about things with someone, and to have a sympathetic ear listen when I didn't know what to do. I wasn't asking for much, I simply didn't want to let down the one person in my life who'd stuck his neck out for me: Liam.

Then a body claimed the space beside me, and with a single snap, I began to feel warmer. That meant it had to be Aspen. I couldn't look up or she'd see the angry tears threatening to spill over, so I kept staring at the dormant grass before me, my hair too little of a shield to hide my face.

Long, thin fingers appeared before my eyes, the nails painted a glittery green, and a fresh orange was clasped between them. "It's not much," Aspen said, "but it's what I have, and I'm willing to share."

I nodded and accepted the fruit, but couldn't make my voice work. The only answer I could give was a sniff. I made it halfway through peeling the orange before I could find a word. The whole time, she just sat there, her shoulder nearly brushing mine in a silent show of solidarity - and it meant a lot.

"Guess I owe you one, huh?" I finally managed.

Her laugh was soft, like wind chimes. "It's less the owing, and more the willingness that matters. A favor done for gain isn't a favor. I don't want your debt, Rain."

Breaking off a slice of orange, I held it out toward her. "I didn't mean to steal your lunch."

She smiled at me. "I already had two, and I didn't want you to be alone."

There was so much concern in that simple phrase. It hit me hard, and coming from such a beautiful girl made it feel like it meant a little more. I shoved an entire piece of the orange into my mouth, then wiped under my eyes to make sure no tears had broken free.

That one little phrase had somehow made the shame feel a little less important.

"Why are you being nice to me?" The words just fell out. I knew I shouldn't have asked, and now it was too late to take it back.

Her eyes jerked out toward the open land and her face stilled. "Because being alone sucks. It's even worse when you're all alone while surrounded by everyone else."

"Like you'd know."

Slowly she nodded. "I kinda do. Torian hates when we do favors for people, but fuck him if he gets pissed."

"I think the jesters hate me because of you four. Because you keep being nice to me."

Her entire face dropped and her shoulders slumped. "Do you want us to leave you alone?"

"No," I assured her. "Aspen, you're kinda my only friend here, and the guys? Well, Torian's an arrogant shit, and I'm pretty sure Hawke hates me, but Wilder has been almost friendly a couple of times. It's just that people like you don't usually talk to people like me. Now, I'm just... I dunno. I don't know what to *do*."

She turned to look at me. "What do you mean?"

"Liam got me in here, and I don't want to mess this up. He went out on a limb for me. I told him I'd make good grades and stay out of trouble, but the only way to deal with people like the jesters is to get *into* trouble! I hate the idea of ignoring it - of letting them think they won like that - but I made a promise to Liam, and I don't break those!"

"So change the deal," she said. "If both parties agree, then there isn't a problem."

My eyes narrowed. "Is that a fae thing or something?"

Her eyes dropped to my lips, and she smiled. "Yeah. Um, you should read the stories about making agreements with the fae. We've gotten better since living here, but some things are hard to change." Then she reached out and brushed my hair back behind my ear so she could see my face. "What do you want us to do?"

"This isn't your problem, Aspen."

Her fingers stilled just above my ear. "But it's our fault, you said. They pick on you because I talk to you. I don't want to stop talking to you, so I need to fix this."

"No, *I* need to fix this," I assured her. "No offense, but if you stand up for me, they'll just get worse."

"So how do I help?" she asked. "I have never been powerless like this in my life!"

"I don't know, Aspen," I said. "Lynn and her friends made it clear they don't want anything to do with me anymore. No more sitting with them at lunch. I mean, not that I blame them, but it still hurts. I'll figure it out, though."

"I'll tell Liam it's my fault," she offered. "I'll make it clear this is on me."

"Aspen..."

Those cold blue eyes of hers turned on me. "He'll listen to me, Rain. At least let me do that? You're so strong and so willful, it's hard to resist, but I want to help because we made this problem. Just let me do this one thing?"

"Ok," I relented. "I just don't want to take advantage of your friendship. I mean... whatever this nice thing is."

But her eyes had just warmed, and her smile was back and brighter than ever before. "Friendship," she assured me. "Definitely friendship."

Chapter Twenty-Four

Unfortunately, my torture wasn't over. The next day, the jesters had to try it again. This time it wasn't the girls, though, but rather a pair of guys in History of Faerie. They kept looking at me, then over to Wilder. One shook his head and the other laughed. Twice, the teacher cleared her throat to make them stop, but it didn't last long. When the bell rang to release us, I finally found out what the big joke was.

"Hey *Lorraine*, we're trying to figure it out. Which one did you fuck to get the special treatment? You eating the pussy or sucking Wilder's cock to keep him off the ice princess? Never would've guessed fucking a normal would be so exciting."

Wilder heard. As the guys were heading through the door, he caught up and shoved - hard - sending the bigger one face down into the mass of students. The boy hit the ground, a very unattractive grunt bursting free even as his stuff scattered around him. Standing braced for anything, Wilder's face turned cruel, and I swore his lips pulled back in a snarl.

"Who I fuck is none of your business. Who Aspen fucks isn't

either." He glared at the second man. "And her name is *Rain!* Tell your girlfriend to stop crawling on Torian. He's not impressed."

Everything seemed to happen at once. The guy on the ground surged forward, but met Wilder's foot in his gut. The second one swung, but Hawke was now at Wilder's side, and he slammed the jester into the wall. Someone screamed, and the next thing I knew, teachers were spilling out of classrooms, including the one we'd just left.

Aspen grabbed my arm - I hadn't even known she was here - and Torian appeared beside her. How the hell had the entire court gotten here so fast? Wilder and Hawke were in that class, so it made sense, but these two? What the hell? My head was whipping around, trying to keep track of what was going on while staying out of the way of the guys throwing fists at each other.

Then Torian simply snapped his fingers. Such a simple gesture, a snap, but not when he did it. My eyes caught a flash of green, the color a match to his eyes, and the world seemed to get stuck in molasses. Everyone else slowed, but I still felt fine. Normal even. I was so busy watching the people moving at a tenth their normal speed that I might as well have been stuck too, until Aspen grabbed my hand and started hauling me behind her, away from that mess.

The whole thing lasted a heartbeat, no different than how things slowed when it was time to panic, but this was seared on my mind. When the teachers finally reached the two guys, I was halfway down the hall, and the rest of the court had vanished like nothing had ever happened. Behind me, I heard someone threatening suspension for fighting, so I kept walking, keeping pace with Aspen. I hadn't done anything wrong, but I certainly wasn't about to get those assholes out of trouble.

When we finally made it to the main hall, Aspen stopped and turned to face me. "Sorry. I know I said I'd let you handle it, but you don't want to get into trouble, and I didn't say I wouldn't help, so - "

My answer was to step forward and hug her hard. "I have no idea how you and Torian got there. I don't know half of what happened, but I am not at all upset. Cross my heart. I like your help, Aspen. I just don't want to rely on you because I'm some useless normal, ok? I will never be upset about you helping me. Maybe embarrassed. Sometimes frustrated because I can't do something on my own, but never upset at you."

"Ok," she mumbled, smiling down at the floor. "Um, get to class. Don't want to be late, right?"

Then she almost skipped backwards a step before turning. The girl wasn't short, but she somehow managed to vanish into the sea of people heading up towards the west side of the building. I turned for my biology class, wondering if Hawke and Wilder were going to get in trouble for that. I really hoped not. And if they did, how would I make it up to them?

Hawke barely tolerated me as it was. Wilder seemed nicer, but he also hung out with Aspen more, while Hawke was basically Torian's shadow. Maybe that said more about Torian than it did Hawke? I honestly didn't know, and with those four, I wasn't really willing to guess.

But in biology, Torian didn't look at me once. Not when I walked into the class, not when I passed by him to get to the desk I was now sharing with his old lab partner, and not even when I sat down. It was such a change that even Jeff noticed. The pair of us kept looking up, proving I wasn't the only one starting to feel a little worried. Halfway through the class, when we were supposed to be dissecting some plant, Jeff leaned closer.

"He's a cool guy, you know."

My eyebrows shot straight up. "Torian? You look terrified of him half the time."

His jaw clenched, and I realized I probably shouldn't have said it quite like that. Jeff was a pretty geeky guy, and I got the impression his magic wasn't on the strong side, but no one wanted to have it thrown in his face - especially not a guy. Unfortunately, I didn't know how to take it back.

"He saved my life last winter." A sigh slipped from Jeff's lips. "We were playing broom hockey on the creek when it froze, but the ice cracked. I fell in, and no one could get to me, except him. Torian never hesitated. He jumped into the freezing water, Rain."

I'd figured Torian to be the kind of guy to wonder what was in it for him, so this was a whole different side to him. Maybe I had the guy all wrong? Granted, Aspen's glamour made me realize freezing cold water didn't necessarily have to feel that way, but it also didn't negate the fact that Torian had been willing to help. There was just one issue with all of this.

"That doesn't mean it's ok for him to snap his fingers and order you around, though." I ducked my head toward him, trying to catch his eyes but failing. "Any decent person would help someone who fell through the ice. It doesn't negate him pushing you around on my first day."

Jeff pushed his glasses higher on his nose. "Funny, because there were eight of us at the creek, but no one else tried to get to me." He cleared his throat. "I just figure the least I can do to make up for it is be nice to him. If Torian wants to have some girl sit beside him, then I'm going to make sure it's easy."

"I think the whole damned school is willing to make things easy for him," I grumbled under my breath.

Jeff chuckled at that. "Yeah, um, you're new here, and I heard you're a *caradil*, not a true Legacy, so it probably doesn't make sense, but - "

I broke in. "What do you mean I'm not a true Legacy?"

"The term typically means someone with no magic who has a fae relative. You're completely human, but you're part of the community. A *caradil*. You didn't get the chance to have magic, so no legacy to inherit. But my point is Torian's more powerful than you can imagine. Magic, influence, and so much more. People are scared of him because even as a teenager, he has more control, more training in his abilities, and more power than anyone else I've ever heard of. He's a true fae. Some people whisper about how his parents must've been nobility. *That* kind of power, Rain."

Maybe I had Torian all wrong. I'd assumed he was an asshole because he was beautiful - and he definitely was that. It had been easy not to crush on him because he was with Aspen. No checking out my only friend's guy and all that. Besides the fact she ignored me whenever he was around, I still wouldn't poach guys from other girls. Then, Torian had done nothing but glare at me, acting like I was either supposed to worship him, fuck him, or fear him. Not really the kind of attitude I found attractive. While a lot of girls didn't agree, I'd always been the type who thought sweet trumped hot any day.

But maybe he deserved another chance? I'd probably shut him down too soon, and his flirting that first day had likely been some test. Hopefully I'd passed. Since Aspen was still talking to me, I was assuming I had. Still, he'd been there when things got out of hand after history, so I at least owed him something for that. I thought about how to make it up to him until the bell rang.

"Torian?" He was sliding off his stool when my voice stopped him.

Slowly, he turned, a tired look on his face. "Yeah?"

I made my way over so I wasn't yelling halfway across the room. "Last period, with the snapping? I know you were probably there for Wilder and Hawke, not me, but I still wanted to say thank you. To you, to Wilder for standing up for me - even if it was mostly for him and Aspen, and to Aspen for making sure I didn't get in trouble. Even Hawke for helping, I guess. I know you'll see them at lunch, so maybe you can pass on the message to the guys for me?"

He chuckled once. "No. I won't tell them that."

"Huh?" I'd honestly been trying to grovel, and he'd just dismissed it? Maybe I'd heard him wrong. "I don't understand. I was trying to thank all of you."

He leaned back against the desk and crossed his arms. "Try it again without using the word 'thank'. I dare you."

Easy enough. "Ok. Would you tell her I appreciate it?"

"Or a synonym."

At this point, I was willing to do just about anything to make the day end. "Can you tell all of them I'm sorry I'm so much trouble, and I know none of you asked for my baggage, but if you ever need something, I will bend over backwards to do what I can?"

"I will," he said gently. "Aspen will like that. Wilder and Hawke will probably be amused. Have a good afternoon, Rain."

Sadly, I couldn't let him walk off that easily. "Hey, what's the deal with the thanks thing?"

He turned, but kept walking backwards to the door. "'Thank you' is the easiest way for people to wipe away a nice gesture. Those words mean they did their part and can forget about it. Why bother putting forth the effort if the recipient doesn't even care?"

"It doesn't always mean that, you know. Sometimes, it's the only way to express the warm feeling in your chest."

He cocked his head to the side. "Prove it. Actions always speak louder than empty words, meat."

Then he stepped through the door and was gone. The class around me was completely empty, but I was not in a hurry today. I had no one to eat lunch with. I had nothing but misery waiting for me in the dining hall. I had an entire pack of jesters waiting to make my life a living hell, and now this.

I vaguely remembered some story about the fae hating being thanked. They wanted to be paid in resources or a trade of services. A thing for a thing. Considering how people reacted when I said the word "deal" around them, it was all starting to make sense. Granted, it wasn't exactly something they included in the student handbook. There was no flyer on how to survive living with a bunch of fae.

But if the court only understood actions as a sign of appreciation, then I could work with it. I didn't know how, and no ideas were springing to mind, but I would definitely figure it out. Mostly, it was because of something Aspen had said outside on that bench. She knew what it was like to be all alone while surrounded by people.

I had a funny feeling she wasn't the only one. I was pretty sure all four of them felt the exact same way. I knew I did.

Chapter Twenty-Five

That afternoon, I ended up working with a practice sword on some pole with sticks jutting out from it. The thing was called a training dummy, but it wasn't quite what I'd expected. Bracken said I was almost ready to start practicing with the other students, so he'd set me to hitting this thing in a set pattern. I was trying hard to do it right, because the whole point was to train my arm and build new muscles.

It was more difficult than I expected too - but in a good way. The overhand shots made my bicep burn. Then, when I finished five repetitions on one arm, I switched to the other. Left-handed, I was a complete mess, but whatever. In just one week, I'd learned the rules of the gym, the names of the equipment, and the warmups for all the combat and defensive styles. I was calling this a win.

By the third time through on my left arm, I was getting tired. Each pass took about ten hits on this weird stick-figure-post thing. It had three clusters of spokes meant to represent limbs, and all were pointing different angles. I was supposed to hit between each one from the top, the front, and from below.

Just as I moved to reach a gap at the side, a guy gasped, "Easy there!"

I turned to see a guy from the class grinning at me with his hands up. Clearly, I'd almost smacked him on the backswing. Even worse, I'd been so focused, I hadn't even known he was there, and this guy was... wow. My eyes dropped down his body on their own, and my cheeks immediately felt warmer when I realized it.

Tall, blonde, and golden-skinned, he was also broad-shouldered, and that black-and-green sleeveless shirt looked *amazing* on him. It took only a split second for me to realize he was very, very fae. Maybe even pure-blooded. Add in the lopsided smile he'd turned on me, and my stomach did a backflip in approval. Sheepishly, I tucked the practice sword - which was basically a wooden stick with a hilt - under my arm and moved over so he could pass by me safely.

"Sorry," I mumbled.

"New girl, right?" he asked, coming closer instead of walking past. Then he offered his hand. "I'm Keir."

"Rain," I said, clasping his hand.

But Keir didn't shake. He leaned over and kissed the back of my knuckles, his lips barely brushing my skin. "AP student, right?"

"That I am," I agreed. "You?"

"Junior. The college kind, since we have both types here." Then he propped his elbow on one of those spokes and leaned against my training dummy. "The whole Institute's talking about you, you know."

I pushed out my breath with a groan. "What did I do this time?"

Keir began listing all of it, lifting a finger on his free hand as he did. "Liam's niece, no fae blood, no magic, picked a fight with the jesters, made friends with the court..." That smile made a reappearance. "Which isn't a small thing around here, so you know."

"Aspen's my suitemate," I explained.

"Rumors say she doesn't hate you. That's pretty big. Those four hate everyone." He lifted a brow, all but daring me to deny it.

Instead, I flicked a finger at him. "Why aren't you on the court? Kinda getting the impression you're pure-blood number five."

Keir just reached up to stroke his chin. "Because of my dashing good looks, huh?" Then he laughed. "I am pure fae. I was also born on Earth, not Faerie. Dad was a gate guardian. Mom was a huntress. Soon as the war started brewing, they escaped for a quieter life - to here. That was the front end of the Exodus. About forty years later, along came me."

"The whole age thing still breaks my brain," I admitted. "How old are your parents, if they waited forty years to have kids? Like, sixty?"

"Two, three hundred," he corrected. "Mom's two thirty-seven. Dad's three nineteen." His smile was getting bigger. "Yes, I'm nineteen. We age the same until about twenty-five."

"Uh huh." Because, yeah, my brain was completely stuck on that. "So, your mom only looks a few years older than you?"

"Yep. Just wait until you find out Ivy Rhodes is in her five hundreds."

I gasped. "No way!"

"Truth," he insisted. "The question is how living in a world with so little magic will affect us. But, I'm sure you don't want to talk about that." He gestured to the dummy he was leaning against. "Frank here needs to be put in his place, and you were doing pretty good."

His eyes made a sweep down my body, but he didn't move away from the dummy. I just rolled my eyes at him. This guy was hot and knew it, but I kinda liked it. I was smiling just a little too much, and the truth was I really didn't mind the interruption.

"Frank's kinda been kicking my ass, you know," I admitted. "I have no idea why, but I thought this whole sword-fighting thing would be easier."

"Mm..." He finally stepped back. "The trick is to use the weapon's weight instead of your muscles." Then he playfully crooked a finger, summoning me even closer. "Let me show you."

I grabbed the hilt of my wooden "sword" again, and moved to stand before the dummy. Keir stepped behind me, pressing in close against my back, then teasingly slid his hand down my arm. My pulse picked up in response, but I refused to show it. I would *not* pant over this guy. Not even if my body really wanted to.

"The trick," he whispered beside my ear as he caught my wrist, "is not to fight it."

I just glanced back, honestly amused. "Does that work for you a lot?"

His face was right there. I couldn't help but notice his eyes. They were blue, but a shade so unique they almost looked violet. Elizabeth Taylor came to mind, yet before I could say anything, he tilted his head at the dummy, getting my mind off of his pretty face.

"Just move with me, Rain," he insisted.

A little bob of my head gave him permission, so Keir guided my arm at the dummy. Slowly at first, so I could feel the pressure of his body twisting. That gave me the chance to match him, and I started to see what he meant. Unfortunately, I wasn't good at it, so the guy dropped a hand across my belly, holding my hips against him. Then he did it again with another swing. Eventually, he moved my arm a little faster, his fingers resting over mine so gently.

All the things the instructor had said were now making sense. Use my hips, twist my shoulders. I sucked in a little breath as the light bulb ignited in my mind, and I got it. I honestly, truly, and completely understood how to make this easier. Keir paused at my gasp and stepped back.

I turned to face him. "That makes so much sense! I don't know why it wasn't sinking in before."

He laughed, ducking his head. "Yeah, um, because they brace up and get stiff in the movies?" Then he stepped back. "Oh, and so you know, that *does* usually work for me. Yesterday, I would've said always, but I'm starting to understand what the court sees in you."

"I'm interesting, huh?" I teased.

He paused only two steps away. "Very. I also noticed you didn't thank me." I opened my mouth, but he lifted his hand. "And please don't ruin it now."

"I was going to say I owed you one," I assured him. "I already got the lesson on the thank yous."

Keir's eyes narrowed. "But not the one about debts, it seems." Pushing out a sigh, he closed the distance between us again, and this time he lowered his voice. "There are a lot of fae here. Pure fae, Rain. The five of us and some of the teachers. Do not make deals with anyone, and don't accept owing a debt. Do not acknowledge it unless you're sure you can handle what they'll ask for when they call it in."

There was an intensity to his voice that made me want to lean back. "What do you mean?"

He shoved a hand through his golden blonde hair. "That? Saying you owe me one? It's open-ended. *Too* open-ended. I helped you see how to swing a sword, you now owe me, so I could call in that favor by asking you to jump off the fourth-floor roof to amuse me. If you don't..." He canted his head.

"Then what?" I asked. "You'd be pissed?"

"I'd be within my rights to make you," he corrected. "A debt. My parents are fae. Real fae, Rain, not the Tinkerbell kind. We don't shit glitter. We amuse ourselves with human suffering. Well, did. Those of us born here learned slightly different rules. I mean, it's hard not to when every other kid in school is human. The problem is, our parents can't understand why the old rules aren't allowed. Half of our teachers are from that generation. The humans - like Liam - temper that, but not completely. And some fae are willing to use it to make themselves look a little more impressive."

"Like the jesters," I realized.

He nodded. "They're the worst. Their families ran from the war, giving up everything, and then thought they could pick up where they left off here on Earth."

"Kinda sounds like the founding of America," I pointed out.

"Probably," he agreed. "All I'm saying is you need to choose your words carefully. The court won't be able to help themselves. The jesters would love to use it against you. The others are jealous because you're the hot topic lately, and I can promise half the guys in my dorm would use that little offer to have you in their room well past your curfew, if you know what I mean."

"But not you?" I asked, unsure how he'd answer.

One more time, his lopsided smile made an appearance, and he stepped back. "I prefer the idea of a willing partner. Kinda why I stopped you. But, if you truly want to pay that debt, then learn. I think you could be good at this, and the fae community needs a few sentinels who can wield iron."

"Just not around you, huh?" I asked.

"Preferably not," he agreed. "Kinda kills the mood." Then he pointed at the dummy before turning away.

I tried to go back to hitting the thing, but I couldn't stop smiling. For some reason, I'd assumed fae boys would have no interest in human girls, but that did not seem to be the case. Sure, maybe he was playing me, but I was cool with that too. Keir was *cute!* No, that wasn't a strong enough word. He was gorgeous. Except that sounded too proper.

While I smacked at the dummy using this new technique, I tried to find the right one. Hot worked. Sensual, seductive, sexy. Why did all the good words start with an S? Regardless, I liked his arms. I'd stolen a few glances of the muscles hidden behind his tight shirt. The only thing I hadn't checked was his ass.

So, when I paused to switch arms, I turned around to see where he'd gone. I expected to find him on the mats, and my big - and not well-thought-out - plan was to make sure he didn't have some flat butt or something. Instead, I found Keir standing beside Bracken against the mirrors.

Both of them were watching me. Yep, my face instantly began to burn, and I turned right back around to focus on the dummy. They'd been looking directly at me. Their heads were leaned together as if discussing my practice - or something. I was clearly the topic of discussion, and if anything, Bracken was even hotter than Keir!

Fuck, living with the fae was going to kill me. One way or another, I would end up making a fool out of myself. And yet, when I finished the next set of hits and changed arms again, I couldn't keep myself from looking back.

Bracken had moved on, but Keir was still watching. The butterflies I was brewing in my belly liked that. Oh, they liked it a little too much, and I was in complete agreement with them.

Chapter Twenty-Six

When class got out, I didn't bother changing out of my workout clothes. Most of us didn't, since we'd be heading back to our dorms anyway. I did, however, grab my coat. I might not need it in the Forge with Tag, or while working out, but the walk was killer at this time of year. Without Aspen to glamour me, I was a big wuss when it came to winter weather.

I was pushing my arm into my sleeve as I headed for the door when Keir fell in beside me. Without a word, he reached over to give me a hand, settling my coat evenly on my shoulders. I flashed him a smile then grabbed the door, holding it open for him to go first.

"Oh, a gentleman," he teased.

I laughed as I followed him through. "Something like that."

Like me, Keir was wearing a pretty impressive coat. I was a little surprised by that, since he was a pure-blood, but winter in the plains got pretty nasty. Yet when I looked at him for the third time, the guy stopped and turned to me.

"Ok, what?" he asked.

"Aspen glamoured the cold away," I explained. "I guess I'm just shocked you don't."

He dropped his head with a heavy sigh. "Ok. First rule about the fae: we aren't all incredibly powerful. Yeah, I can do magic. No, I can't keep up with the court. Kinda why I'm focusing on protection and combat classes. See, convincing you to smell, feel, and hear things that don't exist? It's a lot harder than tricking your eyes. Glamours are simply how the fae lie, and I'm pretty bad at it."

"Huh?" Because I was with him right up until the lying part.

"Lies," he said again. "We can't tell a direct untruth. We can deceive with truth, but we can't flat out lie. It's worse than iron. Also, it's proof we're not perfect or all powerfu - "

A bird swooping between us made him break off as we both jumped back. The thing landed on the ground only a few feet away, then began to caw like it was losing its mind. That was definitely a crow, but the sound was so loud, I couldn't hear anything else. Twice, it jumped up, flapping wildly, and then it hopped toward me and cawed again.

"Are you hurt?" I asked, taking a step toward it.

The crow immediately flew off a few more paces, cawing a little more, but also a little less loudly. I knew they were smart birds, and I'd messed with them enough to know this one was clearly interacting with me. This was not a coincidence, but none of that was the same as knowing what the hell it wanted.

Keir grabbed my arm before I could take more than a step. "Bracken's cat probably got it."

"Then it needs help," I insisted, pulling free to follow after it.

Keir just sighed and followed after me. "Rain, it's a bird."

"I happen to like birds," I told him. "Especially crows. Kinda how I ended up here, which is a long story."

But every time I got closer, the bird flew away again. I was just starting to think it was fine - and screwing with me - when I heard something in the distance. People. No, *girls*. They sounded angry, and that was the exact direction the crow was leading me. I moved a little faster, and my new friend shifted to my side.

Just as we rounded a group of evergreens, I saw them. Six girls huddled around someone else, but they were still pretty far away. They all held something, often thrusting it toward their victim like they were warding them off - and quite a few had on gloves. It only took a second for me to recognize Harper and Katrina in that mess, which meant these were the jesters.

My eyes scanned their faces, able to put names with most, but I'd never actually met all of them. Still, students talked, and the popular girls stood out - these girls. It looked like they were doing their best to bully someone else, and I was so sick and tired of their bullshit after the incident in the dining hall.

"Those bitches," I snarled under my breath and stormed towards them.

Keir kept pace for a few feet, and then he sucked in a breath. "Rain, I can't go over there." When I paused to glance back in confusion, he added, "I feel iron."

I looked at the scene again just as one girl shifted. It was enough for me to see the victim on the ground. Not all of her, but I'd recognize that silver pixie-cut anywhere. It was Aspen! If they had iron...

"Get a teacher," I told Keir before hurrying over to help. "Iron doesn't bother *me*."

I didn't stop to check if he'd obeyed, because someone pressed one of those things against Aspen's arm. My suitemate yelped, jerking back, but the jesters were all around her. There was nowhere for her to go. I wanted to yell for them to stop, but I knew it wouldn't help. I just needed to *get over there!*

As I jogged closer, the wind whipped their words back toward me. I could actually make out some of what they were saying, and it wasn't good.

"Torian's the only thing keeping you safe, you stupid bitch," Harper sneered. "If it wasn't for him, I'd beat your ass every time I saw you."

"Keep your fucking ice shit to yourself!" That voice sounded like Katrina.

Another pair of girls laughed, then one of them said, "Were you out here stalking your new crush? Hoping she'd even notice you? Oh, how the mighty have fallen, huh?"

"I'm telling ya," Harper insisted, "she can't keep her eyes off my tits. Stupid bitch wishes she could get with some Summer nobility. Only person with any interest in *her* is just as cold."

"There's a reason the Winter Court died out!"

"So pathetic," Katrina taunted. "You even look like a damned icicle, you freak. Maybe try making yourself a dildo out of one, because none of us are going to touch you."

"I'd be happy if every last one of you frozen freaks were dead," another snapped.

"The new Summer court will never accept you! This is *our* school. This is *our* world now. The Queen killed your court off for a fucking reason!"

"But you can keep drooling," Harper sneered. "Oh, you're pretty, Aspen, but none of us are desperate enough to get frostbite - yet we know how to use fire magic."

"And this!"

The taunts were getting worse. With each one, a girl leaned over Aspen's crumpled form and thrust what she was holding against her skin. They shoved, one slapped at the back of Aspen's head, and the "weapons" they held all but forced Aspen to take it. Her arms were up and she seemed weak, not like the wild and vibrant girl I'd come to respect.

"Leave her alone," I yelled as I reached them.

Pulling the closest out of the way, I shoved myself between Aspen and her attackers. That surprised them enough that I got the chance to snag one of their torture devices from the hands of a girl I didn't know. Elyssa, I thought her name was. The girl's eyes went wide and she quickly backed up. The thing was just a fucking keychain? No, a *steel* keychain, which meant iron.

But that only pissed me off even more. Turning around, I glared at the group hovering around Aspen, making it clear I was willing to take them *all* on. And just to make sure they weren't confused at all, I lifted up the stupid keychain, clutching it in my bare hand.

"If any of you touch her again, you will regret it," I warned. "I have a feeling this burns you too, huh?"

Elyssa tried to grab my arm and pull. I just shoved the keychain at her, forcing her to leap away before it made contact. Then I glared at the rest of them, holding them off with my presence. When another came closer, I grabbed her keychain too, yanking it right out of her gloved fingers. Nevaeh, I thought her name was.

"Go ahead," I said. "Try me. See, there's one thing this stupid human girl can do better than any of you." And I held up the keychains to show what I meant. "And I'm willing to bet I can punch a lot harder, too."

Because what these girls didn't realize was I'd learned how to be the good girl the hard way - by starting off as the bad one. I could hold my own just fine, and for Aspen's sake, I wasn't scared of the repercussions. What was the worst that could happen, I got kicked out? I had a feeling it wouldn't be that easy. Not once I showed the teachers what they'd been holding.

Besides, when it came to Aspen, getting kicked out seemed worth it. She was the one person who'd stood up for me. Hell, I was only here because she'd insisted. So, if I was supposed to be interesting, then I was going to do a whole lot of *something*, right here, and right now. I just really hoped it worked.

Of course, Harper had to try me. Leaning around my shoulder, she reached for Aspen's face. Her keychain brushed across the bare skin on Aspen's cheek, and my suitemate yelped like it burned. I moved as fast as I could. One hand found Harper's ponytail and yanked, the other clenched into a ball as tight as I could make it. As soon as Harper's face was visible, I swung, aiming for the soft spot around her eye. I got close, and her cheek bone bit back, my fingers caught between it and the keychains I was clutching - but it was worth it.

Harper crumpled to the ground and I turned to the next girl, ducking my head in a taunt to make sure she knew I was ready for her. Elyssa and Giselle lifted their hands and backed away. Harper rolled, clutching at her injury, and Katrina looked between Aspen and me, trying to judge if the fight was still worth it.

"Oh, so you're fucking humans now?" Harper screeched as she got back to her feet. "No one else is going to be with you, bitch!"

Behind her, I could see someone running our way. Coming from another direction was someone else. Then there was the lone figure standing at a distance, watching almost helplessly. That had to be Keir, but he'd gotten us help. I just wasn't sure who the brute was rushing in, or if I was about to get my ass handed to me.

"Just wait until everyone hears what you've done," Katrina sneered at me. "You just picked sides, Rain. In case you missed it, we're the ones who really rule this place."

"Fuck that," I told her. "Fuck your stupid bullying and drama. In case *you* missed it, I'm not scared of you, and your little fairy asses - " Yes, I used the wrong form there. " - can grow the fuck up already."

"Teachers!" hissed the girl whose name I thought was Nevaeh.

The entire group tried to scramble, but it was already too late. They turned one way and saw the brute thundering toward us. Naturally, that made them reverse course to go around the cluster of evergreens in the opposite direction. Right as Harper neared the far side, Liam jogged around the trees to block their escape.

"And you will all stop right there," he panted.

Which was when the brute blocked the other side. "What is going on here?" she demanded. The voice belonged to Tag, but under her winter clothes, she was pretty androgynous. "Who has the iron?"

I lifted my hand with the keychains I'd snagged. "I think they all do. I grabbed two."

Tag held out her hands in the universal gesture for me to throw them over. I did, one after the other, still braced up before Aspen.

The last thing I needed was for someone to come at her again. That she hadn't said anything yet had me terrified this was bad. Like *really* bad.

"All of you," Liam ordered, "my office. Now!" Then he pointed at me. "Take care of Aspen, Rain."

"Call Torian," Tag told me. "I'll make sure this herd figures out iron isn't as powerful when there are people around who don't care about it. C'mon, ladies. Let's see what your parents think about all of this."

The two human teachers escorted the girls back toward the school and I spun around to drop down by Aspen's side. "You ok?"

She didn't look good. There were actual burns on her skin from where the metal had touched. Blisters had appeared on her cheek from Harper's last attack. Aspen's eyes were heavy, and the girl was clearly in pain, but she immediately leaned into me, grasping at my shoulders for comfort.

"It hurts," she whimpered.

"Lemme see," I begged, reaching for her face.

She winced away, her eyes jumping to something behind me. Suddenly, her attitude changed completely. "I'm fine."

When I heard a step on the dry grass behind me, I realized her words weren't for me. A second later, Keir knelt down by my shoulder. "You're not. At least let me do what I can?"

"Fucking Summer Court groupie," she snarled, her voice suddenly feral.

"Earth-born," he reminded her. "Never seen a court, and never had a loyalty to one. Aspen, I can help. Rain's my friend and you're hers."

"I don't want to be in your debt," she told him.

"Then I will be," I decided. "Keir, can you help her for me?"

"Rain!" Aspen whimpered, but Keir had already reached out for the side of her face.

The moment his hand touched her skin, Aspen sucked in a breath like it hurt. There was also a bit of a glow. It was faint and iridescent, but I knew my eyes weren't playing tricks on me, because the blisters were getting better. The red marks weren't fading, but whatever he was doing definitely helped.

Then Keir lifted his hand. "Your debt, Rain..." He tapped his cheek. "A kiss, right there, and we're even."

Without hesitation, I leaned in and kissed the side of his cheek. "You want to help me get her back to our dorm now? Or the nurse? Something?"

"Torian," Keir said. "Aspen, we need to call him."

Aspen's jaw clenched. "No, you need to warn those girls. I *will* remember this. I don't care if they like me. I don't care if Harper thinks I'm into her. I'm not! And I will *not* forget what they did."

"Aspen," I said, turning her face to me. "We're on your side. Well, I am, and I'm pretty sure Keir's on his own, not theirs. Give me your phone, sweetie. I don't have Torian's number."

She weakly reached into her pocket and pulled it out. Pressing her thumb to the screen unlocked it, and then she handed it over. While I looked through the contacts, Keir gestured to her arm, and this time Aspen nodded. Just as he started helping with another of her injuries, I pressed the button to dial and lifted the phone to my ear.

Chapter Twenty-Seven

Torian answered on the second ring with a string of words my mind couldn't process. They definitely weren't English, and sounded worried, but I didn't have time to deal with anything else right now. Aspen needed us.

"It's Rain," I said when he paused for a second. "The jesters were out here shoving iron at Aspen."

Silence hung for a second. "Rain?" he asked. "Where's here?"

"Out by the gym and Forge. I have a friend here with me, so I think we can get your girlfriend back to my dorm."

"Sister," he corrected, "and how bad?"

"What?" Because my mind had just stalled out.

"*How bad is she?*" he demanded. "Can she fucking stand, Rain?"

"I don't think so," I admitted. "Um, Keir, think you can carry her?"

"If she lets me, then sure," he said. "Willing to let me grope you a bit, Aspen? Get my hero complex satiated for a minute?"

She huffed a laugh. "Sure. Rain, tell Tor to meet us at my place?"

"I heard," Torian said over the phone. "Please make sure she's ok?"

"She's wilted, but mostly pissed," I assured him. "Keir did something to make the blisters go away, and I'm pretty sure she just threatened half the school." I tried to laugh, but from the way she'd said it, I wasn't convinced her words had been empty.

"Good," Torian said. "I'm headed to get supplies, then to her room. See you in a minute."

He simply hung up. I looked at the phone, then at Aspen, before passing it back. She tucked the phone into her pocket, then nodded to Keir, giving in. He leaned in, she dropped an arm around his neck, and the guy lifted. Yeah, maybe I checked out his arms as they bulged, and Aspen looked extra-dainty clinging to him like that, but it was all a side effect of them being extra-pretty people, right?

Making sure there wasn't anything left lying on the ground, I hurried to catch up with the pair as we made our way back towards the school. It wasn't too far, thankfully. Maybe a couple hundred yards. Still, there was one thing rattling around in my brain. All of this sucked, but she was safe now, right? Yet her boyfriend wasn't her boyfriend, those girls had said things that made me think someone was a lesbian, and I had some serious questions!

I decided to start easy. "Uh, so Torian's your brother?"

She leaned to look over Keir's shoulder. "What did you think he was?"

"Um, your boyfriend."

Her eyes flicked away and she touched the burn on her cheek, almost as if she were trying to distract herself. "Not really into boyfriends, Rain."

"I didn't know that either." I looked over at Keir, deciding I didn't need too much more awkward here. "It's just that Torian hugs on you so much, it kinda seems like typical relationship cuteness."

"No," she groaned. "It's usually him laughing at me when we're checking out girls together."

"I wish I had a chick to check out girls with me," Keir joked, jerking his chin at the doors we were getting closer to. "Wanna hold those for me, Rain?"

"Yep, got it," I promised, ignoring all the lesbian talk right now.

Hurrying ahead, I realized this put us right next to the atrium, which meant only a few more steps to the elevator. Standing back, I let Keir and Aspen in, then hurried around them again to push the button to call the car down. It dinged almost immediately. Thrusting out my arm kept the doors from closing. Keir stepped on, turned around, and I pressed the button for the fourth floor.

"Not really how I expected to ask for your room number," he teased. "I'm just hoping it's not on the far side."

"Right at the front," Aspen assured him. "She's the second door on the left. Room B403. I'm B401."

"Is that an invitation?" he joked.

Aspen thumped his chest. "Still not into guys, Keir."

"Wait, really?" He looked confused. "I've never met anyone with a hard preference, but ok. Cool, Aspen. Just glad you're starting to feel a little better. That was a lot of iron."

"Fucking cunts," Aspen growled as the doors opened.

Again, I held the doors open so Keir could carry her off, and then I ran to open the double doors that separated the elevator area from the girls' dorm area. Once they were through those, I realized we had one more problem.

"Keys, Aspen?"

"It's not locked," she promised.

So I tried the knob, and sure enough, the door opened. On the other side was nothing but greenery. Keir stepped in and paused, pulling in a deep breath. It only lasted a split second before he was moving to the far side where she had her bed. Carefully, he lowered her down to it.

"Who's the hall chaperone?" he asked her. "Need me to get her?"

"Torian's coming," Aspen assured him.

"Ok. Rain will make sure you're ok until then." He stepped back. "I wanted to help, Aspen. I couldn't, and it fucking sucked."

"I'm in your debt," she told him.

Keir just shook his head. "No debt. It was a favor freely given. Get some rest."

He turned, but I caught his arm. "I'm pretty sure kissing your cheek wasn't enough, so can I at least tell you I appreciate the help?"

He smiled at me. "I'm used to hearing the T word, Rain. I actually get it, and you're welcome." He tilted his head back toward Aspen. "Take care of her. She's weaker than she wants to admit. Iron tears us up."

The moment he left, I closed Aspen's door and hurried to her side. "So what can I do?" I begged.

"You've done it," she promised. "I..." Her eyes darted away. "I just liked having a friend."

"Liked?" I asked. "That sounds as if I'm being told to leave you alone."

"No!" she insisted. "It's just that I know humans have opinions on who people date. I mean..." She glanced back, but her eyes didn't stay on me for long. "I kinda lived with humans long enough to get a few hard lessons."

"So, you're a lesbian, not bi, pan, or something else?" Because I was honestly curious. I also knew this was a horrible time to ask, yet she'd just given me the opening to do so, and I wasn't sure I'd get another. "Just to be clear, I don't care either way."

"Lesbian," she admitted. "Which is not exactly common for my kind either. But that's *not* why I think you're interesting. Maybe it's part of why, but I don't want to lose the friendship we had."

I squatted down before her. "No, that's cool." Because what could I really say to that? "I guess I just figured hanging out with someone like you was, I dunno... Like, there had to be a catch. Girls like you usually don't talk to girls like me. Add in the fae and human stuff, and it only gets weirder. It's cool, though. Aspen, I don't give a shit if you're a lesbian. Honest! But, more importantly, how are you *feeling*? Is this like a bee sting allergy, or something worse?"

She scrubbed one hand across her face. "No, it just makes me tired, mostly. Weak. Like I could go to sleep. Iron fucks with our magic, and we're made of magic. I need some sugar."

"Pixy Stix?" I glanced back, wondering where she'd keep them in this room filled with plants. "Point me in a direction?"

"By the..." She paused. "Big plant, orange flowers, brown pot." I headed that way, and she said, "Yes. Shelf to the left, and up one. There's a box filled with them."

I found it, then pulled out an entire fistful of them. Carrying those back, I tore the top off one and handed it to her. Immediately, Aspen poured the whole thing into her mouth, swallowing it without choking like I would have. When it was empty, she held out her hand for another. We went through four of them like that.

Which was when Torian simply walked into the room without knocking. Behind him came Wilder and Hawke like silent bodyguards. Torian held something, though, making me assume that was what had taken so long. His green eyes jumped over to me, narrowed, and then his sister had his complete attention.

The moment he reached her side, Torian offered her a sizable vial of some brilliantly yellow fluid. It looked like lemonade, but thicker, like honey. Opening the top, he pressed the whole thing into her hand. The concern on his face made me think it had to be some kind of medicine.

"Asp," he said gently, "drink it all, and let's not do this again, ok?"

"Is that like Benadryl?" I asked.

He looked up, piercing me with those green eyes. There was so much rage in them, but I got the feeling it wasn't directed at me. "Something like that. What happened, Rain?"

Aspen grabbed his arm, shaking her head while she swallowed all of the fluid. "I was looking to see if any mistletoe had berries," she said, then stuck out her tongue for the last drop. "The jesters found me. It was almost like they were looking for me, and, well, seems they aren't as scared of me as they are of you."

"Idiots," he snarled.

Her fingers tightened, dimpling his jacket. "This one's mine."

"And Rain can hear you."

Aspen smiled. "But I trust her. Our good little friend throws one hell of a mean punch. She also jumped in without hesitation, took the iron right from their hands, and threatened to use it on them. She's never once tried to thank me, and she thought you were my boyfriend."

Wilder snorted out a laugh behind me. "Kinky."

"He keeps kissing her head," I explained. "Never mind the hugging and hanging on her. C'mon, that's not how most human guys treat a sibling!"

"Human guys," Hawke said, ticking it off on his index finger. "Sibling." That went on the next finger. "Tell me, foster girl, just how much do you know about those?"

"Not much," I admitted. "Well, except what I saw from others in public school."

"So not denying the foster part?" Wilder asked. "Because half the school thinks you're actually related to Liam."

I shook my head. "Never have. Liam calls me his niece, but that's because it's how he got me into the school. Like, credits for the tuition, I guess? I didn't want to mess it up."

The two boys looked at each other. "I don't taste a lie," Hawke admitted.

"Me either," Wilder agreed. "Haven't yet. Well, not for anything important."

"Whoa," I breathed, looking back at Aspen and Torian, then turning to see Wilder and Hawke again. "You can taste lies?"

"It's not really a taste," Aspen said. "It's like a feeling, but there's no word in your language for it. Knowing would be closest, but the sense isn't one humans have. Taste kinda fits better than hearing, so it's just the slang."

"I'm seriously missing out by being a human," I mumbled to myself.

"Look at her burns again," Torian said, "then think about that."

He eased Aspen back into the bed. Once she was lying down, he began to work off her shoes. I'd never seen a guy so gentle with any girl, let alone one who was just a sibling. Aspen let him, but when he lifted a brow, she shook her head. No words were exchanged, but clearly, they understood each other. As if an agreement was made, Torian pulled back her covers and Aspen moved over to slide under them.

She was asleep almost immediately. Whatever he'd given her seemed to be working, though. The red marks on her skin were visibly fading, and all the blisters were gone. The magic Keir had done had helped, but this was definitely a cure. Then, as if that was some kind of sign, the guys all moved to the door, preparing to leave.

I stepped back, aiming for the side door that led through the bathroom and to my suite. Wilder reached the main door first, and Hawke followed, but Torian paused before me. For a moment, his eyes scanned my face. I felt like I was being judged, and I wasn't sure what he expected, so I simply waited.

Then he opened his mouth to speak, but closed it almost as fast. It took a moment before he tried again. "It's my job to take care of her," he finally said, the look in his eyes begging for understanding. "That means I'm in your debt."

"No." I shrugged. "It means you can't be everywhere, and friends take care of each other."

He nodded, accepting that. Then he offered his hand. "Friends?"

I took it. "I'm in need of a few of those."

He just tilted his head at Wilder and Hawke. "How about four? There aren't many people who'd risk themselves for us. Fewer who'd do it so blindly. Every doubt I had about you has just been erased, Rain."

"Aspen's the only reason I'm even here," I admitted. "Torian, I'm already in *her* debt and I know it. I can't seem to forget it. This feels like the smallest way to pay a little of that back. I mean, you have no idea how bad my life was before here. The Sparks were pretty normal for me."

"Shit," Hawke breathed. "Yeah, they were hell. If that was your *normal?*"

"But Aspen didn't stand up for her to help her," Wilder countered. "She did it because..." He thrust out both hands at me. "She's like this."

"Aspen did that for us," Torian clarified. "Ok. Out, guys. Aspen needs to sleep this off. I need to check on what they're doing with the girls who attacked her."

"Liam has them, and while you do that, I'll keep an eye on her," I promised. "Um, if you want to give me your number, I can text you some updates."

He held out his hand, clearly expecting my phone, so I dug it out. Once he had it, Torian flipped to my contact screen, then just shook his head. He started typing, and he kept at it for a little too long. Eventually, he passed it back.

"I added all of us, just in case you need anything." He paused, looking at me for a little too long. "Can I have some time to think of the right words?"

"Huh?" I had no clue what he meant.

An almost shy smile curled his lips and he glanced down. "You know, so I don't accidentally try to thank you. I didn't realize how much harder it is when you're not talking to your family."

"Torian, you can tell me thank you. I know what that warm feeling feels like, and I realize sometimes it's impossible to express it any other way."

"Then *thank you*, Rain," he said softly. "She's the most important thing I have, and I'd be lost without her. She's my family, and the only one I'm willing to claim. I really am in your debt."

"There's no debt," I assured him. "It was a favor freely given, and maybe I did it for my own selfish reasons."

"Which is why you're so interesting," he said before turning and simply walking away.

Chapter Twenty-Eight

I checked on Aspen every hour, just making sure she was sleeping comfortably. I had no clue what the medicine - if that fluid had even been medicine - was supposed to do, but she never stirred. Each time, I sent Torian a message, updating him because I knew he was worried about her.

By the time the sun began to set, her burns were gone. Her skin was pale naturally, but as she slept, it began to get a healthy glow back to it. Not the pasty and pallid look she'd had when we brought her into her room. She was starting to actually look like her normal self again.

I made it back to my own room and had just sat down to read through my homework assignments when someone tapped at my door. Half expecting Liam, I got up and unlocked it. Pulling the door open wide, I paused when the person waiting on the other side was Torian. He held something in his hands.

"She'll sleep through the night," he said, "but you didn't come down for dinner, so I brought something up." Then he offered me the container in his hands.

"Uh, thanks?" I took it and then winced, realizing what I'd said.

"Sorry. Habit." I stepped back so he could come in. "She looks better, but she hasn't stirred at all. I was just about to send you another update, actually."

He stepped in and looked around, examining my private space. When he saw the plant beside my bed, those pouty lips of his curled into a smile. Crossing the room, he reached out to caress the leaves, stroking the thing the way someone would a cat.

And the plant responded. The strange little buds relaxed, revealing what was hidden inside. A soft green glow began to illuminate the corner by my bed - because the funny-looking "flower" bubbles shined like fireflies.

"It glows?" I asked.

"It's a Moon Shine," he explained. "Hard to kill but harder to cultivate. Once you prove you're friendly, it will glow in response. A pretty good night light, actually."

I set the container of food down on my desk and moved to check it out. "Ok, that's cool. I just thought she'd given me a fae cactus or something."

He pointed at one of the leaves. "They like caresses across the wide part, especially the bottom. If you talk to it while you pet it, the thing might become trained to the sound of your voice. Name it. Mine will glow when I say its name."

"That is amazing." Unable to help myself, I reached down and caressed a leaf. "What should I call you, fairy plant? How about Glow, huh?"

Torian just laughed and started to turn away - but he paused halfway. His eyes jumped over my shoulder and his hand snapped out to grab my arm, preventing me from moving. Confused, I tried to look behind me to see what had him so interested.

"Don't," he breathed. "Just stay still for a second?"

So I stood there like an idiot while he watched something. His spring-green eyes darted, clearly chasing something. In my mind, I couldn't help but imagine some fae monsters lurking in the shelves, ready to pounce, yet Torian didn't seem worried about it. It was more like he was confused.

"Slowly," he finally said, "turn your head and watch your shadow."

Trying to be subtle, I looked back to see what he meant. The glow of the fae plant had a silhouette of my shape flickering against the wall. Wait, flickering? The longer I watched, the more it seemed my shadow was trying to do something. Grow, move, or something else, I wasn't sure, but the light from the plant was stable and consistent. There was no reason for my shadow to flicker.

My heart beat a little faster. "Torian, why's it doing that?" Because his shadow wasn't.

"No idea," he said, turning me away so I'd stop worrying about it.

As if it were that easy. Sure, I moved back toward my desk, but I kept looking back, checking to see what my own shadow was doing. Yet the moment it was out of the fae light, the flickering stopped. Clearly, the light bulb in my room didn't cause the same weirdness.

"Why does my shadow flicker and not yours?" I asked.

Torian dropped down onto my bed and made himself comfortable. No asking permission. No shyness about it. The guy took over like it was somehow his right. I sighed, rolled my eyes, and turned back for my meal. For a moment there, I'd kinda hoped he was more like Aspen, but it seemed these siblings didn't share much in the way of personality.

Just as I opened the container of food, Torian finally answered me. "It's interesting, isn't it?"

That damned phrase again! "*What* is interesting?"

"You." He folded his arms behind his head and looked over. "These strange little things happen when you're around. You say you're a human. I heard you tested as having no signs of magic. On the surface, you appear to be a completely normal human girl, but I'm not sure you are."

"And yet *you'd* notice when the teachers missed it?" I lifted a brow, making it clear I could see through that line.

Those lovely lips of his curled a little more as his smile grew. "Yes. I find it amusing how you think our teachers would know more than me."

"And what makes *you* so special?"

He crossed his ankles, clearly not in a hurry to leave. "I was trained in Faerie until I was sixteen by the best tutors in our world." He mimicked my expression, lifting his own brow. "The Mad Queen herself taught me a few things. Mainly, how to see the opportunities in the world."

"Wait, so like, last year?" I asked, quickly doing the math.

"Almost two years ago now," he corrected. "Well, just under. I'm almost eighteen. I left Faerie at sixteen. I managed to get through a gate without getting caught, got picked up by the cops, said I didn't have parents, and was tossed into a foster home." He paused, the smile falling. "The Sparks' place."

"That would be a shock," I said, pulling out the chair at my desk and sitting down.

The entire room separated us, and yet somehow Torian made me feel like I was the guest here. The guy lounged there like some lazy cat, as if he'd be offended if I told him to move. The problem was he looked good doing it. Keir was hot, but Torian was the dangerous kind of beauty. The type that was alluring, but I knew it would cut if I tried to touch.

"Lucky for me," he went on, "Hawke was there. He got out of Faerie when he was eleven, which meant he knew how to work the system. I went from Elysium fields to this box of a room with piss-yellow walls. Couldn't handle it."

"Wait..." That had my complete attention. "Top of the stairs, first door on the left?"

"That's the one," he agreed.

"That's my room now!" I laughed. "No wonder they kept putting iron crap in there."

"Oh, they did that with us too," he promised. "The first time she made me cook, I burned my hand on the pan. Pure iron, and there was so much in that house, I couldn't tell where the irritation came from until I touched it. The color threw me. We don't have cast iron, you see."

"Yeah, makes sense," I agreed. Because if they couldn't touch it, they certainly wouldn't cast it.

"Well, once that bitch realized it hurt me, she began to put little pieces of it around the house. Hawke got burned and lost it. He threw the trinket through the window. She had a fit, her husband tried to berate us, and we were done. In the middle of the night, we snuck out. Made it halfway through town before the police caught us."

"How did you get out of the house?" I asked.

He gave me a confused look. "The window."

"Oh, they've put iron bars on those now. After I got a bird out of the house for them, they even put an iron doorknob on my bedroom door. I was so confused until Liam brought me here."

"Liam..." Torian smiled as he said the man's name. "Mr. Sparks called our case worker, saying we weren't settling in. He intended to send us to the group home."

"Same," I said.

"Well, Liam showed up. He took one look at us and instantly knew what was going on. We were taken to some church for an interview. The Sparks thought Liam was trying to convince us to behave. Instead, he was asking about our history, what we knew of our families, and things like that. When both Hawke and I could tell him everything about our parents - and didn't know enough to limit what we said - he got us in here."

"Wait." I made a circular motion with my hand. "Go back? What do you mean about limiting what you say about your families?"

Torian suddenly tensed. "That," he said as he sat up. "Sometimes, it's easy to get comfortable with a person. The four of us were kids when we left Faerie, but that doesn't mean we didn't understand. We just didn't know how different things are here. What once made us safe now makes us threatened. What had previously been a problem is now a benefit. Everything I knew as a child is reversed here, and while all of these fae ran to escape the war, they also unknowingly brought it with them."

"How?" I asked, lifting a hand so he'd give me a chance to explain. "I don't need to know your secrets, Torian. I get it. I don't want to talk about stuff from my past either. I'm just confused about how I fit into the mess of jesters and courts. Keir said something about running from the bad and trying to start all over as if nothing had changed, and now I'm even more confused."

Torian turned both hands, palms up. "There's the Summer Court," he said, lifting one. Then he dropped that and lifted the other. "Then there's the Winter Court. Right now is the season of Winter, which means the Summer Court has less available power. The opposite happens in the summer."

"Ok..." Because I'd heard about that before, I just wasn't sure how it applied.

"Once, the Queen of the Summer Court ruled fairly. The King of the Winter Court was the same. They accepted their power in turns, aware they were far from weak when it wasn't their season. Fae can touch the power they were born into - either Summer or Winter. For most, it's one season, but the Queen wanted more. Having seen children born from both courts able to use both types of power, she found her answer. The Summer Queen attacked the Winter Court at the beginning of Autumn, when her powers were still stronger than his. The King was defeated, and to save his people, he agreed to marry her, giving her rule over his court some legitimacy - and all of his power."

"Damn," I breathed.

"Oh, it gets worse," he warned. "So, once the Queen had the power of all seasons, she decided to ensure her control. The King was ordered to get her with child. For every year he failed, a member of his former court was executed. Keep in mind our people do not have many children. With the Winter Court nearly destroyed, he finally impregnated her. Once the child was accepted as her heir, the King was executed."

"I'm liking this woman less and less," I said.

"Trust me, I agree," he grumbled. "See, the power of the seasons is channeled through the crowns of each court. The Queen can only wear one, but so long as the other sits empty, the power goes to her. Also, they can only be worn by someone who is recognized as an adult. No infants on thrones in Faerie. But, if the next ruler is her child, the power will be funneled to her as the older relative of the same bloodline. She made a puppet ruler to ensure the Winter Court will forever be hers. If that child *ever* assumes the crown, there's no going back. So long as the Queen lives, her descendants would rule the courts, and she'd get all the power."

"And you saw all of this play out?" I asked.

He nodded. "My father was one of the people executed, Rain. Aspen's mother, Hawke's too, and both of Wilder's parents paid the price. We all lost something, and we saw it. We didn't just hear about it. We watched our parents die and our world turn on itself. I may have been a child, but you have no idea what that's like!"

"I actually do," I admitted. "My father used to abuse my mom. She shot him in front of me when I was five. She'll spend the rest of her life in jail, and I'm, well, here. Granted, she was the victim who won, but she also lost."

He nodded. "So you do understand. Sometimes, there's no good answer. But the jesters are desperately trying to prove to their parents they're fae enough. See, to our kind, magical power is prestige. The fae who came here aren't young. They've lived centuries with the same kind of mentality that led to the Queen going mad. Power is all that matters to them, and to be good little fae children, the jesters chase the same things."

"So they went after Aspen because she's pure fae?"

He chuckled, but it was a cold sound. "No. It's because people love their tribes. The history and traditions of where we came from are what give us pride about who we are and an expectation of who we should be. In other words, it's all we know. Well, they. Aspen is one of the last obvious children of the Winter Court. Most of the refugees are from the Summer Court - or peasants who had no court."

"And because the four of you were born in Faerie, the jesters think you're some kind of threat?" I asked, trying to make all this new information fit what I knew.

He opened his mouth, paused, and then sighed. "It's a little more complicated than that. Aspen is powerful, but she's untrained. Before she came to Silver Oaks last year, Harper was the most powerful girl in this school. Now she's not. Worse, Aspen's power is Winter magic."

"So, they attacked Aspen because Harper's jealous?" I grumbled under my breath. "Well, fuck them. I hate bullies, and I'm sick of them pushing people around. Just tell me how I can help?"

"You already have," he promised as he pushed to his feet. "I'm going to go check on my *sister* while you eat that disgusting mess."

"What?" I looked over to see a roast beef sandwich. "Uh, what did you do to my food?"

"Nothing," he promised, walking backwards towards my bathroom door. "We just don't eat it." He gestured to my meal. "Iron."

"So what the hell do you eat?" I asked.

"Fruit," he said. "Sugars. Like little butterflies."

"All pure-blood fae are vegetarians?" I asked. "Then how the hell do you get the muscles?"

"Maybe you should start joining the court for meals and you can see." He jerked his chin at me. "But good to know you were looking." Then the bastard grinned, turned, and stepped through the door.

Chapter Twenty-Nine

That evening, it started snowing. From the window in my room, I could see the flakes piling up on the glass roof of the atrium just above. Torian was still in Aspen's room, and I could hear the pair talking softly, so I didn't want to disturb them. He'd said she'd sleep through the night, so I wasn't sure if he'd woken her up to check how she was doing or if there might be a problem.

Either way, I felt useless, and I hated it. So, grabbing my tablet, I decided to get out of my room for a bit. I thought about the study area, because I knew it would be quiet, and yet my feet carried me the other way. Taking the elevator downstairs, I stepped into the darkened halls of the first floor and my eyes went right to the atrium. In the moonlight, with the snow collecting on the panes of the glass roof, the place looked even more magical.

Using the side door, I stepped in, wandering through the warmth and vegetation until I found a soft spot. There, I activated my tablet and tried to read, but I couldn't stop wondering about the jesters. Had they been punished for what they'd done? My eyes scanned the text for my Literature class twice, but none of the words made it into my brain, so I just gave up.

Leaning back, I tensed at the sound of the door opening again. Quickly, I dimmed my tablet, hoping I hadn't set myself up by coming out here alone. I'd seen what those girls had done to Aspen. If the boys decided to show me that being human wasn't the same as being strong, I'd be so fucked.

But the person who walked around the trunk of the massive silver oak wasn't a student. It was Bracken, my combat instructor. His eyes found me easily, and he made his way closer. Where I sat with my back against the stones of the fish pond, he moved to use the lip as his seat, keeping about an arm's length between us.

"I saw you heading in here, so I came to see how you're doing after that scare today," he said, getting right to the point.

"Scare?" I shook my head. "No, I was angry."

"Maybe it's more traumatic for us. The use of iron against another like that is..." He paused, pulling in a breath as he carefully chose his word. "Unexpected."

"Yeah. I heard it's a power struggle thing." I turned so I could see his face.

Because if fae couldn't lie, and Bracken was a fae, then his words would be true. That didn't necessarily mean they wouldn't deceive, and I wasn't quite sure how all that worked, but I wasn't stupid. Something about his posture, his face, or what he refused to talk about would give me an answer. Might not be the one I wanted, but I'd seen enough foster parent evasions to muddle through this.

But Bracken surprised me. "It is," he agreed. "How's Aspen doing?"

"She was sleeping until her brother came to check on her."

He nodded. "Those two are good for each other. Opposites in so many ways, but they keep each other from becoming too extreme. I'm glad we found her."

"Wait..." That was something I hadn't heard before. "What do you mean 'found?'"

Bracken leaned over his knees to get a little closer. "You aren't the only foundling, Rain. Liam spends a lot of time combing through the records of foster kids. His job here allows him to work as the primary case worker for Plainsboro, which gives him access to all of this district."

"Yeah, Liam mentioned he's been looking for fae in the foster system," I said. "What about the parents, though?"

Bracken made a noise like I was missing the point. "A lot of fae are taken by the Wild Hunt. Their part-fae children end up in the foster system. Then there's the ones from Faerie."

"Kids from Faerie, you mean?"

He nodded. "Most refugees now are kids. Long ago, if a fae wanted to protect their child, they would steal a human infant and replace it with the fae baby. The foster system makes that pointless. Just leave a kid somewhere, call for help, and presto, the police handle the rest. It's easier to slip a kid out than an adult, so if a parent has to choose..."

"Huh, which is why Liam thought my record mattered." I bobbed my head, thinking about that. "So, fae kids kinda bounce around a lot once they're in human foster homes, huh?"

"Iron makes us grumpy. Most of your homes have a lot of it. We're not always easy to deal with."

"I dunno," I countered. "I kinda think you're easier than most of the humans I've met in my life."

The man actually laughed at that. "Which is why you definitely belong here." Then he leaned back again and sighed. "So, the girls were all reprimanded. They're restricted from after-hours activities, confined to their dorms for the next week when not in school, and their parents or guardians have been called. Two were sent home for a week. Giselle and Elyssa. Tag says you planted yourself right over Aspen and took the iron from their hands?"

"They had keychains," I explained. "Normal, regular things you can buy in any gas station. I've held a million of them, so it wasn't that big of a deal."

"Was to Aspen," he countered. "Keir said he could feel the itch of it from fifty yards away."

I gestured up. "But the building doesn't bother you?"

"Not much iron," he assured me. "This whole place was built with brick, stone, mortar, aluminum, and some bronze. Oh, there's iron in here. It's impossible to avoid it all, but the original refugees tried to limit it as much as possible. If an alternative could be used, then it was."

I nodded to show I'd heard, but I was less interested in the building than the jesters. "So, what happens when they try it again? You know those girls won't like the fact they got in trouble."

"They won't," he agreed. "I want to say you should come tell a teacher, but I think we're both realists, right?"

"Yeah," I mumbled.

"But Liam said you're worried about getting into trouble. He made it clear you have a history of standing up for yourself, even when it means you might pay the price. So, let us talk like fae, not teacher to student, hm?"

"Ok?"

I turned a little more, then hugged my knees. I wasn't quite sure what he meant by that, but I was more than willing to listen. Bracken had been fair to me so far, and the fact he was cute made me not mind talking to him. I just wasn't sure where he was going with this.

"There are times when being fae makes us very, very weak. There are times when being fae makes us very strong. The same is true for humans, which you demonstrated today. Aspen is a powerful young lady. She could level this school if she wanted to. However, a keychain brought her to her knees."

"Yeah," I grumbled, hating that.

"So, if you are defending another student, I will give you my word you will not be expelled from Silver Oaks. *Any* other student, but it needs to be for a valid reason. You can't scald a fae with iron because they bumped someone in the halls. Like for like, Rain. Can you agree to that?"

"I can," I said.

He nodded slowly, as if thinking. "Then I want you to start training against multiple opponents in my classes. Tag said she's going to start teaching you various metals. She wants you to be able to identify the harmful ones at a glance." He looked over and smiled. "You impressed a few teachers today, so you know. That doesn't mean we'll go easy on you. In fact, it means we all intend to push you - because you have potential. Our school is not like what you're used to. Here, we're teaching you how to fit into a fae community while blending with human society. You could be very useful in *any* fae community that will take you, and I'm sure a few would love to."

"What if I want to stay here?" I asked. "Be like Liam, you know? Help find foster kids who had a hard time. Maybe some humans who've dreamed of finding out they're a fairy princess or something?"

"Or a guardian for the fae," he suggested. "There are always jobs at Silver Oaks. I can't make promises about anything else, but if you become a part of this community, we will *rely* on you."

"I just like it here," I admitted. "It's like, for the first time in my life, you're all willing to listen to me. I'm not always assumed to be belligerent or difficult because things go wrong."

He murmured to himself, looking over at the large tree that was the centerpiece of the atrium's garden. "I'm going to tell you something, and Liam wouldn't approve, but I think you need to know." He paused, then finally looked over. "We need warriors. Against the Hunt, against the possibility of the gates reopening, and against the pain of so much iron all around us. That's why we offer combat courses here. The fae weren't meant to live on Earth, but we don't have any other option now. We will either have to expose ourselves or we'll be burned alive by the civilization that's taking over the remaining open spaces. We need warriors, Rain, and you have the heart for it."

"But I don't know anything," I reminded him.

"I can teach you," he swore. "You aren't like most of the humans we see here. You're more like the fae in some ways, and yet you grab iron without flinching. Liam checked your parents, and there's no chance of fae ancestry, yet you're..."

"Interesting," I finished for him, the word a grumble.

Bracken just chuckled at me. "It's an appropriate word. You remind me of myths of old. See, the fae have stories of humans who entered our world. Merlin, as an example. Men and women with great power who crossed through the gates. There's just something about you I can't quite put my finger on, but I can almost feel it."

"I'm kinda special in my own way, huh?" I asked.

He nodded. "So, think about it. Take the weekend, and if you do want to learn to become a sentinel, let me know. If you don't, then simply pretend this conversation never happened."

And he stood. Bracken paused to clasp my shoulder as he passed, clearly heading for the exit on the boy's side. Just as he reached the silver oak, I remembered how nervous I'd been when I realized I wasn't alone down here. Before he left, I decided to ask about that.

"Hey, Bracken?" I called out.

He paused, looking back. "Yes?"

"Am I going to get jumped by the jesters if I run around alone? Like, real talk and all?"

"Not tonight, but I wouldn't rule it out," he said. "You might consider a keychain for your room key."

"Yeah," I groaned. "I need a job."

"Or to make something besides a sword in Weapons-Crafting," he countered. "After all, the best weapons are the ones no one would worry about." His teeth flashed in the pale moonlight, then the man kept going.

I sat there for a bit longer, thinking about that. Were *all* the jesters in trouble tonight? Otherwise, why wouldn't they come after me? Maybe they just assumed I'd be hiding upstairs? I had no idea, but the longer I was at this school, the more complicated everything was becoming.

And to think, I'd assumed magic would be the hardest thing to get used to. Instead, I was now surrounded with fae politics, some warped hierarchy of ancestry and rank, plus all the nuances of teen drama. Yep, welcome to Silver Oaks Institute, home of a little insanity.

The strange thing, though, was that I wouldn't change it for the world. Somehow, this mess made me feel useful, as if I'd finally stopped bouncing around and landing in dust bunnies to be forgotten. Here, I was somebody. Maybe I wasn't someone important or fancy, but I wasn't a nobody, and that felt pretty good.

Plus, I had friends. A smile touched my lips as I thought about that. Four of them. Five, if I counted Keir. Oddly, they were all the pure-bloods. Well, look at me. I was the fae-whisperer!

Chuckling about that, I woke up my tablet and got back to my textbook. This time, my eyes didn't skip over the page. If my best friend was being bullied because of fae history, then I needed to not just pass my History of Faerie course - I needed to *understand* it. I needed to wrap my mind around everything that was going on.

And something was *definitely* going on. I just had a feeling all the truths my fae friends were saying left out a few important details. The big question was which ones.

Chapter Thirty

The next day, Aspen was doing much better. I woke to the sound of her in the shower, whistling. Just hearing it made me think of the plant she'd given me, so I rolled over and petted the leaves. The thing actually moved, stretching like it enjoyed the sensation.

"Morning, Glow," I told it. "I wish I knew how often to water you."

Of course, the plant didn't respond. It might be from Faerie, but it was still a plant. Although it was kinda cool that it seemed to like me. Thinking about the number of strange things I'd begun to take for granted, I got up and did my own morning routine. When I finished, I thought about checking on Aspen, but her room now sounded strangely empty.

She'd probably gone to visit the guys, to show them she was ok or something. I shouldn't have felt upset about it, but I kinda did. I'd spent all evening worrying about her. I couldn't count the number of times I'd checked on her through the night, feeling so helpless, and not even a thank you?

Of course not. She was fae, and fae didn't do that. Laughing at my own foolishness, I headed over to check my phone, only to find a message from Liam. Just like Bracken had last night, Liam wanted to make sure I knew what had happened to the girls who'd been busted for bullying my suitemate. Then he added he was proud of me, and it made everything else ok.

Liam was *proud* of me for getting into trouble. Oh, he called it standing up for someone else, but it had always been "trouble" when I'd done it before. That put a little smile on my face as I got dressed and put on some makeup. Then I went back to studying. I'd never been this kind of student before in my life, but at Silver Oaks, I felt like my classes were actually useful.

Instead of asking stupid questions all the time, I could just read the book. Considering they were all digital, that meant I could even highlight stuff and mark places to reference later. By doing my homework, I was learning what I needed to keep my head above water with all this magic stuff.

And it was still kinda boring. I'd been here for two complete weeks now, and I only had one real friend. Yes, Torian and his two nearly-silent shadows had offered their friendship last night, but we'd only spoken a few times. It wasn't quite the same. Here I was, surrounded by all these hot guys, with no one to talk to about it, no one who knew me well enough to giggle about things I liked. Not even a pal to watch movies with in the common area. Even worse, I didn't actually know how to make fae friends. I kinda wanted to mope about that, but I was more of a doer type than a whiner.

Then, just before lunch, I heard something. Confused, I headed to the window to see what was going on downstairs in the rest of the school. My room had a view that looked into the atrium. The glass roof was not far above, and the panes were completely covered with snow, but inside, something was thumping steadily. A cluster of students streamed towards it, proving that whatever this was, it was meant to draw attention. I decided to join them.

Like everyone else, I headed that way, my curiosity insatiable. Living so close to the elevator, I managed to catch the car before the group of people heading up the hall caused a lineup. When I made it to the ground floor, I realized the thumping was bass, and it came from the garden. That was why everyone was heading there. At least twenty people were already clustered around, smiling like this was a welcome surprise.

I followed the herd of students through the glass doors and into the warmth of the greenhouse. There, it became obvious the bass was coming from a simple set of speakers. The small, ordinary, Bluetooth type. The intensity made me think they might be magically enchanted, though. Beneath the trees, people were starting to dance. It was mostly swaying and bouncing, but it counted. It wasn't until I got closer that I figured out who'd started all of this.

Torian sat on the rocks by the fish pond - almost the same place I'd been last night. His arms and body moved to the beat. The volume was so loud conversation was almost impossible, but no one seemed to care. The strangest thing was Torian's smile. It was honest and cheerful, not cold like most other times.

On the other side of the pond, I saw Aspen's silver hair. She spun in Wilder's arms, doing something almost like a pirouette. Beside them, Hawke had found another girl and was grinding against her like he was trying to get a date. They weren't the only ones, though. I saw Lynn and her friends, plus plenty of people whose names I didn't know.

But I got spotted quickly. Aspen broke away from Wilder and hurried over to catch my arm. Grinning, she pulled me back to the space they'd taken over, then gestured for me to start moving. Laughing, I gave in and joined her. The music wasn't really my style, being a little more dubstep than I typically went for, but I could bounce to it.

When the song ended, Torian stood, making everyone look at him. "What's next?" he called out.

"Is this a common thing?" I asked Aspen.

She nodded. "Used to be. He did this pretty much every weekend last year. First time this year, though."

Then Hawke leaned in so his mouth was beside my ear. "Decided someone deserved a little fun." When I glanced back, he was pointing at me.

"You did this for me?" I asked, completely confused. "Why?"

"So you'll get your nose out of those books," Wilder said as a slower song began to play.

Aspen opened her arms in an invitation to dance. "Wanna?"

But the look on her face was braced for rejection. Just yesterday, I'd learned she was a lesbian. She assumed that meant I'd be weird about having fun with her, but this was Aspen! She was the prettiest girl in school, possibly the most fun person I'd ever met, and my only real friend here.

I stepped in awkwardly and began to sway with her. "Have I been dubbed a nerd or something?"

"No," she said softly, draping her arms around my neck. "It's just that we don't wipe away favors. We wanted to pay you back, and you seem lonely. Torian said you're our friend. All of ours, so we're celebrating that. The rest of the school just gets to enjoy the side effects."

She glanced away and a shy smile touched her lips. When pink appeared on her cheeks, I realized she was being self-conscious, and it was kinda cute on her. Something between us had changed yesterday, but I wasn't quite sure what. I knew she liked girls. I'd stood up for her. I had every intention of continuing to do so, too. I could see how that would be a little weird for her, but her shyness made me feel a little protective.

"I realized something last night," I said as we slow-danced. "I can't remember the last time I had a best friend, and I kinda think of you that way. I mean, I know we don't really know each other that well..."

She hugged me tighter. "All my friends are guys, Rain. I just don't want the fact that I kinda think you're cute to be weird."

"Not weird," I promised. "Besides, I've seen some gay couples around the halls since I've been here. See? Not weird at all. Believe it or not, I'm ok with you - or anyone else - liking whoever you like."

Her teeth caught her lower lip, yet she still managed to smile around it. "Back at my last school I got in so much shit for it. I couldn't be out, wasn't allowed to take a girl to dances or things like that, and..." She tipped her head back to where the atrium was full of people. "Now they give me shit about having Winter magic. It's like I can't win. Ever since I got to Earth, things have just been hell."

"I thought you were just a baby when you left Faerie?" So how would she know about those things?

Aspen laughed. "That's what I mean! There, marriages are contracts only. Not for love. Relationships are free and open. Sex and families aren't the same. A person can be married and still have five lovers. My mother was with a woman. My father had an entire harem of lovers."

"Wow," I breathed.

She nodded just as the song ended. "And that's one more thing that makes you interesting, you know. You're so much like the fae, and yet you're also completely human." Then she pointed down. "And they seem to like you."

I followed her finger to see a flower leaning into me. Thinking of Glow upstairs, I leaned down to pet it. That made Aspen laugh, but Wilder playfully tugged her back and moved before me. A new song began to play, this one a little faster.

"My turn," he teased, spinning me around so he could press his chest up against my back.

And we danced. After Wilder came Hawke, then I found myself with Jeff from my biology class! Slowly but surely, I moved from partner to partner. The music changed from pop to metal and then to country. Others joined in. Plenty of the students were older, clearly the college-age type, but everyone was here to have a little fun.

A pair of guys were grinding on each other with the pulse of the music. Girls spun each other around. Friends clustered together, groups were forming, and smiles seemed to be everywhere. Musically, everything possible was offered. At one point, I ended up with a guy who didn't look any more fae than me.

Eventually, I waved off the next offer and moved toward the base of the silver oak to catch my breath. The sight of a tall golden man leaning against the trunk made me smile. It was Keir. He saw me, then turned to grab something. By the time I reached him, he was holding out a red plastic cup filled with something that looked a lot like thin syrup.

"What the hell is that?" I asked.

"Taste it," he teased.

My eyes narrowed. "Isn't eating and drinking your stuff supposed to be a bad idea?"

Keir just laughed. "Only in Faerie. On Earth, I hear it's a mortal insult to refuse. Taste it, Rain."

I took a careful sip, then twitched in surprise. Yes, it was sweet. It also tasted like honeysuckle nectar. That was the closest thing I had to compare. Impressed, I took another drink. This one was bigger.

Keir reached up to press a finger against the bottom of my cup, lowering it from my mouth gently. "Go easy. It packs a punch."

"Is this like fae alcohol?" I asked.

The grin that claimed his mouth was all the answer I needed. "Since it's not alcohol, and it only comes from the silver oak here, you're allowed to have it. We can also get in trouble for getting you young'uns drunk on it. Think wine at meals, not sloshed in the halls."

I shifted to stand before him. "I see. So are you trying to get me drunk, Keir?"

His grin grew, if that was possible. "Damn you, woman."

"You are!" He couldn't say no, because he couldn't tell a lie. So I stepped around his legs, getting close enough to tap his chest. "What's your nefarious plan, fae-boy?"

His arm snaked around my lower back. "To see you laugh."

Oh, but I was figuring out how this worked. "And?" I asked.

He chuckled. "The next pretty human girl I meet, I'm not telling her about fae quirks."

"Stop changing the subject," I teased, definitely catching that part about pretty. "And, Keir? What's the rest of your big plan?"

He tugged my hips against his, then leaned in toward my ear. "Stop trying to get me in trouble. I promise my plan has all your clothes still on your body - and that's all I'm saying."

I leaned back to meet his eyes. He didn't even look embarrassed. No, he met my gaze like it was a dare. That was what made these guys so tempting. There was this arrogance about them, and yet it wasn't like most guys I'd met, the kind who wanted to put me in my place.

Then there was his mouth. Those full lips that curled more on one side than the other. Before I did anything stupid, I lifted the glass and took another drink, but I didn't pull away.

"So, how much am I going to regret drinking this later?" I asked.

"Unlike the crap you people drink, ours is revitalizing," he promised. "It's why we're allowed to have it. Promise you won't need coffee tomorrow."

"I'm gonna need a lot of this, huh?"

The words were barely out of my mouth before an arm snagged around my waist and I was pulled away from Keir. Turning, Torian simultaneously shifted me over while placing his body between us. Then he shoved at Keir's chest.

"What the fuck are you doing?" he snarled.

Keir pushed right back into him. "I'm having fun. I'm teaching her about oak syrup. I also told her to go slow, so back the fuck off, Torian."

The pair just glared at each other for a moment. Torian was dark like the moon at night. Keir was golden like the sun in the middle of the day. They were about the same height, just as muscled, and yet so very different. They were also beautiful, but braced up like this, there was no doubt in my mind they were of equal power.

"If you try to use her ignorance against her, I will make sure you pay," Torian snarled. "She's *ours*, Keir."

"You don't get to own everything pretty, Torian," Keir warned him. "She's hers, and I will stand up for her right to prove it." He leaned just a bit more. "I'm also not scared of you."

"You will be," Torian warned, turning to catch my arm. "Let's go, Rain. You need to pick your friends better."

Chapter Thirty-One

Torian didn't ask. Using his grip on my arm, he simply hauled me through the crowd and away from Keir. Even when I tried to pull away, I couldn't break his grip. Without slowing down, he all but dragged me to the farthest corner of the atrium, to the back wall that looked out over the grounds.

The moment his fingers released, I pulled my arm away. "Dick," I snapped.

"You foolish little human girl," he grumbled, those green eyes flashing in anger. "That? You're making yourself a target."

"In case you missed it, Keir's the one who carried Aspen back last night," I said, thrusting an arm back in the direction of the silver oak. "*He* is the one who got two human teachers to deal with the jesters and their iron!"

"What?" Torian seemed completely confused.

"Keir helped me in my offense class. He's been *nice* to me." Then I pushed into Torian's face the same way Keir had. "He's cute too, and I don't care if you like it. I also don't need my best friend's brother cockblocking me."

His hand snapped up to catch my jaw, holding my face right

before his. "Magicless little girls shouldn't pick fights they can't win," he warned.

Yeah, too bad for him, I was already figuring out how things worked. "Well, this magicless little girl is protected by her friend. The sister you wouldn't dare upset, and I'm more than willing to use *that* to my advantage. Tell me, Tor, who's more powerful, you or Aspen?"

His fingers relaxed, his jaw clenched in frustration, but he didn't let go. "She would never hurt me."

"And you'd never hurt her," I said, proving I got that much. "I kinda figured that part out. It also means that so long as I'm in Aspen's good graces - which is my definition of friendship, so you know - you don't *scare* me. Stop acting like a bully."

Shaking his head, he finally pulled his arm away. "Fine, but if you hurt her, I will destroy you. I will make sure you regret it."

"Yeah, I figured that out too," I assured him. "You and Aspen are close. I get it. You want to protect her. Cool. And so you know, *this*? Yanking me around, snarling at me like some fucktoy? It's not my definition of friendship."

He just huffed out a laugh, those green eyes watching me intently. "You know, they all think *she's* the crazy one." He leaned in a little more and dropped his voice to a deep rumble. "They're wrong."

I'd been about to leave, completely ready to walk off, but that stopped me before I could even turn. "What do you mean?"

"Aspen," he explained. "She channels her magic into her plants so it doesn't spill over. She was never taught how to control it before she came here, and..." He glanced back, checking to make sure we were alone. "She's stronger than any of the teachers, even Ms. Rhodes."

"And you're stronger," I guessed.

"More controlled," he corrected. "I don't think I'm stronger. Her magic was never tethered. It knows no bounds. They call it untamed, but she was raised *here*. She knows how to live in *this* world." His eyes searched mine. "I don't. I went from Faerie to the Sparks' for a matter of months, then here - surrounded by fae. You're not fae."

"But I thought you said I act like it?" I was completely lost now.

Torian shoved a hand over his hair, pushing it out of his face. "You do. That's the confusing part. If you bumbled around like a normal human, I wouldn't forget."

"So how about you treat me like you'd treat your sister," I told him.

His eyes dropped down my body, the look anything but subtle. "I don't think that will work."

"No?" I hooked a finger under his chin to lift his eyes back to my face. "Let me make this very clear to you, Torian. There are a lot of very pretty boys at this school. You're one of many, and pretty is only skin deep. I prefer a kind attitude to sharp jaws and high cheekbones. Act like a dick, and all your flirting will be pointless. So you know, dragging me away from my friends counts right up there on the dick levels."

He just laughed. "And you thought I was Aspen's boyfriend. Shit, that makes more sense."

"What?" He'd changed subjects too fast for me to follow.

"Why you shot me down that first day," he explained. "You thought I was trying to get a side piece. I see."

"Were you?" I asked.

He stepped right into me, so close our chests almost touched, but I wouldn't back up. I had to tilt my head so I wasn't staring at his amazing chest, though. Damn, how did he get muscles like that eating nothing but fruit? And no, I definitely should not touch them. I was trying very hard to make a point, but I kinda wanted to poke him at least once, just to check if his pecs felt as solid as they looked.

"No, I was not hunting for a side piece," he assured me. "I was trying to see just how easily you bend, but I think you have a little drool..." He reached over and wiped at the corner of my mouth.

It was supposed to be a taunting gesture, poking fun at me for checking him out a moment ago, but his touch was a little too soft. My heart skittered a bit faster as I looked at him. His hand paused, his thumb just touching my lower lip, and Torian cocked his head ever so slightly. I refused to turn to jello at his good looks, but that only seemed to confuse him more.

"What are you?" he breathed.

I stepped back, breaking the contact while trying to keep my pride. "That's supposed to be my line."

He nodded, but his expression was still confused. It was like he knew the steps to this dance, but his mind was elsewhere. "Still doesn't answer the question, though. Rain Brooks - that can't be coincidence. Your name is made of nature."

"Coincidence or not, sexy or not, your little ego needs to come down a peg," I told him. "Believe it - or not - but I can still think when my panties are wet."

The smile returned. "Are they? Wet, I mean?"

"No," I said, stepping back just to point at my chest. "Human, remember?"

"Lies," he tossed after me. "I can still taste them, Rain."

"Doesn't stop me from saying them," I called as I continued walking.

Because I would *not* chase after that boy. I refused to be controlled by my vagina. First, he was my new best friend's brother. Messing around with him was a great way to fuck up this friendship I'd just started. Second, he kept acting like he thought he was better than everyone else. Not just me. Torian seemed to want to be the king everyone accused him of, and I wasn't interested in becoming anyone's bitch.

Then a form fell in at my side, offering me another red cup. This one was completely full. "Not a good idea," the guy warned, making me look over to see Hawke.

"Aren't you supposed to be his silent shadow?" I asked.

He just lifted the cup in a clear gesture for me to take it. "No. I'm supposed to be his friend. Nothing about that requires silence. It's just nectar, Rain. Oak syrup sent by Aspen."

"Yeah..." I paused, turning to face him. "Why would I trust that again?"

Hawke groaned. "It's safe. Before you doubt that, remember I'm fae. It's completely safe, it was sent by Aspen, and I'm supposed to deliver it so she doesn't look like a stalker. I also know she'd prefer I didn't tell you all of that, but I can see the doubt on your face."

And he couldn't lie. That was easy to know, yet hard to believe. Still, I accepted the drink, sliding this cup inside my now empty one. When I lifted it to my lips for a taste, Hawke stepped around me, putting his back to most of the people in the atrium.

"Taunting Torian's a bad idea," he warned.

"He taunted me first," I countered. "And what's the deal with Keir?"

"Fuck..." Hawke groaned. "I was trying to be nice, Rain."

Which had exactly nothing to do with my question. Yep, I was starting to see how the fae avoided things. "Keir's my friend. He's been nice to me. If the four of you think me being friends with Aspen means I'm not going to talk to anyone else, you're wrong."

"*This* is why I play the silent shadow," he said.

I just took another drink, refusing to budge and not needing to say anything. It didn't take long before Hawke cursed under his breath, true annoyance on his face. Yeah, that was intimidating, but I had a feeling the same rules applied to him as to Torian. He couldn't be a dick to me without risking Aspen's wrath. Since I'd seen her snap once, I had a feeling these guys wouldn't risk it.

Surprisingly, Hawke caved pretty easily. "Fine!" he groaned. "It has to do with a girl. Keir dated her. She dumped him for Tor. Tor dumped her, and she went right back to Keir, who said no. To the rest of the school, though, it said Keir was second place."

"Not you or Wilder?" I asked.

"Wilder only started here last spring," he told me.

"And you?" I couldn't stop my smile, because picking on these guys was kinda fun.

"I was with her friend," he finally admitted. "I also have no problem being second to Tor."

"But you do to Keir," I realized. "Why's that?"

Hawke just leaned in. "In case you missed it, I don't have to be nice. I could completely ignore you."

"Which means you won't answer that." I nodded. "I'm liking this 'no lies' thing."

He looked me over, then huffed. "I'll tell you something else instead. Fae women are lean and lithe. All of them. Humans, however, have these amazing curves. Hips. Tits. Asses. Unique, beautiful shapes that beg to be touched." He stole the cup from my fingers and took a gulp, holding it up like he was deciding if he should give it back. "That's why there are so many faelings here. The jesters know it, and they will never stop hating you for having the curves they will never get."

I took my glass back. "So, I stand with you or I get bullied by them?" I asked.

"I'd prefer lying to standing." He said that a little too casually. "And no, there's no ultimatum. Just a warning."

My heart stammered for a split second before I could get it under control. "I find it amusing how you all assume I'm just going to fall into your beds."

"No assumptions," he promised. "However, I like how you assume my bed's empty."

His grin was wicked, but he left me standing there before I could think of a comeback to that. The music was still playing, and Hawke faded into the crowd of people bouncing to the song currently on. I watched him, deciding I clearly had a thing for fae men. Torian was "prettier," but there was something a little predatory about Hawke. Probably how he'd gotten his name.

Where Torian was moonlight and shadows, Aspen was snow and ice. Wilder reminded me of the bare branches of a tree in winter, colored in shades of cool browns. Hawke was different. His skin was olive, both warm and almost cool at the same time. His hair was rusty, caught between brown and red, but he didn't have that same warm look as Keir.

Hawke's features were harder, his eyes more piercing, but he was broader than the others. Not much, since the fae came in different shades of lithe instead of bulky. The problem was I hadn't figured out yet how to ignore their good looks. Torian, Wilder, Hawke, and Keir were all just different shades of sexy.

But this was supposed to be a party. It was my chance to meet some people and make a few new friends. Taking a bigger drink from my cup, I could feel a nice little glow from this stuff. It was too sweet to drink too fast, but still tasted pretty good. I wandered around for a bit, stopping to talk to faces I recognized. They introduced me to more, and I kept going.

When my cup was finally empty, Aspen appeared with another. Her eyes were as glassy as mine felt, but since no teachers were heading down to break this up, I decided it must be ok. Accepting the drink, I lifted it out toward where her brother was once again manning the music.

"I think your guy friends were hitting on me," I said.

Aspen laughed. "Oh, they are. No question about it. Pretty sure they're going to start trying to one up each other soon."

"Torian tried to pick a fight with Keir," I said.

Aspen groaned. "Why do guys have to think with their dicks? So, you're into Keir?"

"I'm into enjoying all of this," I told her. "For the first time, I'm pretty sure I won't be moving before I get to know people. I also feel like I'm kinda buzzed on this stuff."

"Me too," she said. "C'mon, let's give the boys something to drool over."

Then she pulled me toward where people were dancing and started bouncing to the beat. I joined right in, doing my best to dance and drink. Aspen just laughed, lifting her glass to drain it in a single chug. When she was done, she tossed the empty cup and made a gesture with her fingers.

The whole thing simply vanished. I gasped. "What did you..."

"Sent it to the trash," she explained.

So I lifted my glass and drained it as quickly as I could. "Do me?"

A devious little smile curled her lips. "Tease." But she flicked her fingers at my now-empty cup, and it disappeared right from my grip.

"And now," I said, stepping back and crooking a finger for her to follow, "we can actually dance."

Lifting my hands over my head, I didn't care if I looked stupid. I felt just good enough that it didn't matter. I was also having fun. Pure, simple, uncomplicated fun with a friend. For me, it was basically what I'd spent the last few years wishing for. I wasn't going to let this pass me by.

Chapter Thirty-Two

Somewhere along the way, people began to leave. I didn't notice it happen, which meant it had been a slow thing, but with the fae drink making me feel a little giggly, I didn't care. Instead, it was the setting sun that made me realize I'd spent most of my Saturday down here having the best time.

I also hadn't eaten a thing. No morning coffee, no breakfast or lunch, and now it was pushing dinnertime. I wanted to ask for another glass of what Aspen kept calling "nectar," but which seemed to be tree sap or syrup, yet I knew better. I was inebriated and wiped out - a dangerous combination. Aspen might be able to dance for hours, but Torian had been playing some pretty jumping stuff, and I couldn't take anymore.

Waving her off, I made my way back to sit down and catch my breath. I was pretty sure I'd seen a bench out here somewhere, but not finding it, I turned around a set of shrubs to claim a boulder. I knew where that was. I'd found it a few times today, and all by accident.

Once my rump hit the stone, I kicked my legs out before me, leaned back on my hands, and gulped for a little air. It didn't take long before Aspen found me like that - and she looked worried. Coming over, she crouched down by my knees.

"I'm so sorry," she said, clasping my leg. "I completely forgot. I was just having fun, and you kept up, and I didn't think about the stories of us dancing humans to death. Please tell me you're ok?"

"I'm fine," I promised, huffing out a weary laugh. "Little hot and sweaty, but that's it. I was having fun too."

"I just don't want to hurt you," she admitted, reaching up to push back my sweaty hair. "I kinda like you, Rain."

I glanced over to find her eyes waiting for something. She looked worried, so I smiled. Like that was some kind of signal, she pushed up and in, her hand finding the side of my face a moment before her lips took mine. Shocked, I gasped, and her tongue took the invitation. The kiss was hot, fast, and the most passionate thing I could imagine, but I had no idea what to do! This was Aspen. She was my friend. I'd never kissed a *girl* before!

I tensed and she felt it. I didn't push her away or scream. I simply froze. Immediately, Aspen pulled back, pushing to her feet in a single motion.

"I thought..." She took a step back. Then another. "Shit. I just ruined everything!"

She spun and was gone. There was no flight, no mad dash through the plants. Aspen just took one step and vanished in the most fae escape I'd ever imagined. I hadn't even had the chance to say a thing, and I wasn't sure what I would've said. Instead, I lifted my hand to my lips, right where she'd kissed me so hard.

The kiss had lasted a split second, but her lips had been so soft, nothing like a guy's. Her touch had been so tender. Nothing like a guy's. She smelled like honeysuckle and a fresh breeze. She looked at me like she saw me, not a conquest. All of those things were so different, and again, nothing like a guy.

Aspen Fox liked me like *that*, and I didn't know what to do about it. She was so pretty, so different from anyone I'd ever known before, but was I even into girls? It didn't bother me if she was, and I couldn't care less about Liam having a boyfriend. I was cool with anyone being with whoever they wanted. And I'd seen a few gay and lesbian couples around campus, but I'd always chased guys. I noticed *guys*! I could tell the girls here were pretty, but Harper was a bitch and Aspen was my suitemate.

I had no idea what any of this meant, so I sat there a little longer with my fingers resting against my lower lip. Long enough I must've looked dazed or something, because Keir found me like that. Heading through the atrium, he angled his path toward me, stopping by my feet when I didn't look up.

"Rain?"

Finally, I pulled my hand away and realized he was waiting for me. "Yeah?"

"You drunk on that stuff?"

"Buzzed," I admitted. "And you forgot to warn me about dancing with the fae."

"Ah." But he crossed his arms over his chest. "Pretty sure that's not your only problem."

"Just trying to decide if I should have a shower before dinner," I told him. "And who I'm going to eat with, and how much it sucks to not know what the hell is going on."

"I usually sit near the back," he said. "Closer to the doors to the gym. If you ever want to, you're welcome to sit with me. I'll even introduce you to my friends. Believe it or not, I have some, but I'm voting for a shower first." He grinned. "You're a mess, and the last thing you need is anyone thinking you earned that hot and bothered look doing something else."

"Good point," I agreed, pushing to my feet. Then I paused. "Hey, Keir?"

"Mm?"

"I yelled at Torian for being a dick. I mean, just so you know."

He chuckled. "Believe it or not, I'm not worried about Torian Hunt, but I'm still glad to hear it." Then he stepped the other way, aiming for the boys' side doors. "Shower, Rain. I dunno, get pretty or something."

"I'm always pretty," I teased, turning to leave.

But he called after me, "You are. Kinda my point."

That should've been thrilling. Keir was everything a girl wanted in a guy. I knew he wasn't lying, because he couldn't. I should have a giddy feeling in my chest and butterflies in my stomach. Instead, my mind immediately jumped back to Aspen's lips on mine. Her hand pressing against my cheek. The way she'd said she liked me - and how I now realized that meant a very different kind of "like" than I'd first thought.

As I headed up to my room, I tried to make sense of what I felt. It was all a jumble, tangling up with itself in my head. I always had fun when I was with Aspen. I thought she was beautiful. I owed her for getting me into Silver Oaks. I'd just never kissed a girl before. I liked that she liked me, but did that mean I liked her back?

Most of all, what was I supposed to do now?

Not worry about it, I decided. Grabbing a quick shower, I pulled on an old tee and a pair of yoga pants. It was the weekend, so we were given a lot more leeway on what we could wear, and this was comfortable. My hair went into a messy bun, and I didn't bother with makeup. I was honestly too hungry.

But when I walked into the dining hall a few minutes later, I realized everyone was down here. Most of them were wearing casual clothes, like me. Sadly, that meant there wasn't much empty space. Apparently this was the official dinner hour. I usually ate a little later, which meant I could typically find a table all to myself.

Or maybe it was because we'd been partying all day? Either way, step one was to get myself a meal. Moving into the line, I walked past the options, looking for something good. I noticed the large array of fresh fruit, though. Sure, it had always been there, but I'd assumed it was a healthy thing, not a fae thing.

I went with a vegetarian pasta, and the server was just passing back my plate when, of all people, Wilder stepped in beside me. He'd completely cut the line, but no one complained. Yet when I turned to get myself a drink, he followed me.

"You're eating with us."

I looked down at my meal. "Uh, you sure about that? It's not fruit."

He moved around me while I filled my cup from the dispenser. "Aspen's worried about something. You vanished. She said she thinks she danced you too hard. Tor's grilling her because she won't let him *see*. Hawke's grumpy. Come eat with us?" Wilder begged. "Please spare my sanity?"

"I was going to eat with Keir," I admitted.

The guy gave me an exasperated look. "What is going on?"

"Nothing," I insisted, but I saw him wince.

"Try that again," he told me.

"None of your business."

Wilder actually laughed. "You're a little too good at this. Rain, most people would jump at the chance to be invited to our table. You're formally invited. Come sit with the court and amuse our little princess?"

"Ok!" I relented, gesturing for him to lead the way.

Because it wasn't that I didn't want to. I wasn't mad at Aspen. My problem was I didn't know how to act or what to say now. I wasn't sure how I felt about that kiss, and things would be super weird, but clearly Aspen hadn't said anything either. Still, the fact Wilder was worried about her and Torian was grilling her meant she needed a little backup. Aspen was still my friend, and friends stood beside each other, so I was going to do this.

When I made it to the table, I saw the collection of sweets and fruit. Overly aware of what was on my plate, I took a seat directly across from Torian and Aspen. Basically, the furthest from the fae I could get. There was an empty chair between me and Wilder. Same thing on the other side with Hawke.

"You look clean," Hawke immediately teased.

"I smelled *very* bad," I explained. "I figured that if I didn't get a shower, my hair would be crusty when it dried."

"Please tell me you're ok?" Aspen asked.

I glanced up out of habit, and our eyes met. She was worried. No, terrified was a better word. I jiggled my head in a nod, not wanting to actually say anything, because I wasn't sure. The two of us knew she wasn't talking about me dancing too much. She meant the kiss, and yeah, I was ok. Confused, but ok.

"I'm not in that bad shape, I promise," I told them all - which was true. "No one danced me into the ground, let alone to death. No one hurt me." I glanced at Aspen again. "I just didn't know what to expect."

"So, saying we should have more dance parties on the weekends?" Torian asked.

"Dunno," I said, shifting my attention to him. "I made a few new friends, and Keir invited me to eat with him too. Looks like I have options."

Hawke sucked in a breath. "She doesn't know she's pushing your buttons, Tor."

"She does," Torian said, watching me. "I'm also missing something, and I'm not sure what it is."

I just pointed at my food. "Still disgusting?"

"No meat," Wilder said. "It's weird, but not disgusting."

So I bent and took a bite, trying hard not to care if they were watching me. "I'm kinda curious how you managed to eat in foster homes?"

"Vegetarians," Hawke explained.

"Picky," Torian said.

I nodded. "And is there a reason Liam doesn't simply ask about that during his interviews with foster kids?"

It was Aspen who answered, her voice a bit softer than usual. "Faelings - the half-bloods or less - eat like you. Foundlings are more common than you can imagine. I think at least half the school came from the foster system."

"Changelings, right?" I asked.

Wilder shook his head. "We were changelings. Fae children slipped into the world and lost among humans. Foundlings are those from here."

"Because that's not confusing at all," I said.

"It's easy," he assured me. "Changelings from Faerie. Foundlings from Earth. How much fae blood they have isn't important."

"So, you're all changelings then?"

Around the table, they nodded. "We spent different amounts of time in the system," Hawke explained, "but yeah. I think Aspen was in the longest."

"Since I was five," she admitted. "My guardian was killed, and so it made sense. I never thought to look for a fae community."

"But I was looking for you," Torian said. "I knew you were out there somewhere."

I pointed between them. "Did the foster system name you or something?"

"No, why?" Torian asked.

"Hunt and Fox? You're siblings, but don't have the same last name. Part of why I thought you were a couple, you know."

"Uh..." Torian looked over at Aspen.

She just shrugged. "Not our real names, Rain. That's why everyone from Faerie has these pretty names. We pick them. Our real names have too much power over us, so we leave them behind. They also don't blend in."

"Oh." Because what else could I say?

The guys went on about how it was a common practice, and how knowing someone's full, real name could be used against them. I heard them, but I found myself glancing over to Aspen while they talked. She didn't look back, but I could tell she knew I was watching her.

I just couldn't stop thinking about how she'd kissed me. Was I bisexual? Had I liked it? Would this make Harper and the jesters target me the way they had her? Not that iron would hurt me, but I had a feeling there were a lot of other things which would. Most of all, why couldn't I stop thinking about it?

About *her*.

It distracted me enough that it wasn't until I was done eating when I realized the entire table of jesters was staring at me. I was sitting with the court. No one sat with the court, and all four of them were talking to me. I hadn't pushed myself in. It was clear I'd been invited. And staring right at me was Harper, watching it all.

Well, it seemed I'd made an enemy. Too bad for her, I had bigger things to worry about. Namely, whether or not I'd lost my best friend before I really got her as one.

Chapter Thirty-Three

Things were awkward that weekend. On Sunday, I went to use the shower just as Aspen came out. We met in the pass-through area in front of the sinks - and she was wearing nothing but a towel. Our eyes met and we both looked away quickly. She blushed, which made me blush, but it was like neither of us knew what to say. I was convinced she was mad at me, or upset, or disappointed. Something.

Then, Monday in our math class, she passed me a Pixy Stix. For a brief moment, our fingers brushed. An innocent and accidental gesture, but it felt like a zap of electricity straight up my arm. I smiled. She smiled. That was it. I couldn't even explain how huge of a moment it was, but I felt it.

For the rest of the day, I kept thinking about that touch. Then about the kiss in the garden. I liked it, but I wasn't sure if I liked the boost to my ego, the simple fact someone liked me, or if I actually liked her as more than a friend.

Because Aspen was beautiful. She had the type of charisma that made her stand out in a crowd. Something about her felt almost infectious, as if she drew my eyes right to her. Now, after that kiss, I kept thinking about more. About the plant she'd given me, the way she'd pushed back my hair, and how she was always on my side.

I just liked her - but like was such a fickle word. I felt stupid, giddy, and most of all confused. I'd never kissed a girl before. It certainly hadn't been disgusting, but did I want to do it again? More? Needless to say, by the time we got to lunch, I ended up stealing glances at her all through my vegetarian meal. Even worse, Wilder noticed.

I was seventeen years old. I'd been to dozens of schools - literally - and I'd never been attracted to a girl before, so this had to be a fae thing. Maybe some fae magic? A compulsion? I'd heard people mention those, and I knew Enticement was one of the many magical specialties they could have. Because I had none of that, I'd focused on learning the things which actually mattered to me every day. Things like how not to say thank you to anyone.

But my distraction made me take a beating in Self-Defense. The faeling girl I'd been paired with had no intention of going easy on me. She attacked, forcing me to dodge and evade, but my brain kept getting stuck on my suitemate. The way Aspen had smiled at me so shyly. Aspen wasn't a shy girl, but she'd turned that way around me ever since we'd kissed, and I kinda liked it.

When we broke to get ready for my last class of the day, Offensive Combat, Bracken pulled me aside. "Rain, I want you to work with Keir today."

"Ok, why?" I asked.

The combat instructor just stared at me. For a little too long, he said nothing. Then, "Whatever is distracting you is going to get you hurt. At least with Keir, I know he won't break anything. Liam would not take it well if you got hurt. But I'm hoping that maybe you'll decide to talk to someone. I don't even care who."

Which was how the pair of us ended up alone in one of the non-mirrored training rooms. Keir held a pair of martial arts sticks. Another set waited in the middle of the room. When I walked in, he gestured for me to close the door, making this session private.

"You seem to have Bracken worried," he said. "I was told to go easy on you."

"Pretty sure that's not going to help," I grumbled as I picked up the sticks and tested their weight.

"What happened between the brave and brazen savior on Friday and this distracted and flighty girl today?" He pushed away from the wall. "Swing at me while you talk."

"It's nothing," I said.

So he took a poke at my side with his stick, making me block it. "Lie. Try again."

"How about none of your business?" I asked, striking out at his elbow in one of the few moves I knew.

He simply twitched his arm, proving he was much more skilled at this than me. "I'm guessing you had a wild make-out session with..." His eyes narrowed. "Torian Hunt?"

"No," I said, throwing my best combat moves at him.

Of course, he dodged them without even trying. "Hawke Woods?"

"No," I said again, this time aiming for his legs.

So he decided to make me sweat a little. Three hits came at my chest, each one forcing me to focus to get away from them. I got the first two, but the third he managed to just poke my belly. I nodded to show he connected, so Keir stepped back and flicked a pair of fingers around a hilt, taunting me to come at him harder.

"Must be Wilder Reed then." Thrusting out his lower lip, Keir nodded. "Not a bad choice from the court."

"Not Wilder either," I said.

"Huh." He smacked one of my sticks, forcing me into motion. "Aspen Fox."

I swung, trying to catch him off guard, but that was pointless. I'd had exactly one week of weapon training. Keir had been raised on this stuff. I knew he'd been taking Bracken's classes since he got to Silver Oaks, which meant at least three years, maybe four. I kinda got the impression he'd been sparring with his family even longer.

My sticks swung for his arms, his legs, his chest, and even his head. The clack of our weapons connecting turned into a nice rhythm, and Keir moved me around the room, forcing my feet to work as much as my hands. For just a moment, he had my complete attention, and my week of practice began to fall into place.

All the hits at the training dummy had taught my body how to move. His pressure engaged the rest of me. What had started as some wild flailing was quickly becoming a little more. My sticks got closer to where I wanted, my brain began to see the openings and opportunities he left. Then I finally managed to get a tap on his thigh. He blocked most of it, but I still saw him wince when my stick thumped him.

"It's Aspen," he said, waving me off. "So you're into girls?"

"No!" I insisted.

He stopped hard. Those nearly violet eyes of his weighed me, then he said softly, "That's the truth."

"Yeah, it is," I grumbled.

"Or you *think* it is," he corrected. "Rain, we only hear the deception. If you believe something is real, even if you were deceived, it feels like the truth to me. But let me ask you this. If you're not into girls, then why has your mind been so scattered today that even Bracken noticed?"

"Because he's a good teacher?" I guessed.

"So, you don't want to talk about this?" Keir asked, stepping back and towing me into the center again.

I just sighed. "And say what?"

"Well, you could start with what happened," he offered.

"But that's the thing. I can't," I told him. "Anything I say to you will get to someone else, and then someone else, right up until it's back to Harper or Katrina, and they'll be trying to brand her with keychains again!"

In two steps, he closed the distance between us, peeling both sticks from my hands without trying. After tossing the weapons out of my reach, Keir stood there, making me look at him. Gently, he reached up and pushed a stray strand of hair away from my cheek.

"I am not a jester. I'm also not in the court." Then he tilted my face up a little more. "I give you my word, with no conditions, that I will not share your secrets without your direct permission."

There was a tingling in the contact between us. Some sensation that was more than my imagination. It trembled in the air around us, yet it ended where his skin touched mine. What he'd said was important. It was big, and I'd felt it.

"What was that?" I breathed.

"A vow," he explained. "Fae are careful about promises for that reason, Rain. This one, I think I can make."

"Why?" I asked. "What do you even care? I'm just the boring human girl who does nothing fancy."

"Mm..." He wobbled his head from side to side like I didn't have that quite right. "You do a lot of things fancy. You're human, but that gives you a different set of skills. It also gives you an allure of 'other' to us fae. Plus, you're..."

"Interesting," I finished for him.

"A good word, but not the one I was going for," he assured me. "I was going to say appealing. See, the jesters are all trying to prove themselves. The problem is, they're judging by the wrong yardstick. They want to be fae. They can't be, because they're part human. It's like a fish wishing it were a bird. You, however, are a human trying to be a human among fae. It's oddly refreshing."

"So, I'm like an animal in a zoo or something?" Because I wasn't sure I liked that.

Keir just laughed. "No. You're like a friend, Rain. There's this rawness about you. I won't deny the curiosity, though. It's definitely there. Those pretty brown eyes are nice, too. So, since I've given you that much honesty, don't you think you owe me at least a little back?"

"That's manipulation," I pointed out.

He leaned in. "I'm fae. Of course it is. Talk, Rain. What happened with Aspen?"

He was right. I knew he was, so I simply gave in. "She kissed me in the atrium. She said she liked me, I thought she meant friend, and I don't even remember what I said back, if anything, but she kissed me."

"Ok, and now it's awkward?" he asked.

I looked away, my hand moving to my lips. "I don't know how to know if I liked it."

"Yeah, well, I do." He stepped back, moving to pick up all four of our sticks. "See the way you touched the memory of her lips on yours? The way your mind refuses to settle? Isn't that how you feel when you have a crush on a guy?"

"But I've never been into girls before," I pointed out.

He came back, offering my sticks to me. "So?"

"But I'm not a lesbian. I *like* guys!"

"And?" he asked, a smugness to his tone.

I just groaned, knowing he was pushing me. "She's supposed to be my best friend, Keir. Never mind that we live in the same suite! Talk about awkward. I mean, I walked into the bathroom just as she was leaving the shower area. We're going to bump into each other, and I don't know what to say!"

He grinned deviously. "Yeah, I'd love to see that. Even better, both of you in that shower together. Maybe a little mutual washing? Lots of suds."

I rolled my eyes at him. "So now you're all team Aspen? What happened to the flirting, hm?"

He made a gesture with his stick almost like a backwards circle. "I'd like to remind you that you just said you like guys. This, however, is a separate issue. See, this girl I'm into has this problem, and I'm all about the long, deep, and meaningful conversations."

"About me having a crush on someone else?" I scoffed.

But Keir pointed his stick right at me. "And she admits it!"

"No, I meant hypothetically," I tried.

His lips curled into that lopsided smirk he did so well. "Lie."

"Fuck you, Keir," I snarled, turning for the door.

But he grabbed my arm, spinning me back to face him. "Hit me. Don't run from me. Use those sticks and beat the frustration out. Pretty sure I can block anything you'll throw, and if I don't, well, healing is one of my skills." Then he gestured for me to come at him. "You like the idea of having kissed a girl, right? All exciting and new and dangerous?"

"Taboo," I agreed, smacking at him.

He blocked with a loud clack. "And Aspen is beautiful. I mean, you can't deny that. She's also powerful, which is what most people would be chasing - but not you. Ever think that's why she's so drawn to you?"

Our weapons kept moving. Not as fast as before, but this was now a consistent pace I could actually keep up. It was a lot like the sets Bracken had given me for the dummy last week. I leaned into the pattern, letting my muscles move from memory, and actually thought about what he was saying.

"I don't know if I like her or if I'm just flustered," I finally admitted. "Mostly, I'm freaking out about our friendship."

"Truth," he said. "So let's break it down. Do you still like hanging out with her?"

"Yes."

He twitched to evade a shot that was a little too close. "Do you think she's pretty?"

"Definitely," I agreed. "I wish I looked like her."

"I happen to like how you look just as much," he assured me. "Do you think her tits are nice? Maybe her ass is sexy?"

"No," I said. "Well, not like that. I'm not some guy who wants to jerk off to her. I think she's nice, though. She's probably the most caring person I've ever met, but she doesn't know how to show it. Torian said something about her being untamed in a way, and it fits. She gave me a plant my first day. She raged at Liam to make them let me come here. Like, she's just so... real, you know? I was starting to think of her as my best friend."

"So be her friend," he said. "Did the kiss disgust you?"

"No," I admitted. "It was more shocking. I just didn't expect it."

"Did you like it?" he asked next.

"That's what I've been trying to figure out!" I snapped. "I don't know! I mean, girls kiss nothing like guys. Well, at least she doesn't. It's kinda weird."

"How do guys kiss?" he asked, refusing to let up with the swords.

My arms were getting tired, but I pushed through it. "Hard. Deep. Guys pull girls against them, take what they want, and feel so strong. I kinda like that part."

"How does she kiss?" he asked next.

Our weapons collided over and over while I thought about that. "Soft," I finally said. "She's just smaller. Her lips feel completely different. Her tongue didn't thrust like some sexual proxy, you know? More of a caress and swirl. Like, tender."

He waved me down, lowering his weapons. "Would you let her kiss you again?"

"Maybe?" I scrunched up my face, hoping that wasn't the wrong answer.

"That felt like an untruth," he pointed out. "Would you, Rain? No judgment. I'm just asking."

"Yeah, I think so, but I could be wrong."

He just nodded. "Truth. So stop worrying about it. Be Aspen's friend. If you end up cuddling, then see how it goes. If you kiss her, then let it happen."

I huffed at him. "And you're all for this because you're hoping for some threesome, right?"

"And you're assuming my opinion matters at all?" he countered. "Rain, before Friday, I suspected Aspen wasn't into guys, but it's not open knowledge. Back in Faerie? It's normal for most people to enjoy both sexes. Being gay is as uncommon as being straight. Me thinking two beautiful women together is appealing is no different from you thinking two sexy men are appealing. It's normal. It's natural. Two is better than one, after all. Right?"

"Yeah, I guess?" I admitted. "But guys are always pushing girls to be in a threesome for them. You know, whether they like it or not. That whole thing. Like seriously objectifying us."

"Trust me, I know," he assured me. "I was born on Earth. I grew up with those guys, and I know it's what you're expecting, so I'll tease you about it. Why? Because when I say it, you stop and think. Because the idea of you with Aspen *is* appealing, but probably not for the reasons you think."

"Then why?" I shot back.

He murmured, clearly choosing his words. "For the fae, pleasures of the flesh are one thing. Pleasures of the mind are another. Pleasures of the heart are a third. Responsibilities of commitment - fae marriages - are something completely separate. They are not exclusive of each other, and each has its own appeal."

"Ok?" Because now I was lost.

He chuckled softly. "I'm saying I don't see a conflict with my friend chasing something that pleases her. I don't feel like I should have to hide my approval of your choices, but you clearly do. Rain, I'm saying I like you, but I also *like* you. Believe it or not, my favorite things are these long, deep conversations. Well, and the bashing each other with sticks. I'm saying I can be your friend. I promise it doesn't bother me at all to talk about some cute fae girl - with a cute human one."

I just nodded. "Am I going to be in your debt for this?"

"Yep. For being willing to listen to you, I expect you to repay me by talking to me." Then he gestured to the sticks again. "I think it's a fair exchange. Now, are you ready for another round? I'm going to hit back this time."

"Deal," I told him, lifting my sticks back into position. "For both."

Chapter Thirty-Four

Keir wore my ass out. The guy pushed me hard and kept me talking for the rest of the class. The best part was that it helped - both the swordsmanship and the mental crap I was stuck on. And the more I told him, the more sweet words of wisdom he had. At one point, he mentioned that it didn't matter if I was straight, a lesbian, or something else. I was me, and liking someone wasn't ever guaranteed. Being straight didn't mean I'd be into every guy in the world, did it? Being excited about a kiss didn't mean I had to be more to Aspen than a friend.

It was such an obvious thing, and yet hearing him say it made me feel so much better. When the last bell rang and we put our weapons away, I actually felt like I had my head on straight. Keir just patted my back and turned me toward the door, only for us to find Bracken leaning against the wall on the other side.

"So?" he asked, looking at Keir.

Keir smiled at me. "Being new at a fae school is easier said than done. She's adjusting. We worked through it."

"Good," Bracken said, turning his attention on me. "If, at any time, you need help or advice, I am here to talk. I also know that sometimes bashing it out helps more. Keir has keys to the gym, and since he's a junior, he's allowed out here as late as he wants. I'll make sure both of you are cleared for after-hours use. If it's after curfew, Rain, you'll have to get permission from me or Liam first, ok?"

"Easy," I agreed.

"Sounds like I just got a promotion," Keir teased.

Bracken just chuckled. "If you truly want to be my teaching assistant next year, consider this your first student assignment. I'm thinking of your future."

"And hers," Keir said.

Bracken lifted one shoulder like he was almost dismissing that. "Need to get her caught up to the others. It's a good excuse."

Keir patted the man's shoulder. "Yep, it is. So you know, I'm walking Rain back to the dorms."

I followed beside him until we were out of Bracken's hearing. "Oh, you're just taking that onto yourself, huh? Because I might not make it back on my own?"

He grunted, clearly unimpressed. "So Bracken doesn't try to make me help clean. I'm using you, Rain. Get used to it."

"Good to know," I teased, grabbing my coat.

We each got dressed against the winter in silence. Keir looked back twice, checking on Bracken, and then we left. Yet the moment we were outside, he moved to walk at my shoulder again.

"Sounds like Bracken thinks you have potential, you know," he pointed out.

"Mhm." I had a feeling the man was just being nice. "Sounds like you plan on becoming the teacher's pet. Trying to get an easy A or something?"

"No," he assured me. "I'm honestly hoping to become a weapons instructor one day. The gym could hold twice as many classes, but most people focus on the magic instead of the combat. Who needs a sword in this modern world of yours, right? Who wants to take a gym class? And yet, the Hunt keeps coming back. Some things aren't scared of human police or lead bullets. We fae brought things into your world that someone has to stop."

"How often does the Hunt come?" I asked.

"Too often," he said. "Usually about once each - " Then he ducked. "Fucking bird!"

I turned to see a crow land just on the other side of him. This time, however, the bird didn't caw. For all I knew, it was the same one as last time, and it seemed to like picking on Keir. I bit my lips, trying hard not to laugh.

"Did you piss off the crows?" I teased. "You know they recognize faces, right? Upset one and all the rest will make your life hell."

"I didn't do a damned thing to - "

"Jack!" the bird croaked.

My heart stopped in my chest, and I gave the bird my complete attention. "What? Hey, birdy... Did you just caw at us?"

"Jack!" it said again, hopping toward me. "Jack, Jack, Jack Jack!"

"It fucking talks?" Keir asked.

I glanced back at him, then to the crow again. "So, that's not just a normal crow sound?"

"You're the fucking crow expert, Rain," he reminded me. "How the fuck do I know? But it sure sounds like the damned thing thinks its name is Jack."

"Jack!" the crow said again, taking to the air to come right at me.

I went to throw my arms before my face, but the crow wasn't trying to attack me. Instead, I felt its little feet close on a spot just above my wrist, and then Jack folded his wings and simply let me hold him. He was actually kinda heavy. And big. And black. Not to mention right in front of my face.

"There's no way you're the same crow from my foster home," I said softly, daring to reach up and pet the thing's back.

The bird made a clacking noise and leaned into my caress. His little eyelids closed, and I was convinced the bird looked happy. When I stopped, it ruffled its feathers and leaned toward me just a bit more.

"Jack," it croaked, making it sound like an order.

"Is that your name, bud?" I asked. When the bird nodded its head quickly, I almost dropped my arm. "And I'm guessing you're a 'he' huh?"

Jack nodded again, although that probably wasn't the right word. It was more that he slung his bill up and down as fast as he could. Still, he got the point across - or it was a great coincidence. I decided to test it.

"Are you just here trying to scare me, Jack?" I asked.

The thing tilted its head, blinked, and then made a no gesture, much like shaking its head. I hadn't expected that. Oh, I'd tried, but I'd honestly expected the bird to just nod again, some avian antic my human brain was trying to turn into my language. The fact Jack seemed to say yes and no on command? Or at least gesture in a way that meant such things? Mind. Blown.

"Keir?" I asked. "Do weird things like this happen a lot around here?"

"No," he assured me. "I mean, I've seen some birds around, but mostly like, robins, and usually when Sheeba - Bracken's cat - catches one."

"When did the crows come here?" I asked.

"Jack!" the bird announced.

Keir chuckled at that. "Um, couple of weeks ago?"

Which was about when I'd moved here. There was no way this was the same bird, was it? The Sparks lived on the other side of Plainsboro, which was at least half an hour away by car. Then again, cars were stuck to roads, and there was a saying about "as the crow flies" for a reason.

"Jack?" I asked. "Did you follow me to Silver Oaks?"

He nodded again, bigger this time. Then he bent to nibble one of my fingers. I flinched, his talons gripped my arms and his wings flared, but the bird didn't fly away. He also didn't bite me. It was almost like he was looking for... Food. I'd fed him bread! I'd made friends with this bird when I'd given it a bookmark and some treats.

"I don't have any bread, buddy," I told him. "But when I come to class tomorrow, I'll bring some, ok?"

The bird tilted its head the other way. "Jack?"

"For Jack," I agreed, hoping that was what he meant.

Then the crow cawed and took off. My entire arm was shoved down at the force of his lift off, but it was kinda cool. That was a big crow, and he looked like he was in good shape. The one at the Sparks' place had been the same, but most crows were big, and they were always black. I couldn't exactly tell them apart that well.

Still, I watched Jack fly over the gym and find a spot in one of the large evergreen trees behind it. The ones that looked right over the building, which meant he could see us walking between the institute and the gym. Eerie. Sure, it was probably a coincidence, but a strange one!

"I think you have a friend," Keir teased.

I just blew out a breath and began walking back towards the dorms, not surprised when he followed at my side. "So, the reason I'm here is because a crow flew into my foster family's house. I got it calmed down and outside, but they thought it was witchcraft or something and called my caseworker."

"Liam," he realized.

"Mhm," I agreed. "Thing is, there was this crow that kept coming to my bedroom window. I mean, there were iron bars on it..." I debated mentioning how Torian was the reason for those, then decided to skip that part. "Well, the crow said 'Jack,' just like that one. I assumed he'd been socialized by people. Maybe injured and rehabilitated or something. Now he's here?"

"So sure it's the same crow?" Keir asked.

"Not at all," I assured him. "It's just that while they make some noises, saying 'Jack' isn't one. To have two crows, in the same town, both do it? Did someone named Jack rehab a lot of crows or something?"

Keir pulled in a breath, shifting just a little closer so he could lower his voice. "So, this might not be the advice you want, but I think you should ask Aspen. She knows about a lot of the conservation stuff, or how to find it."

"Yeah?"

He just nodded. "Yeah. Besides, you two do need to talk. Avoiding her isn't going to make things any less awkward, and the longer you take, the more weird it will be."

"Why are you being so cool about all of this?" I finally asked, turning to face him as my feet stalled out.

He reached up, running his fingers through his golden hair. For a little too long, he didn't answer, but the expression on his face said he wasn't avoiding my question. Rather, the guy was trying to figure out what to say to me.

"All of this?" he finally asked. "Do you mean the magic taught in class here? Do you mean the way we all flinch from iron? The magical plants growing in the atrium we all pretend are just tropical exotics to outsiders? Rain, a crow is pretty normal. A problem with a suitemate or someone liking you? Just as normal."

"But why are you, I dunno, helping me?"

He stepped in a little closer. "Have I been too subtle? I like you, Rain. You're cute. You're this strange mix of too serious and so naive about all of this, and I can't get enough of hearing the awe in your voice. I like you, and it only took me two seconds to figure out you aren't the kind of girl to beg for attention." He ducked his head a bit. "That only makes me more interested."

"So you're being cool about the weird crow stuff and the weird suitemate stuff because it makes me interesting?" Yep, no matter how many ways I looked at that, it did not compute.

"I have a different yardstick to measure by," he countered. "The crow thing? Maybe the magic here is affecting the local animals? Maybe the same reason we fae find you interesting applies to those birds. They used to cross the gates, you know. One of the few animals found in both worlds."

"Really?"

Keir nodded. "Kinda why I think Aspen is a better resource for this than me. I'd say Torian, but..." He made a face. "I'm not opposed to you thinking he's a dick."

"So you *are* hoping for a threesome," I realized.

Keir caught my arm. "I am *not*. Aspen said she's a lesbian. I may be a guy, but I get what that means: not gonna happen. So take everything you know about human guys and flush it, Rain. I'm not human. I will never be human. Neither will Torian, Wilder, or Hawke. For some reason, you keep being pulled toward those of us who are pure-blood, while the part-bloods despise you. Well, as a general rule. I'm sure some are ok with you, but the jesters *definitely* hate you. And in the middle of all of this is one pretty girl who doesn't say thank you. Who doesn't flinch when I speak the truth or call her out on lies. Who isn't scared of her suitemate's magic."

"I take it that's not normal?" I asked.

"Nothing about you is normal," he admitted. "You're so close you can pass for it if you tried, but there are all these little things. The plants reach for you. The birds come to you. Are you pulling at us as well? You are something new, and new is interesting. You're beautiful, smart, and bold in a way I can't get enough of. I'm helping you because I can't stop thinking about you. Is that honest enough to ease your worries?"

"Yeah," I breathed. "It's just kinda weird because I've only been here a little over two weeks."

"I didn't say I was in love with you," he pointed out. "I said I like you. I have a crush on the new girl." He turned me back toward the dorms and leaned in toward my ear. "And I think the new girl smiles a lot when she looks at me. Makes me wonder if she might have a crush on the 'other' pure-blood fae. I also don't expect an answer to that." He moved his hands to my shoulders, guiding me from behind. "After all, I don't want to make things weird. Kinda sounds like you have enough to worry about with Aspen."

I just ducked my head and let him steer me to the doors at the back of the building. "Somehow, you don't make this weird," I admitted as I reached out to open one.

He followed me in, then reached over to push the button for my elevator. "Friends first," he told me. "That's all I'm going for. I just think it's nice to know someone who gets as excited about slinging around those sticks as I do. But that's the thing, Rain. Friends first." And he glanced up pointedly, indicating my suitemate. "And if you need an ear, I'm in room D412. Good luck. Hope she can help with your bird."

With that, he turned away, walking off just as the elevator dinged to announce the car had arrived.

Chapter Thirty-Five

I made it to my room, thinking Keir had a really good idea. First, the weird crow thing was an excuse to talk. Second, friends first was a pretty smart way of thinking about this. For both him and Aspen. The hard part was how to start this talk. I was mulling over a few ideas when I stepped inside my room - and saw a new plant on my desk, just inside the door.

This one was small, blue, and covered in little pink flowers. It was clearly not like anything found on Earth. I also knew it was from Aspen. I never locked the door that led to the bathroom. I hadn't felt the need to, with Aspen on the other side. It had been my way of encouraging her to visit, and clearly she had.

Glancing back, I saw that not only was my door open to the bathroom, but on the other side, hers was as well. Anxiety hit me like a wave, so I reached out to pet the plant, hoping for a little encouragement. She'd gifted me another of her beloved flowers, so she couldn't be mad at me, right? This was like her way of apologizing, or saying we needed to talk, or something?

Pulling in a steadying breath, I decided to just get it over with.

Still, when I turned for the bathroom door, it felt like the distance between me and it grew. I was sweaty from my weapons class. Pulling off my coat, I dropped it on the back of the chair and debated changing, but that would only delay the inevitable. The distance hadn't grown, my nervousness had - and I was not going to wimp out now.

I marched forward with all the determination I could muster. From the bathroom, I could see her feet on her bed, so I paused on her side and tapped at the door frame. Immediately, she twitched, shifting things around out of sight before sitting up.

"Yeah?"

"Hey," I said, peeking my head into her room. "I saw the flower. I also wanted to ask how often I should water Glow."

"The Moon Shine will roll up its leaves when it needs attention," she explained. "The Avalon Petticoat will want some once a week. I usually do the weekends."

"Cool," I said. "I'll learn how to grow them one day. Um..." I shifted in place, feeling my pulse racing. "So, I also wondered if you knew anything about crows, and I kinda wanted to, um, apologize for Saturday."

"You can come in," she told me, moving to sit on the side of her bed and looking about as nervous as I felt.

So I crossed the threshold and stepped into her room. "I didn't, uh, expect that. You to kiss me, I mean."

She nodded, staring at her hands in her lap. "I don't know what I was thinking. I'm not sure I *was*. You were just - " She stopped, her eyes jumping up. "I like being your friend, Rain."

So I moved to sit on the bed beside her, turned so I was facing her. "I like being your friend too, Aspen. I'm not mad you kissed me. I'm really not. I'm just confused."

She nodded. "I hate myself for that."

"No," I breathed, reaching over for her hand. "Aspen, I've never kissed a girl before."

"Because you're straight," she said. "Figured that out. It's just you're so open and accepting. You never make me feel like it's weird for you, so I just hoped that maybe..."

"It's not weird," I promised. "Well, not weird that you like girls. I..." I laughed because we were both doing the same thing. Stammering, basically. "I like you, Aspen. I just don't know what kind of like it is, and I don't really know you that well. You're like this icon of the perfect girl. The popular one I always wanted to be, you know? And then you keep being nice to me, and I like it. I like when you share your Pixy Stix with me, and I keep thinking about you kissing me."

"Bad?" she asked.

I shook my head. "Confused. See, I kinda like someone else too."

Her eyes narrowed. "Keir, right?"

I jiggled my head. "He's been really nice. I just know Torian hates him, and you and Torian seem to be inseparable, so I have no clue what I'm doing here. Not the social stuff, not the romance stuff, or any of it. I'm just trying to keep up with the magical things, and I'm not saying I don't want to."

"Then what are you saying?" she asked, her voice almost timid.

"That I'm a mess, and I know I want to be friends. I'm not ruling anything else out, but I *do* think of you as my best friend."

"Keir's cute," she pointed out. "Kinda low-born, and his magic is pathetic..."

I laughed, feeling all my tension vanish as she teased me. "Yeah, and this other person I'm kinda thinking about has some insane magic."

"Torian?" she asked.

"You," I breathed, the word almost without sound.

I saw her swallow, and those glacial eyes of hers met mine. The tip of her tongue darted out to moisten her lips, then the corners flickered back. It wasn't a smile, but it looked like, if she was a bit less nervous, it would've been.

Her thumb slid over the back of my hand. "I don't want to lose my new best friend."

"Me either," I agreed. "I'm just saying I'm ok with whatever this is. Friends with hand holding. I kinda like it when you say nice things about me. I think I liked when you kissed me, but I was too shocked, you know? Basically, I'm not ruling anything out."

"This isn't why I told them to let you into the school," she told me. "I just need you to know that."

"I know. I also don't care," I promised, reaching up to cup the side of her face. "I don't want you to ever stop being you. Flirty you. Angry you. Plant-loving you. I like you because you're you."

Moisture began to pool in her large, blue eyes. "I'm so tired of hiding everything," she mumbled. "All the things. Torian warned me about how much people hate Winter magic, too. They think that because my magic is different from theirs, I'm evil, or pathetic, or something. Girls turn their noses up at me, you know? And then Ms. Rhodes made it clear I couldn't talk about my mom or my magic. I just..." She blinked, trying to hold back the tears. "All I've had are my plants and the guys, and they're always over there while I have to be here. Alone!"

"Not anymore," I swore.

She surged into me, hugging me tightly. "You don't care about any of it. You're so pretty, and so nice, and you barely lie at all. You aren't scared of me, but you aren't trying to be friends because I'm powerful. You're just..." She pressed her face into my cheek and pulled in a breath. "You're as lost as I am, but you act like it doesn't bother you, and I like that."

I wrapped my arms around her back and held her. "Then let's be lost together, Aspen. Best friends?"

"Best friends," she agreed.

"Us against the jesters?" I added.

She huffed a laugh, struggling to get it through the tears that were trying to take over. "Always."

Then I guided her back enough that I could kiss her brow. "And flirting's allowed. Just don't laugh at me too much if I'm stupid, ok?"

She sniffed, then reached up to wipe at her eyes. "I give you my word, Rain. But if I can flirt, then you can talk to me about boys. Just don't laugh at me too much if I make faces. Do we have a deal?"

"We do," I decided.

And that tingling thing happened again. It was stronger this time than it had been with Keir, making me look up. The air around us crackled, but there were no sparks. My hair didn't stand on end or anything, yet it felt like the moment before a lightning strike, as if there was power just waiting to be unleashed.

Because there was.

"What's that?" I asked, gesturing to the space around us.

"Fae magic," she explained, letting me go so she could scoot back and grab her tablet. "Powerful agreements with the court are binding."

"Just the court?" I asked, lifting a brow.

Aspen made a noise, correcting herself. "Back home, positions on the court were decided by levels of power. Monarch, major nobility, minor nobility, courtiers, and all the way down to peasant. More magic meant more status. So, I'm not talking about the nickname they gave us here at Silver Oaks. I'm talking about the fact that me, Torian, and Wilder are all strong enough, magically, that when we feel strongly about an agreement, it becomes a spell."

"But not Hawke?" Since I'd noticed she'd left him out.

"His magic is stronger than he thinks, but he's the weakest of us. It's why he takes the combat courses instead."

"I never really see him in that class," I admitted.

"Classes," she corrected. "And he's in the advanced stuff. Means he's not in the same room you're in. Bracken separates the novices to one side, the middle group gets that main room, and the experts are usually on the other. He moves between them."

"Which is why he wants to have a teaching assistant," I realized.

Her eyes narrowed. "It would be a good idea, but we're not giving up Hawke."

"He said something about it to Keir, actually," I explained. "Before we left today. He's kinda got Keir working with me."

"And you don't mind at all," she teased, gesturing for me to come closer. Then she rolled onto her stomach and woke up her tablet. "Crows, you said?"

"Crows," I agreed, telling her all about the birds from the Sparks' place, and then the one I'd just met outside.

Aspen nodded while I talked, occasionally pausing to type something into a search. A few times, she glanced over, her eyes meeting mine. Sometimes, she'd smile, making me do the same. Eventually, I lay down like her, our heads together over her tablet, our feet in the air behind us.

"I'm not finding anything about a bird rescue in the area," she admitted. "That doesn't mean there isn't someone doing it out of their house, but it's usually found on Google." Dimming the screen, she pushed it away. "You said it could answer questions, though?"

"Only nodding or shaking its head," I explained. "It also says, 'Jack,' and pretty clearly. It's just weird that a bird from the other side of town would move here. I mean, I haven't seen a whole murder of crows or anything."

"There are more now than there used to be," she admitted. "When I was walking the grounds on Friday, I kept seeing them. Maybe half a dozen? I'm pretty sure we didn't have any before you came."

"But I'm normal," I reminded her.

"And crows keep showing up in your life," she countered. "When was the first time, Rain?"

I blew out my breath as I thought back. "I don't really know. I mean, I had a set at a previous foster home. Different city, so no way it's the same ones. And, um, I remember throwing Cheerios to them when I was a baby. Mom would give me a handful of cereal for them. Like, on my tray, because I was little. It's all a blur, though. I just remember the handful of Cheerios, then me throwing them off the back porch and crows coming to eat them. It's why I fed the first group."

"Because they remind you of your mom." She looked over at her plants. "Pretty sure I get that."

"Yeah, which is why I feel less stupid telling you. Most people would think I'm completely nuts."

She laughed at that, the sound so beautiful. "You? In case you missed it, you're at Silver Oaks Institute, a school for the fae folk. 'Nuts' is something we're going to have to redefine. Besides, they're crows. If it was sparrows or something, I'd see where you're coming from."

Which reminded me. "Keir said they're one of the few things that could cross the gates."

Aspen nodded. "Fae and crows. The Queen - back before she was mad - tried to lock all animals from crossing through. Too many things terrorizing ancient Earth, you know? Her spell worked for everything but crows. They're nulls, you see. It's not that they're immune to magic. It's that they convert it, so our spells are useless on them."

"Crows do magic?" Because that was the most unbelievable thing I'd heard yet.

"No!" she laughed. "No more than your Moon Shine does. Some things simply co-exist with magic. The silver oak uses it to live longer and grow bigger. Fae plants are fertilized by it. Crows? They seem to be more of a catalyst." Then she sucked in a breath. "We need to mark your friend. Jack. He needs a leg band so we can tell him apart, just to make sure he's the same crow."

"How?" I asked.

"Well, you said he landed on your arm. Maybe we can convince him to let you put something on him?" She shrugged. "It's worth trying, right? I'll ask Mr. Moss about it tomorrow." Then she rolled onto her back. "I'm glad you're not mad at me anymore."

I flopped down beside her. "Never mad. Nervous, I think."

Aspen reached over, using the tips of her fingers to toy with mine. "Me too, but I missed you. It was a long few days."

I shifted to lie on my side, her tablet separating us. "Yeah." Then I moved my fingers to tease the tips of hers. "I really do like the new plant."

"I really like you," she breathed. "And we're going to figure out your crows."

"Might make me less interesting," I warned, silently hoping she'd never think that.

Aspen just shook her head. "Not at all."

Chapter Thirty-Six

The next day, everyone was talking about Thanksgiving. I hadn't even thought about it, in all honesty. For some reason, I'd assumed the fae wouldn't bother with such a human holiday, but it made sense. Aspen said the fae used it as a chance to be thankful they had a safe world to hide in. Keir told me the important thing was the long weekend.

And Jack was still there for classes that afternoon. I'd grabbed a couple of rolls from the dining hall. One, I fed him on my way to Weapons-Crafting. The other I saved for after my last class, giving Keir a chunk to bribe the bird so Jack would stop dive-bombing him. While Jack didn't seem completely convinced Keir was his friend, he was more than willing to accept the bribe.

When I got back to my room that night, Aspen produced a pretty little ring. It was made of iridescent metal, and she explained how she had a mismatched earring she'd reformed. I wasn't sure a bird needed a hunk of some priceless *eltam* on its leg, but she was adamant. Mostly because it would allow us to track him if he ever went missing.

So, on Wednesday, I packed a baggie with bread, meat, and some fruits. Google said crows would eat almost anything, and I wanted to make sure I convinced Jack this was a good idea. Like he had the day before, my feathered friend flew to meet me as I headed to my first class after lunch, cheering with his name.

Then, when Offensive Combat got out, I pulled the little leg band Aspen had made from my coat pocket and slipped it onto the tip of my pinky finger. It didn't go all the way around, but the split would allow me to wrap it around his leg without problems. Then, with the offering of food ready to go, Keir and I went outside to do this.

"Jack!" the bird said, hopping around the doorway as if he'd been there for a while.

"Hey, Jack," I said, turning to the right, aiming for a more secluded area. "I have something for you."

"Jack!" he said again.

Keir just chuckled. "He's more like a parrot than a wild bird, I think."

Jack shook his head, clearly not a fan of that idea. He also followed, alternating between hopping and flapping a few paces to keep up. When I got far enough, I just sat down on the ground, crossed my legs beneath me, and placed the bag of food in my lap. Opening it, I could smell all the good stuff from the dining hall, and Jack's attention made me think he could too.

"We have to make a trade," I told the bird, looking up to see Keir lean up against a tree to watch me.

"Think he understands you?"

I could only shrug. "If he can learn words, then maybe?" I looked back to the crow and showed him the thing on my pinky. "You want a pretty, Jack?"

Caw!

That was a yes if I'd ever heard one. So, I reached down for a little piece of chicken. "You like meat?" That got tossed onto the ground by my feet.

Immediately, Jack hopped over to peck at it. Finding it was good, the crow used a foot to hold half down while he tore a chunk off and just swallowed it. Needless to say, it didn't take long for him to finish the whole thing. It wasn't that big.

Then I patted my knee. "Will you sit here?"

Jack cocked his head, thinking about it. When I patted my leg again, he ruffled his feathers, and then gave in. It took two hops, and then he was perched on my knee. I held up my hand between us again, letting Jack see the pretty colors on the *eltam* band.

"See this? It's pretty, right? It fits on me so I don't lose it and I don't have to think about carrying it." Then I slowly reached down to pet his foot - half expecting the bird to peck at me. "Can I put it on your leg? It'll make sure no one hurts you, ok?"

Jack swiveled his head, blinking at me like I'd lost my mind. "Jack!"

"Yes, Jack's a pretty bird, and I want to keep him safe." Carefully, I slipped the band off my pinky.

Jack bent down to watch while I slowly and carefully moved it to his leg. Once, he tried to nibble at it, tugging like he wanted to pull it from my hands. I held on tight enough he couldn't steal it, so he fluffed his feathers again. When he still didn't leave, I decided to just be brave.

Holding the little band between my index finger and thumb, I pressed it around his leg, closing the gap quickly. It wasn't perfect, but if he did fly away, the metal wouldn't be lost. But Jack didn't fly. He cawed instead, right into my face.

"Ok, hang on," I begged. "I'll make it fit better, but not too tight."

I mashed the sides, thankful the metal was thin so it would flex. The bird nudged at my fingers with his beak, but he didn't peck or bite at me. When I thought I had it good enough, I reached for a piece of bread and tore off a nice hunk about the size of my thumb.

"See, you were a good bird, so now you get some treats!" I praised.

Jack just lifted his leg and examined the new band. He pecked at it, then rubbed his beak against it, proving it could rotate around his leg. Then he chittered at me as if grumbling and took the offered bread.

Keir chuckled. "Your new pet has an attitude."

"Seems I have a fondness for that," I teased.

He slapped both hands over his heart. "Oh, I'm wounded. Are you calling me arrogant?"

"Maybe a little," I joked. "So what do you think? Will you be able to see the band when he's flying around?"

"Yes," Keir assured me. "I'm more worried about the other birds picking on him. It's shiny, it's colorful, and crows are known hoarders, right?"

"But this is Jack's hoard," I countered, petting the bird's back as I offered him some more food.

It seemed Jack liked the meat and bread the best, but a grape was a hit too. I hadn't really picked too much fruit, but the bird wasn't impressed with most of the vegetables I offered him. Then, when he finished the last bit of what I had, Jack hopped closer to rub his face against my hand.

"I like you too, Jack," I said. "But I think I'm going to have to get better crow treats. I'm pretty sure this stuff isn't that good for you."

"Jack!" the bird told me.

"I know, bud." I didn't, but it sounded comforting. Then I moved him off my lap.

Surprisingly, the crow allowed me to pick him up. I felt his wings flex against my hands, but he didn't really fight me. It was more like he was trying to balance as I lifted. When I set him back on the ground and stood, the silly thing tried to peck at my shoes. He was kinda cute.

"You know," Keir said, flicking a finger at me, "that's kinda sexy."

"The bird pecking my shoes?"

"The girl being so kind to animals," he countered, pushing himself away from the tree. "Also, tomorrow is Thanksgiving. What are the chances you'll consider spending a little time with me and my friends?"

"Uh..."

He wrapped an arm around my back and turned me for the Institute. "Bye, Jack. I'm stealing your girl."

Caw!

Keir chuckled. "That's definitely your bird." We walked a few steps more, then he looked over. "So, what's the status on you and Aspen?"

"Good," I assured him, but it was a little too fast. When his violet eyes kept watching me, I sighed. "It's good, Keir. I'm not sure what it is, but I know it's good."

"So, any more kissing?" There was a devious sparkle in those eyes.

So I poked him in the ribs. "No!"

But damn, that boy was solid. My teeth found my lower lip and I tried to play it off as being embarrassed about Aspen, yet even as he ducked away, his expression said he knew better. The guy looked at me for just a little too long and then rushed back in. I yelped, trying to dodge him, but I didn't stand a chance.

His arms wrapped around my waist from behind, and he lifted. I tried kicking out, but Keir was laughing a little too hard. Desperate to get down, I reached back, hoping to tickle him again. My fingers found his waist, but there was nothing soft to torment there. I poked, I grabbed, and I squirmed. Stretching a bit more, I struggled to do something - anything - to get loose. That was how I ended up grabbing a little too low.

"Easy now," he teased as my finger poked right into his dick. "Caress, don't jab."

"Keir!" I squealed.

He finally set me down, but he didn't let go. With his mouth right beside my ear, he said, "Virgin?"

"What?" I asked, spinning around to face him.

"Are you a virgin?" he asked.

"No. Why?" The moment the words were out of my mouth, I started to wonder if that was a bad thing.

"Truth," he told me, his smile softening some. "I'm just trying to figure you out, Rain. You blush. You get flustered. You flirt and then evade. I'm simply trying to make sure I don't chase you off."

"I'm hard to chase off," I reminded him.

He nodded. "Yeah. I'm getting that impression." Then he turned and started walking again. "So, you've never done it with a girl. When you need some advice about finding the clit, ask. I happen to know where it is."

"Keir!" This time, I smacked him. "You pig!"

"Fae," he countered, ducking away. "There are some similarities, but I like to think I'm a bit more obnoxious than swine." Then he came back. "I'm serious, though. Oh, and don't try to push both breasts together. Girls don't like that."

This time, he got two smacks. "Man!"

"That, I am," he agreed, but his grin was as big as mine. "I also noticed you didn't say it would never happen."

All I could do was throw up my hands. "I know this cool guy who said friends first was a good idea. I'm kinda going with that."

"And this 'cool guy,' is he fun to hang out with?" He glanced over without turning his head.

"He is," I decided. "I might even have to start alternating time between the court and his friends."

"Uh, no. You will not seduce my friends. I promise they are not worth your time, most are mere faelings, and I would be forced to steal your attention away from them."

"But what if I like these friends of yours?" I asked, bumping his shoulder with mine.

He draped his arm around my back, holding me against his side. "Then it would suck for me. I don't do so good talking about cute boys. Cute girls, however, I am an expert on."

"Fine," I said, giving in. "Then I'll come talk to you at some point. You, not your friends."

"Timeshare with Aspen, huh?" He leaned in and lowered his voice. "I'd keep that to yourself, just so you know. A few people at this school do not approve of those with Winter magic being allowed to attend."

"Which is why they're shitty to Aspen." I nodded to show I understood.

"But if they start anything," he told me, "I'm on your side. I will stand up for both you and Aspen."

I nodded, trying to accept that, but there was one thing I couldn't really wrap my mind around. The pair of us kept walking, his arm still around my back, and I knew I should let it go. I should just accept this hot guy was flirting with me without being pushy. I should take what I could get and enjoy it. Sadly, I'd never been that kind of girl.

"Why?" I asked, stopping a few feet before the door to the dorms. "You don't want me talking to your friends, but you're totally chill with me and my suitemate? I'm missing something, right?"

He grunted, turning halfway to the door, then he stopped again. "Why can't you just be oblivious like everyone else, Rain?"

"Because paying attention is what kept me out of trouble," I said. "Why, Keir?"

He pulled in a deep breath, then forced it out through his nose. "My friends are faelings. They went to normal schools for most of their lives. Most are fosters. They didn't grow up knowing what they were. They grew up knowing cute little human girls thought they were attractive. They realized it wasn't hard to get a girl in bed, and they didn't need to commit. You see, faelings can lie."

"So, only pure fae can't? What about hearing the truth?" I asked.

"If they focus, some can. Some can't. It's not directly tied to blood, either."

I mulled that over for a moment. "So you're ok with me and Aspen because she's fae?"

"Because I know she means what she says. She won't try to glamour you for the wrong reason. She's not looking to get fucked,

Rain. The guys I know? They are. They're my friends because we're all in combat classes together. Some are in defense and offense with us. Some are in tracking. I can't say they're all bad, or that they'll all take advantage of you, but I also can't say they won't."

"So you're looking out for me?" Because that didn't really make sense.

Keir glanced away then scratched at his jaw. "I also know that if you're with Aspen then you're not with Torian."

"And there it is," I realized. "Yeah, that makes more sense." I turned, walking backwards for the door. "So how many other girls are you flirting with like this, Keir?"

He just tossed up his hands and followed. "Not answering that, Rain."

"Because it's a lot, huh?"

"Nope."

I pulled open the door and slipped in, scampering over to my elevator. "Two?"

"No."

"Three?"

He walked right up to me, standing close enough he could kiss me if he bent only a little bit. "None. Seems that about two weeks ago, something pretty caught my eye and then my mind. It's a dangerous combination."

My heart stalled, I lifted my chin, waiting for him to lean in that last bit. Instead, Keir smiled and his gaze shifted over my head.

"Hey, Aspen," he said, taking a step back. "Glad to see you're doing well."

She skipped over to my side. "Are you flirting with my best friend?"

"I was getting grilled. I think you just saved my pride. Don't get into too much trouble, ladies." Then he turned and walked away.

Aspen leaned in close. "I like him. He likes you. He's not even subtle about it."

Ducking my head, I simply reached over and pushed the button.

Anything I said now would get me in more trouble. The saddest part was I had a feeling the fae were trying their hardest to be nice. I couldn't imagine how much shit I'd be in if they decided to fuck with me like the stories said they did most people. This was bad enough.

Chapter Thirty-Seven

Aspen had picked on me about Keir, but she dropped it as soon as I didn't play along. Hauling me into her room after her, she began telling me all about what I should expect for the fae version of this holiday. Nice clothes were a must, but we weren't expected to wear uniforms. Most of the school took this as their chance to show off. Just one problem: I didn't have much but t-shirts and jeans now. Not after Mr. Sparks had trashed my wardrobe.

Aspen said not to worry about it. Then she told me about the feast. Everyone would be allowed to drink nectar from the silver oak with our meal. One glass, though. No more than that for those of us under eighteen. Every food imaginable would be served, from a traditional human style meal to a mass of fresh fruits and even flowers!

More importantly, the instructors would all be involved. There would be a few speeches, but nothing too insane. Mostly, it was a complete holiday. Those with families were allowed to go home if they chose, but not many did, she explained. Most of all, the dining room would be fancy, not just the usual stuff we were used to.

And I felt like a duck out of water. Surely, I wasn't the only kid with no family to spend money on them and no expensive clothes to show off? If most of us were here on scholarships - which was what it sounded like - then they'd all understand. I was pretty sure I had a nice pair of dark jeans, and I could just use one of my white shirts for my uniform, and I'd be fine, right?

I spent the night worrying about it, making it hard to fall asleep. That meant the next morning, I slept in. Not a problem, since the meal wasn't until two in the afternoon. But when I opened my eyes, the first thing I saw was a dress hanging on the bathroom door. It was a periwinkle-blue color, simple, and so very beautiful.

I crawled out of bed and staggered over, still in my jammies. Hell, I was barely awake, but when I reached out to touch it, half expecting the dress to vanish when I woke the rest of the way up, I heard a giggle. Turning, I saw Aspen in a pair of long pants and a tank. Her hair was a mess, making it clear she hadn't been up for long either. She was also smiling at me.

"Like it?" she asked.

"Where did this come from?" Because I was pretty sure the fabric was silk.

She moved behind me to wrap her arms around my shoulders, then rested her chin beside them. "You may not have a fairy godmother, but you do have a fae best friend, Rain. I really want to make a joke about getting home before midnight or it will vanish, but it won't."

"Oh, me standing there and poof, my clothes are all gone. You'd like that, huh?"

She pressed her lips to my shoulder to hold in a giggle. "I refuse to respond to that. I have a feeling Keir wouldn't mind either. Could get a little awkward to explain to the teachers, though."

I turned around and hugged her. "Thank you, Aspen. The Sparks threw out anything I could've worn. You're a life-saver." Then I paused. "Shit. I used the T word."

She just cupped my cheek. "It's ok. I'm starting to realize that for you, it's not a way to ignore the gesture. It's... the voice of your heart."

I had no idea what came over me, what I was thinking, or if it was simply that I wasn't functioning on all cylinders yet, but I leaned in and kissed her. I just pressed my lips to hers, but she froze. When I pulled back a second later, Aspen's eyes were searching my face almost desperately.

"Sorry," I breathed, pulling away.

"Please... Don't..." She blinked. "That's..." Then she just smiled. "You kissed me."

I groaned and turned back to the dress. "And now I'm embarrassed. I messed that up, didn't I?"

"No," she said softly, shifting closer, and I felt her arms side around my waist and towards my back. "That more than makes up for any debt the dress may have carried. I'll also let you have the shower first, since you have more hair to dry." Then she kissed the side of my neck and all but flitted back to her room.

I lifted my hand to touch the spot and a smile claimed my lips. I'd kissed her. She'd wrapped her arms around me like that. I was so used to boys always pawing and wanting to make out and grope instead of talk or do things, but Aspen wasn't like that. She was... amazing. My mind spun as I headed into the bathroom and took that shower.

Aspen was the most generous person I'd ever met. Sure, she was selective about it, but I didn't blame her. She also never asked for half as much back as she gave. With her, it was the little things. The way she noticed if I was worried about something or how she knew the right way to show me I wasn't fucking up - like with the comments about Keir.

I just liked *her*.

When I was out of the shower, I leaned into her room to let her know it was her turn. She ran her eyes over me in my towel, then shooed me out. I warned her she had to wait for the big reveal, then closed the door on my side. I had two hours to get ready. That would be enough time for my hair to dry, but also to screw up my makeup at least once.

When I finally looked as good as possible, I put on the dress. Like magic - and probably because of it - the fabric shifted to hug my curves, fitting perfectly. The long sleeves were made of some sheer fabric with a pattern of vines stitched into it. That accented the neckline of the sheath dress that fell to just above my knees.

It was elegant, appropriate, and looked so good on me. When I looked in the bathroom mirror, I felt like I was seeing someone else staring back. My long, dark hair fell in soft waves. My eye makeup made my dark eyes pop. My lips were in a nude shade, just because I knew eating wouldn't work well with lipstick. I looked like some valedictorian ready to give a speech, not the new girl at Silver Oaks.

I was standing there as Aspen returned. She paused, her mouth falling open. "Wow," she breathed. "You are the most beautiful girl I've ever seen."

I glanced at her reflection in the mirror. "I love the dress."

"There's just one thing you need," she decided, hurrying back to her room.

Confused, I turned to follow, but she was back before I could do anything else. Holding up a pure white flower, she placed it against my throat, then made one of her little gestures. Something raced from her fingers, up around the back of my neck, and then stopped. Turning to the mirror, I found I now had a necklace, and the flower was the pendant.

Then Aspen moved beside me. The two of us were almost the same height. She might be a half inch taller at most, but where she was so pale, I was dark. My skin was olive, my hair was a natural black. My dress was a purple shade of blue. Hers was a yellow shade of green that made her look even lighter - but it worked.

Then she looked at my feet. "Oh, no!" Aspen declared. "You can't wear your school shoes!" Once again, she spun and left the bathroom, returning a moment later with two silver leaves from some plant. "Shoes off, Rain. Stand on the leaves."

"Is this how Cinderella's godmother worked?" I asked even as I obeyed.

"Close," she admitted. "See, I dump some of my magic into the plants. That means when I need to use more, I always have it around my room." Then she closed her eyes and scrunched up her face before snapping her fingers.

The leaves changed, shifting to shoes. I was looking down to watch and got to see the straps grow from nothing, racing around my feet and ankles to make the most amazing silver heels I'd ever seen. They were intricate, with loops instead of simple crisscrosses, and looked exactly like something a "fairy" would make.

"Oh, those are nice," I said.

Aspen just kicked out her own foot, showing a matching pair. "I might like the style." And then she offered her arm. "Can I take you to dinner, Rain?"

"Like a date?" I asked.

She nodded once. "Just like a date. Maybe a secret one, but I am honestly dying to show you off."

"Then I'd be honored." And I took her arm.

The pair of us made it down to the dining hall with five minutes to spare. From the sounds inside, everyone else was already here. Well, everyone except the three guys leaning against the wall, watching us come closer. Torian wore a crisp black-and-white suit - his sleeves even had cufflinks! - but there was no other color on him at all. Surprisingly, it made his eyes seem even more vivid.

Then there was Wilder. His tie was in a green-and-yellow pattern that complemented Aspen's dress nicely. His shirt was black, his suit was a steel grey, and the only other color on him was a pocket square that matched his tie. With his darker skin, the whole look was very, very impressive.

I turned to Hawke just as he desperately made a face at Torian. With a sigh, the "king" made a small gesture and Hawke's tie and pocket square changed color, shifting from red to lavender, and settling on a periwinkle color that perfectly matched my dress. His coat and pants were charcoal, just a bit lighter than Torian's black, but it worked with the new colors.

"Now Rain doesn't look like the misfit," Hawke said.

"Trust me," Torian told him, "she didn't before." He let his eyes run down my body. "Aspen, you are evil."

"I am, huh?" she agreed, moving to catch my arm again. "Now, let us show you how to make an entrance. Ladies first and all that. Just remember to keep your chin up, Rain, because the jesters *will* be watching."

It was like one of those scenes from a teen drama movie. The ones where the popular girls walk in slow motion down the halls, except this was us. Aspen stepped off and I stayed at her side, but the three guys fell in behind us. Torian was in the middle with Wilder flanking Aspen and Hawke just beside and behind me.

The five of us marched down the aisle, heading to the court's usual table. Things had been moved around, but not enough for me to get lost. I tried not to gape and gawk, but I still noticed everyone turn to see us. Aspen's expression was damned near regal, so I did my best to match it.

As we passed, people began to talk. The conversation was soft, like a wave that followed behind us, but it was impossible to miss. We'd been noticed, and I had a feeling that had been *very* intentional. Then, when we claimed our spots at the table, Torian moved me to his side, bumping Hawke down one chair. It also put him between me and Aspen, but I decided that was ok. The way we were sitting, my back was against the wall, which meant the entire room spread out before me.

The beautiful room. Unlike the Thanksgiving decorations I was used to, autumn wasn't the theme here. This was all about winter. White flowers served as accents, but so did bare branches, holly, and berries. Mistletoe was everywhere, as were fat flakes of snow that drifted through the air but never reached the tables.

Things shimmered: the lights, the accents over the doors, and so much more. It was like living glitter had been used to add a little sparkle. The plates, table cloths, and most of the decorations were white. Everything else was silver. I tried to take it all in, but that was impossible. There was just enough magic to make this wondrous, but not enough to make it impossible, and I loved it.

"Best Thanksgiving ever," I breathed.

"Welcome to the fae celebration of winter," Hawke told me. "We do something similar in the summer for the Fourth of July." Then he looked across the table at Aspen. "Happy winter, beautiful."

She smiled at him. "Happy winter to all of us," she said. "This year, I've decided we should be thankful for Rain."

Chapter Thirty-Eight

This time, the meal wasn't a buffet we could wade through. The kitchen staff actually came around with trolleys of options. When they got to us, it was Wilder who made the choices. He pointed to me and asked for a traditional meal, then gestured to the rest of them and said simply, "Fae."

Five plates were quickly handed out. The first four were theirs, filled with fruits soaked in honey and syrup. There was an arrangement of little flowers on the side, and it looked like the kind of thing someone would take a picture of for social media. Then the server reached for a lower level of her cart, picked up a plate with a silver cap, and set that before me.

Once she left, my curiosity got the better of me. Lifting the lid, I found the typical Thanksgiving style meal. Turkey, ham, stuffing, sweet potatoes with marshmallows, and even a green bean casserole. There was just one problem. My fae friends didn't really do meat eating. Nervously, I checked to see if anyone was staring.

When I looked to my left, Hawke leaned in. "You're fine," he assured me. "No one's going to steal your meal."

"No, it's - " His look made the words die on my lips.

"Aspen has made it clear you're allowed to be as human as you want. We're allowed to be ourselves. Stop trying to be nice, Rain. It's really not your style."

"It kinda is," I assured him.

His eyes dropped to my lips and he smiled softly. "And it seems I'm your unofficial date for the night."

"Uh..." My eyes jumped across the table to Aspen.

"Unofficial," he said again. "Believe it or not, we know more than you can guess. Her highness over there talks to us."

I rolled my eyes at him. "You were almost being nice, Hawke."

"I'm being as nice as I can," he promised. "This?" He ran a hand down his tie. "It's called plausible deniability. Might even keep the jesters off you for the weekend."

"So what's the deal with that?" I asked. "Why do they hate you four so much?"

A smirk took over his face just as someone began tapping at a crystal glass. All around us, the room fell silent, and the entire court turned to look in the same direction. Following their eyes, I realized the entire end of the dining hall had been turned into a long table for the teachers. Ms. Rhodes sat in the center. There were a few teachers I didn't know on either side of her - and they all looked very fae - and then more I knew sitting further down.

Liam caught my eye. He sat next to Bracken. Tag was on Bracken's other side. Oddly, the three of them were looking our way. I smiled at Liam and lifted my hand, hoping to let him know I was aware of the inspection. He smiled back and then leaned towards Bracken.

But Ms. Rhodes had stood. "For those of you new to Silver Oaks this year, I would like to wish you all a happy winter. Regardless of the court you or your parents supported in Faerie, here winter is allowed to be a time of renewal. As the power of summer slumbers, a few among us will enjoy increased strength. This is the natural way of things, and not a cause for strife. Think of it more as a time for reflection."

She paused, smiling at the room filled with students. "Most importantly, as tradition dictates, there will be no classes tomorrow. Because of this, curfew for our AP students will be moved to midnight tonight." She lifted a finger. "Do not assume that means we won't be watching. All other rules - including the opposite sex in your rooms - will still be strictly enforced. For those of you leaving this evening to spend time with your families, you will be expected back on Sunday by nine p.m. For everyone else, the grounds are open. This semester is almost over, and midterm exams will be coming faster than you think. Please keep in mind that passing grades are required to continue attendance here. And, as always, the Winter Solstice will be celebrated the Monday after the term ends. Please plan your winter holidays accordingly." The woman smiled as murmurs filled the room. "And with that, let us all be thankful we've found each other. Happy winter, everyone. Enjoy your meals."

"Short, sweet, and to the point," Wilder said, reaching to pluck a slice of glazed orange from his plate. "Gotta at least give her that."

"Ms. Rhodes?" I asked.

"Yep," Torian agreed. "The *dean* of Silver Oaks." He said that like he knew something.

"She's supposed to be our floor's chaperone, right?" I asked, because I'd never seen her there. Maybe that was it?

Aspen leaned in. "She is. She actually does a few things here. See, that woman designed this entire school. She's the reason Silver Oaks exists, so she's dedicated to keeping it running smoothly."

Ah, well, that explained it. She wasn't merely the dean. She was the architect of all of this. Ok, that was pretty cool, and if the rumors were true, she had a little experience to draw on.

So I looked between my friends. "I heard she's like five hundred years old."

"At least," Torian admitted. "I know she served the Queen for centuries. Believe it or not, she used to be a general of the Summer Soldiers."

"Ivy Rhodes?" Yeah, that was hard to believe.

"The same," Torian said. "On Faerie, there were stories of her abilities. She merged magic with weapons to become an unstoppable force. When the Queen went mad, Ms. Rhodes slipped through the gates, assumed a new name, and vanished. Not many people know that, though."

"So don't tell Keir," Aspen added.

Yeah, there was something hinky about that. "How do you know?"

Torian chuckled. "I recognized her from a painting in the Summer Court."

That wasn't what I'd expected. "So, you've been to the Summer Court?"

He nodded. "I told you the Queen trained me herself. It wasn't an exaggeration, Rain. It's also why I spent everything I had to get out. I saw firsthand what the Mad Queen was doing, and I heard her rants about why. Faerie is no longer the haven we all like to pretend."

"I'm sorry," I told him.

Something in his expression softened. It was almost as if he'd expected to debate with me, and my sympathy caught him by surprise. No one else at the table moved until Torian nodded, making it clear he wasn't upset by my words.

"We like to think of home as this perfect place, but that doesn't make it true," he finally said. "I think you're one of the few people here who can understand that. Most fosters imagine that if they were still with their parents, then their problems would be solved. If we were still in Faerie, then we'd all be happier. It doesn't matter what goal they chase, but having something be out of reach makes it seem sweeter for some reason."

"But we were all taken away for a reason," I agreed. "For me, it was brutal enough I never had that dream. I can only imagine if it was an entire world and civilization I'd had to leave."

Aspen just pointed her fork at my plate. "Eat. I want to see it happen."

"Oh, make me feel extra self-conscious," I grumbled playfully. "Thanks, Asp. No, really."

"I just don't know how it doesn't burn your mouth," Wilder said.

"Should've seen her grab iron," Aspen told him. "Like it was nothing. She hesitates more when touching *eltam*."

They all began talking, so I cut off a piece of the turkey and shoved it into my mouth. Immediately, all of their eyes went right back to me. I just chewed, lifting a hand to cover my mouth, then swallowed as quickly as I could.

"Stop!" I insisted.

"Is it good?" Wilder asked, tossing what looked like a miniature daisy into his mouth.

I nodded. "It really is. It also doesn't taste like dirt, which I can only imagine that flower does."

"It really doesn't," Hawke assured me, picking up another. This time, he held it out. "Try it, Rain."

But before I could reach for it, he held it to my lips. I still plucked the flower from his fingers, but there was something intimate in the fact he'd even tried. When I popped it into my mouth, I realized he was watching me intently. His eyes were technically brown, but in that same warm and rusty shade as his hair. Chestnut wasn't quite right. This was more like autumn, with a mixture of browns, reds, oranges, and warm golds.

Then I chewed. The flower was crisp-tasting and sharp. The closest thing I could think of was a cucumber. Maybe a honeydew melon, since it was a little sweet. Humming in surprise, I reached for my glass to wash it down.

"That's actually kinda good." I gestured to his plate. "Not a daisy, huh?"

"Not a daisy," he promised.

"Bet she'd share the bird," Wilder teased, flashing a devious look at Hawke.

Hawke just huffed. "Not happening."

So Aspen leaned around her brother to offer me a bit of fruit. "Try this!"

I leaned in, feeling a little playful and caught her wrist. Instead of taking the food from her fingers, I used her hand to guide it to my mouth. Torian murmured and leaned back. Hawke chuckled. Wilder shifted in his seat, but a shy smile curled Aspen's pretty little lips.

"Teasing the boys now?" she asked.

I sucked the slice of fruit from between her fingers. "Not intentionally." My eyes held hers, making it clear who I'd intended to tease.

"That's my *sister*," Torian groaned.

"Sucks to be you," Wilder told him, "because that was hot."

"Very," Hawke breathed, glancing over at Wilder.

Wilder nodded, that pair sharing some secret thought, but it didn't take a genius to figure it out. Boys! I rolled my eyes at the both of them, and went back to my own meal. It really was good, but so was the fae food. Sadly, I couldn't survive well on nothing but sugar and fruit. I'd either blow up like a blimp or fade away to nothing. Possibly both at the same time - too much where I didn't want and not enough where I did, knowing my luck. It was the bane of being a girl.

"So," Hawke asked a little while later, "when are you going to spar against me in offense, Rain?"

"I'm doing pretty good to not hit myself with those sticks," I admitted.

He grinned. "I can help you learn, you know. You don't have to keep running to Keir."

"Fucking Keir," Torian said.

"No," I snapped, cutting him off. "Don't start that. I will have you know I stand up for my friends. Right now, that's Aspen and Keir. Hawke's working his way higher. You?" I looked at him pointedly. "You're acting like the same kind of brat as Harper, and I'm still not scared of whatever mystical power you have over this school."

"Be nice, Tor," Aspen warned.

So Torian leaned in, dropping his elbow on the table as he looked right in my face. "Are you fucking with my sister?"

"Nope." I lifted my chin and dared him to keep going.

"Good. Don't," he warned. "There's just one little downside to your plan, though. I don't share with family."

Wait, what? What the actual fuck was he even talking about? I jerked back, confusion taking over my face, and shook my head. Aspen grabbed Torian's arm and yanked him back, pressing him into his chair. The spark in her eyes had just become the dangerous kind.

"Unlike everyone else here, Rain doesn't have a plan. She's not chasing you, Torian, and you're going to have to get used to that. She doesn't need you, and from the way you're acting, she doesn't even *like* you. I don't care what you think you deserve. Has it ever crossed your fucking arrogant mind that maybe I deserve a little something too?"

"Aspen..." he tried.

She just shoved at him again. "I will fight you for this, and it's my season."

"Mine too," he reminded her.

"Half yours," she corrected. "All mine. Leave my girlfriend alone."

"Whoa," Wilder breathed, leaning away a bit. "Tor, you need to back off fast. She's getting icy."

"Breathe, Aspen," Hawke said. "He's just jealous."

But Tor didn't back off. He turned to his sister and cupped her cheek. "I will never steal from you. I just wish you didn't have such good taste. And *Keir?*"

"She likes him," Aspen said.

My head was whipping between them, trying desperately to keep up. "Please tell me I didn't make some fae fuck-up?"

"You're fine," Wilder assured me. "This time, it's Tor who blew it."

"And I still don't know what's going on," I admitted.

"Fae politics," Torian assured me. "*This* is the problem when the other half of a soul doesn't agree." He caught Aspen's hand and lifted it to his lips. "I'm trying to be good, Asp."

"You're a shitty baby brother," she told him.

He chuckled. "It's three days. Don't think that counts." Then he stood. "Trade places with me?"

The pair shifted their things, moved over, and then Aspen was beside me. She also kept fidgeting with her plate. I kept eating while Hawke and Wilder tried to discuss their plans for the weekend. I got the distinct impression they were trying very hard to ease the tension that had just flared up.

"What did I miss?" I asked Aspen.

She bit her lower lip and those big blue eyes looked up at me. "I didn't mean to say that out loud."

"Which part?" I teased.

"Girlfriend," she breathed.

Under the edge of the table, I caught her hand. "I'm not scared of the jesters."

"I really do like you," she said softly. "I'm just not being a very good friend."

So I traced my thumb over the back of her hand. "I like you too. I just feel like I don't know half of what's going on."

"It's ok," she promised. "My brother's an ass. A cute one, I know, but he's still pompous, arrogant, and full of himself."

"With good reason," Torian added. "I'll make up for it, Aspen. I promise."

"Wait, so they all know, um, about us?" I whispered to her.

She nodded. "I did warn you that we talk about cute girls. You're cute. You're a girl."

I could feel my cheeks getting warmer. "Right. I'm so bad at this."

"You're perfect," she told me. "I also think you should hang out with Keir today and really make the jesters confused." But she shifted her hand so her fingers slipped into the gaps between mine. "Later, though. For just a minute, let me enjoy the fact you didn't say no."

With my other hand, I reached up to brush a lock of hair behind her completely round ear. "I didn't," I agreed, taking in this beautiful girl so close to me. "It's just because I want to keep the dress, though."

She laughed. "Blatant lie!"

"Completely," I agreed.

Chapter Thirty-Nine

By the time the food was done and we'd all finished a glass of nectar, the whole table was laughing. Mostly, they were laughing at me, but this time I was just as bad. Hawke had tears coming from his eyes, and Wilder was making a gesture, trying desperately to get my attention.

"Do it again!" he begged.

"I'm a boy," I said.

Torian snorted, shaking his head as he waved away whatever sensation they got when I lied. "That's so wrong!"

"The sky is pink," I tried next.

Aspen grabbed her waist, a smile plastered on her beautiful lips. "How do you even do that?" she begged.

"They're just words," I insisted.

Hawke wiped at his eyes. "With meanings and intentions," he pointed out. "You can't feel the dissonance?"

"That's a good way to put it," Aspen giggled. "Like really bad music, but in the back of my mind."

I just shook my head at her. "Nothing."

"Wait." Torian leaned across the table to look at me. "So, how can humans tell if someone is lying?"

"The look on your face," I explained. "I don't know. We just see it."

"Show me?" he begged.

I looked to the snowy ceiling trying to think of something else. "Aspen and I are just friends. There's nothing there."

Torian's eyes narrowed. "I know that's a lie, but it feels like it wants to be the truth."

"No," Wilder said. "The buzzing feeling. It's subtle, but she's using a loophole."

Aspen gasped. "You're lying like the fae! It's almost true, but not quite."

I just pointed to my face. "But did you see the expression? How I look away, don't want to meet your eyes, and there's something too stiff about it?"

"So you like my sister, huh?" Torian asked.

I glanced at her, feeling my lips split into a smile that was a bit too big. "Maybe."

"And while true, that feels like a lie," Hawke told me. "Tor, sorry, but I'm so into this idea. They're cute."

Torian groaned. "Of course you are." Then he looked at me. "Do it again. I want to see."

From beside our table came a deep laugh. "Of course you do, Tor."

"Keir!" I gasped, turning to see him.

"What has this table giggling loud enough the whole dining hall is watching?" he asked.

"Your face is purple," I said just as calmly as I could.

Wilder actually tittered, the noise coming from him three octaves too high. Torian howled while both Hawke and Aspen slapped their hands over their lips.

"Are you drunk on oak syrup?" Keir asked.

I shook my head. "They're curious about lies." I turned back to Aspen. "I'm gonna go meet his friends."

"Go!" she insisted. "I've monopolized you enough. Wouldn't be a good fairy godmother if I didn't make you show off that dress!"

"Fairy bestie," I corrected.

She just smiled. "It's a good title. Better than the one I used. Also causes less issues."

"My thought exactly." Then I pushed my chair back. "So, where are your friends, Keir?"

He didn't turn immediately. Instead, he looked over at Torian. "Let's not make a scene, hm?"

"Agreed," Torian said, flicking a hand as if shooing me away.

"Dick," I grumbled, grabbing Keir's arm to tow him away.

He turned me slightly, knowing which table his friends were at. "That was for me, actually."

"What is the deal between you two?" I asked, because there was clearly a little animosity.

He chuckled. "Call it a culture clash." He smiled down at me. "And let me introduce you to most of the offensive combat class. Rain, these are the guys. Guys, Rain Brooks."

The table before me was set toward the side, but only one row away from where the teachers sat. I was overly aware of Liam watching me, but he wasn't actually my uncle. Oddly, I felt more concerned about what he thought than I ever had most of my foster parents, though. Glancing up, I found him talking animatedly with Bracken and another teacher down the table. Then I turned my eyes back to the group of guys all inspecting me.

"She's cute," one said. "Human, right?"

Keir groaned. "That's Fin, short for Finley. He's my suitemate. Over there is Daivon, Axel, Bran, and Pascal."

I lifted my hand in the dorkiest of greetings. "Hey."

"Seriously," Fin insisted. "You're completely human?"

"Yep," I agreed, turning when Keir gestured for me to take a chair. Thankfully, he claimed the empty one beside it. "So, I take it I'm the only one here?"

Pascal nodded. "At the table, yeah. There are a few of your kind in the school, but this *is* a fae place."

"Faeling," Keir corrected. "Don't try to make yourself sound all impressive, Pas."

"Didn't mean it like that," Pascal insisted.

The one Keir had called Axel scoffed. "If she's hanging on Keir, pretty sure you don't have a chance."

"And Torian..." Daivon teased. "So, you two chasing the same girl again?"

"Fuck off, man," Keir warned him. "And to think, I said nice things about you guys."

"Not many," I admitted.

"At least two, so it's true," he pointed out. "I told you they were my friends, and I'm pretty sure I said you should hang with us."

"You just wanted her away from your archnemesis," Bran said before turning to me. "Last year, he and Torian were ready to tear down the entire school. Should've seen Torian's face when he realized Keir can hold off his magic."

"Do what?" I asked, turning to Keir. "You two got into a fight?"

Keir grinned. "He mentions Torian throwing magic at me, and your response is to call it a fight?"

"Isn't that what it was?" I countered. "I mean, most guys I grew up with used fists, but I've already figured out things work differently here."

"Kinda like Torian casting that slow enchantment awhile back?" Bran sighed. "I got caught in it. Was three minutes late to class. Almost got detention."

"In the D wing?" Pascal asked. "Heard about that. Couple of teachers were stuck in it too."

"That's why he got away with it," Daivon pointed out. "Fucking dick. The teachers won't shut him down because they can't."

My head was bouncing around like I was watching a tennis

match, but I was pretty sure I was keeping up. "So, Torian is trouble, huh?"

"Says the one girl invited to the court," Bran muttered. "Yeah, trouble's putting it mildly. I just want to know how you got in. They only talk to fae from Faerie. No one else."

"Aspen's my suitemate," I explained. "She was kinda the only person I knew for the first week."

"And?" Bran asked.

Fin waved him down. "He's just jealous. We thought we had those four figured out. With you being included, we don't."

"Ok?" And now I was lost.

Keir sighed. "The rumor was that the court was actually from the court. Like, children of nobility sent here to grow up. Real changelings. Even their girlfriends were kept on the outside. That's why you sitting at their table causes such a stir with the jesters."

Yeah, two plus two equaled four. Didn't take a genius to figure out the big reveal there. "Who used to date one of the jesters?" I asked.

Keir's mouth closed quickly, but Fin leaned back in his chair and laughed. "Oh, you didn't tell her about that, huh? It's great, Rain. See, Keir was banging Harper Valentina. Torian smiled at the girl once and she dumped Keir's ass and moved onto greener - or maybe Elysian fields."

"Elysian fields?" I'd heard that before somewhere.

"Home of the Summer Court," Keir explained. "Considered the perfect landscape by some."

"Ah." And yet, the rest of that hadn't passed me by. "So you and Harper?"

"Don't want to talk about it," Keir said.

"All last year," Fin went on, completely ignoring him, "all I heard from his side of the suite was Harper squealing. 'More, Keir. Harder, Keir.'"

"I'm going to make you regret that," Keir told him.

Fin just laughed. "And now you're unknowingly following in

Harper's footsteps, Rain. Flirt with one pure-blood while hooking the other?"

"Torian's a dick," I told him, stopping that before it could even start. "Aspen's my friend. Best friend. I'm trying to decide if Hawke and Wilder are worth my time yet."

"Hawke's pretty cool," Daivon assured me. "Intense, but not a bad guy."

"He's got some wicked moves," Bran agreed. "Kicks my ass on a regular basis."

I just pointed around the table. "So are all of you Legacies or something?"

"Nope," they assured me, but Pascal was nodding.

"I am," he admitted. "If the stars align, I might be able to fizzle something. My magic's so weak, it doesn't even count."

"Enticer," Fin said with a smirk.

Then Keir took over. "Daivon and Axel are Glamours, Bran's an Enchanter."

"And you?" I asked. "Because I've never seen you in your uniform. No tie to tip me off."

Keir chuckled. "Yeah, um, I rate as a Conjurer, but I promise it's not impressive. Minor healing, and the rest is all defensive."

"Wicked defenses," Axel corrected. "Keir's talent is dispelling. What about you, new girl? What cool tricks can you do?"

"Completely magicless," I admitted, pretty sure that wasn't what he was asking about. "Not even a flicker of light."

"Heard you got in as a favor to Liam," Fin said. "And since he's never going to have kids..."

"Fuck off!" Keir snapped. "Seriously, Fin? Could you be more of a dick? This is why I never bring girls around. You make sure to chase them off."

"No, you just sneak them down to the Never," Fin shot back, flicking up both brows. "Trust me, Rain, if he asks you to go downstairs, just do it. Can't hear the screams from down there."

I smiled and leaned over the table toward him. "Virgin, huh?"

"What?" Fin asked.

But the rest of the guys were losing it. Even Keir. I was struggling not to smile. "I mean, that's usually why a guy is so completely oblivious as to when he's making an ass out of himself - or his friends."

"No..." Fin tried, looking over to Keir as if he expected help.

Keir was still laughing. "You are all on your own, man. I warned you she's something else. Now do you believe me?"

"Big tip," I told Fin. "When you finally do get a girl to talk to you, she doesn't want to know about the others you've chased, fucked, or failed at impressing. We're not conquests, Fin. We're also not here for your amusement."

Fin just stared at me, his eyes narrowing. Daivon tapped Pascal's shoulder, flicking a finger at Fin. Keir's jaw clenched and he glared at Fin in warning. Something was happening, but I wasn't sure what. Confused, I looked between the guys, desperately trying to get some hint.

Then Keir slapped his hand down on the table, making all of the guys jump. "Lay off, Fin."

"It's not fucking working," Fin grumbled. "I was just going to make her squeal like she was getting off, but I couldn't get into her head."

"What?" I asked.

Keir's complete attention was on his suitemate. "If you fuck with her mind at all, I will kill you. Stop and listen to that again, Fin. Kill. I'm pretty sure Aspen would help me make sure you disappear, so do *not* try your tricks with her."

"Was just a joke," Fin grumbled.

But Axel sucked in a breath. "And shit just got real."

Keir didn't care. Shoving back his chair, he turned and offered me a hand. "This was a bad idea. Let's get out of here?"

I pressed my palm against his and let him help me up. Without a word, Keir turned me away, but his jaw was still clenched. We passed a few tables before he shifted his arm and tilted his head, making it clear he wanted me to take it. I looped my hand inside his elbow like some elegant lady, but we didn't stop until we left the dining hall.

It seemed we weren't the first. A few students hung out in the halls. Most were couples or mixed groups. Keir just turned toward the atrium. I thought that was where we were going until he turned us up that hall.

"Um, I kinda wanted to talk," he admitted. "If I invite you up to my room for a bit, will you please not make your decision based on my asshole of a suitemate?"

"I'm not scared of Fin," I assured him. "He's pretty much like every guy I've ever known before."

"With the ability to fuck with your mind," Keir reminded me. "Rain, Enticers can convince you that you're someone else. They can change your mind for you. They can compel you to do things you wouldn't ordinarily do - like him."

"You mean... like date rape?" I asked.

"Worse," he said. "Fin's strong enough to make sure you don't say anything. Kinda why I'm still his suitemate." He glanced over. "And why he's still a virgin. Seems my ability to dispel things is a powerful one."

I gestured to the boys' elevator. "Then let's go. Seems I've made the right friends."

"You're not bothered by that?" he asked.

"Oh, I'm bothered," I assured him. "I also don't blame you for being a decent guy. Fin's a dick. I'm just wondering how many girls he took someplace besides his room."

"None," he promised. "I've made it very clear that if he crosses that line, I won't just get him expelled. I'll make sure the Hunt finds him." He pressed the button to call the car down. "We were paired by chance our first year here. He tried it once - just to get a girl to kiss him. I put a stop to it and made sure Bracken knew. Bracken made sure he's stuck with me now. Ironically, the girl he tried to steal a kiss from? One of the jesters. Talk about burning his bridges before he could get in with any crowd, so now he's stuck with the sentinels."

The door opened and he led me on, but when he pressed the button for the fourth floor, I realized there was something else I needed to know. "What exactly are sentinels, Keir? I keep hearing that term, but I'm not sure how it fits into all of this."

"We're the ones training to stop the Hunt," he explained. "It's how Bracken made his fame. He helped break the Wild Hunt into a few smaller groups. Still dangerous, but a group of us can fight back five or six. We can't stop the Hunt as a whole. You see, they can't be killed."

"Doesn't sound like a good career choice," I pointed out.

He lifted one shoulder in a mock shrug. "I did mention I have a thing for being a hero. I also can't lie." Like an exclamation point, the door dinged, announcing we'd reached the fourth floor.

Chapter Forty

Keir's room was nothing like mine. The floor was hardwood. The rug was brown and grey. He didn't have a window looking over the atrium - he was on the wrong hall for that - and the bed was in a completely different space. Then there was all the personal stuff.

A set of leather armor hung on a rack in the corner. There was a collection of swords on the wall. None of them were iron. His shelves were adorned with so many pictures. Plenty had a pair of beautiful people who I would've guessed were in their mid-twenties. Late twenties at most.

"Are those your parents?" I asked.

He chuckled. "Yeah. Um, I call them my aunt and uncle now. In a few more years, they'll be my brother and sister. Well, in public."

"They don't look a day over a hundred," I joked.

He ducked his head. "How are you so ok with all of this? You ask questions, accept the answers, and then just move on."

"The only stable thing in my entire life has been change," I admitted.

"Makes sense." He reached up to release his tie, sliding that off just to toss it into the corner. "So, um, you look nice today."

I made a slow pirouette. "Aspen created it for me."

"Uh huh, and Hawke matched. Trust me, everyone noticed." Then he pulled out the chair at his desk and dropped onto it backwards. "How are things going in the girl dorm, anyway?"

A groan fell out and I moved to sit on his bed. It was the only other space. "I took your advice about friends. I mean, it's been a week, but I kinda kissed her this morning. Not like a real kiss, though. I just..." The words faded away when I realized I was rambling.

Keir stood to drag his chair a little closer, then dropped into it again. "You know you might want to keep that to yourself, right? You and Aspen?"

"Why?" I quickly asked.

"Because if the instructors find out, they'll move you. Couples aren't allowed to share a suite."

"Well, then I'm safe, because I'm not sure there is a me and Aspen," I pointed out. "Oh, I know there could be, and she kinda told her brother I'm her girlfriend, but I feel like a complete idiot around her."

"Like when you had your first crush on a guy?" he asked. "Don't know what to say, what to think, but you still like being around her just because she's amazing, or wonderful, or beautiful? That sort of thing?"

"Yes!" I gasped. "How do you know?"

"Uh, I've had a crush on a girl before," he assured me. "One or two, at least."

That earned him both a grunt *and* an eye roll. "You know the strange thing?" I shifted to lie on his bed, turning sideways so I wouldn't accidentally flash anything with this short dress. "I don't have parents to upset. I don't have anyone to judge me because I might like a girl, or not be straight, or whatever. There is no reason I can't just do what I want, and my legal guardian is gay." Then I sucked in a breath, realizing what I'd said.

Keir waved me down. "I know about Liam. It's not a secret here."

"So why am I second-guessing this?" I asked. "I mean, I could probably hook up with some guy and it would be a lot easier, but I just *like* her, Keir. She's..." I lifted my arm just to let it flop back to my side. "Free, fun, spontaneous, beautiful, and all those other things. When I'm around her, I feel like the world is a little brighter."

He moved from his chair to sit on the end of the bed, then reached over to unbuckle the strap of my shoe. "Because you've probably been told it's wrong. Girls like boys and boys like girls. Here's the thing. The moment you realized they were attacking Aspen, you forgot to worry about anything else. Six girls, and you charged right in there."

"Yeah, but - "

"No," he insisted, cutting me off. "Listen, Rain." He slid my shoe off and dropped it down beside the bed. Then he moved to the other. "When she's around, *you* seem a little brighter. It's not a friend thing, and I get that. You look the same way when you're talking to that stupid bird."

"Jack," I laughed. "I promise Aspen is nothing like a bird."

"No, but the closer you two get, the more chances there are that Harper will notice."

"And?" I asked. "If there's nothing wrong with it, then why should I act like there's something wrong with it?"

"Think of it like high school drama with fae arrogance," he explained, removing that shoe just to place it by the first. "See, there are a few things going on here that you need to understand."

"Ok?"

"First," he said, "Aspen's magic is Winter. Most of the Winter Court is dead. Hers is strong and mostly untrained, but still terrifyingly strong. Since she's at her peak power when the Summer Court is fading? That's seen as a threat. Combined with those who believe the Winter Court was killed off so Silver Oaks should be for Summer magic only?" He canted his head. "So we have magical discrimination."

"Figured that out," I admitted. "Yet Torian, Wilder, and Hawke don't care?"

"Wilder also has Winter magic," Keir said. "Torian is her sibling, and Hawke is, well, Hawke. He's an outlier who's loyal to Torian."

"Gotcha."

"The second problem," he said, "is Harper. She's the leader of the jesters right now. No, she's not the first leader, and I'm sure she won't be the last. But her family are well positioned in fae circles. They are powerful, have ties to the former Summer Court, and strong magic. The Valentinas are one of the most outspoken about banishing Winter magic. Plus, Harper likes to win, and she's been spoiled enough she never learned there are any other options. Her mother's miracle baby and all that."

"Because *of course* she is," I grumbled.

Keir grunted in agreement. "The problem is Harper thinks the best way to impress her mother and solidify her future in our society is to pair with a 'real' fae. Ideally a guy, so her children will be more than mere half-bloods. We also don't have a pure fae woman around with Summer magic - except the teachers - and her hate for Winter is strong enough to blind her. That leaves three options."

"Four," I corrected. "You, Torian, Wilder, and Hawke."

"Three," he countered. "Wilder also uses Winter magic, so he's just as bad as Aspen."

"Oh." Yeah, I didn't think that through.

He nodded. "But she dumped me to be with Torian. She and Torian broke up because he was ignoring her for his sister. She hoped it would teach him a lesson. Too bad for her, he didn't care. From the drama of the breakup - which happened in the dining hall at lunch - I can tell you it wasn't pretty. She made it clear she gave him her virginity. Trust me, she didn't. He asked why he should care. She tried to turn Aspen into a frog. Well, she did, but Torian reversed it almost immediately. Then he completely lost it."

"Lost it how?" I asked. "Are we talking about yelling or spell throwing?"

"Both," Keir said. "People were running for cover, teachers couldn't stop him, and it was a mess. The end result was that no one in the court will give her the time of day. So she's determined to make them. She's also realized hurting Aspen hurts Torian. It's the only time he's lost control. Most of us saw it as a sign to be real nice to the girl. Harper decided it was his weakness."

"So tormenting Aspen gets Harper her revenge," I realized.

Keir nodded. "Yeah. Anything she likes, Harper hates. And just so you don't find out later, she wanted to get back together with me. Evidently I'm a decent backup plan, even if I'm 'only' Earth-born. I'm also not interested in being a trophy boyfriend. Torian's pissed at me because her virginity?" He lifted his hand. "That was me. Then the idiot tried to tell Torian I was better in bed anyway. He came at me. I held him off, and we ended with a peace treaty of sorts. I ignore him, he ignores me, and the Institute stays standing."

"Sounds like I missed a lot last year," I teased.

Keir flicked a finger at the spot beside me. "Am I being a jerk if I join you over there?"

I just shifted over. "Nope. I may have a girlfriend, though."

He lay down on his back, his arm resting beside mine. "Torian is an asshole, Rain, but he's one for the right reasons. He's also the most fae person you'll ever meet. He's tempered by Aspen, but she's mellowed by him, I think. You don't get one without the other. They act more like twins than half-siblings."

"Half?" Then I groaned. "Right, three days apart in age. They have to be." Then I sat straight up. "Shit. Tor said something about the Mad Queen killing his dad! That was Aspen's dad too!"

"She killed a lot of people," Keir said. "Thousands, Rain." He reached over to shift a lock of my hair away from my face. "You know that right now those guys think we're up here breaking a few rules, right? I'll deny it, they'll try to figure out how I'm deceiving them, but the rumor will spread. It won't take long before the school thinks we're more than friends."

I turned my head to look at him. "So I'm your way of getting even with Torian?" I watched his face, praying he'd deny it.

"No," he assured me. "I'm saying Harper will think you're with me, not Aspen. I'm trying to tell you I'm ok with that."

"Why?" I asked, because there was a little too much evasion in his words.

"If I said it's because you're beautiful and I'm intentionally incurring debts you'll owe me for, would you buy it?"

"Nope." I lay down, and turned on my side to see him. "What are you doing, Keir?"

"I'm being intrigued," he admitted, his eyes searching mine. "Think of this like chess. We've all moved our pawns, but I'm playing for checkmate."

"Keir..." I sighed. "I'm serious."

"I'm learning more about my new friend?" he tried next, but the curl of his lips betrayed the deception.

So I sat up and swung my legs off the bed. "Yep. Good talk. Too bad for you, I'm not interested in being a political puppet for stupid drama."

He caught my arm. "I'm fucking *protecting* you," he snarled, that fae temper showing itself for the first time. "Don't you get it? You're helpless in this fight. Torian and Harper could both *destroy* you and you'd never stand a chance. I like you, Rain. I keep *saying it,* and I don't know why that's so hard for you to fucking understand, but I do. I like you enough that I'm being as human as I can. I'm making sure you're not walking around this school blind. I'm also stepping right into Torian's sights to make sure the girl I'm into doesn't become his target! *I like you,* and I'm waiting for you to figure out if you like me back."

"But Aspen..." I tried.

He tugged me back toward him just enough so he could lean into my face. "Which is why I'm calling myself your friend. Figure out if you're playing by human rules or fae. I'll respect either one. I'm also making sure that if anyone wonders, the pretty new girl at school isn't spending all her time locked alone with public enemy number one."

"Because you're scared of Harper," I realized.

"There are three people in this school who aren't," he assured me. "Torian, Aspen, and Wilder."

"And me," I added.

"Then you're a fool." He released his grip. "Harper has no limits, a fae temper, and the power to make sure she's never caught. Let me be your friend and your beard until you figure out what you're doing. I *like* you, Rain. I will even say it again. I *do* like you, enough that I'm not pushing. I'm just moving a pawn so I'll win either way."

I scanned his face, convinced I was missing something, but his answer had always been the same. The more complicated all of this got, the more consistent Keir was. He didn't seem to mind at all that I liked Aspen romantically. He didn't have a problem with telling me how he felt. So why couldn't I just accept this and move on?

"I'm in over my head, aren't I?" I realized.

He nodded slowly. "Yeah, but I actually think you can handle it. You get this. I'm not sure how, but not even the faelings can grasp the nuances as easily as you do. There are politics, power, and popularity dynamics here. Magic isn't just for making snowflakes swirl over dinner, Rain. Most of us have heard the stories of life in Faerie. We know how easy it is to go too far. Unfortunately, Harper doesn't have limits, and you just got her in a lot of trouble."

I nodded to show I understood. "So what do I do?"

"Tell Aspen about this talk. Let everyone else think what they will. It's one less reason for the jesters to come after you. It's one more reason for me to get a little time with this crazy girl who is nothing like I expected." Then he shifted a little closer, lifting onto his knees to do it. "You've been in my bed now, Rain. You were lying with me. I'm willing to tell those truths, if that's what you want."

He loomed over me, our positions forcing me to look up at him.

There was power in his expression, but also a gentleness I could almost feel. My problem wasn't what he'd said. It was that I had no clue what I was doing. I did like Aspen. I didn't want to ruin things when we'd just started talking again. I also liked Keir. He was so... manly. Strong, powerful, beautiful, and slightly dangerous. The kind of guy I'd always been drawn to.

Unfortunately, it felt like I was going to make a mess of this no matter what I did, so I really had nothing else to lose. Things with Aspen had been nice lately. I might feel nervous about it, but she always made it easy - and like I was being cute instead of stupid. Keir was the same, but the other way. It was this mess with jesters, courts, and magic that messed it all up.

"I think I need to study more, huh?" I asked, because ignorance was not bliss here.

"You need to..." He paused, lifting his eyes. "Fin's back."

"Asshole," I grumbled.

But Keir reached for my face, cupping my cheek. "You need to lie back," he breathed, pulling me down onto his bed.

And he followed. My heart picked up, the position so sensual and promising, but before my body was all the way down, I heard a door open. Keir stopped, looking over with a glare of warning.

"Lock that," he snapped.

I turned to see Fin grinning at us. "Don't want to hear any screaming tonight," he teased.

"Don't worry," I assured him. "I'm not a screamer. Well, not usually."

He laughed and pulled the door closed, then Keir dropped down beside me, the seduction gone as fast as it had started. "Sorry, heard his feet heading this way."

"So this is now a thing," I realized.

"Yeah," he agreed. "Worry less about the histories, Rain. Maybe have Aspen make you a protection charm, and learn how to defend against magic. Defense comes before offense, but sentinels *can* hold our own. Even if we can't stand against their magic, we can find ways to evade it."

"My weapons classes," I realized.

He nodded. "It's the best way for a Legacy to stay safe. I have a bad feeling you're going to need it."

"Fucking bullies," I grumbled. "I thought college was supposed to be different!"

"You thought this was a normal college," he countered. "It's not. This is a school for the fae, which means politics is as much a part of things as it is in any high school."

"Fuck," I groaned. "Ok, so how long before you can walk me to my room?"

"Give me at least thirty minutes so I'm not laughed at?" he begged.

"Should I start yelling now or later?"

He lifted himself up to look at my face. "Remind me again that you have a girlfriend?"

"I have a girlfriend," I told him.

"And now it's official," he pointed out. "No yelling, though. That would get us busted, and neither of us wants to explain this to Bracken. Trust me, he'll make us work it out in weapon-style detention."

"No yelling," I agreed. "But you can tell me more about the jesters."

He flopped back, shoved an arm beneath me, and tugged me over so I had to roll to face him. "I think you should tell me about Rain Brooks, the girl who seems to have entranced all the fae at Silver Oaks."

"There's not really much to tell," I insisted.

"Tell me anyway?" he asked. "Let's call it my price for keeping my hands off you."

"You are a bad, bad boy, Keir."

He simply murmured in approval. "I'm a good one. A little naughty at times, but very good."

"So!" I was losing and knew when to give in. "I was born in Des Moines..."

As I began to talk, a smile claimed his lips. This beautiful, gorgeous, and pretty amazing guy listened, and the whole time, he looked like he actually enjoyed it. Fuck. I liked him a little too much. I was already making a mess of things with Aspen. I kept making a fool of myself in front of Keir.

So why did all of this make me want to smile?

Chapter Forty-One

I stayed in Keir's room for another hour. Before we left, I made a point of messing up my hair, which made him laugh. Then, just to keep the ruse we now had going, I reached over and unbuttoned the top of his shirt before wiggling my fingers through his hair. With a groan, Keir tried to smooth it back into place, but I grabbed his hand and tugged him toward the door before he could fix it.

He laced his fingers with mine the moment we reached the hall, because it was crowded. Guys leaned against walls, doors were open and people called through them to the room across the hall. Naturally, we got noticed. I did my best to act like I didn't care, and Keir smirked as he escorted me to the elevator.

I expected him to leave me there. Instead, he rode all the way down and walked me through the atrium and to the girl's side. It was the most visible way from one side to the other, and I had a feeling part of this was for anyone watching. They'd see a cute if shy couple. When he offered to take me up to my room, I waved him off, making it clear I wanted to break this to Aspen on my own. He nodded and stepped back, but there was a look in his eye which proved he wasn't completely faking this.

The guy liked me. Me! Weird, boring Lorraine. The foster girl who was never cool. Somehow, I'd ended up at the most elite school I could imagine, and I'd fallen in with the least likely group ever. I wanted to joke around and say magic had to be involved, but I was pretty sure it wasn't. Mostly.

But when I walked into my room, I realized Aspen wasn't alone. The sound of guys' voices ruined my plans to explain everything. No matter how close she was with her brother, I didn't want to do this in a crowd. Instead, I headed to the bathroom to wash my face, but her door was open. Wilder turned, catching my movement.

"Rain's back," he said.

So I peeked my head into Aspen's side. "Hey. I was just going to get comfy."

She immediately hopped up and hurried over. "I'm sorry the guys were jerks at dinner," she said when she reached me.

I caught her arm. "It's fine, but um, when you're done hanging out, I wanted to talk. Not a rush. Can wait until tomorrow."

"You can come hang out if you want..." She tilted her head back in a clear invitation.

I just shook my head. "I kinda have a lot to think about. Keir told me about Harper."

She nodded. "I can come over when the guys are gone, if you want?"

"Yeah," I decided, catching her hand. "And there might be rumors."

A smile claimed her lips. "True ones? Because your hair looks like a bad case of bed-head."

"No!" I insisted. "I mean, it was supposed to. Kinda the reason for the talking thing."

"Yeah." She shifted her fingers to hold mine. "So you know, I sorta want to kiss you right now, but turn around and I can at least get your zipper."

I turned, and she lowered it just far enough for me to do the rest on my own. When I turned back around, I decided to just go for it. Leaning in, I kissed her. It didn't feel graceful or elegant. In truth, I felt stupid as all fuck, but I still did it. Aspen quickly caught the side of my face with her other hand, and then her lips parted.

The first time our tongues touched, it felt like a zing of electricity. I smiled against her mouth and her hand slid against my cheek. Soft. Tender. Just a cautious moment of affection, but I felt like my insides had turned to jelly and butterflies were pinging around at light speed inside me.

"I'll kick them out soon," she promised, the words whispered against my lips.

There was another one of those sparks shooting right up my spine. Why was being with her so different? So amazing and wonderful. It felt exciting and dangerous, but in the best way. Just being near Aspen made me want to smile, and kissing her? I was a giddy, nervous wreck and loving it.

"I have a feeling they'll figure out how to stay well past curfew," I warned. "Just don't get in trouble, ok?"

"We never get in trouble," she promised. "And you're welcome to change your mind. You're one of us, Rain. I'm not sure how, but we all agree on that. You're a part of the court."

I took another step back without releasing her fingers, our arms stretching between us. "Explain that to me later, ok?"

"Promise," she said, finally pulling her hand free.

When I stepped into my room, I closed the door behind me, but I made sure it wasn't locked. I also did a stupid little dance of excitement. I fucking liked this girl. Somehow, she made me feel like I was on top of the world. And yet liking her was completely different from liking a guy.

While I changed into my sleep shorts and a tank, I thought about why. The moment Keir had leaned me back onto his bed popped into my mind. He was strong, big, and powerful. When I was around him,

I felt delicate and pretty. Touching Aspen was easier, less intimidating, and actually felt safer. There was a happiness to being around her. It was definitely a thrill, but a different flavor than being near Keir.

Touching her was soft. Talking to her was easy. Being around her made me feel seen, but not physically. It was as if she saw the real me, not just my tits or ass. Like things between us were a little deeper than guys usually went for. More emotional, maybe?

Then there was Torian. He made my pulse race, but it was always caught between anger and intimidation. Somehow, he always knew the right way to get under my skin. Was that lust or frustration? The guy was as beautiful as they came, with his dark hair and neon eyes. I crawled into bed trying to figure it all out.

Hawke was sexy, but in a more brutal way. His features were sharp, and "pretty" wasn't a word that sprang to mind with him. He was ripped, though. Muscled more obviously than the others - even Keir. Wilder was the opposite. His dark skin was so smooth it looked impossible, like he had a perpetual Instagram filter on. While he was fit, his build reminded me more of a dancer or swimmer. The guy was nothing but elegance.

But that was the thing, wasn't it? I liked pretty. I'd never gone crazy for square jaws and dimpled chins. I liked high cheekbones and long lashes - on both guys and girls. I had a weakness for the lithe look of the fae. Aspen was a waif, the kind of girl who would've made a perfect ballerina, with her lean form and long legs. She didn't have big breasts or a bubble butt.

I liked her eyes, though. I couldn't get enough of the icy blue color. It reminded me of pictures I'd seen of glaciers. Her hair was just dark enough at the roots to not be platinum blonde. The cut of it was a little punk, making the slip of a girl look like a tough little wild spirit.

And her lips. Ever since she'd kissed me, I'd started to think about them. When she painted them pink or red. When she left them bare to show the natural blush color. The way they curled so easily, always ready for a smile, and how they felt when touching mine. How soft they were, the feel of her breath sliding over them.

I flopped down on my bed and sighed heavily. I was a mess. When I'd come to Silver Oaks, I'd convinced myself that pretty didn't matter, but I was wrong. There was only so much perfection I could take before I succumbed to the temptation. But of all the pretty I could be chasing, the one who kept drawing me in was also the sweetest. I honestly liked Aspen as a friend - and more. So much more.

I meant to grab my tablet and read about faelings. I needed to know what Harper could do to me. I'd considered looking up the defensive options for Legacies in combat. Instead, I closed my eyes and tried to imagine what it would be like to be out as Aspen's girlfriend. My mind filled with images of laughing as we ran through the halls, slipping into corners to steal kisses. Lying out in the sun - never mind that it was winter - and talking for hours with our hands intertwined.

Somewhere in there, I forgot to open my eyes again. When the lights went out, I finally did. Sucking in a breath, I stared into the darkness before remembering my plant.

"Glow," I breathed.

The thing immediately unfurled its buds and a soft green glow filled the room, about as bright as a glow stick. Halfway across the room, Aspen smiled at me. The light from the plant allowed her to navigate her way toward me a little easier.

"You didn't even make it under the covers," she said.

So I shifted around to do that, then slid back. Her eyes jumped from the open spot in the bed to me and then back. "Rain? What are we doing?"

"I don't know, but I like it," I admitted.

She lifted the edge of the blankets and slipped in beside me. "I'm confused," she breathed.

I just scooted a little closer, until our faces were almost together. "I like you, Aspen. I turn stupid when you're around, and I know I'm acting like an idiot, but that's why. You kissed me, and then I thought you were mad at me, and now you aren't, and it all keeps coming back to that."

"What about Keir?" she asked.

I shrugged. "He told me about Harper making your life hell. He said she bullies you because your magic is Winter and because she knows it gets under Torian's skin. Sounds like pissing him off is her real goal."

"Revenge," she clarified. "But being with me doesn't stop that."

"I know," I assured her. "That's why my hair was a mess. Keir said to let people think what they would. It would buy me some time to learn how to defend myself - and maybe you."

"I can defend us," Aspen promised. "That's why they came at me with iron. It's the one thing I'm weak to. I just can't always be there for you, and I don't want you in the middle of my mess."

"What mess?" I asked, palming the side of her face. "I can tell there's something going on, Aspen. I know there are things deeper than how much fae blood and what magic you four can do. This isn't just about you using Winter magic, is it?"

She pressed her cheek into my hand. "I can't tell you that," she breathed. "I really can't. I promised Liam."

"Is this because Harper dated both Torian and Keir?" I asked.

"No," she said softly. "Harper's a bitch, but who she sleeps with isn't why. It's not about jealousy or competition. It's because she's convinced they think she's lesser because she's half human. We do think she's lesser, but it's not because of her parents. It's her selfishness. She's the same kind of crazy we ran from in Faerie."

"That's a hint, isn't it?" I asked.

Aspen nodded. "It's the best I can do, sweetie. Believe it or not, I'm trying to take care of you."

"When do I get to take care of you?" I asked.

"You already are," she promised. "Please don't let me push you too far, Rain?"

I moved a little closer. "I've never made out with a girl before. How can I know what's too far unless I try, hm?"

I caught a flash of teeth in her smile, and then Aspen leaned in. Our lips met in the middle, the kiss more intense than the last one we'd shared, but just as amazing. This time, she led. Her tongue swirled against mine like a dance. My fingers moved into her hair, and for just a moment, nothing else mattered.

Her legs tangled with mine, our arms wrapped around each other, and we kissed until I forgot about the rest of the world. Her lips, her cheeks, and down her neck. Every time my mouth roamed, hers took that as permission to explore. The give and take was so sensual as we learned each other. I felt her chest pressing against mine. My pulse dropped lower, and it wasn't weird at all.

This felt right. Every guy I'd been with had been chasing one thing. Aspen wasn't. Every time she touched me, I felt like she was touching *me*, not the currently available way to satiate her lust. Her fingers trailed down my arm, exploring my skin. Her eyes shined in the soft glow, watching me as we moved.

No words were spoken, but none were needed, not until we'd kissed ourselves out. I was breathing harder and she couldn't stop touching me, drawing little circles on the skin of my arm. The entire floor was quiet, only the shifting of the building proving time hadn't stood still, and all I wanted to do was look at her a little more.

"Be my girlfriend?" she whispered softly. "My best friend too, but also my girlfriend?"

"I've been thinking about it since you said that earlier," I admitted, "but Keir says we can't. If we're official, we won't be allowed to share a suite."

"So be my girlfriend and we won't tell anyone?" she offered next.

"Yeah," I breathed. "I like 'girlfriend.'"

"Then let me stay the night?" she asked next.

"Definitely," I agreed.

So she shifted to shove her arm under my neck, moving a little higher. Without thinking about it, I moved closer, cuddling against her side. She wasn't a big, strong pillow like a guy, but that didn't make it any less amazing. Her arm curled around my back, mine wrapped around her waist, and we fit together so well.

"I kinda hate that we can't make this public, though," she said softly.

"Mhm," I murmured against the side of her neck. "I know the court knows. Keir knows."

"I like him," she told me. "He makes you happy."

"He flirts with me pretty much constantly," I admitted.

She giggled. "Rain, *I* flirt with you pretty much constantly. Pretty sure my brother does too."

"Yeah, but you're my girlfriend and your brother's a dick most days."

"There's that," she agreed. "And you're my *girlfriend*. Go to sleep, beautiful one. Give me one more thing to be thankful for today."

I closed my eyes and she whispered a string of words in another language. The glow from my plant faded, obeying her command without question. Just as I drifted off to sleep, I realized she'd spoken Faeril. It was even more beautiful than I'd imagined - kinda like my first girlfriend.

Chapter Forty-Two

The next morning, I woke up alone, but Aspen was flitting around the bathroom. She skipped, twirled, and looked like she was in the best mood ever. I couldn't help but smile. She was adorable in so many ways. Powerful in others, but it felt like she let me see her softer side.

We decided to have breakfast together. Fruit for her. Fruit and yogurt for me. There wasn't a lot of talking about what had happened last night, but I may have found myself giggling for no reason. I was nervous, excited, and a little shy - yet it felt like I was on cloud nine.

At some point, Wilder showed up. He found himself a meal and moved to join us. Aspen giggled, flashing a glance at me. My cheeks turned warmer, and the guy hadn't even said a thing. His dark eyes scanned the both of us, then he just nodded.

"So, good night in the girls' dorm, huh?"

"Hush!" Aspen said, tossing a grape at him.

He caught it much too easily, then tossed it into his mouth. "So, guess this means we get to chase the peasant off now?"

"No!" Aspen gasped. "She likes him."

"Kinda my point," he countered.

Which was when I realized they were talking about Keir. "No, he, uh, knows." Wow, I sounded like a moron. "I mean, some people saw me in his room so no one would... you know."

"He's playing your beard?" Wilder asked. "Why?"

"We share a suite," Aspen pointed out.

"And?" Wilder asked.

Aspen just huffed. "Wilder! You know they'd try to split us up. Someone would complain about the Winter bitch getting what she wants and all that. I mean, you at least have Torian to back you up."

"You do too," I reminded her.

"Sorta," she said. "Different dorm, different hall chaperone. Ms. Rhodes would not be as understanding as Liam."

"Who chaperones us," Wilder added as explanation.

"Ah, ok." Because Liam was a bit of a pushover. I knew that firsthand.

"Besides," Aspen said, "Keir's being cool. He's helping out."

"Huh. Didn't expect it of him." Wilder popped a piece of melon into his mouth. "Hawke's not going to be happy."

"He'll get over it or step up," she assured him. "Don't worry, Wilder. You're still my main man."

"Means an easy date to school functions." Then he leaned in. "Can I pretend to take you to the Winter Solstice, Aspen?"

She reached over and tapped under his chin playfully. "Always, Wilder. Who's Torian taking?"

Wilder's eyes jumped back to me. "Yeah, I'm no longer sure." Then back to Aspen. "Knowing him, he'll make a production of going alone. Might make Hawke feel better, though."

So Aspen turned to me. "Has Keir asked you to go with him yet?"

"Don't even know what you're talking about anymore," I admitted. "Aspen, I'm so lost. When is the Winter Solstice? Most of all, what's so special about it?"

"It's the most powerful day of winter," she explained. "Our last exams are on Friday, and technically the semester is over after that, but with Winter Solstice being the Monday afterwards, everyone will stay until Tuesday morning. It's..." She paused as if searching for the right words.

"It's a powerful holiday for the fae," Wilder explained. "It's the shortest day of the year. The pivot point where Winter starts to recede, so those who use Summer magic celebrate their power returning. Those who use Winter magic celebrate it as the strongest day of the year. Different reasons, same party. There will be drinking, dancing, and making very merry. It's held out back near the gateway. We'll have bonfires, warmth glamours for cuddling in the dark, and a lot of rules always get broken."

"Oh, god," I groaned, realizing something else.

Wilder leaned back with a devious smirk. "Oh, you can call me that if you want."

I rolled my eyes at him. "Dream on. No, I just realized I have to go back to the Sparks'!"

"Nope," Aspen said. "We can stay here through the winter break. Most of us do."

"Thank god," I breathed.

"And again," Wilder joked. "You do know you're supposed to be under me when saying that, right?"

I didn't even get the chance to smack him before Aspen did. "Find your own girl!"

He grabbed his bowl and stood. "But I like yours better." Then he moved to kiss her cheek. "Promised Hawke I'd bring something back for him so he can eat in peace. You two, don't have too much fun today. Remember to close the door if you don't want company."

"Promise," she said.

The pair of us finished eating, but there was something else I wanted to do. So, grabbing a pair of rolls, I told Aspen I'd catch up with her. I wanted to make sure Jack knew I hadn't forgotten him. Aspen's face lit up, though, and she asked if she could come feed him with me.

Why did that make me want to smile so much? Unable to hide

my expression, I linked my arm with hers and we headed the long way around, aiming for the door closest to the gym. The weather was biting outside. Not just cold - which her glamour could fix - but also windy. When I suggested it, Aspen didn't seem to mind at all.

We were walking down the main hall, heading for the library, when someone scoffed loudly. We both looked up at the sound in time to see Harper pulling a suitcase behind her. The scorn on her face was made of pure hatred.

"Maybe I should turn you two in to the dean. There are rules against sleeping with your suitemate, you know," she sneered.

I couldn't help myself. My feet stalled out and I turned to face her, letting go of Aspen's arm. "Kinda like the ones against burning another student with iron? Wait. You think those apply to everyone but you, right? Well, let me explain to you how the real world works." I pointed back at Aspen. "That's my best friend. If she and I want to go feed the birds, be giggly, and maybe talk about boys, then that's what we'll do. If you don't like it, you can fuck right the hell off. I dunno, tell your mommy or something."

"My *mother* is nothing to trifle with," Harper snapped, storming into my face.

But I didn't back up. "Don't know. Don't care. Did you miss the memo about how I'm just a plain, boring little human?" Yeah, there was a bit of attitude in my voice. "I also *really* hate bullies, Harper."

"Oh, so going to go tell your 'uncle' Liam?" She snorted at that. "Please. We all know he's your caseworker, just like he is for half the school. Only reason you got in is because you're diving into Aspen's muff."

I reached up to pat Harper's cheek. "Funny how you think that's so wrong - or are you jealous? Besides, you were jumping on a few dicks just to get a bit more fae in you, huh? At least own it, Harper. Sheesh. Do I need to teach you how to be a mean girl? Well, the first step is to make sure it can't come back and bite you in the ass later." I refused to look away, making it clear I wasn't worried about her accusations. It was the only way to keep her from calling my response "proof" of anything.

"Bitch!" she hissed, shoving me back

Then everything seemed to happen at once. Lightning crackled between Harper's fingers. A split second later, the entire hall turned cold enough for my breath to fog in front of my lips. Aspen moved beside me, her shoulder just in front of mine, and she looked like she'd frosted over. Her hair was paler. Her skin shimmered like it was glazed with ice. Her blue eyes, however, were luminescent.

"Try it," Aspen dared. "We're in *my* season now."

"You have no control!" Harper shot back.

Aspen's lips curled into a terrifyingly feral smile. "So? I will turn this world inside out if I have to. She stands with the court. That means *the court stands with her!* Do you hear me? *With* her!" People were starting to gather, the hum of magic enough to draw them near, but Aspen didn't seem to care. "I've also learned a lot in a year."

The electricity on Harper's hand froze over with a flick of Aspen's finger, then the sparks cracked and fell to the ground. Harper's eyes went wide and the girl actually took a step back, but it was too late. We'd been spotted. Teachers ran toward us and *something* began to happen. The cold was being sucked away, dissipated by all of them. Tendrils of frost began to spiral back towards each teacher, declaring their location.

"Aspen!" Ms. Rhodes yelled, her tone an order to stop. "Control yourself, girl." Then she stormed right into the middle of the three of us. "Harper, your mother should be here soon. Go wait on the front steps." Next, I became the center of her attention. "Do you think this is helping?" And finally, she turned back to Aspen. "Let the power go."

Aspen relaxed and the cold quickly vanished. It didn't take long, but the presence of so many teachers had to be pretty good incentive. I tried my best to stand beside Aspen loyally, but every instinct told me to fade back so I wouldn't get in trouble. Then again, I'd started this, and I wouldn't let Aspen go down for me.

"I'm sorry, Ms. Rhodes," I said. "I started that. Aspen was just standing up for me."

"Girls..." Ms. Rhodes grumbled. "You are to report bullying to me. We'd like the school to keep standing, Aspen. And you, Rain, need to worry more about your grades than your peers. Now, go on. Whatever you were doing."

Aspen quickly grabbed my hand and pulled, hauling me up the hall towards the library. I followed, glancing over to see at least three of my own instructors among the crowd of kids. How had this turned into such an ordeal so quickly?

Yet the moment we stepped outside, Aspen began giggling. "Did you see Harper's face?" she squealed.

I was still in a state of shock. "What the hell just happened, Aspen?"

"Oh, she was going to singe you a bit. Nothing fatal. I just made it clear you have my protection. She..." Aspen turned to clasp both my arms. "Harper had no idea I've gotten this much control over my magic!" She paused, but her grin made it clear there was a little more she was excited about. "And now everyone knows you're a part of the court! Show me where we find your bird."

I took her hand again and led her that way. "Do you even realize that half the time I have no idea what's going on?"

"It's ok," she promised. "I do. Harper just wants everyone to think she's the most powerful girl of her age. She's one of those people who wants others to fear them, not befriend them. She also saw five different teachers try to siphon my power."

"Not normal, huh?" I asked.

Aspen shook her head. "No, only Torian's that strong, and I'm getting close. He's going to be so proud!"

There was something about her excitement that was infectious. Never mind how beautiful she looked with her eyes shining like this. It made me laugh with her. It didn't matter that I had no concept of how strong she was or what it would even be good for. I could follow the basic concept.

Most of all, though, Aspen looked like she'd just accomplished something she'd been struggling with her entire life - and *that* was something I could wrap my mind around. She'd succeeded and she was thrilled about it. As we hurried across the open lawn between the school and the outbuildings, I laughed with her.

Then we reached the back of the gym. "Jack?" I yelled, hoping he'd hear me.

"Why do you call him Jack?" Aspen asked.

"It's the one word he can speak. I mean, it could just be a crow call that really sounds like Jack, but he repeats it a lot." Then I raised my voice. "I brought you some bread, Jack, to make up for being gone yesterday!"

Caw!

The sound came first, and a moment later the bird swooped in, landing down by my feet. He made quite the production of ruffling his feathers and putting his wings back, chattering at me like I was in trouble. Then he simply stopped. In one hop, he turned to face Aspen, and then his head twisted to the side.

She pulled in a little breath before kneeling down before him. "Hello, Jack. I see your band. It's an honor to meet a friend of my friend."

"Jack," he croaked before lowering his head in what I could only describe as an avian bow.

"Whoa," I breathed. "He's never done that before."

Aspen just reached over to pet his back, stroking the length of his feathers. "Things that live near the gateways often are touched by magic," she explained. "Isn't he big for a crow?"

I could only shrug. "No idea how big they're supposed to be. Google doesn't really help much with that."

"I have a feeling he's the most magnificent bird here." Then she pulled out the roll I'd given her and pinched off a piece. "Friends, Jack?"

Caw! he agreed.

Then Aspen rolled onto her butt, sitting on the cold ground like it was completely normal. When she looked up at me, I decided to join her. She shifted over, leaned her head onto my shoulder, and broke off another piece of bread for "my" bird.

"This is why you're interesting," she said. "Jack seems to know it."

"Can you talk to him or something?"

She laughed. "No! it's just that the fae folk are known to be friendly with animals. It's why we don't like the idea of eating them. They have minds and thoughts and opinions. Not like plants. Most people don't notice that - but you did."

"He made sure of it," I admitted, tossing him a piece of bread from the roll I had.

"Jack!" he agreed.

Aspen sighed, relaxing into me. "You're so fae in some ways, and so not in others. I don't know how else to describe it, but we all feel it. It's why Keir keeps wanting to talk to you too."

I moved my arm around her shoulders, hugging her against my side. "I kinda told him I'm into you."

"He figured it out when you saved me from the iron." She looked up. "It's ok, Rain."

"I was talking more about him always flirting with me, and how I've kinda ended up in a situation where it'll keep happening," I admitted. "I like you, Aspen. I..."

"Don't want to cheat," she realized. "No, this isn't cheating. Fae don't think like that. I want your time and attention. So long as I'm not missing out, why do I have any right to say who else you can enjoy being around?"

"Yeah, but it's different," I admitted. "Um, I like guys too. I mean, I've always liked guys, and you're kinda the first girl I've thought about like this."

"Like how?" she teased.

I shifted my hand to push her hair back. "The way I always want to hold your hand. How I notice the sparkle in your eyes and I smile when you whistle or hum to yourself. The way you make me feel like an idiot, but the smiling kind. You know, like a girlfriend."

She tossed the rest of her roll at Jack. "Small pieces, my friend."

Caw!

Then she turned toward me, our hips still side by side. Gently, her hand traced the line of my cheek, her face so close. My eyes jumped between hers, making her smile softly.

"I know I shouldn't, but I like when you're nervous," she admitted. "You say more, and I can feel the truth in it. Rain, I have only dated one girl in my life. We were fifteen! I don't know what I'm doing either, but I really like doing this with you. I feel..." She gestured to her chest. "Giddy? I didn't think you'd like me. I thought you'd like Torian, and I keep waiting for you to change your mind. I don't mind that you like Keir too. I get it, ok?"

"Get what?" I asked.

"You like boys," she said with a little shrug. "Boys like you. So, let's make a deal. A binding one, Rain. We will be friends first. We will accept and understand the other as much as we can, and when we don't, we'll ask. I may be your girlfriend, but I'm your friend first, and if you like a boy, or kiss a boy, or anything else, you will tell me. If I like a girl - or any boy happens to catch my eye, which isn't likely - I will tell you. We will be friends first, and we will celebrate each other before all else. And while we do, we will still be this. Still be happy and excited to see each other."

"I like that," I agreed.

"Is it a deal?" she asked. "Do you agree to the terms, Rain?"

"I do," I breathed, and the power rushed over us, spiraling through the currents of the wind and locking our words somehow.

Aspen just smiled. "Then tell me about this boy you like." She shifted to lay her head in my lap. "I think it's cute when you get all blushing and giggly."

"What about this girl I like?" I asked, running my fingers through her hair.

"Oh, you can do that too," she agreed, "but best friends sometimes talk about boys, right?" She was smiling just a little too much. "That's what you told Harper. Besides, if some guy wants to hit on my girlfriend, then I deserve to know about it. So which guys at school do you think are cute?"

"Well," I said, leaning over to kiss her forehead. "I think Wilder looks like he's been airbrushed. The guy is too pretty to be so masculine!"

She giggled. "I know, right? And his big, black eyes."

"He reminds me of a tree in the snow." I let my eyes close as I thought about it. "He's stark in a way, and crisp, but also elegant in his simplicity."

"He'll like that," she breathed.

I gasped. "You're not supposed to tell him!"

"Ok, ok!" She giggled, the sound absolutely beautiful. "Keir reminds me of a sunset."

"No, midday," I countered. "All golden and shiny. He has some amazing muscles, too."

"Blech," she huffed, clearly not impressed. "He has nice lips, though. Kinda like yours."

"Jack!" the bird snapped, making us both look. "Jack, Jack, Jack!"

"More bread," I realized. "Fine!"

So I picked off another chunk and tossed it at him. While he ate, Aspen and I kept talking. For every guy I mentioned, I made her talk about a girl. She tried not to, but I wouldn't let up, and we laughed. This was why I liked her. Being with Aspen was so easy. It was so natural.

It was just so right.

Chapter Forty-Three

The rest of the weekend was just as nice. Aspen began going out with me to spoil Jack. The bird liked her, but he made it clear he liked me more. On Saturday, he began riding on my shoulder, pecking at my hair almost affectionately. Sunday, he tried to follow us back to the school and got pissed off when I said he couldn't come in.

The bird was just too smart for his own good. Maybe Aspen had something with the whole magical absorption thing. It was pretty much all that made sense. Granted, Keir had mentioned crows were one of the few things that could cross the gates into Faerie. Or at least they had been before the gates closed.

I really liked that idea, but since Jack clearly had not been around in the seventies, it didn't really work. Still, how cool would it have been to meet a bird who'd been to Faerie? Either way, he was special, and I liked how Aspen understood my fascination with him.

Sadly, the weekend didn't last nearly long enough. Before I was ready, students were coming back to the dorms. Harper made a scene of it, of course. Towing her stupid little suitcase behind her, she banged on the doors as she passed, yelling, "I'm back, bitches!"

It wasn't just my room or Aspen's. Nope, she pounded on all of them, as if there should be a parade for her safe return or something. It was almost like she was daring me to hate her more than I already did. Then, when I peeked my head out to see what her deal was, I couldn't help but notice the fancy new clothes.

The girl had on things that looked designer. For all I knew, they could've been knock-offs, though. She even wore a pair of tortoise-shell sunglasses on her head, and I was pretty sure there was at least one new ring on her hand. Subtle things, but signs she had money while most people at Silver Oaks were still technically in the foster system. People like me.

It was no surprise when she decided to target me on Monday. Aspen and I headed to the elevator together for first period. Of course Harper was already there, surrounded by her gaggle of jesters. I shared a glance with Aspen, and we turned for the stairs, knowing it wouldn't be worth the headache of waiting for the elevator.

One of the girls saw us, and reached out to grab a handful of my hair. I didn't even think. I simply spun and slapped her across the face. The crack was loud enough to make everyone shut up and stare. Then I shoved my finger right in the girl's face. Nevaeh, I thought.

"You hurt me and I will hurt you, get it?" I glared, making it clear I expected a response.

"Then don't flap your ponytail in my face," she shot back.

My hand lowered, but I stepped even closer. "Yeah? And how far did you have to jump to make sure that happened? Just hope I don't have iron in it next time."

"Rain?" Aspen begged, tilting her head. "Don't want to be late, right?"

So I wiggled my fingers at Nevaeh and skipped off to follow. Yeah, the bouncy little strut thing was forced, but it got the message across. When I was far enough down the stairs Harper couldn't see us, the first giggle slipped out. Aspen joined me a moment later, looping her arm through mine. We didn't even care about the other students and what stupid rumors they might start.

It felt like we were partners in crime, doing something amazingly daring. We weren't. We were simply standing up for ourselves, and maybe taunting Harper a bit, but that was all. Still, Harper wasn't impressed. When I headed for my third-period class, making my way across the building on my own, she decided she'd had enough.

I felt her shoulder slam into me as we passed in opposite directions. The contact was hard enough to make my arms slip, and my tablet went sliding. So did the notebook I was carrying, a pen, and a highlighter. Naturally, they all went in different directions.

"Watch where you're going, Legacy," Harper sneered.

I'd been about to chase after my tablet, but her voice stopped me. Slowly, I turned to face her, aware of the students moving out of our way. The bitch stood there proudly, daring me to try something else.

"Is that the best you have?" I asked her. "My name, in case your little brain can't remember it, is *Rain*."

"No, it's Lorraine," she countered. "Sitting at their table doesn't make you a part of the court, or didn't you know that? There are some things you must be born into. Power is one. Blood is another. You? You're just a piece-of-shit human Silver Oaks took pity on."

"And you're just a self-absorbed cunt. What's your point?" I asked.

"You..." She lifted her hand and threw, but there was nothing in it.

"Harper!" Ms. Rhodes yelled, slinging out her own hand from up the hall.

Magic washed over me. I could feel the static of it, heard the sizzle, but none of it touched me. In that split second, I'd braced for the worst, remembering the story of how she'd turned Aspen into a frog for a moment, but nothing. Had Ms. Rhodes somehow dispelled the effect before it reached me? Had Harper been faking, wanting to make me scream and flinch or something? I didn't get to worry about it for long.

"Both of you!" Ms. Rhodes bellowed as she stormed toward us on her too-high heels. "Office! Now!"

"I have a quiz in Algebra," Harper told her.

"Not anymore," Ms. Rhodes said. "You've just failed it because you didn't think of that first. Rain?"

"I..." Spinning, I hurried to find the things of mine that had hit the ground. "She made me drop my stuff."

Ms. Rhodes clasped the back of Harper's blazer, turning the girl toward the stairs. "Then find it and join us. Five minutes."

"Yes, ma'am," I mumbled, a sinking feeling in my gut.

Considering she was my teacher for third period, if she was doing this now, it couldn't be good. Never mind that her office was downstairs, one of the many rooms in the glass administrative area where I'd enrolled. It also just happened to be across from Liam's, which meant he'd see me in there. I was so busted. I really hoped it wasn't the kind that got me expelled from the Institute!

I found my tablet, kicked up next to the wall. My highlighter came next, and a delicate girl held out my notebook nervously. I made it clear I appreciated the help, knowing better than to simply thank her. She'd saved it before all the pages got bent and warped. Since my notes about my midterms were in there, she was a lifesaver. My pen, however, was gone.

Giving up, I made it to the stairs as the halls began to clear. By the time the bell for third period rang, I walked into the office. Ms. Rhodes was waiting.

"Rain, you need to speak to your guardian. Yes, he's already been informed." Then she pointed Harper into her room.

I watched as my bully went, then I took a deep breath, bracing for the worst. When I turned for Liam's door, he was standing there. His arms were crossed, his jaw was set, and from the look in his eyes, I was in some very deep shit.

"Sit," he ordered.

I took the chair across from his desk, waiting while he closed the door and claimed his own chair. The whole time, my heart was thudding in my chest. He was pissed. I seriously liked Liam, and I'd said I wouldn't cause problems when I came here, but that had changed in the last few weeks. I hadn't even considered it when I'd smarted off to Harper, but I had a feeling Liam remembered.

"This is the second fight you've tried to start in a month!" Liam snapped. "You've just made Ivy send a substitute to cover her class while she's dealing with this. It is a *big deal,* Rain. Do you not realize you have no way of defending yourself against *magic?"* He groaned. "I knew it was a bad idea to let you come here, but Aspen demanded it."

"You know Harper's been bullying Aspen, right?" I asked.

Liam paused. "What do you know about that?"

"Harper dated Keir. She decided Torian would be a better catch, so she moved on to him. When Aspen came here - after she was found, they say - Torian ignored Harper, which pissed her off." I paused to lick my lips, my nerves causing my mouth to feel dry. "They broke up, and to get even, Harper's been tormenting Aspen because it's the only thing that seems to get under Torian's skin. Supposedly, it also makes her mommy proud because that family thinks Winter magic is evil or something."

"Uh-huh..." he leaned back in his chair. "I'm not sure how any of this is your business, though."

"Bracken asked me to stand up for people," I explained. "I hate bullies, and they can't tear me down because I have nothing. Well, and I like Aspen. She's..." I glanced back at the door, then to him again. "Um, I like her."

"Rain..." he breathed, leaning forward to push his face into his hands. "Ivy - Ms. Rhodes - said Harper cast an allergy conjuration at you."

"Yeah, but I'm fine," I pointed out.

"Because the dean happened to be walking down the hall!" he snapped. "She wasn't sure her defense would reach you in time. How much would you like being covered in poison ivy right now? Maybe going into shock from a reaction to the air around you? I'm sure Harper will say it was something minor - but you do not understand what the fae can do!" His voice became a snarl and I flinched back.

"I'm learning," I insisted.

"You stopped them from using iron once," he said, frustration wrapped all around his words, "and now you think you're unstoppable? That's iron. It's where we're strongest, but unless you plan to walk around all day wearing a suit of it, you need to realize that sometimes sucking up is safest."

"I'm not going to suck up to a bully!" I shot back. "Kick me out, Liam. Send me to the group home. I don't care. I promised Bracken I'd stand up for others, and that's what I'm doing!"

"Promised?" he asked.

I nodded. "He talked to me in the atrium that evening. You know, after the whole keychain thing. You were dealing with the girls who'd burned Aspen."

"Shit," Liam breathed, not even caring that he'd just cursed in front of me.

Then he got up and headed right for the door. Yanking it open, he stormed across the hall, knocked on Ms. Rhodes', and entered without waiting for a reply. I leaned back, trying to see what was going on, but I shouldn't have bothered. Their voices were loud enough to carry all the way back.

"She made a promise to Bracken!" Liam said, pointing back my way even though his head was looking at someone inside. "Rain has agreed to stand up to bullies or something. I don't know the words of their agreement, and she won't remember, but it's binding."

"Then Bracken can deal with this," Ms. Rhodes said. "Explain things to her, Liam. Make it very clear what she's done. I'll deal with Ms. Valentina."

Liam stormed back, all but slammed the door, and then threw himself into his chair. "What did you promise?"

"Like for like," I explained. "No excuses that were stupid, like beating someone up for an accidental bump. Why? Liam, what's going on?"

"Politics," he grumbled, reaching for his personal phone. He tapped and swiped, then lifted it to his ear. "Brack? Hey. Yeah. I have

Rain in my office. What deal did you make with her?" He paused for a moment. "Yeah? Well, she just called out Harper in the middle of the halls. Yeah. Oh, I know. She doesn't, but I do. Yeah, I'll tell her to make time for it. Thanks. Bye."

"But we were talking about Harper when he said he'd make sure I didn't get expelled," I said as soon as he was off the phone.

"Fae," Liam grumbled. "He knows, and he explained it. Rain, he just doesn't understand how vulnerable you are right now. I'm not mad at you, ok? I'm worried *for* you. Harper Valentina is a very dangerous girl. She's one of the strongest part-bloods this school has seen in a while. She has abilities in at least three categories. She is not the kind of person you want to face alone."

"Which is why she made sure I was alone before starting something," I countered.

"You. Could. *Die.*" He lifted a brow to make sure I'd heard him. "I'm not talking a bloody nose or social embarrassment here. I'm talking about death, Rain. So, since Harper will be getting detention for this, so will you - with Bracken. If he intends to make you his warrior, then you'd better put in the time."

I nodded. "Ok. Today?"

"Today," he agreed, "and all week long."

"Yeah..." I swallowed, looking up at him. "I'm sorry, Liam. I know I said I'd try to be good, but I kinda forgot. I mean, Harper hates me and there's nothing I can do about that. She's been starting stuff since I first got here. Am I really supposed to tuck my tail and run from it?"

"Sometimes, yes," he told me. "Bracken said Keir mentioned getting a charm from Aspen?"

"I forgot," I admitted.

So Liam pulled open his top drawer and passed me a simple braided bracelet. "It has one use. One single spell can be broken by that. Do not wear it in training or it will discharge. If that happens, Bracken can charge it again."

"How will I know?" I asked as I slipped it onto my wrist.

Immediately, it fizzled, sounding like a bad radio station, and a spark of light flashed off of it. Liam just sighed and gestured for me to give it back.

"Like that," he said. "So maybe Ivy didn't stop the spell. For all we know, you could've had fish for lunch and gone into anaphylactic shock. We'll have to get you another one to keep on hand." Then he grabbed a pad and started writing something. "Stay away from Harper unless you're with Aspen or Torian. Both is better. Do not pick a fight with her again today. Take the long way. Be late to class. I don't care, and I'll handle things with your teachers if you get in trouble." Then he ripped the note off and passed it to me. "Now go to class and give that to the sub. It will keep you from any more detentions."

"Thanks," I said as I stood. "I hope I didn't get you in trouble."

"You didn't," he promised. "You got *you* in trouble, Rain, and it may not be the kind I can do much about. Welcome to being a human in the fae's world."

Chapter Forty-Four

The court wasn't impressed to hear about Harper coming at me. Oddly, it was Torian who was pissed because Ms. Rhodes had punished me too. I could see her point, though. Bullying often made the accuser look like the victim, so unless both parties were held accountable, it would only get worse. I'd fallen into that trap a few times, looking like I was starting something when I was just standing up for myself.

Aspen said she was sorry. Hawke was annoyed. Wilder told me he'd been worried when I was late to third period. It was kinda nice. I couldn't remember the last time I'd been someplace long enough to feel like I actually fit in. Sure, maybe the social circles at Silver Oaks were a little more complicated than at a normal school, but this feeling? Knowing I was included? It made it all worthwhile.

At least until I made it to sixth period, my self-defense class. Bracken was there, waiting for me. He put me into a group with two sophomores attacking me. Worse, they'd been taking classes with him for a few years now. I had to block and hold them off with nothing but my bare hands. The fact that he stood over me, calling out directions and stopping to teach me new moves, ensured I couldn't even take a breather.

In seventh period, things got out of hand. I was back on the training dummy, this time with two sticks, and told to alternate without pause. The steady taps of my training weapons on the wood spokes were almost relaxing, and then the sound in the room changed. I paused, but the clacking of wood on wood kept going, meaning it wasn't just me.

When I turned, I found Keir in the center of the main room, and his sticks were a blur. Across from him was Hawke. Something about their expressions made it clear this wasn't all in good fun. It wasn't merely a training session. They were trying to one-up each other. The moment Hawke threw a kick into Keir's stomach, shoving him back, I was sure of it.

"Be careful what you ask for," Bracken said from behind me.

I spun, shocked that he'd appeared there almost silently. Where had the man come from? Never mind. I was honestly more worried about Hawke and Keir taking things a little too far. Most of us moved slower, trying to learn where to put our weapons and how. Not them. They were aiming for each other's bodies, blocking, and then throwing their own attacks.

"You stood up for Aspen twice," Bracken said, his words soft enough they wouldn't carry. "The court is now in your debt, even if they won't admit it. Keir has been spending too much time with you."

"Aren't you going to stop them?" I asked.

Bracken actually chuckled. "No, I'm not. Keir needs to prove himself. Hawke needs to realize it's not always about who you know, but rather what you've learned." He moved to stand beside my shoulder. "Why did you taunt Harper today, Rain?"

"She's been trying to cause problems," I said.

"More," he demanded. "We have a deal, remember?"

I sighed. "It's complicated."

"Still not good enough," he told me. "Rain, our agreement was that you'd help other students. This time, you started something for your own shallow pride. What I want to know is why I shouldn't be offended?" He dropped his hand on my shoulder. "And I know about Aspen."

"And me?" I asked, looking over.

His eyes flared, making it clear he didn't know that. "Ah, so that's how it is, huh? By taunting Harper, you think you're taking the heat away from Aspen? You think you're protecting her?"

"A little," I admitted, unsure how exactly he'd taken my comment. Still, I wasn't about to tell him we were dating if he didn't know. "It's also that Harper picks on Aspen to upset Torian. She picks on me to upset Aspen. Thus, she picks on me to upset Torian." I shrugged. "Complicated."

He rubbed the spot under his hand gently. "Not as much as you might think, and more than you know. Harper Valentina wants power. She'll take it anywhere she can get it, and a fae from Faerie is more impressive than one from Earth. A pure more than a half. In her mind, Summer is more important than Winter. Rain, she ranks things by how much bragging power they have, and bringing down Torian Hunt is a lot of bragging power."

"Why?" I asked, still watching Hawke and Keir.

"The same reason those boys are fighting," he told me. "Think of the fae like a pack of dogs. Some of us rise to the top because we have sharper teeth - more magic. Others survive by showing their belly and pleasing those with sharp teeth. The fae are a wild people. We're very civilized in some ways and almost feral in others."

"Ok?" That all made sense so far.

Bracken dropped his hand so he could gesture at the guys. "By birth, their ranks should've been equal. By social status, they're not. Hawke rose while Keir faded. Now, the shiny new thing has shifted the balance. Keir has been allowed to not only train you, but socialize with you."

"Allowed?" I asked with a huff.

"I'm still relating this to dogs, Rain. The alpha bitch allowed that mongrel to play. The other mongrel feels slighted. His only recourse is to make it clear he's just as fast, just as strong, and just as worthy."

"Worthy for what, though?" I asked.

"That is a question for you to ask *them*," he said. "And Hawke will win. Keir will let him to keep the peace. Hawke will know it, but the rest won't. You see, Keir knows that sometimes, the best way to defeat an enemy is to let him - or her - think they defeated you. Consider that the next time you're alone, with no one to shield you from magic, and trying to piss off the fourth strongest fae at this school."

"Who's the third?" I asked.

Bracken smiled. "Wilder, of course. Now, back to your lesson. Don't worry, you'll get a chance to use it in detention."

With a groan, I turned and began smacking the dummy again. I may have shifted around so I could also watch the guys sparring. I definitely missed a few of the spots I was aiming for. Still, the fight dragged on long past what I could've handled. The guys were slick with sweat. Hawke's shirt clung to him, making every muscle on his body stand out. Keir's hair had turned a shade darker from the moisture.

They were gorgeous. Not surprising, since they were both fae, but it was still hard to ignore. I'd always imagined "fairies" to be scrawny little things. Instead, they were lithe and fit. Not massive like action heroes in the movies, but still the kind of bodies that made women drool. Just to be sure I wasn't, I wiped at my lip and started another round.

Then, sure enough, Keir took a hard hit to his gut. The guy doubled over, dropping to a knee, and Hawke followed with a set of bashing blows to Keir's back. Waving him off, Keir admitted his defeat. For a long moment, Hawke just stood there, waiting, watching. Yeah, he knew Keir had thrown that. I didn't know how, because the hit looked legitimate to me, but Hawke had been in the middle of it.

Then Hawke thrust out his hand, offering to help Keir up. I saw them talking, the tension between them fading. After a few seconds, both of them turned to look right at me. I tried to act like I didn't notice, focusing on the pattern with my sticks, but I was pretty sure I failed.

For the rest of the class, the pair worked together. It seemed Bracken was right. They were a lot more like dogs than I'd thought. The dominance had been settled, and now the guys acted as if nothing at all had happened. Thankfully, seeing the other students glance over made me feel a little better - like I wasn't the only one confused about whatever issues they were working through.

But an hour of beating a training dummy with sticks left my arms feeling like mush. Even worse, when the final bell rang and everyone else got to leave, I had at *least* another hour of detention. I took the chance for a break, dropping my weapons on the floor and bending over just to let my aching arms hang.

"You have ten minutes to get a drink, bathroom, or anything else," Bracken told me as he moved down to the center area and began cleaning up the mats. "Then I'm going to teach you how to deal with magic."

That had my complete attention. "Yeah? I'm good."

Hawke came out of the changing room and started helping. "How long you keeping her, Bracken?"

"One hour today," Bracken said. "From there, we'll see how it goes."

Hawke nodded. "We don't want her walking back alone. Can Keir really dispel well enough?"

"I can," Keir called as he made his way out.

"He can," Bracken promised. "Now you boys get out of my classroom. Rain?" He pointed at the ground. "Tie your hair into a bun. You won't want it in the way for this."

"What's this?" I asked as the room began to empty.

Bracken just chuckled and walked away. Yeah, clearly I was not getting an answer to that. I watched Keir and Hawke leave together, something about that making me a little anxious. The entire middle area had been cleared, leaving nothing but a wooden floor. Not the best footing, I'd been taught, but I'd work with what I was given.

Then Bracken picked up a single stick and moved to the edge. "There are three ways for a true Legacy to prevent magic. The first is iron, and it's not something students are encouraged to carry in school. I've gotten an exemption for you, but if you abuse it, you will be right back here for another week, am I understood?"

"Yes, sir," I agreed.

Bracken pointed to a rack by the door. "There's a keychain there. Pick it up when you leave, because that is not the option we're working on today. Now, the second way is to have a charm or enchantment that will negate a spell. Liam told me he offered you his own charm and it went off. That means Harper's spell got through. We have no way of knowing how serious it would've been, but it's gone now."

"Ok, so I'm assuming that's not what we're doing today either?" I asked.

"It's not," he agreed. "Today, you are going to learn the hardest way to keep a fae from enchanting, conjuring at, or cursing you - by interrupting it."

"What?!" I gasped. "How?"

"For every bit of magic we do, we must first visualize it. More power means more effect. It's one way of being strong. Control, however, is the key. The more control a person has, the more predictable the result. The faster they can make it happen. The more specific the effect. Control is nothing more than managing the magic to obey the way we want it to instead of the way we feel it should."

"Ok?" I was keeping up so far.

"The less control a fae has, the longer it will take for them to activate their power. Trying to figure out what they want to happen, imagine how it will look and the way it will be released, is all the time you have to stop them. Seconds, Rain. So, to practice this, I will be casting at you. The spells will not hurt, but there will be a lasting effect. When you leave here, everyone will see just how many times you were hit with magic."

I groaned. "Ok, and I just rush you or something?"

"A push, a distraction, or startling me will break my 'casting,' for lack of a better term. Now, how far away was Harper this morning?"

"Only a few feet," I admitted.

Bracken moved closer until I gestured that was about it. Then he lifted his hand. "Are you ready?"

I pulled in a breath then nodded.

"Then stop me," he ordered.

His body tensed and I rushed in, trying to shove at his arm. It didn't work. I was a half-step away when something popped over my head and a torrent of tepid fluid rushed down my body. In shock, I gasped, turning to look, only to find bright pink... paint? Like someone had dumped a glass of it over my head, and it was soaking through my clothes!

"Oh, that's gross," I moaned.

"Then do better," he said. "Reset."

I tried again, jumping and yelling to spook him out of his control this time. The pop over my head was softer, but it still came. Even worse, the powder that rained down around me sparkled. Half of it drifted to the floor. Hanging my head, I checked, and yep, that was glitter.

"You just glitter bombed me?"

The man's expression finally cracked and a laugh broke free. "Oh yeah. This is the most fun I've had all week."

"Bracken!" I whined.

"Again, Rain. More paint is coming. Lucky for you, it will all wash off with just water. But if you keep failing, I'll just add extra sparkly glitter."

"Fine!" I took my spot, and we did it again.

Then again, and about a dozen more times after that. Running at him wasn't working, so I experimented. Since I was still holding my sticks, that gave me a little extra reach. Twice, I managed to thump

Bracken hard enough to break his control. Those were simply rewarded with a reset.

And then I got doused in rainbow glitter to make up for it. Lime-green paint came next. So did white, brown, black, orange, and a whole lot more pink. So much pink! Probably because I'd made a face when I saw the color, so my instructor was intentionally trying to piss me off.

I simply wasn't fast enough to stop him. I got the idea. What I didn't understand was how to reach him. Then it hit me. The next time Bracken had me reset, I was smiling, because I had a plan. He nodded, and I reached up to swipe a handful of paint from my body and slung it at him.

Technicolor, glitter-coated goo landed right across his neck and chest. Bracken just opened his mouth and groaned. "That is honestly disgusting. It's... warm!"

"You made it!" I reminded him.

"And you just got a new idea." He looked down and checked his shirt. "Just glad it washes out. Again!"

This time, I was done messing around. When Bracken tensed to cast, I tossed one of the sticks at him, standing my ground. The thing bounced off his shoulder, making him jerk his head up in surprise, and then he began to nod.

"That," he said. "That works. Your tablet, a book, or anything else. Hit them and it will distract." Then he flicked his finger at the door. "Go home and have a shower."

"Is it bad?" I asked.

He just laughed. "Oh, it's *so* bad. Have fun explaining it to everyone you pass. Maybe tomorrow you'll have a few more ideas, because you won't get the weapons. Have a nice night, Rain."

"I hate you, Bracken. You know that, right?" I grumbled, tromping over to get my things.

"At least I'm not making you clean up the room." Then he pointed to the rack. "Don't forget the keychain, because I'm not touching the thing again!" I turned that way just as he added, "And so you know, Aspen's control is fragile, but Harper's isn't. Pick your fights wisely for the next few days."

Not what I wanted to hear. Not at all. Even worse, when I reached the door, I realized it was well into twilight outside. That meant cold, and this was going to be a miserable walk home.

Chapter Forty-Five

I did not put on my coat. Hell, I was mortified I even had to hold it, let alone slip the cute little butterfly keychain into the pocket. Paint dripped off my clothes in wet, glitter-filled globs. Granted, Bracken had warned me, and it could've been worse. I just had a feeling I was going to spend this entire week covered in something.

I was barely out of the door before a snorted laugh made me look up quickly. The motion made another drop of goo slide down my arm. Standing across from me, watching the exit, Keir saw it all. The bastard didn't even try to hide his amusement.

"So, did you learn how to block at all?" he asked, walking over with his arms out. "Let me have your coat. You are a complete mess."

"Jack!" the crow said before rattling in some crow version of amusement.

Ok, it probably wasn't a laugh, but it sure felt like one right now. All I could do was sigh and give in. Keir took my coat, the bird flapped around me, and I just started walking back toward the school. I wasn't ashamed, but I was disgusting, and all I wanted was my shower.

"Rain?" Keir asked, jogging to catch up.

"I stopped a couple," I told him. "Bracken actually laughed at me, though."

"I can't say that I blame him," Keir admitted. "Is that glitter?"

"Asshole glitter bombed me more than paint."

Keir not only snorted this time but he sputtered to go along with it, all but spitting as he tried to hold back his amusement. "I see. But he let you out early, so that must mean you did well, right?"

I just stopped and spun to face him. "Why are you here? Class was over an hour ago."

"And I promised Hawke I'd wait."

My eyes narrowed. "Explain that. Why would Hawke care?"

Hanging his head, Keir gave in. "Hawke takes care of Torian. Torian adores his sister. Aspen will be worried about you, thus..."

"Hawke wants to make sure Harper doesn't try to jump me out here alone," I finished. "Ok."

"And he's worried you're in too deep," Keir added.

That was not at all what I'd expected. "Hawke? Like, autumn-colored guy, eagle eyes, kinda looks like his namesake?"

"The second member of the court. Yeah, same guy," Keir agreed. "Why?"

"Because he doesn't *know* me!" I threw up my arms, but that sent a glob of glitter ooze flying.

Keir quickly stepped back, and the slung mess splattered onto the dry grass. "Raincoat tomorrow. Gotta remember that," he teased. "And let me break this all down for you. Aspen claimed you as the court's. Sounds like a possession, works like a title. Hawke is the soldier of the court. Then there's the fact that this girl he's supposed to be watching out for is..."

"Interesting," I supplied.

"Sexy," Keir corrected. "I mean, do you have any idea how your shirt is clinging to you right now?"

"Trust me, I know," I promised, walking again. "It's also starting to get cold."

"Trust me," Keir repeated as he moved back to my side, "I know."

I scoffed. "I'm wearing a sports bra. You shouldn't be able to see much nipple."

"Well your right one's definitely lower than the left, but they're poking out pretty good."

"I am going to hug you," I threatened.

He laughed. "Tempting, but I'm going to pass." For a few steps, he said nothing, but he kept glancing over. "Rain, can we talk about what happened with Harper yet?"

"She caught me between classes and slammed her shoulder into me hard enough to send my stuff flying. I didn't appreciate it," I informed him.

"She waited until you were alone, singled you out, taunted you in a way she knew would get you to react, and then set you up to get either expelled or destroyed," he corrected. "Which was it?"

"Destroyed," I admitted. "She cast some spell on me."

"Conjured or enchanted," he said. "We don't actually 'cast.' We're not mages, Rain."

"Same shit to me." I stopped again. "Keir, I don't tolerate bullies. I am not going to duck my head and ignore it when she goes after Aspen. I'm not going to grovel before her like I'm somehow less worthy." I almost stopped there, but I just couldn't help myself. "She thinks I'm going to be scared of her, but there's one thing she's missed. I have nothing to lose and everything to gain."

He took a half step closer, his smile completely gone. "What do you mean?"

"I have spent my *entire* life trying to find a safe place. My home wasn't it. My foster homes gave up on me almost as fast as they got me. The one good foster parent I had got transferred out of state for work. What is the worst Harper can do to me? Kill me? So fucking what! This, Keir, is all I have. Liam cares about me more than anyone else in my life ever has. Aspen is the first friend who hasn't tried to change me so I fit in. You!"

"What about me?" he asked.

"You give a damn, ok?" I said, glancing away. "The fact that you're even out here? All the little things you do that make me think you're a good guy? And I like it, but I'm waiting for it to all go wrong. I'm going to end up expelled if Harper has anything to say about it."

"Sounds to me like Bracken has you covered," he countered. "I know the court does, and do not discount their power."

"They're just students," I hissed. "I don't even get how that works!"

He stepped even closer and cupped the side of my neck, ignoring the splatter that I knew coated it. "No one does. Don't you see, Rain? That's why everyone watches them. Is it because they're really that strong? Is it something else? We don't know, no one's talking, and the guesses are flying."

"What guesses?" I asked.

"That they own this place. That they have some secret way of tapping into the power of Faerie. That their magic is all a bluff - but I've seen it. I can assure you it's not." He leaned in just a bit more. "And those four think *you* are interesting. They have claimed you as one of theirs. Hawke made it very clear to me that if I'm not good to you, then he's coming for me. They have claimed you, and that's not a small thing."

"I don't..."

"I know," he assured me. "The part you don't get is that we don't truly understand them either. We know there's *something*. We can fucking feel it when they walk into a room. Just like you feel dark. Not depressed. Not dangerous. You feel dark the same way you said Hawke looks like autumn. It's a feeling in the same place we sense lies. Rain, something is going on, and you have planted yourself right in the middle of it."

"No, Jack did," I corrected. "I wouldn't even be here if that crow hadn't flown into the house. Hell, it may not have even been him! It was *a* crow, in *a* house, and now I'm here caught up in this, and all I know is that bullies suck, Harper is one, and I'm not backing down!"

"Then don't back down," he told me. "I made it clear I'll keep an eye on you." He lifted his hand and stepped back. "Before you get all defensive about that, know it's just while you're learning how to keep Harper from stabbing you in the back. I can dispel. Hawke has enough magic to shield you. Torian, Wilder, and Aspen have enough to break Harper. All we're doing is standing up for you, because this is one time you can't stand up for yourself."

I jiggled my head in a weak nod. "Ok. I just don't want to become some damsel in distress, you know? Some little bimbo who falls down when the bad guy - or girl - is chasing her."

"No," he assured me, "you're not a damsel. See, that's the thing with friends. We look out for each other. It means you don't have to do it alone, and you've got a few of us now."

"I barely know the guys of the court, though," I said again. "Seriously, the most I've talked to Torian was after Aspen got hurt. Well, and when he pulled me away from you by the tree."

"I was going to steal a kiss, too," Keir teased. "Asshole ruined my moment, and now you're banging his sister."

"No banging," I assured him as we both began walking again. "It's different with her. It's not about getting off, you know?"

"Not at all," he joked. "I happen to like getting off. I know a lot of girls who like it too."

I thumped his arm, leaving a shiny pink spot on his sleeve. "I mean that doesn't trump talking or curling up with her."

"Are you two sharing a bed?" he gasped, making a mock-production of it.

"Once," I admitted. "And it was to sleep, so quit. I just..." A groan fell out because I knew I shouldn't ask a guy this, and yet I had no one else. "How do I know?"

"When she's ready, or when you are?" he asked. "Rain, you know when you know. It's ok to take it slow. There's nothing wrong with enjoying spending time with her. Maybe she's interesting, fun, and nice to look at. Maybe talking to her is its own reward. You don't have to prove yourself."

"What if I'm not really bi?" I asked. "What if I'm just desperate or crazy? What if it's a fae thing?"

He grabbed my arm. "Stop. It's ok to be wrong. It's ok to try it out. It's ok to be unsure. It's ok to not know what you like and to experiment, but I think you like her. Maybe you won't like sex with her. Maybe you will. Doesn't matter. You like her, and you clearly like her in a way that's more than just a friend."

"I feel so stupid when I'm around her," I admitted. "I can't think of what I should say, and then I try too hard. It's like, it all makes sense in my head, and then I feel like I'm completely screwing it up, but she still smiles at me so sweetly."

"Welcome to being the one who gets to ask, or start, or go first." He chuckled. "We guys go through this in like ninth and tenth grade. Well, some are still trying. We think we're supposed to know all the right words and moves, but you girls think it's cute when we're just honest, so try that?"

"Yeah," I said as we reached the door. "Bye, Jack!"

"Jack!" the bird replied, proving he was out there in the darkness somewhere.

Thankfully, Keir opened the door so I didn't have to. When I stepped through, he moved right to the elevator and pushed that button too. The moment it opened, he followed me in and reached for the fourth-floor button, tapping it as well.

"What are you doing?" I asked.

"I'm walking you all the way home, because you are not allowed to touch anything in the state you're in. The fact it's not dripping does not mean you aren't a mess."

"At least it's pretty?" I asked as the elevator stopped on my floor.

Keir waved for me to go first. "It's sparkly? The colors have become some pink-and-shit-stain combo. Bracken did not do you any favors." Together, we made it to my door, then he looked at my coat. "Keys?"

"Don't reach in that pocket," I warned. "Bracken gave me an iron keychain. Um, if you lean it over here..."

"Fuck it," he mumbled before flicking all five of his fingers at my door knob. I heard it click, then he reached over and pushed my door open. "I'll do it my way."

"I thought you only had defensive magic," I gasped.

"That counts," he assured me. "There's no attack in unlocking things, putting out lights, and a few other tricks. I'm pure fae, Rain. My version of weak is a faeling's dream of power. I just got all the inward skills. The non-aggressive ones."

"Good to know," I said, stepping through and pointing to my desk so he'd know where to put my coat. "And no offense, but I need a shower."

"Aspen!" Keir called out.

Immediately, I heard movement, and then the bathroom door burst open. "What..." Her eyes landed on me and the sentence died as the laughter took over. "Rain!"

"She needs a shower," Keir said. "Tell Hawke I got her back safe. Make sure she doesn't drip any of that on the floor. It's Bracken's special mix, so it washes off with straight water, but that doesn't mean it won't be a mess. I don't even want to think about how long this place will have glitter in it."

"Fucking Bracken," I groaned.

Aspen just tugged me back toward the bathroom. "You did good, Keir," she called back. "Night!"

"Night, you two," he said as he left.

Then she pointed to our bathing nook. "You are getting in the tub to take all of that off. I'll start the shower and get towels. Oh, Rain... next time duck or something."

"I was learning how to stop someone from throwing magic at me," I explained. "It's my detention for picking a fight with Harper." I caught her arm before she could even react. "And this is my fight, ok? She's coming after me because she thinks I'm weak. I'm going to make sure she knows I'm not. Let me have this?"

She nodded. "Ok, but if she hurts you..."

I climbed in the tub and started toeing off my shoes. "I'd kiss you right now if I didn't think it would make more of a mess."

"No," she told me, backing away. "You keep your splooge to yourself, woman! Not even you are that cute. Close, but not pink-and-brown glitter cute. Bathe! Then you can kiss me."

Chapter Forty-Six

For the rest of the week, I came home covered in paint and glitter. Thankfully, it was less each time. By Thursday evening, I'd somehow avoided all the paint, and I only had three colors of glitter on me, but the stuff was in my *hair!* I'd found little sparkles all over my room lately, and I was pretty sure this was a lesson I'd never forget.

But I was getting pretty good at preventing Bracken from tossing his magic at me. An hour or more every night had me lunging faster. I'd figured out standing close was better than a distance. Smarting off gave me an excuse to push into his face. So far, I'd called Bracken a toad-eater, a nunu head - with gusto - and a potato peeler. It was the best I could do on short notice.

I also had my "crew" walking me to class. Aspen took me from our suite to first period. Then Torian walked me to second period. I was actually starting to warm up to the guy. He wasn't always a dick, and he adored his sister in a way I hadn't thought possible. Unfortunately, our chats were mostly shallow and generic stuff.

After second period, Aspen walked me to the end of the hall where Keir waited to take me across the building to third. There,

Hawke and Wilder walked me to fourth period, and Torian stayed with me as we headed to lunch. Easy, right? Not so much, because Harper noticed. She glared. She tossed out insults every chance she could, and only half of them were at me.

Then, on Friday, Harper decided she wasn't going to get the chance she wanted, so she decided to make one. Keir and I had just passed the atrium when she swooped in from the side, clearly having planned this. She wasn't aiming for me, though. Her complete attention was on Keir.

"Hey," she said, catching his arm so he'd stop.

I paused with him, both of us turning to face her. Keir moved to drape his arm over my shoulder, holding me against his side. I shifted in closer, hugging his waist with my own arm. For a moment, Harper's jaw clenched, but then she got control of her face again.

"So, I need a date to the Winter Solstice," she told him, completely ignoring my presence.

"Good for you," Keir said.

"Are you going with someone?" Harper pressed, her eyes flicking over to me.

"I am," he assured her.

But my guts clenched. It was stupid, and I knew it. That still didn't stop the intense feeling of disappointment, because he hadn't asked *me*. The idea of him taking another girl to this event? I didn't even know what the big deal was about, but there was still a part of me that wanted him to be *my* date - even if it was just as a cover excuse.

"Well, if you change your mind," she said, stepping closer to trail a finger down the middle of his chest, "let me know before midterms. I remember our last solstice together." She winked and tapped right over his heart.

"Oh, back off," I grumbled, pulling her hand away from his body. "You had your turn. You screwed it up. Get over yourself already!"

"Stay out of this, Rain," Harper snarled. "Haven't you realized just how helpless you are? The only reason you're still walking the halls is because *I* let you!"

"Keep dreaming," I grumbled.

But Keir was having none of it. "So, you're jealous of her, Harper, is that it? Rain shows up and all the pure-bloods can't keep our eyes off her. Well, while you've been chasing power, we're chasing something better: a personality. I promise fucking you wasn't that impressive, and it's certainly not worth the headache that comes with your spoiled ass."

She huffed. "You liked it!"

"Of course I did," Keir chuckled. "You chased me. You bent over for me. You dropped to your knees for me. What's not to like? Even a bad orgasm is still an orgasm. Just one little problem with your big plan." He leaned into her face. "You still don't rule this school, and I'm not into groveling."

He glanced at me and turned, the pair of us continuing on our way. Behind us, Harper huffed in frustration a few times, then she squealed in rage. I glanced back just in time to see her brace up and pull in a deep breath.

"Keir!" I hissed, reaching for something to throw at her, because that was the first step in casting!

But my big, strong guardian didn't seem concerned at all. He looked back right as she flung her arm and a shield of rainbow light flashed up, vanishing just as quickly. That was when Keir finally let me go, so he could storm back toward her.

"Are you fucking insane?" he demanded. "You know I can stop you every time. You know the rules forbid magic in the halls! I don't care how important you think you are, if you become a menace, I will throw you out for the Hunt myself. Do you hear me?"

"Fuck you, Keir!" Harper snapped before shoving at his chest.

I moved to join him, unwilling to make Keir do this on his own. The guy thrust his hand back, gesturing for me to keep my distance. I stopped, but damned if I didn't hate it.

Then he pointed at Harper's face. "Try me. I dare you. But if you come after Rain again, I will make sure you regret it. She's under my protection, Harper. Mine - and the court's. The one thing that can bring the five of us together... is her."

"A stupid human girl who can't even wipe her own ass!" Harper growled.

Keir caught her face, squeezing her cheeks between his fingers and thumb. "She's prettier than you. She's nicer than you. She's also a lot smarter than you. Fuck your half-blood ego. You're still just a faeling in a world of humans. Grow the fuck up already."

Then, using that grip, he pushed her back and stormed toward me. As he passed, he caught my hand, pulling me back up against his side, and we kept walking. Everyone saw. The stares of the others in the hall were a mixture of awe and fear, because Keir wasn't happy. This easy-going man looked damned near feral.

The strange thing was how much I liked it. I wasn't scared of being beside him. However, I was a little worried for him. When we made it far enough away, I pulled my hand from his so I could grab his arm.

"Are you ok, Keir?"

"No," he said, slowing his pace. "I hate her, Rain. I try not to, but every time she talks to me, I hate her even more. That she tried to conjure you? Fucking *bitch!*"

"Hey," I breathed. "But I'm ok, and that's why you're here, right? I mean, and the whole light show was pretty impressive, in all honesty."

That finally made the scowl on his face ease. "Yeah?" he asked. "You don't even know what it was."

I just shrugged. "Pretty lights and a safe girl. I got that part. Plus, my friend makes a damned good hero."

He chuckled, slowing as we reached the door for my third-period class. "Yeah. So, since she already brought it up, I was going to ask you this weekend. I'm sure you'll be mingling, and it's your first solstice, but would you like to be my date?"

The air rushed from my lungs. "I thought you were going with someone?"

"Yeah, um..." He pushed his hand into his hair, shoving it all back. "Fae lies. I told the guys that if I couldn't get a date, I'd go and hang with them. So, I'm definitely going with *someone*. I was just hoping you'd be the one on my arm when we arrive." Then he leaned in. "And Aspen's later. I get that."

"I'd love to," I said. "I just didn't want to expect it, since... you know."

He nodded, then lifted his hand to trail his thumb across my cheek. "Expect it, Rain." Then he tilted his head at my class. "Get in there before you're late."

"Yeah," I breathed before pulling away and turning for the door.

Behind me, Keir made his way to his own class. I had a feeling he wouldn't make it in time, but I kinda didn't care. They weren't as strict on the older students. Plus, I couldn't stop smiling, and those butterflies were back.

I was *supposed* to be going with Aspen, though we couldn't do it publicly. Well, we could if we wanted new room assignments. Keir seemed to understand. Yet I didn't know how to deal with the fact that both of them gave me the same silly feeling - or how much I liked it.

But the moment I walked in, Hawke and Wilder were watching me. Hawke was sprawled in his chair with his feet on the edge of some guy's desk across from him, blocking the aisle. His eyes watched me, tracking my movement across the room. When I turned down the row to get to my seat, he didn't move, his legs effectively blocking my path.

"Hawke, please?" I asked.

"What was that about?" he asked. "You and Keir."

"He's been walking me to class all week," I said. "You know that."

Hawke just turned to look at his friend. "Wilder, can I get an assist?"

Wilder lifted his hand and snapped. A burst of white light flared and everyone else in the room slowed to a crawl. "You have five minutes," Wilder told him. "I can't hold it forever like Tor."

So Hawke pulled down his legs and pushed to his feet, right into my face. Gone was the lazy attitude of a second ago, replaced with something dangerous, and he was leaning in towards me. His pupils narrowed, turning oblong. His body tensed, bulking up like he was ready to pummel something, and I felt like I was staring into the face of a bird of prey.

"What was that at the door!" he demanded, snarling like some kind of wild monster. "That was not walking you to class. That was not kind or gentle. That was crossing the *fucking line,* and you're *ours.* I gave him the smallest privilege, and if he thinks he can abuse it, I will *tear him apart,* so what the fuck did he say?"

Holy.

Shit.

I had to swallow before I could make my voice work. "He asked me to be his date to the solstice thing. We'd talked about it before, but after Harper tried to make a scene in the halls, he officially asked if I'd go with him."

"And?" Hawke asked, the warning clear in his tone. "What. Did. You. *Say?*"

"I said yes," I told him quickly.

"You're with Aspen!" he roared. "If you think I'll ignore this - "

I had no idea what came over me, but I reached out to clasp his arm, halting the tirade. "She knows," I assured him. "Keir's my official date. She's my unofficial one. He knows that. He made it clear."

Hawke just looked down at my hand on his bicep. For a long moment, he didn't move. His eyes, however, relaxed, changing back to something much less animalistic. Then they jumped from my hand back to my face.

"Have you ever experienced fear, Rain?"

"Yeah," I assured him, wondering if this was a warning.

"When was the last time?" he asked gently.

I swallowed. "When Harper tried to throw something at me a moment ago and I was too far away to stop her."

He pressed his hand over mine, the monster inside him now gone. "I was going to ask you, so you know. Wilder's taking Aspen. I was going to be your date, and I do not like him."

Keir. He didn't like Keir. "Why?" I asked.

Hawke just shifted to the side, giving me the space to pass. "Because he's taking you." Then he looked over and nodded at Wilder.

Another snap made the rest of the class move again. The girl in the desk behind Hawke jumped, surprised to find him suddenly standing, but then she looked back down as if trying to ignore it. I rubbed Hawke's arm gently.

"Next time," I promised him. "You just have to ask."

The guy's face softened a bit, but I kept moving. I made it beside my desk as the bell rang, so I hurried to drop my rump into it. A moment later, Ms. Rhodes walked in, looking around to make sure everything was ok.

"Who has been conjuring in my class?" she asked.

"That was me," Wilder said. "I needed a moment of privacy."

"How about you learn patience instead?" she told him. Then she turned to the rest of us, acting like it had never happened. "Today, we're going to talk about the three types of magic in Faerie."

I pulled out my notebook and pen. This sounded like the kind of thing that would be on the midterms. The ones that were coming up much too fast, and which I was not prepared for at all. Flipping open my spiral notebook, I began writing quickly. Summer. Winter. Wild. Those were the three types.

"As many of you know," Ms. Rhodes explained, "Summer and Winter magic comes from the court we're born to. Many of common birth have access to both, but it's never as strong as those who have sworn themselves to a season."

"What's Wild magic?" someone asked.

She tipped her head toward them, acknowledging the question.

"That is the raw magic of the untamed side of Faerie. It is the antithesis to everything you all know about magic and works in very different ways. We fae cannot touch it, only the Wild ones and their agents. Wild magic is something you will probably never see, but it is real. When I was still a child - back when the Mad Queen was newly coronated - I attended the funeral of Joan le Fae. On Earth, she was called Joan d'Arc. She was the last person known to wield Wild magic."

Yeah, this was why I loved going to school here. Classes I'd once thought were boring had just become interesting. Knowing about this parallel world turned history into an adventure, and I was dying to know more. Looking up, with my pen ready, I was hanging on Ms. Rhodes' every word.

But in his chair, Hawke sat twisted, looking back at me.

Those eyes. I'd watched his pupils turn to slits, almost like a cat's but going sideways. Talking about Wild magic made me wonder about him. The memory of that change was etched in my mind, and yet those eyes seemed... warm, not scary. Passionate, for sure, but when he'd asked me about fear, I hadn't even considered he might be referring to whether I was scared of him.

I only hoped I'd answered the right way.

Chapter Forty-Seven

Harper stopped trying to catch me alone after that. Instead, she and her friends resorted to the old tried-and-true methods of bullying. Every time they saw me, they would turn to each other and giggle about it. Usually while looking back to make sure I'd noticed. Harper wasn't the only one doing it, either. Katrina was just as bad. Elyssa, Nevaeh, Gabrielle, and another girl named Sierra all did their best.

Too bad for them, I honestly didn't care. They could laugh about me all they wanted. So long as they weren't coming after Aspen or throwing magic at me, I was willing to call it a win. That didn't mean I wasn't pissed about it, but I figured I had bigger problems.

Three of my teachers made it clear being new wouldn't be an excuse for a failing grade. On the upside, it was Literature, math, and biology. On the downside, there was enough fae knowledge in there I was going to have to bust my butt - or get kicked out of the Advanced Placement program I was in. Silver Oaks was a school for the fae, and since I wasn't a fae, my only chance of staying here was to make some impressively good grades.

While I could now stop someone from casting a spell, Bracken made it clear that if I wanted to learn more, he was definitely willing to train me. Since Keir was always hanging around, he got pulled in to be my partner. This time, thankfully, there were no glitter bombs. Instead, it seemed I was now in Bracken's accelerated learning program.

It was kinda fun, but fun didn't stop my body from hurting every morning. On Wednesday, I was barely out of bed when the sound of a crow had me looking out my window. It wasn't Jack. Although, sitting on the glass roof of the atrium were about five or six crows. They were all pecking at the reflections, their feathers ruffling in the winter breeze.

The forecast called for some intense snow tonight, but right now, it was still blue skies and sunny outside. That wasn't the same as warm, so I found one of the Silver Oaks sweaters, my favorite plaid skirt, and pulled on some thigh-high socks just to make sure Aspen did a double take when she saw me.

Sure enough, the moment she walked into my room, she did. She also purred in a way that made my pulse pick up. I still had to put on my makeup, but like always, she was beautiful. This girl would've given me a complex if she hadn't made it clear she felt the same way about me.

At the elevators, Neveah started the tittering and glaring. I rolled my eyes, though, because Aspen had let me in on a little secret. Evidently Neveah used Winter magic. The only reason *she* wasn't an outcast was because she was Harper's cousin, so loosely tied to the Summer Court. Not that they got along! It sounded to me like Neveah was trying a bit too hard to "prove" herself, so she was going over the top.

After first period, however, it was Sierra trying to shame me, earning her a warning look from Torian. That actually made her stop and turn away, which was a little impressive. Then again, she was the newest addition to the jesters - and a high school junior - so Torian probably intimidated the hell out of her.

Which meant they'd sent the weakest links after me. That was probably supposed to be some kind of insult, but whatever. Let the jesters do their stupid little high school bullshit. This was college, and while it felt like half the students here were on this Advanced Placement program, plenty of others were old enough - or smart enough - to ignore the pathetic attempts at drama.

Just as we turned down the hall to my second-period class, something rapped on the window behind us. I didn't think anything of it, but Torian swung around like he was bracing for a threat. When I looked, I found Jack sitting on the second-floor window ledge, tapping at the window. His little leg band reflected a rainbow of colors, making me positive it was him and not one of the other birds.

"What the..." Torian breathed.

"That's Jack," I told him. "I feed him when I go to the gym. He's a little spoiled."

"Yeah," Torian agreed, forgetting about it almost immediately.

I decided I'd bring him something better today. Clearly, Jack was hungry. Considering it was well below freezing outside, his options had probably all disappeared. I needed to figure out how to buy some bird seed or something. First, because it would keep Jack from getting too attached, and secondly, the other crows weren't as pushy but were probably just as hungry.

When Keir walked me past the atrium to third period, I got proof of that. Another half dozen birds were sitting on the top of the atrium roof. From down here, they looked like little black specks, but I knew what they were. Had something happened outside? Because that was a *lot* of crows.

Then, in fourth period, everyone was talking about the birds still on the atrium roof. Our teacher said it was probably their way of soaking up the warmth, yet people were muttering about it. On impulse, I decided to sit next to Torian again, earning a smile from him, but I was here for information.

"Is this something that happens every year?" I asked. "The crows, I mean?"

"No, it's not," he assured me. "I'm not sure if anyone's mentioned it, but crows are one of the - "

"Few things that can go to Faerie," I finished for him. "Yeah, Keir told me. But the gates are closed, and they've been closed, so this isn't some mystical thing?"

"The two are not always related," he said. "What do you think about walking past the atrium before heading to lunch?"

"I'm thinking they're hungry," I told him. "Something happened to their normal food source. Insects froze, or something?"

"Possible," he agreed. "It's been cold lately. We can just look."

Which was how the two of us ended up standing before the main entrance, staring up four stories to the top. Everyone else was going to the dining hall, but there were so many birds up there now the roof was almost completely black. While we watched, more and more kept arriving. I hadn't even realized there were this many crows on the grounds!

The sound of thumping behind me made me flinch. Torian turned first and sucked in a breath. When I looked, I found Jack hopping back and forth, his little beak opening repeatedly like he was making a ruckus. Without warning, he launched into the air, banging right into the exterior glass doors.

"Jack!" I gasped, but Torian was already moving.

He shoved through the inner doors and made his way to the one Jack was in front of. Opening it wide, he let Jack fly right in. Now I could hear him cawing in the space between the two sets of doors, and it wasn't quiet.

"What are you doing?" I asked Torian through the glass. "If he gets loose in here - " I didn't get to finish because Torian opened the inner doors and Jack was immediately in the air. "Torian!" I groaned. "We'll never get him out of here now!"

Then Jack swooped back down, aiming right for me. "Jack!"

The bird landed on the ground before me, bobbed his head at Torian, then cawed a few more times. Each one was different, like he was trying to do something. I just bent before him and offered my hand as a perch. Surprisingly, he took it. When I stood back up, he only flared his wings for balance. He didn't try to take off.

Caw! he bellowed in my face. "Jack!" Then he ruffled his feathers, looking at me with some kind of inhuman intelligence. "Hunt!" *Caw!*

With that, Jack pushed off, flying through the halls around the atrium. "Hunt!" the bird screamed. "Hunt! Hunt! Hunt!"

"Oh, fuck," Torian breathed, just as the cold front hit.

The birds on the roof all scattered at the intensity of the wind, and yet they tried hard to come back. Like a sheet being fluffed over the building, the crows were covering the glass roof, almost as if they were protecting it. Beside me, Torian was whipping his head around frantically like he was looking for something.

"It's the fucking Wild Hunt, Rain!" he snapped even as his eyes found his target.

Confused, I stood there as he ran toward the wall beside the office, pulling a green box that looked a lot like a fire alarm. Immediately, a screeching noise filled the entire school. A moment later, my tablet and phone both went off. Swiping at the screen of my tablet, I found an emergency student notice plastered at the top.

Emergency Lockdown Procedures. Return to your rooms. Shelter in place if you cannot.

Students were pouring from the dining hall, heading to the stairs like a tidal wave. Teachers were streaming from the office, and Ivy Rhodes was at the front. The woman was amazingly beautiful, but right now she looked like some kind of warrior in office attire. Her head snapped over to the alarm, finding Torian right beside it.

"What are you doing?" she yelled, her voice barely audible over the sound.

Torian just pointed to the top of the atrium. "They say the Hunt is coming. I need my court."

"Go," she ordered before turning to me. "Rain, I need your help."

I jiggled my head, and she pointed at the back doors, the ones beside the boys' elevator. "Close everything that leads to outside. Make sure it's locked."

"I got this," Liam said, pushing in beside her. "Get to cover, Ivy."

"Do we even know it's the Hunt?" Ivy asked.

"Better safe than sorry," Liam said. "I'm just glad it's now, when we're all in the building."

Which was when Jack came back, swooping in to land on my shoulder. "Hunt!" he screamed. "Hunt, Hunt, Jack, Hunt!"

"What the..." Liam just shook his head. "Doors, Rain. Check everything that leads outside. Lock them. If there's someone out there, let them in, but make sure they're one of us, ok?"

"How will I know?" I asked.

He turned me toward the hall and pushed. "You'll know!"

I ran, my Mary Janes slick on the tile floor, but this sounded important. I'd know if they weren't us? What the hell was this? More importantly, why was everyone freaking out? I'd heard stories about the Wild Hunt, but they only chased bad people, didn't they? Fuck! I should've studied more!

Halfway there, the alarms suddenly went quiet. The students had moved faster than I'd ever seen before, and the halls were eerily silent. I made it to the back side to find the door flapping in the intensity of the wind. Pulling at the part which served as a handle, I yanked it in and turned the deadbolt. It clicked, but didn't feel right, so I turned a little more, finally feeling the thing secure itself.

"Hunt!" Jack screeched again, sounding even more frantic.

Well, fuck going all the way around the atrium. I ran through, ducking between the flowers and bushes meant to make the space feel meandering. Jack flew, keeping pace with me much too easily. When I reached the other side, he had to make a circle while I opened the door, and then he streaked through it, turning for exactly where I needed to go.

"I got the library!" Liam yelled. "Dining hall's secure."

The whole building creaked with the force of the cold front slamming directly into it. Normally, it wouldn't have worried me, but this? Everything about this felt like panic. The teachers were gone. The school wasn't even this quiet in the middle of the night, and the light coming down from above was an eerie sort of shadow. That was from the crows, and there were so many I couldn't even see the sky through the glass roof. Just birds. So many birds.

"Hunt!" Jack yelled again.

I grabbed the door and pulled, scanning the yard between here, the gym, and the Forge. It was desolate, only a few broken branches, long fallen leaves, and swirls of dust moving out there. No students. No teachers. But the clouds rushing in over the line of trees looked dark and much too ominous.

I pulled at the door, spinning the deadbolt. That first click happened, but the wind made the door rattle open. Another gust hit, yanking it out of my grasp and it opened about a handspan. Cursing under my breath, I caught the bar and pulled, fighting the weather to make it happen - and that was when I saw the first one.

Like something out of a movie, the horses were ghastly things made of hanging flesh and gaunt bones. More followed after. So many more. On my shoulder, Jack began to scream and rattle, clearly pissed off, but I needed to get this damned door locked before they got here!

I pulled, a break in the wind finally making it easy, and then I spun the dial just as fast as I could. The horse was racing straight toward me, looking like it was going to come through the glass, but I wouldn't budge. Not until I heard the click. Another spin, and finally the whole thing locked into place right as the man on the horse jumped off.

The horse veered, but the man stormed closer. He wore all grey. Even his skin was grey, and there was something strange about him. He had the lines of the fae, with their beautiful angles, but this man looked like he'd dried up. White, necrotic eyes stared straight at me the same way Hawke did so often.

My heart was racing. My fingers were trembling. At least I hadn't forgotten to breathe, but I was panting instead, and the man kept coming. When he reached the door, he thrust both hands onto the glass like he was going to push through it.

"Come with me," he said, the words sounding hollow, ghastly. "Ride with us."

"Jack!" my bird screeched, flying at the door.

His talons were out like he was ready to attack, but they simply skittered on the glass. Still, the Huntsman flinched back, his attention turning to the crow. A snarl crossed his face, and then the Huntsman banged the flat of his hand right at where Jack was trying to get through.

And he spoke again. This time, I couldn't make out the words. I knew they were in Faeril, and whatever he said sounded like a threat, but he couldn't get in! The Hunt couldn't get inside with the doors locked. I just hoped all the others were completely secure. I hoped I'd done it right.

"Jack!" the crow yelled again. "Rain. Jack!"

Hearing my name from the bird shook me out of the stupor, and I stepped back, thinking about reaching for my phone. Instead, my fingers brushed against the keychain Bracken had given me. Iron. A weapon. If this thing spoke Faeril, then it had to be fae, and they didn't like iron.

So I wrapped my fingers around the butterfly and thrust it out before me. "You have nothing to hunt here," I warned. "Leave."

"But I see you," the Huntsman said, his attention back on me like a switch had been flipped. "You and your bird."

"Rain?" This time, my name came from a man, and he sounded worried. Liam, I realized, but I didn't dare look away.

"Go!" I yelled at the *thing* on the other side of the glass.

And then I pressed the keychain right up against it. The Huntsman hissed, jumping back two paces as fast as he could. Yeah, it seemed iron did work against them. I felt my breath fall out in a rush, but I didn't get a chance to enjoy my small victory. Jack began fussing again, and then he flew up, straight up, aiming for the other crows still hugging the roof of the atrium.

The crow cawed like it was a battle cry. Immediately, the other birds took to the air. Groups went off in different directions, and a large cluster shot straight down. Before my eyes, the Huntsman began to retreat, but he was still on foot. The crows targeted him, each one swooping in to peck, claw, or grab at anything they could reach.

Around the school, others were doing the same thing. I knew they were screaming like a murder of birds, but inside, I couldn't hear it. If anything, that made the scene even more surreal.

"Rain?" Liam asked, moving to clasp my shoulder. "It's ok. They'll leave now. It usually doesn't last more than fifteen minutes. They have to ride the storms. It's the only magic they have to get around."

"What are they?" I asked.

"They used to be the Wild Hunt," he said. "Then the Queen enchanted them, and now they're... this."

"Jack!" my bird said, coming to land before me.

He slid on the slick floor, grumbled about it with his ticks and clicks, then turned back around. When he tilted his head to examine me, Liam examined him. Then Jack turned to look at my guardian.

"Jack," he said, hopping closer. "Rain. Jack."

"That's the bird from the house," I explained. "He followed me here."

"How'd he get inside?" Liam asked.

I licked my lips nervously. "Torian let him in right before he pulled the fire alarm."

"Hunt alarm, but yeah," Liam said.

"Hunt. Jack!"

"Yeah, and he keeps saying that," I added.

Liam just crouched down. "Did you warn us about the Hunt coming, Jack?"

The bird nodded his head vigorously.

"Were you trying to help the king?' Liam asked.

This time, Jack shook his head no. "Rain!"

"You were warning Rain about the Hunt." Liam pushed out a breath. "You know they won't come after her, right?"

Jack nodded, but this time it was only one bob of his beak. "Hunt. Hunt Hunt! Jack Hunt Hunt."

Liam just looked up at me. "I have no clue what that means, but one thing is very clear. It seems you have a familiar. Evidently, you aren't only interesting to Aspen. You're interesting to the crows as well. Now, c'mon. We need to check the other doors, and I think Jack will keep up."

"Jack!" the bird agreed, flapping up so he could land on my shoulder. "Rain Jack."

As I followed Liam, I reached up to pet him. He'd earned it, after all, because the Hunt was a lot more terrifying than I'd imagined. I might not be able to see them any longer, but the wind was still blowing, there were still crows on the roof, and I had a feeling we'd be in lockdown for a little while longer.

And then I'd melt down. Not until this was over. I might be scared shitless, but right now, this was something I could do and my friends needed me. My enemies too.

Chapter Forty-Eight

The rest of our classes were canceled after that. No one wanted to go back outside, and the exterior doors remained locked. There was a subtle anxiety running through the student body, yet headcounts showed we were all accounted for. Because it had been lunchtime, even the teachers from the outbuildings had been inside to grab a meal.

Evidently, we weren't usually this lucky. I headed to my room to check on Aspen, but found our suite empty. When I started asking others in the halls if they'd seen her, one girl said she was pretty sure she'd been with her brother. I didn't know what rooms the guys were in, and I didn't care. Running down the hall, I finally used the double doors separating the boys' side from the girls', and kept going.

"Where's Torian's room?" I asked the first guy I saw.

"Near the elevators," he told me. "I don't know the number!"

So I kept going, and Jack flew behind me. Since the doors were locked, he was still inside, and it seemed no one was upset about that. Someone jumped out of the way, not expecting a bird to be trailing me, but that was about it. When I made it halfway up the hall, I started asking again.

"Where is Torian's room? Or Hawke. Wilder?"

"Last ones on the atrium side," the guy said. "Last two suites before the elevator."

I reached the first one and banged on it. When there wasn't an immediate answer, I did it again, thumping my fist against the wood until it was finally opened, revealing Wilder on the other side.

"Rain," he breathed, pulling me in.

"Jack," my crow said, slipping through the gap in the door.

"Jack!" Aspen called out excitedly, proving she was in there.

I stepped around Wilder to see her sitting in the middle of the floor. Torian was beside her, sprawled like he'd been hugging her. Both of his legs were bent, one behind Aspen's back, and his chest faced her shoulder. She was turned toward him just enough so it was personal, but not that kind of personal.

Hawke was lying on his side across from them, and a game of Monopoly was spread on the floor between them. They'd been gaming while that went on? Seeing it, I sighed in relief, moving over to sit on whoever's bed this was.

"You weren't in your room," I told Aspen.

"I didn't want to be alone," she admitted, climbing to her feet. "Tor said you were helping."

I nodded. "That was the most terrifying thing I've ever been through."

Aspen came over and kissed me gently. "Thank you," she breathed against my lips. "The glass is enchanted to keep them out, but they've cracked it before. It never lasts too long, but it always feels like an eternity. Are you ok?"

I hugged her waist, not caring if the guys were watching. "Yeah. Jack helped. He's kinda my hero right now. I think he got the other crows to attack them, but that's probably stupid, huh?"

The words were no more out of my mouth before Jack decided to land in the middle of their game, scattering all the pieces. Hopping in place, he turned to inspect the three boys around him. Wilder stood there, his hands out - which made me think he'd been winning. Torian and Hawke just watched the bird.

Then Jack turned to Torian and lowered his beak to the ground. In response, Torian dipped his head. As if that was a signal, Jack turned to Wilder and did the same, but he didn't bow quite as low. Probably because he was exhausted. Wilder dipped his head respectfully. Finally, Jack turned to Hawke, swiveling his head as he inspected him.

"Jack!" he cawed loudly.

"Hawke," the guy replied. "It's a pleasure, sir."

"Rain Jack."

"Really?" Torian asked.

I just gestured to them. "What are they doing?"

"Talking to Jack," she said as if that should've been obvious.

"A bird?"

"A very special bird," Torian corrected. "Are you the king?" he asked.

Jack shook his beak violently.

"Prince?"

That made Jack blink.

"Duke?" Torian offered.

Another no.

"So, maybe you're an unrecognized prince of the Crow King?" Torian asked.

"Jack!" the bird replied.

"Then it is my honor to meet you, Prince Jack." And Torian said something in his native language.

The words were lyrical and fluid on his tongue, a bit different than I'd heard before. Not that I knew what any of it meant, but when Torian said it, it sounded like diamonds instead of glitter. Just a little more crisp and defined, a bit more flair. In all honesty, it sounded like the most amazing thing I'd ever heard.

"He was born speaking Faeril," Aspen explained. "There's a good chance Jack understands it as much as English. I'm getting the impression your friend is the son of a fae bird, or a line of fae birds trapped here."

"Which is why he's so big?" I asked.

"Probably," she agreed, moving to sit beside me, and then shifting to wrap her arms around me. "You ok, sweetie?"

"I honestly don't know yet," I admitted, turning to her while the guys continued to talk to Jack in words I didn't know. Then I told her about what had happened at the door.

Aspen just reached up to smooth back my hair. "Once, the Hunt looked like us and rode between worlds as they needed. Now that they're locked here, the magic isn't fueling them, so they're all decaying. The Hunt doesn't stop, you see. They ride, and they always ride until they catch their target."

"Which is all the fae on Earth," Torian said, proving he was listening in. "The Mad Queen sent them here to collect the defectors. The gates were closed, and I don't think she did it. She has her guards watching them, though. That's how most of us slip through, often by bribing a guard to not notice. A few gates can open partway, and the one on the far side of the property is how I got here."

"So, doesn't that mean the Hunt can go back?" I asked. Because if they could open a bit, then wouldn't the Hunt use that?

"Can't open them at all from this side," he explained. "From the Faerie side, with enough magic, they can be wedged open for a few seconds. People have died because they didn't get through fast enough, though. The question is if the risk of staying is worth the risk of leaving."

"Ok..." I was pretty sure I was following along, but my head felt full, and I knew there was something I was missing. "If the Hunt is supposed to catch fae and take them back, but they can't get back, then why kill them? Why don't they just *give up* when the door doesn't open?"

"Well," Aspen said. "We're criminals, remember? We broke the Queen's law about not leaving, so we must be punished. If we can't be brought back for the Queen to execute, then the Huntsmen will do it in her name. They get to the gate, Rain, and when they can't get through, they kill us."

Yeah, that was the piece I couldn't wrap my mind around. "Then how do you stop them? I mean, this has been going on for how long?"

"Can't be killed," Hawke pointed out. "Part of the enchantment, and why they need so much magic. No aging, no death, no stopping because they need to rest. It's the *Wild Hunt,* Rain."

"And I was never a huge fan of fairy tales," I told him. "Not really in my daily dose of human upbringing. I will probably forget half of what you tell me a few times because, guys... This is a lot."

But I was feeling better. Just seeing my friends made my anxiety fade a bit. Leaning back into Aspen, I hugged where her arms wrapped around me. They were all so used to this. To them, it was no different than me doing a fire drill. Sometimes it was annoying, sometimes it was fun, but in the end, it wasn't even memorable.

Unfortunately, I didn't get to stay long. Liam texted me saying to meet him at his apartment. Considering that was pretty much where I was, I told him I'd be there in a moment. He replied back to bring Jack. In other words, I was about to get a lecture about the bird with a mind of his own.

"C'mon, Jack," I said, holding up my arm. "We gotta go talk to Liam about you breaking in."

"I let him in," Torian said. "And if they have a problem with that, they can talk to me about it." He caught my eye. "Tell them that, Rain."

"Let's hope I don't have to," I said. "Aspen, you going to be here for a while?"

"Until dinner," she said. "Coming back?"

"If I'm not in too much trouble." I gave her one last kiss and then left.

From that room - whichever guy it belonged to - I passed one more door in the hall, then stepped into the elevator area. Straight ahead of me was one last door: the one for the chaperone's apartment. With Jack balanced on my arm, I stepped right up to it and knocked.

Two seconds later, the door opened, but it wasn't Liam on the other side. "Rain?" Bracken asked.

"Uh... I was supposed to meet Liam. I thought this was his place." I looked back, making sure I was on the fourth floor of the boy's wing.

Bracken just opened the door wider. "It is. Come in."

I stepped past him to find a real apartment. The entryway had tile, and not the crappy stuff they used in the halls. There were pictures on the walls, and over there was a set of hunting bows hung decoratively. But when I made it into the main room, I noticed carbon fiber swords, a set of daggers, and a shield hanging next to the dining room table.

Yep, I was confused. I had no idea Liam was into weapons. The more I looked, the fewer signs I saw of the guy I'd thought I knew. But then I noticed a picture on a shelf. When someone else knocked at the door, I took the chance to see if that was really what I thought it was.

Sure enough, it was Liam, but he was in a graduation cap and gown like from high school. Standing just behind him, hugging him closely, was a slightly younger version of Bracken. The pale hair was a dead giveaway. My mouth dropped open in shock.

And then the front door opened again. "Brack?" Liam demanded as he rushed in. "You ok?"

I turned in time to see Liam throw his arms around my combat instructor's shoulders. Bracken hugged him back. "I'm fine. Rain's here too."

"Good. I told her to meet us here." Then Liam pulled back. "Ivy, any problems?"

"None besides my heart trying to pound out of my chest," she promised as she rounded the corner, clearly having come in with Liam. "Now, where's this bird?"

"Jack!" he announced proudly, making them all turn to see me holding the picture.

Liam just chuckled. "Do not pick on me for being a kid. That was when Bracken and I became public."

"You..." I looked over at Bracken. "And you?" Wait. Holy shit. "*He's* the boy you met?"

"The same," Bracken said. "I thought you knew?"

"I knew he was dating *a* fae guy, which was how he ended up working here. I didn't know *who!*"

Liam ducked his head and scrubbed at his face. "Yeah. So, I guess that makes Bracken like your other uncle. It's why he's been training you, Rain. I asked him to make sure you wouldn't get yourself hurt your first year."

"Preferably any year," Ivy said as she moved to the couch. "Put the picture down, Rain, and come sit. I want to know about this bird."

"Jack!" he declared again.

I set the picture back where I'd gotten it, then took the chair directly across from her. My insides were twisting up, because the only time I'd ever really talked to Ms. Rhodes was my entrance exam. Oh, I'd listened to her a million times in class, but this felt different, like I was in some very deep trouble.

"Um," I said, moving Jack to the arm of the chair because he was starting to get heavy. "I didn't let him in. Torian did."

Damn it! I hadn't meant to fold that fast. I'd intended to take this calmly, but Ms. Rhodes had a way of looking at me that made me feel as if I was five years old and about to get a spanking.

"I'd like to know how you met him," she clarified.

"I'm not sure, exactly." I glanced at the bird who was preening himself. "I know that when I lived with the Sparks, my last foster home - well, current, I suppose - he was at my window. That was the first time he told me his name, but I've kinda always had crows around, and if he followed me from there, then I dunno if he's the one from the previous time."

"How many times?" she asked carefully.

"When I was a kid, I used to throw cheerios to them, so I guess that's first."

Caw! Jack agreed.

"And then there was another foster family where I fed them a bit. Crows are really smart birds, and because I moved a lot, I wasn't allowed to have a pet, so I kinda taught them to come to the window. I got kicked out of that home for my foster mom losing an earring."

"The theft I told you about," Liam explained.

But Bracken moved over to kneel down beside Jack. "Was that the first time, Jack?"

Jack shook his head.

"Were you there when she was a kid?"

Jack nodded as big and as fast as he could. "Jack. Rain. Jack-Rain."

Bracken's eyes narrowed. "You need a few more words, my friend."

"Torian said he's Prince Jack," I added.

Ms. Rhodes lifted a brow. "I see. Your Highness?"

"Jack!" he corrected.

"Jack," she agreed. "What do you mean about the first time?"

Jack ruffled his feathers, looked at me, scanning my body as if searching for something, then his attention turned to the room around us. He was eerily intelligent, and it was fascinating to see him like this. Finally, he decided something and took off, flying over to the bookshelf. Picking up a coin, he flew over to Ms. Rhodes. That, he dropped into her lap, then pecked at her ring.

"Jack!"

"You want to trade?" she asked.

"No..." Bracken breathed. "He wants to make a deal. Is that what you did, Jack? Did you make a deal with Rain?" The bird nodded, so Bracken kept going. "Was it when she was little? Smaller than now?" Another nod. "About this big?" Bracken asked, holding his hand up about toddler height.

"Jack! Rain!" the bird agreed.

And there was no doubt it was an agreement. Just to prove the point, he picked up the coin and returned it. Not that he got it in exactly the same place, but it was still pretty impressive. Then he flew straight for Liam, landing on his shoulder. Evidently, that meant my "uncle" was safe enough to work as a perch.

"I think that settles it," Ms. Rhodes said. "If he's a prince, then he's clearly fae. If he made a deal with Rain, then we can't separate them. We don't know the agreement. The problem is how to care for him."

"I've been feeding him bread," I admitted.

"So we will have to make sure you have better options," she told me. "If he's going to be living inside with you, he will need to be fed inside with you as well. We'll get something for your room, but he can also eat from the buffet." She turned her attention to Jack. "And no droppings on the floor. Atrium only."

Surprisingly, the bird nodded. My mouth just flopped open. "But he's a bird!"

"No, Rain," Bracken said. "He's as fae as I am. He may have been born here, but that bird is closer to a nature spirit than any common animal. Treat him as such."

"Wow," I breathed. "And you chose me, Jack?"

"Rain!" he croaked, looking rather pleased with himself. I decided to take that as a yes.

Chapter Forty-Nine

At dinner, I went to check on Keir before anything else. He was surprised to see Jack with me, but said it all made sense. Rumors were running through the dorms about the crows on the roof, and how they'd fought off the Hunt. Keir assumed it had all been exaggerated. I assured him it wasn't, and then explained how Jack had flown in yelling about the Hunt. I'd always thought he could only say his name.

Naturally, Jack was more than happy to prove he could also say my name. That led us to talking about what Jack could eat, and Keir suggested I ask him. So, when I went to get my meal, Keir came with, carrying a plate we filled for my bird. Not that he was my possession, but he did seem to have a fondness for me.

I debated going back to Keir's table for a moment, a little too aware I'd completely forgotten about him in the insanity of the Hunt. He, however, turned for the court's table, leading the way with Jack's food. When he got there, he set the plate in the middle, clasped my arm, and said he'd see me tomorrow. In other words, he wasn't upset.

And Jack was thrilled. Evidently, he liked chicken, most berries, and he had a weakness for hard-boiled eggs. The bird ate himself stupid, and with the court offering him things from their plates, he was exceedingly happy. So happy he wanted to be carried - on his *back* - when I headed up to my room that night.

When I got upstairs, I found a small bag of puppy food sitting outside my door with a sticky note that said it was for Jack. There were also two little bowls. Clearly, this was from Liam. Unfortunately, it was all I had for keeping a bird, and I had a feeling it wasn't enough.

Jack decided my headboard was a good enough place for him to sleep. I decided I wasn't quite over the fright from earlier. Aspen and I wrapped ourselves in each other's arms, whispering that we didn't want to be alone, and before I knew it, I was asleep. The Hunt had scared me more than I wanted to admit, and with the adrenaline gone, I simply had nothing left.

But sometime in the middle of the night, I woke to a soft nibble on my ear. I giggled under my breath, moving away from it, but that wasn't Aspen. Sucking in a breath, I opened my eyes to find her right in front of me. Moonlight through the window turned her into an icy dream. With her eyes closed, she became something almost delicate.

I couldn't help but reach out to stroke her face. I had a girlfriend. A beautiful one. Her lips were parted as she breathed softly in sleep, and I wanted to kiss her awake. I also wanted to go back to sleep myself. Then the nibbling came again. That was when I realized it was Jack.

"Go to sleep, bird," I whispered.

He ticked his disapproval and flapped over to the door. Hopping before it, he made another noise, this one sounding a little more urgent. Shit, he needed to go to the atrium. Ms. Rhodes had told him he could only go out there, and he couldn't get downstairs without me. Damn it!

So I slipped out of Aspen's arms, grabbed a sweater to go over my pajamas, and slipped on a pair of shoes. As quietly as I could, I opened the door, not bothering to lock it, and let Jack fly ahead. He went straight for the elevator, landing on the ground before it, still hopping. That made me walk a little faster

"Ok," I breathed, pushing the button.

The doors opened immediately, and Jack hopped in, not even bothering to fly. He was like the strangest mix of a puppy, a kitten, and a bird in some ways. Nothing like I expected a crow to be, and yet everything like one. Kinda like the fae, I supposed.

When we reached the first floor, Jack was off again, and this time I jogged to keep up with him. The moment I opened the atrium door, he was gone. The poor thing. I had no idea how often crows needed to have a potty break, but Jack had been running around with me all afternoon, and I hadn't even thought about it.

I was a bad bird-mom. I'd learn, though, and I had a feeling Jack would definitely teach me. But, while he flew and did his thing, I moved over to the base of the weeping willow, and leaned back against it. I hadn't brought my phone or tablet, so I had nothing to keep me distracted. Instead, I let my eyes close.

It couldn't have been long before I heard the atrium door open again. My eyes jerked open and I was instantly awake, scanning for whoever had just come in. On the boy's side, I could see the plants reacting. Some glowed, the effect more obvious in the darkness. Others whispered, sounding almost like their leaves were brushing together, but I had a feeling that wasn't the cause of the sound.

Then Jack swooped down to greet the visitor with a soft caw. The guy sucked in a breath, and then he chuckled. "Jack?" he asked. "Where's Rain?" I recognized the voice as Torian's.

"What are you doing up?" I asked, revealing myself by the sound.

Torian turned my way. At first, I only heard him, then he came around a set of tall shrubs, and I saw Aspen's brother dressed like he expected no one at all to see him. He wore a pair of grey sweats and a shirt that was thin, soft, and a little too tight. My eyes dropped to take in the lines of his perfect body, hoping he couldn't tell in the moonlight.

"I had to check the protections," he admitted. "I know they've been checked and checked again, but..." He paused before me to rumple his own hair. "We didn't know they were coming," he finally said.

"The Hunt?"

"Yeah." He knelt down before me. "What are you doing?"

"Jack evidently poops," I grumbled. He huffed at that which made me smile. "It seems I open doors for His Highness."

So he held out a hand. "Come. Talk while I do this?"

I accepted, letting him pull me up. Together, we wandered through the garden to the back. The wall was glass, but it didn't matter much. The plants had claimed this place, taking over almost everything. Once inside, it was a very secluded spot - for the most part. I had a feeling the only reason it wasn't the preferred make-out place was due to the dorm windows, which made it possible to see everything.

But when we reached the back, Torian moved right to the large panes of glass. Pressing his hand to one, he let his eyes close as he focused, and the glass changed. I wanted to say it fogged over, but it wasn't that. It was more like the glass changed to something blue and milky, creating a very similar effect. And there, in the middle of it all were a jumble of shapes and patterns I couldn't quite make out.

Torian simply moved his finger to a smudged spot and concentrated again. A soft green glow flared inside the glass, too dim to really count as a glow, but bright enough I could make it out. Almost like an aftereffect of seeing a bright light. It matched the pattern that was already there, sharpened it, and then the glass cleared again. Torian simply moved on to the next pane.

"What are you doing?" I asked.

"The glass is enchanted against the fae," he explained. "Means the Hunt can't break it. The enchantment is still good, but I'm refreshing it."

"Why? Don't the teachers, or staff, or adults do that?"

He spun to face me. "What if they got in, Rain? What if they got to Aspen? I would much rather do this than risk it. I know what would happen!"

"Sorry," I breathed, leaning back. "I don't know any of this stuff, Torian. I'm just trying to figure it out, ok?"

He slapped his hand against the next pane, working faster this time. He also kept talking. "Why are you here, Rain?"

"At Silver Oaks? Because Aspen said I'm interesting."

"No, why were you even at the Sparks' to get Liam's attention? How did you manage it?" he demanded, still pressing on the glass.

"Because I punched a guy for grabbing my ass," I said. "I'm not about to just tolerate being groped!"

He yanked his hand back and turned to look at me. "Do you see how coincidental it is? Your record was perfect. Just like a fae's. A girl in the foster system, can't settle into a home, makes decent enough grades, doesn't have any outstanding problems like assault or drugs, but she just can't settle. That's what *we* always look like."

"Yeah, I've heard," I said softly.

"And now you're running around with a prince among crows. A bastard one, I'm pretty sure, but still a bird who is more than you can imagine. What. Are. You?"

"I'm nothing," I said softly, taking a step back.

Because I didn't need to deal with his shit. Every time I was around Torian, it always went weird somehow. Jack had to be done by now, but the stupid bird had gone silent. I scanned the air for him, then my eyes moved to the trees, but finding a black bird in the middle of the night? Yeah, not likely.

Torian simply moved to the last pane of glass. "You're not nothing." He paused for a long moment, but his next words were enough to keep me from leaving. "You don't feel like everyone else."

"I don't even know what that means," I admitted. "Aspen says I'm interesting. You say I feel like something. Jack seems to think I'm cool enough. I don't know how to break it to any of you, but I can't do magic. I'm not part fae. I'm just a normal, ordinary human girl."

He turned to face me one more time, scrubbing at his face.

"Human, I'll give you," he said, dropping down to sit on one of the many decorative boulders. "Ordinary, you are not. The problem is you're covered in darkness, and that scares the shit out of me."

"What?" That made absolutely no sense.

"Do you remember your shadow?" he asked. "That's not the first time I've seen it move. The more power around you, the more you seem to flicker. It's what Aspen noticed, along with the plants trying to greet you. You don't thank us. You understand deals and promises. You hear the lies in our truths - and the evasions. You are not ordinary."

"But I'm not fae," I insisted.

"We agree on that," he said again.

Just as I was sure this conversation was going nowhere, Jack decided it was time to return. I sighed, ready to leave, but then he dropped something before me.

"Jack!" he declared.

"Shh," I reminded him. "The whole school is sleeping, bud."

So he tried it softer. "Jack." And he nosed the thing again.

It was small, but it sounded like metal against his beak. The grass almost hid it, so I bent down to pick up whatever he had. Jack ruffled his feathers excitedly, then nosed my hand, guiding me right to it. Feeling around the grass, I found it. Hard, metal, and round. Lifting it up, I found a ring.

"Jack, did you find this?"

Caw!

Yeah, whatever that meant. "We should leave it so whoever lost it can find it."

But Jack lifted up his little leg. The one with the band. When I did nothing but squat down before him, he tried again, making grabby motions with his foot. I shook my head, still unsure of what this bird wanted, so he nudged my hand, nibbled at the ring, and then did the same to my index finger.

"Oh, you want me to wear a ring like yours?" I asked.

Torian chuckled. "Yep, he's got you trained. No wonder he likes you. I think the bird has a bad case of 'I'll show you mine if you show me yours.'"

"Funny," I told him before talking to Jack again. "So, you want me to try on the ring, huh? Fine, and then we'll take it to the lost and found in the morning."

Yep, that made Jack happy. He clicked rapidly, hopping around before me. Just to keep the peace, I pushed the tarnished-looking ring onto the index finger of my left hand, the same side as the leg Jack had banded.

"Like that?" I asked.

"Rain," he said approvingly.

Oddly, the ring fit. I lifted my hand to see it, but it was nothing special. Just a thick, almost masculine band with something stamped around the edges. Hoping Jack was happy enough for me to go to bed, I stood back up, tugging the ring to take it off.

It didn't budge.

So I tried again. It would spin on my finger easily, and it didn't fit tightly at all. In fact, the thing fit perfectly - yet when I pulled, nothing happened. Absolutely nothing. It was almost like I couldn't quite grab it, or if I did, my fingers slid off. The ring wasn't stuck, per se. It was immoveable.

"Shit," I breathed. "Tor? It won't come off."

"What is it?" he asked.

So I thrust my hand out to him. "I don't know. Is it iron?"

He came closer and took my hand while Jack hopped around beneath us. Carefully, Torian tested the ring, and then he tried to slip it off - clearly able to touch it. Nothing. Just like with me, he couldn't seem to get a grip on it. Then he did something else.

Waving his palm over my finger, a pale green light glowed. The metal of the ring reacted, shimmering wildly across the surface. It wasn't like *eltam*. This was very, very different.

"Magic," Torian breathed. "Rain, I don't think you're getting it off."

"But it's not iron, right? I can still touch Aspen?"

"I have no interest in hearing what you do with my *sister*," he snapped. Then his temper cooled. "But no, it's not iron. It's not even metal, Rain. That ring? It's made completely out of magic. I've never seen anything that powerful in my life."

"Then where the fuck did Jack find it?" I asked. "Has it been lost out here for decades?"

He let his finger caress the surface again. "This is old. There were artifacts in the palace like this. Stuff made from powers we have long ago forgotten."

"Jack!" my crow interrupted.

"Is it going to hurt her?" Torian asked the bird.

That got a very obvious shake of the head.

Torian just sighed. "Then go back to bed, Rain. I'll see what I can find out. Ask Aspen if she can tell anything about it. I have a feeling this was either lost by someone out here, or maybe left by someone to be found."

"Harper?" I asked. "Would she really leave something like this laying around to get me in trouble?"

"I can't rule it out," he admitted. "It's the kind of thing she'd do, and we all know crows like shiny things. Trust me, everyone knows about your bird already. You're getting the attention she wants, so what better revenge than to make your new friend bring you down?"

"Fuck," I grumbled. "Yeah, I clearly need to sleep before I deal with this. But hey, at least it's comfortable, right?"

"Better than painful," he agreed as I turned for the girl's side door. Just before I reached it, he called out, "Have a good night, Rain."

"Your sister's in my bed," I called back.

He laughed once. "I have a feeling you're going to be a pain in my ass that just won't go away."

"Count on it," I agreed. "Good night, Torian." And I pulled open the door to let Jack lead us back home. Fucking bird.

Chapter Fifty

The next day, we were back to classes as normal. I showed Aspen the ring while we got ready, but she agreed with Torian. It was made of magic, so taking it off meant we'd have to break the enchantment. The bigger question was what the enchantment did. Sadly, Aspen couldn't figure it out. She admitted that was really more Torian's area than hers.

Jack was thrilled with me wearing this new ring, though. Considering that after I washed it, I found out the engraved marks on it looked like birds, well, it made sense. He seemed to be a rather vain crow. The material of it was strange, though. The ring looked like metal, but it was dark. Not truly black, but definitely a black-metal color. Charcoal, possibly?

It was a wide band, but the edges were smooth. Probably worn that way by time. Then again, did a magical material do that? Thankfully, if I didn't think about it, it didn't bother me at all. The problem was I kept thinking about it. Just the idea that Harper was somehow going to use this against me made me a little crazy. When I told Aspen my theory, she actually laughed at me.

"Do you seriously think Harper would have access to something like that?" Aspen shook her head, giving me the answer. "It's more likely it was lost when they were building Silver Oaks. A lot of the fae back then had just come here, and they'd carried everything of value on their bodies. There wasn't any other option."

"But it doesn't come off," I reminded her. "Kinda hard to lose a ring that doesn't come off, right?"

"Not how it works," she assured me as we headed to class. "Enchanted items, especially ones made of nothing *but* an enchantment, often decide when their task is done. The bearer no longer meets the criteria, so the part holding it with them releases, waiting for the next person they can help."

"Yeah, but Jack found this." I lifted a brow. "He's not a *person*, Aspen."

"He's still fae," she reminded me. "So, he's kinda a person."

And Jack was another problem for me to worry about. He refused to leave my side, which meant I had to tell each one of my teachers about him. Luckily, Ms. Rhodes had warned them, but that didn't mean Jack knew how to act in class. He had opinions, and didn't mind stating them in the middle of a lecture. Usually, it was with a caw or his name - since his vocabulary was limited.

The students laughed at his antics, frustrating the teachers. I tried to get him to behave, but without yelling at him, I wasn't sure how. Jack liked all the attention. I, however, didn't. I'd just started to feel like I was fitting in, and now he was making me stand out again. Between classes, people stared, whispering behind their hands, and I knew I was once again the talk of the school.

The moment I walked into third period, Wilder and Hawke asked to see my ring. It seemed Aspen had told them both about it. Hawke said the birds looked like crows, which was what I was thinking. Wilder said he'd never seen anything like it and suggested I show it to Ms. Rhodes. I was pretty sure that would be a bad idea. I really didn't need any more drama, not with the end of the semester coming so fast, so I'd just ignore it. If this ring was as much of a problem as I suspected, it might be the final straw to convince the staff I didn't belong at Silver Oaks.

So, when Ms. Rhodes walked into class, I said nothing. I simply took my chair and tried to convince my crow to be quiet. Ms. Rhodes noticed. The first thing she did was address Jack, making it clear he could perch on the back of her chair, my chair, or the cabinet in the corner. Then she explained that if he interrupted her, he would spend class hours alone in the atrium.

Jack ruffled his feathers, letting her know he wasn't pleased, but he kept the commentary to a minimum. Mostly it was flapped wings and excessive preening. Once, he made that clicking noise, but when Ms. Rhodes glared at him, Jack stopped immediately. I had to struggle not to laugh. He got the point, though, and in biology, he didn't make a peep.

Then, in my weapons courses, Bracken told Jack to make himself at home, stay out of the way of the weapons and students sparring, but otherwise he was free to do what he wanted. Naturally, Jack found a perch at the top of a training dummy, the wood spokes the perfect size for his feet to wrap around. The few times I checked on him, I got the impression he was napping.

Like always, Keir offered to spar with me. That was why he noticed my ring. Mostly because he told me wearing jewelry was a good way to get a finger broken. When I said I couldn't take it off, he asked me if my "significant other" had given it to me. He meant Aspen, so I explained it was something Jack had found.

"Your crow found a ring with crows on it?" He threw a punch, making me block. "You don't think that's weird at all?"

"I think it's *completely* weird," I assured him. "A ring with crows, from a crow, and now it won't come off? Yeah, my first thought was that Harper had to be setting me up."

"Not if it's enchanted," he assured me. "She wouldn't spend time making something like that and then give it away."

"Unless she made it just to get me in trouble," I countered. "Keir, she hates me. She hates that you're protecting me. She's livid that the court pays attention to me. Besides, it has crows all over it. Doesn't take a genius to realize Jack would try to collect it. Crows do have a reputation."

"And so does Harper," he reminded me. "She's pretty, but she's not a genius, Rain. I'm not saying she couldn't be, but that girl is too fixated on proving how powerful she is. Look, all I'm saying is that if it hasn't blown up yet, then it's not Harper's style."

Ok, he had a point there. "So I just wear it?" I asked.

He shrugged. "Jack gave it to you. Jack is a fae of sorts. We call creatures like him wildlings, and they have their own power. So, who's to say it's not his way of marking you so the other crows know who you are? Kinda like that band you put on him, right?"

Which made so much sense. Jack had made it a trade. I'd assumed that was just him being a crow, but everyone said he was a very special bird. He was smart. He could talk a little bit. Then there was how he'd held out his banded leg, making it clear he still wore the *eltam*, and then he'd told me to put the ring on. The question was why I'd even done it.

"Could Jack have made something like this?" I asked.

"No idea," Keir admitted. "Could *a* wildling make something like that? Yes. Without a doubt. Is Jack powerful enough or trained enough to do so? I don't know. I haven't seen him doing anything magical."

"So, not all wildlings are magical?"

"Nope," Keir said. "Well, yes and no. They're all carriers of magic. They can't all do anything with it. Kinda like me. I can defend, but not attack. Well, not successfully. Some people can dance. Others sing. Our talents vary, and the same is true for wildlings. And no, wildlings with powerful magic are not common. It's why our people rule Faerie, because we can all use the power in some way."

That actually made me feel a little better. I was pretty sure Jack had no magical ability of his own. Otherwise, he would've used it by now, right? But if he was a wildling - or a prince wildling - then he'd certainly recognize an artifact made by his kind. Right? So, if Aspen was right and the ring had been lost when the atrium was being built, the fact Jack found it was a lot less shocking.

Then Keir began to push me a little harder. All throughout self-defense, he made me not only block his free-hand attacks, but also interrupt his casting. Thankfully, the few times I missed, the result had nothing to do with paint or glitter. He just made glowing shields appear around me. I still got the point.

Then, when my offensive class was over, Bracken called for me to stay behind. Keir flopped down on a bench, clearly intending to wait, and the rest of the students quickly filed out of the building. With everyone watching, I ducked my head and made my way to Bracken, wondering what I was in trouble for this time.

But Bracken just hooked a finger under my chin, lifting it back up. "I wanted to say that I'm proud of you. Liam told me how you faced down not just a hunter, but *the* Huntsman himself. Rain, the man on the other side of the glass door? That was the leader of the Wild Hunt. He's a scary bastard, so don't ever be ashamed of your fear, ok?"

"I had no idea what to do," I admitted.

He nodded. "And yet you still *did*. I want to set a time for you to be trained in our full lockdown procedure. What to do out here, if you're in the yard, or in the main school." He paused, sighed, and then gestured to a bench. "Keir, you can stop pretending like you're not listening. It's fine."

Bracken moved me to one of the resting areas, and because he'd said something, Keir got up to join us. The three benches were placed in a C shape, the spot next to the water for a place to sit while taking a break. Each of us claimed the middle of a bench, and then Bracken kicked his legs out and leaned back, making this feel a little less formal.

"First," Bracken said, "Keir knows I'm committed to Liam. He's been my apprentice since he came to Silver Oaks years ago. I had no idea you didn't know, Rain."

"I just want to know why you two aren't married," I admitted.

Keir bit back a laugh - proving how inappropriate my question was. I winced, realizing it only after the words were out of my mouth. Thankfully, Bracken didn't look upset. He seemed more amused than anything else.

"Well," Bracken explained, "to the fae, marriage means something different than it does here in America. It's more like a job than a relationship. Marriages are usually to produce children, to ensure titles, or for a specific goal, and they're arranged like any other deal between the fae. An exchange of services, which are clearly listed before the agreement is made. That's not how I feel about Liam. I love him, I am with him because I love him, and there are no expectations other than that."

"Oh." That actually sounded pretty sweet. But sticking my foot in my mouth once a day was enough. I quickly got back to the subject at hand. "Um, so, when the Hunt comes, you hide in your apartment? I mean, for lack of a better word, because 'hiding' sounds bad, but I'm curious how that works."

"Yes, we hide," Bracken assured me. "You see, if the Hunt has proof there are fae in an area, they will let the storm pass them by. They will stay here and keep trying to get in, and the school isn't a fortress. If a fae is spotted, then the sentinels will come to defend. That's called stage two. Stage one is to simply give them no reason to miss their 'ride' to the next place.'

"The storm," I realized.

Bracken nodded. "Exactly. There are a few rare instances where the Wild Hunt can come without one, but now that the gates are closed, there's just not enough magic for them to be used often. Once a century sort of events. The question, though, is if you're willing to do that again. Rain, will you risk facing another hunter to make sure the doors are locked and the school is secure?"

I nodded quickly. "Yeah, of course. I mean, if I help, then Jack helps, and it seems like if he helps, then the other crows do too, right?"

"Exactly," Bracken said. "You may not realize it, but the crows saved us. The only reason we knew the Hunt was coming was because of Jack."

"Jack!" the bird said, proving he was listening too.

"Yes," Bracken agreed. "You saved all of us." Then he turned back to me. "But if you're going to do this, I'd like to keep up with the after-hours practices."

I groaned. "It's almost midterms. Bracken, I have *got* to study. I'm so far behind. I want to, and I'm ok with it, but what if I fail my classes? Literature, math, and biology aren't grading me on a curve!"

"We'll help," Keir promised. "I definitely will, and I'm pretty sure the entire court will. I mean, Aspen will all but demand it."

Bracken's eyes narrowed. "Aspen?"

"Her, uh, best friend," Keir explained. "And you know that if Aspen wants something, Torian is willing to give it."

Bracken chuckled. "That he will. The offer for lessons is there, Rain. I don't want your other classes to suffer, but since you're going to be here over the winter, then we can just plan for then. How does that sound?"

"Perfect," I agreed. "And if I have a free day, maybe I can sneak something in then?"

"I'm always available," Bracken promised. "Mostly because Liam would have my balls if I wasn't." With a grin, he shooed us away. "Get out of here, you two. Keir, talk to the court. Make sure she has everything she needs."

"Yes, sir," Keir agreed, waving to the door for me to go first. "C'mon, Jack. Let's let you stretch your wings for a bit."

Chapter Fifty-One

That evening, someone knocked on my door. Confused, I got up to answer it, but Aspen was in her room reading through her botany lesson. That meant it had to be Liam, because no one else came to visit me. Although when I opened the door, it wasn't him. In fact, the guy standing on the other side may have been the last person I'd ever expect to seek me out: Hawke.

In his hand was a strange pole of sorts. More were laying on the ground beside him. My brow furrowed, and I looked from one thing to the other, then back to him. I couldn't even figure out what to say.

"Hawke?" I finally asked.

He cleared his throat awkwardly. "So, Aspen said Jack was perching on the headboard." He bent to grab the smaller poles on the ground. "It's a roost, Rain. A place for him to sleep, and I figured Aspen can make some grass grow beneath it so you won't have to wake up in the middle of the night."

"What? Why?" I asked, stepping back so he could come in.

"Because if he shits in the grass, it's fertilizer?" Hawke asked.

"No!" I laughed. "I meant why are you making Jack a roost, silly."

That earned me a little smile, and it may have been the first one

I'd ever had him turn on me. His gaze softened for a split second, then he moved to an empty space in my room. One right next to the window.

"What about here?" he asked. "I can probably make a little opening in the window for him..." He paused. "Torian could, at least."

"Not that magical?" I asked, moving over beside him.

"Plenty magical," he assured me. "I just don't have a knack for delicate work. Glass is delicate, so... Yeah."

I gestured to the spot before him. "Well, that works for me, and I'm kinda getting used to the idea of keeping Jack happy." I reached for the table beneath the window. "There's no reason this can't move over, either."

Hawke's hand landed on mine, stopping me from what I was about to do. "I can move it," he promised. Once again, I was stuck looking deep into his eyes. Strange, caramel-colored eyes. "I can help with your math course too," he added.

My lips curled into a smile on their own. "Yeah? Who told?"

"Keir," he admitted. "We've been parsing out your classes. Wilder said he's got Literature. Torian and Keir are debating History of Faerie, but I think you should let Torian have that. He kinda lived there his whole life. Bracken should pass you in Self-Defense and Offensive Combat. Tag will give you something for your skillset, because she's the most fair human I've ever met - " He paused. "Right. You're human."

"Hawke?" I asked, aware he seemed off. Nervous, almost.

He turned his attention to the poles that would become Jack's roost. "Why aren't you scared of me, Rain? The faelings are."

"Why should I be?" I countered. "I thought you could be trusted."

That made him look back. For a second, his strange eyes measured me, and then he let go of the poles. One step put him right before me. Slowly, he reached up to trail his thumb over my ear.

The nail was thicker than I expected, but it didn't tangle in my hair. He was gentle, but the intensity of his gaze wasn't. Of all the fae I'd met, Hawke seemed the least human, but was that simply because he didn't try to fit in as much? Was that why he expected me to fear him?

"Not even a shiver," he said softly, moving his hand again. "That's what makes you interesting, because I have a feeling your lack of fear has nothing to do with a lack of intelligence."

"Was that a compliment?" I asked.

His eyes dropped to my lips, then they slid down to hang on my pulse for a second before the guy simply turned and started messing with the poles again. "Did the Hunt scare you at all?"

"Freaked me right out," I admitted. "The Huntsman looked like he wanted to break through the glass and get me. I mean, it could've been Jack he wanted to get, though, since he's a fae thing. Still, I'd never seen anything like that."

His hands were quickly screwing the pieces of poles together to make a large, T-shaped structure. "What do they look like now? The riders, I mean."

"Um, grey. Everything about them is this storm-grey color, including their skin and hair. White eyes, like dead. Like the worst cataracts ever." Then I paused. "But his teeth were nice. Not rotten or anything. It was just that his skin was all shriveled up."

"The magic being sucked out of them," Hawke explained. "The storms were assumed to give them just enough to keep going, but from the sounds of it, that might be wrong. If they're withering, then it could be a case of running on a deficit, draining themselves to complete their task."

"Why is it different for you?" I asked. "I mean, if they need magic to survive..."

Hawke chuckled. "So do we. Sunlight is a good one, and it's stored in fruit. The sweetness of sugar is another. Our diet consists of the small magics Earth makes. Faelings can thrive on your food, but they'll still go for fruits and sugars for the magic. They are part fae and part human, after all."

Then he finished the last piece and stepped back to show me a rather typical bird perch. It had a sturdy base so it wouldn't fall over easily, and the T meant there was plenty of room for Jack to walk from side to side. When I moved to look at it, Hawke stepped around me to shove the table over. That left a nice space before the window, so he moved the roost there.

"Hey, Jack?" he asked, turning to search the room for the bird. "Wanna try it out and give me your opinion?"

Jack immediately left his perch on my shelf and sailed down to land on the roost. Rattling in pleasure, he bobbed his head and walked the length of it, then turned around and came back the other way. That made him caw with excitement. With a little hop, he turned around to look out the window.

"Jack!" he proclaimed. "Rain, Jack! Jack-Jack!"

"I get the impression he approves," I said. "That was a kind thing. I have no idea how I'll repay you."

"The debt belongs to Jack," Hawke assured me. "He can make his own amends."

"But where did you get the stuff?" I asked.

Hawke sighed and ducked his head. "Wilder convinced one of the trees in the atrium to help. He grew it, Rain. I just made the holes and added the screws to secure it."

"And sanded it," I said, reaching over to feel the smooth wood. "A little finishing work. Kinda hard to remember that doing things the mundane way is just as impressive as the magical one, huh?"

His reaction was not the one I expected. The words were barely out of my mouth before his eyes trapped me again and Hawke stepped into my body. His hand found the side of my face and he leaned in, closer, but his mouth never met mine. His eyes also didn't let go.

"I want to kiss you right now," he breathed, the air warm against my lips. "To watch as your eyes close and your body relaxes. I'm just not sure that's what would happen." His thumb brushed across my cheek, almost daring me to close the gap. "I already know my lover would approve, but I think you'd push me off because you don't realize yours would."

"Hawke..."

His pupils were constricting again, the process oddly enticing. "I can't imagine you being scared of anything, and I like that a little too much. Tell Aspen to grow grass."

My heart was hammering. I knew I should pull away, but instead, he did. Without stopping to look back, saying nothing else, Hawke simply marched out of my room. The door closed softly behind him and I still stood there, trying to figure out what the fuck had just happened.

Why did he think I should be scared of him? What was he thinking saying he wanted to kiss me? He knew I was with Aspen! The entire court did! If I told her about this, would she rip him a new one? I would if the situation was reversed. The idea of someone trying to steal my girlfriend from me? A *friend* trying to do it?

Pushing out a breath, I turned to look at Jack's new perch. It was well made. Nothing fancy, but still done with care. Sitting on it, Jack tilted his head, examining me. I reached up to pet him, but the ordeal with Hawke bothered me more than I wanted to admit. I just didn't understand *why*. It made me feel like I'd done something wrong. I hadn't, though. I knew I hadn't, but I still felt like it.

"Why couldn't they all have been hideous?" I asked Jack. "That would remove the temptation."

He murmured at me softly, the sound rather croaky, yet cute in its own way.

"So what do I tell Aspen, Jack? He's her friend!"

"Who is?" Aspen asked, picking that exact moment to walk into my room.

I just groaned and ducked my head. "Hawke made Jack a roost."

"Yeah, he was talking about it in fourth period," she said. "Wait. Did he do something else?"

Pulling in a deep breath, I turned to face her. I didn't want to talk about Hawke, but I needed something to fix this. To keep this from happening again. Most of all, to remove this annoying guilty feeling. My mind settled on one thing.

"Why can't we come out, Aspen?" I asked. "Why can't we tell everyone we're together? It's not like Harper will pick on us less, and with the whole court watching out for us, what can she do?"

She looked at me for a long moment, then made her way over. "Rain? What's going on?"

"I just feel like if we were more open then people would accept it," I said, wondering if that actually would've made Hawke pause. He'd mentioned my lover, so he *knew,* which might invalidate my theory. I still kept going. "Make it clear I'm with you and I'm not going to cheat on you."

"You'd have to move," she told me. "There's a rule that we couldn't live together. They'd move someone else in here and you in with another suitemate. Sure, we could date, but we wouldn't be able to spend the night anymore. It's underage immorality and all that."

"I don't think Liam would care," I insisted.

"No, but other parents would," she countered. "Harper's mom, as an example. Allowing kids to have sex and not stopping it. Encouraging us, and all that shit. Why? Rain, what *happened?*"

Yeah, there was no getting out of this. "Hawke said he wanted to kiss me."

"And?" she asked. "Did he pressure you?"

"No!" Fuck, I was making a mess of this. "He's completely fascinated by the fact that I'm not scared of him. I think it turns him on or something. He stepped in like he was about to try, and I was ready to push him off, but he just said he wanted to kiss me. He mentioned his lover approving, which is wrong on so many levels, and..." I just flapped my hands beside me. "I know he's your friend, and he didn't really do anything, but I didn't even know he's dating someone! I just... Aspen, if we were out, he'd know better, wouldn't he?"

"No, he wouldn't," she said gently, guiding me over toward my bed. "Rain, we're not married. I don't have any right to stop you from doing what you want. I trust you enough to include me, even if that's just being honest about it. That's what fae consider a relationship. It's not me owning the rights to your body or you owning mine. You didn't sell yourself to me when we started this. You simply offered to care, and I think you do."

"I definitely do," I promised her.

"But that's the thing," she continued. "We were all old enough when we left Faerie to know how our parents loved, and to think of *that* as normal. My mother had three lovers - I think I told you that before. Two women and a man. Hawke's mother was a courtier, which is like very minor nobility in a way. She had a few lovers, and they were all together, even though none of them were his father. My point is, the fae are mostly pansexual, kinda like you. They love who they love, and gender is less important than attraction." She paused to lick her lips. "Which is why you didn't know Hawke was dating someone. You see, we're not allowed to be intimate with our suitemates."

My mouth fell open. Sure, she'd told me some of that, but all the bits and pieces were starting to finally make sense in my head. Hearing her mother had been with a woman was one thing. Her dad didn't really sound like he'd been in the picture, after all. And while I knew he was dead now, I wasn't sure *when* he'd died. But like this? She made it sound like it didn't matter either way, as if sharing was their way of caring or something.

Never mind that bombshell about Hawke! "He's with a guy?" I asked, making sure I'd heard her right.

"Yeah," she said, dragging the word out. "See, Torian and I are only attracted to girls. Not that it can't change, and maybe one day some guy will change our minds, but it hasn't happened yet. Most pure fae don't think like that, though. Fae tend to love who they love, regardless of gender. They are with who they want to be with, not just as a couple. Cheating can only happen if someone else has the rights to your body, but I will never *own you,* Rain. If you want to kiss him, then kiss him. If you want to have sex with him, then do."

"What? But..."

She caught my hands. "Rain, I really like you. Probably more than I should. I don't, however, want to own you. I want to hear you giggle about it. I don't mind the idea of seeing you pressed up against some big strong guy either. I want to be your partner, not your owner, and I want you to feel the same about me."

Licking my lips, I nodded. "I want to. I just..." Yeah, how could I say this without sounding like a horrible person? "The idea of you being with someone else scares me. What if you like them more? What if you decide I'm not as good?"

"That's not how it works," she laughed, the sound gentle and comforting. "Rain, I like you just like I enjoy Pixy Stix. I also like oranges and honey. Having only one would not be as much fun as having all three, right?" She leaned in and kissed me quickly. "And if I ever like someone else, I'd tell you first. I'd talk about it, share it with you, and include you. That's how fae do things."

"So you want another girlfriend too?" I asked, feeling a whole new form of anxiety begin to build.

"No," she assured me. "Never mind that I'm a pariah because of my magic. Without even considering that most of Silver Oaks is scared of me. Even if I was just like everyone else here, I still wouldn't, because none of these girls make me feel so stupid and happy. They don't make me like them, Rain."

"Oh." Yeah, ok, that made me feel better.

"But I like you," she promised, her words heavy with the truth I knew she was offering. "I like you because you're beautiful, sensitive, and wonderful. I just *like you,* Rain. Enough to be happy if you hook a guy as well. I mean, if you like both, why not enjoy both, right?"

"I'm sure you'd like it more if I was just with you, though," I countered.

"No," she assured me. "The idea of you trusting me with that? Of letting me be a part of the rest of your life? It makes me feel so much more important than having you deny something because you think it's what I want. I simply want to be your other half."

"I think you are," I said softly. "*I* just don't want to be greedy."

"Be greedy," she told me. "It's a very fae trait." Then she held up her phone. "And it seems I'm going to be teaching you biology, which is kinda why I came in. You're going to make at least a B on all your midterms. You have my wor- "

I kissed her before she could make that promise. "Don't overestimate my test taking abilities, Aspen. How about we just try to study?"

"Every night until midterms are over," she agreed. "With only a little kissing to keep you from getting stressed."

To prove her point, she kissed me again. Damn, but I liked this girl a lot. More than I'd ever thought possible. Knowing she wasn't mad about Hawke just proved how amazing she was. And the rest of that? I'd worry about it later.

Chapter Fifty-Two

After classes on Friday, I headed to the study hall. Midterms started next week. The weather outside was disgusting - not quite snowing, but too solid to be rain - and the sound of it on the windows was relaxing. I had my tablet resting on the provided stand, charging in the available port, and I was trying to read everything I'd missed in History of Faerie before I'd transferred here.

My eyes were starting to get tired when a paper cup appeared by my elbow. I wanted to say magically, but there was a hand attached to it. Following that up, I found Torian looking back. He tipped his head at the chair beside me, so I nodded.

"You're not an easy girl to find," he said, turning the chair to face me. "Aspen thought you were in the library."

"So how'd you find me?" I asked.

He flicked a finger to Jack. "Asked where the crow went. A few girls saw him fly in here." Then he reached over for my schedule. "When's your history test?"

"Tuesday," I told him.

"What's Monday?" he asked.

I groaned. "Math. The class I share with Aspen. Hawke's supposed to be helping me with that, I think." Then I paused. "Yeah, he's probably not anymore, huh?"

"He is," Torian assured me. "You're going to spend most of your day tomorrow in the atrium. Sunday as well, and every evening until you've passed your midterms."

"And who made this decision for me?" I asked.

His lips curled into a devious smile. "Well, I did, of course. Aspen thinks better around the plants. Relaxes her. I have a feeling you think better when Jack isn't distracting you."

"And you?" Because I wasn't sure I liked his tone. "Do you just think well all the time? Is it some impressive guy-talent you have?"

He chuckled once. "No, Rain. I study in a perfectly silent room with nothing moving, no sound, and exactly zero distractions. Wilder likes music. Lots of very loud music."

I couldn't help myself. "What about Hawke?"

"Yeah, he doesn't study," Torian admitted. "Bastard sees it and remembers it. So where are the notes for your upcoming exam?" he asked.

I flicked at the screen to open that app. "Aren't you taking History of Faerie?"

"Tested out," he explained as he scanned the list of what would be on the test. "And it's Ms. Rhodes, so this will be long-answer stuff. A paragraph, written or typed. So, how about we start here?"

The girl across from him groaned. "Can you do it quieter? I'm trying to study for my own classes."

Torian's eyes immediately jumped to her. "Then do it somewhere *else*." The words came out as a snarl.

I grabbed his arm. "In case you missed it, this is the *girls'* study hall. This is where she should be studying." Then I grabbed my tablet, cord, and papers. Pushing to my feet, I gestured pointedly at the door. "If we're talking, then *we* can leave."

"Thanks, Rain," the girl said.

I didn't have a clue who she was, but she looked like the same person who'd saved my notebook that day in the halls - although it didn't really matter. This was a communal space, which meant communal respect. Torian groaned like I was putting him out, but he stood to follow. As soon as I headed for the door, Jack took off, wanting to beat me. He swooped through near the top, but still low enough to make someone rounding the corner squeak in surprise when he barreled out.

"Damn it!" Shit, that was Harper's voice.

Even worse, she came into view just as Torian and I were about to step through. We all stopped to keep from hitting each other. Two other girls were behind her, Elyssa and the new one, Sierra. They flinched back, but Harper's eyes went right to Torian. For a moment, they glared at each other, and then she turned her attention to me.

"You're fucking *this* now, Tor? Taking your sister's sloppy seconds?"

"Better than Keir's," I mumbled under my breath, unable to help myself.

But that was more than Harper could take. She stepped right into my face. "What did you say?"

So I leaned into hers. "Oh, you heard me. What, am I not supposed to know you've been throwing yourself at the pure-bloods? Do you even care if they're nice guys?"

"Do you?" she asked. "Because you're building up quite the little collection there, aren't ya?"

"Enough!" Torian snarled, pushing Harper back. "Let me make this clear. We're done, Harper. I'm not about to become some quiet and submissive piece of arm candy for you to brag about. You're not about to shut your fucking mouth, and unless there's a dick in it, no guy's interested - so move on already."

"You went from me to her?" she asked him. "I'm almost as strong as you, and her? What, she takes it up the ass or something?"

"Oh, I can bang three at once," I said before she could try to pull all the typical slut slurs. "Going for the group play, you see." Then I nudged her shoulder, pushing her back.

She turned to me and pulled in a breath, but I pushed at her shoulder again. "Try calling magic on me, and I'll use my fist next time. And if you do it a third, I'll pull out the iron. Burns you too, huh?"

"Fucking cunt," she grumbled.

But all of my pushing had nudged her out of the doorway, effectively removing the barrier. Just on principle, I shoved her one more time - a little harder, simply because it felt good - then kept walking. Ahead of me, Jack cawed out his approval, and Torian had to stretch his legs to keep up.

Harper simply stood there, sputtering in frustration. The girls with her looked confused, as if they weren't sure how to handle me, but that was kinda the point. Bullies expected their targets to always cry, whimper, or run away. As a foster kid, I'd learned early on how to protect myself. If it didn't seem to hurt me, then it lost all appeal. It was as true for bullies as it was for foster siblings and parents.

"You should've let me get that," Torian said as we turned for the stairs.

"And have her think I'm helpless without some big strong fae around? Don't think so," I told him.

But I noticed he held the door a bit wider so Jack had a straight shot. That was a little endearing. Still, there was something about this guy that made me feel like I needed to prove myself. Almost like he was constantly judging me - and pretty much every other person around him.

"So," he said when we reached the bottom of the stairs, "the founding of the current Summer Court happened in what you'd consider the mid-fourteen hundreds. I want to say fourteen thirties? We keep track of time by the reign of the monarch. In our case, that was the first year of Titania. The Winter Court would've called it the seventeenth year of Oberon."

"So you're from the Summer Court, huh?" I asked.

His face stilled. "I was. Now I'm from Earth."

"Ok, so am I crazy," I asked as we reached the first floor and stepped out in view of the atrium, "or are there ethnic differences between Summer and Winter fae?"

"What do you mean?" he asked.

"Race," I said. "Look at Harper. She's clearly from the Summer Court, with her pretty blonde hair and peaches-and-cream skin. But Aspen, on the other hand, is definitely Winter, right?"

"Right..." he agreed.

"You have those spring-green eyes, your skin's a cooler shade of olive, and your hair is natural black. It could go either way, but I'm guessing Summer because of your magic. Wilder's dark, but a cool tone, so more Winter. Keir's Summer, though. Ms. Rhodes is Summer. I mean, it seems like most people are Summer."

"What about Bracken?" Torian countered as we reached the atrium doors.

"Oh, that's tricky," I admitted while he held them open so I could enter first. "I want to say Summer, but he's got that icy hair and there's something about his eyes."

Torian paused to let Jack in. "Good eye. He has a parent from each. What about Hawke?"

"Autumn," I said without hesitation.

"There is no Autumn Court," Torian said. "Only Summer and Winter. So, if you had to put him in a court, where would you place him?"

"Summer, but only because he seems permanently attached to your side." I shrugged. "Granted, Nevaeh is Winter, but she's Harper's cousin, and I'm not sure how that works."

"She inherited Winter magic," he explained, "but her father was tied to the Summer Court. She got her grandmother's magic, though."

"So, she's Winter?" I asked.

"She's Summer here," he said, "but in Faerie, yeah. She would've been Winter. See, it wasn't uncommon to marry a member of the other court for material or political gain. For peasants, it made the rural villages stronger, giving them access to power in all seasons. For nobility, which these fools like to pretend they're descended from, it decided allegiances."

"And the color of the magic determines which court?" I asked.

"It's a little more complicated than that," he admitted. "But yes. Summer magic comes out green. Winter magic is white. That's determined by the tap it comes from, like hot or cold water from a sink."

"Which is why you have green magic," I realized. "Aspen's is white, but yours is green. But you're siblings?"

"Exactly," he said as he led me toward the large weeping willow. There, he sat down and gestured for me to join him. "Rain, can I ask you something?"

"Sure, but I might not answer."

He nodded as if that was fair. "Why Keir?"

That was not at all what I'd expected. "He's my friend."

"He doesn't want to be merely your friend, and we both know you're not a stupid girl. Why Keir?" he pressed.

I set my tablet in the grass beside me and reached over to pluck a blade. "Because he's nice. He explains things to me without making me feel stupid for asking - or like he's judging me when I don't know something."

"I'm not judging you," Torian said.

I shrugged. "I'm also dating your sister, so it doesn't matter either way."

"What?" The look on his face was pure confusion. "No. That's not how this is supposed to work."

"Which this?" I asked, pressing my advantage.

"You," he told me. "Aspen said you're into guys."

I thrust out my lower lip and nodded, doing my best to look like I was debating that. "Yeah, guys are ok. So is Aspen, it seems. I mean, Keir's pretty hot." Then I tapped my sleeping tablet. "In case you forgot, I'm out here to study, not get laid. I happen to have a willing partner up in my suite for *that*."

"The Queen's reign," he said, getting back to my lesson, "started well enough. For the first century, she was considered to be one of the best rulers, and the Summer Court flourished under her rule."

"What happened?" I asked.

"Officially? She fell in love with Oberon. They met at a Winter Solstice celebration. The pair danced. He charmed her with glitz and glamour. She was a young and vain queen - most fae are vain, so you know - and she adored the attention. When Oberon decided he should consider an heir, and thus a wife, she put herself forward. Unfortunately, marriage between the crowns isn't done. It would've confused the magic."

"But isn't that what's happening now?" I asked.

"It is," he agreed, "and the Queen has gone mad because of it. But, that's just the official story. The unofficial one is that Titania felt embarrassed because Oberon's power was greater than hers. It was his season, after all. When the Summer Solstice came, he was busy elsewhere, and probably in someone's bed. The man was well known for his lovers. She didn't get the chance to show him up, so she began searching for ways to store power to use off-season. And thus, the woman became obsessed with power, always wanting more. The crown on Oberon's head offered it. The natural solution was to force him to marry her."

"She sounds kinda like Harper," I grumbled.

He dropped his head and sighed. "Please don't say that. Harper is petty, malicious, and self-absorbed, but I promise she's nothing like the Mad Queen. Titania has goals, she has contingency plans, and the woman is nothing but one scheme on top of another."

"Was she terrifying?" I asked, aware he'd actually met her.

Torian nodded. "Very. The whole fairytale about the mirror? It's based on her vanity. She loved no one but herself and her own reflection. She only wanted a child as a means to get control of the Winter crown, you see. And failure was not tolerated around her. If she bestowed her favor on you - like offering to teach something - she expected nothing but excellence. Anything else would reflect poorly on her, as if she might not be a perfect teacher."

"Is she why you left?" I asked.

He nodded again. "Yeah. She figured out that threatening children was the easiest way to force her court to obey her. Normally, killing children is an abhorrent thing to the fae, but Titania didn't care at all. The rules were hers to create and break as she pleased. Harper has that about her, and it's what I couldn't tolerate."

"Is Harper related to the Queen or something?" I asked.

The look he gave me was appalled. "No! Her mother was the Queen's maid. Nothing more. Granted, the woman tells everyone she was the Queen's handmaid and keeper of her secrets, but her duties were preparing the Queen's clothes. If she ever talked to Titania, I'd be surprised. She also left before I was born."

I spun the little blade of grass between my fingers. "You know, all of this is interesting, like some wild fairytale or something, but there's one thing I don't get about all of it."

"What's that?" he asked.

"Why do we care? Why am I learning about the history of a world that's locked away? What difference does it even make?" I asked. "Why do all of our teachers act like knowing this is very, very important? It's not like you'll be going back, and *I* certainly won't be!"

Torian leaned forward to hug his knees. "Well, they say those who ignore history are doomed to repeat it." He sighed deeply before looking over at me. "And the hope is to go back, Rain. Humans live long lives there. Faelings would be no different than fae, and their children would be born into the magic again. We *do* want to go back, but we also want to return to a world where the Queen isn't in charge."

"So what then?" I asked. "Kill the Queen and get a new tyrant? I mean, isn't that how monarchs work? All-powerful and shit?"

"No," he promised. "The crowns tie the rulers to their power. From there, it's dispersed to the courts. It's like a focus stone, I guess. Like a magnifying glass. The crowns were made long, long ago to gather all the magic so our people could all have some. Those with more are expected to do more in Faerie. Nobles aren't special just because of birth. They're ranked because of their power, and because of their title, they are beholden to those under them."

"A pyramid scheme," I realized, chuckling at the idea.

"Kinda," he admitted. "The difference is that before Titania, those at the top lived busy, challenging lives. Not easy ones. The life of luxury belonged to those who worked with their hands, lacking the power to be responsible for anything but their own existence."

"And who polices it?" I asked. "Because if Titania went rogue, who's to say someone else won't?"

"It used to be the wildlings," he said. "And through them, a champion. In Faerie, the world finds a way to balance itself. Tilt the scales and be ready to pay the price. I like to think it means the Mad Queen will pay very, very dearly."

Chapter Fifty-Three

On Saturday, I spent most of the day in the atrium. The place was becoming more popular as everyone crammed for midterms. So was the panic. Over and over again, I kept hearing people mention academic suspension or even expulsion if we didn't pass our courses. When added to the fact that I had no special abilities besides an overly friendly crow? Well, to say I was nervous was putting it mildly.

For the most part, Jack behaved himself. Once, he stole a guy's keys. Some college guy had set them down beside where he was sitting, and Jack had been fascinated by the shiny metal. Before the guy even knew what was happening, the bird swooped in, grabbed the keys, and flew off. Thankfully, he brought them right to me so I could give them back.

Which pissed Jack off. He was not at all impressed that I'd returned the gift he'd stolen so fairly. The chattering and cawing was enough for me to send him up to the top of the atrium. He still grumbled, but at least up there it wasn't quite as loud.

The first half of the day, Aspen and I both spent with Hawke. He wasn't in our math course, but he was taking an advanced class, so our stuff was easy, he said. While he sat propped up against the fish pond, Aspen and I both claimed his legs as pillows for our heads. She lay stretched out one way. I went the other. Hawke assured us he didn't mind *at all*.

Then he grilled us on math problems from Aspen's tablet. When I stumbled, he paused and broke them down for me. When Aspen had a question, he always answered it. The guy was smart! I'd only ever paid attention to him in my offensive combat class, but I was starting to think I was missing out.

Intermittently, he'd rest his hand on my stomach or Aspen's. The first time he did it, I looked up to find his eyes waiting. I smiled, he relaxed, and neither of us said a thing, but it was kinda nice. I got the impression he was mostly doing it for Aspen, making everyone else think she was flirting with him. Or maybe that he was flirting with her, I realized once I remembered he was with a guy.

No, not *a* guy. His suitemate. Since Torian was supposedly only into women, I had a feeling the other guy was Wilder. Then again, for all I knew, Torian and Wilder were suitemates and Hawke was with some faeling guy. I was dying to ask, but I was neither stupid enough to try nor rude enough to think I deserved to know.

We studied math for three hours. My brain was so full of numbers I was starting to do worse just as Keir arrived. He came over to stand above the three of us, but his smile was the honest kind.

"So, looks like you lucked out, Hawke. How'd you get the best-looking girls in school on your lap at the same time?" he teased.

Hawke just looked up at him. "I offered to explain numbers. Seems women like a man who can... teach them things."

There was a definite tension there between them. Keir just shrugged it off. "Well, since I'm sure you can only handle one of them at a time, I'm stealing Rain for a bit."

"You are?" I asked.

"I am," Keir assured me. "I did promise to help with your courses, and I've passed all of them once already."

"Go," Aspen told me. "Let me have this hottie, and you can crawl on that one."

I looked over to find her smiling up at me. The expression on her face was honest and... excited? She looked just like a best friend encouraging me to talk to the cute guy I liked. The problem was I liked *her*. Ok, so I liked a few people. So what? But that fear hit me again. The one that felt like I was doing something wrong.

"You don't have to," Hawke said as the worry set in.

I shook my head. "No, I probably should. And if I don't learn anything, I'll come back for help, Hawke."

He caught my hand. "Rain, we're all just trying to help, not push. You don't *have* to. There's nothing to be afraid of."

My heart stalled out at his words. How had he known I was nervous about this? Was it written on my face or something? Never mind the slightly protective note in his voice or the way he kept looking at Keir as if he was a threat.

"She wants to," Aspen said, shifting over so she could sit beside Hawke. "She's also waiting for someone to get jealous because she's human. She's *still* human, Hawke. I'm simply reminding her that it's cute when she's all happy and acting like one of us."

My teeth found my lower lip and I caught her eyes. "Giggling, right?"

"Much giggling," she insisted. "I can't lie, remember? Go, Rain. Have fun. See if you can make Keir blush."

"I don't blush," he told Aspen. "I'm also just a friend. Let Rain set her own pace." Then he offered me a hand up. "Get your tablet. I'm pretty sure I don't think like Hawke, and my way of muddling through your... is it Comprehensive Math?"

"Yeah," I grumbled. "Like a catch-up course for all the stuff I missed in public school. Supposed to have me ready for trig next year."

"And you're in the same one, Aspen?" he asked.

She nodded. "Yep. Got put into basic math last year. Aren't you glad you didn't have a crappy public school education?"

"I went to public school until the eleventh grade," he countered.

"Here," she reminded him. "I was in the middle of nowhere, at a school where the football coach taught all math, and no one failed. Crappy's the key word there. Couldn't risk the players being benched for grades, after all." She waved me away. "Go play, Rain! I need some good gossip this evening."

So I clambered to my feet, grabbed my tablet, and let Keir lead the way. He showed me to a nice little spot beside the glass wall at the back. Vines grew on one side that smelled a lot like Aspen. On the other was a hedge of some fae flowering plant. It had to be at least four feet tall, possibly five. When we sat down, the space was amazingly secluded.

Then Keir flicked his fingers, and the sound around us softened to barely a whisper. "What was all that about?" he asked.

"Uh..."

"The conjuration gives us privacy," he promised. "You clearly knew what Aspen was talking about, so I'm asking to be let in."

I moaned, dropping onto my back. "I'm trying to balance everything," I said. "Classes, mean girls, courts, learning weapons - both how to use and how to make them - and guys with my girl."

"Culture shock," he realized.

"She says she wants me to giggle with her about guys. She knows I'm into them, she's not, and she basically said she doesn't own me."

He shifted down and rolled over onto his stomach, lying parallel to me but the other side up. "Is that what *you* want, though?"

I lifted up my hands and let them drop. "I'd have to be an idiot to say no, but at the same time, I'm waiting for the catch."

"The catch is that living with fae takes practice," he explained. "I say this because I had to learn the other way around. When I had two girlfriends in middle school, I didn't see why I couldn't tell the first about the second. I tried and got slapped, called a cheating dog, and so on. For you, it's the other way around, right?"

"Oh, so you were a junior high slut?" I teased.

He chuckled. "Fae boy among humans. It seems we have an

appeal." Then he tilted towards me and playfully lowered his voice. "So do humans, though. More masculine men and curvier women. It's all about wanting what you can't have, or so I hear. Talk to me, Rain. What's going on in your head?"

"Hawke wanted to kiss me," I blurted out.

"Not surprised at all," Keir said.

"Aspen thinks you intend to be more than just a friend to me," I tried next, not knowing how else to explain the weirdness of my girlfriend being ok with that.

He nodded. "I do. I also have respect for your relationship with her."

"I don't know what I'm doing with her," I admitted. "Not why I'm with her - *that* hits me every time she walks into a room. It's more the 'what to do' part of actually, you know, being with her."

So he turned on his side. "Tell me?"

"It's like she's so beautiful," I said. "I've never been attracted to a girl before, but with Aspen, it's this subtle happiness that's there when she's around. My eyes are always drawn to her, and I find myself smiling like an idiot. I want to hold her, listen to her, and spend every moment with her. Being with Aspen is like being with a best friend, except I want to kiss her and touch her any chance I can get. She gets me excited, but that's where things always fizzle out."

"Because neither of you knows how to make the first move," he told me. "She's giving you space to figure things out, and you're making yourself nervous because you're overthinking. Do you want to sleep with her, Rain?"

"Yeah," I breathed, looking over at him. "I'm just convinced it's going to be a mess."

The sweetest smile lifted one side of his mouth. "Kiss. Start with her lips, work your way to her neck. When she relaxes, then keep going down. Take your time. Don't rush for the end goal. Enjoy each kiss and touch you get. When neither of you can breathe, tease her nipples. Use your leg for her to grind against. Pull her in, up against your body. By that point, you should both be shedding clothes, and then see where it goes."

"Why are you telling me this?" I asked.

"First, because the idea of you and Aspen going at it is sexy," he admitted. "There's an appeal there, although it's probably not the one you'd expect."

"The girl-on-girl fantasy guys always have?" I asked.

"That's exactly what it's not," he assured me. "It's more the ranking of competition. Aspen? She's impressive. Beautiful, intelligent, powerful, and all the things we judge ourselves against. For you to be attracted to her makes sense. Shoot for the best, right? But you also flirt with me, which implies a compliment you cannot understand. One that ranks me near her, in a way. One that says I'm also beautiful, intelligent, and powerful."

"But aren't you?" I asked. "And how is that sexy?"

"I'm not that powerful," he clarified. "As for sexy? How is it not? You are beautiful. She is beautiful. I am not blind, and I do have a very good imagination. It's basically the majority of a young man's sex life, you know."

Which made me laugh. "Ok, fair enough. I just feel like this whole dating thing is the one part of fae life I'm struggling with."

"Well, I do have an ulterior motive," he said. "You see, we're having a relaxed conversation about you with a lover. One that isn't me. It's nice. I feel included. The same thing works the other way around. This? The friendship? The *companionship* is the pleasure of the mind. It's one of many beautiful things about our society."

"Do your parents have other lovers?" I asked.

He shook his head. "No, but they raised me to think of it as normal. My mother married my father to get away from her old life. That was their agreement. My parents love each other very much, and while they wouldn't stop the other from taking a lover, they've just never had the chance. They were from two very different communities, you see. A Romeo and Juliet type of story. Their relationship wasn't accepted by either group, which made it so easy for them to come here."

"That's sweet," I said.

"It's sad," he corrected. "All the happiness they lost because they dared to be true to themselves." Then Keir reached over to shift my hair over my shoulder, and he changed the subject. "I talked to Bracken this morning."

"Yeah?" I turned to face him, shifting to my side so we mirrored each other. "What about?"

"He's making me his TA," Keir said. "As a teaching assistant, I'll be doing less learning and more instructing next semester. Well, so long as I keep my grades up. If I'm good enough, he'll make me the head of the sentinels for my final year here. It's all but setting me up to become the junior weapons instructor after I graduate."

A smile immediately claimed my lips. "Yeah?"

He nodded. "That's what I want. It doesn't hurt that it means more time working with you and the other AP students." This time, when he swept at my hair, it was beside my cheek. His touch was soft, almost a caress. "What I'm saying is there's no rush. I like being your friend. I like listening to you talk about Aspen. I really like that you let me touch you."

"You know I'm going to tell her all of this, right?"

He nodded. "I'm counting on it. Now, how about we make sure you're still here next year? Math, is it?" He woke up my tablet and tapped the icon for my school books. "And so you know, I'm waiting for you to make the first move."

"That's kinda the part I'm bad at," I admitted.

"And yet you're lying a little closer to me today than you were last time. You're not bad at anything, Rain. You're just overwhelmed. All I need is for you to set the gap between us, and I'll believe you. That, beautiful, counts as a first move."

I was smiling and my cheeks were starting to feel warm. "Yeah, so how about some math while I lie here blushing?"

He shifted so he could whisper in my ear, "I like your blushes. As much for her as for me." Then he flicked the page. "Ok, so geometry sucks, but to get the most points on your exam, you'll want to write out every step of your proof. The more you put on the page, the less points you'll lose."

"Thank you," I said softly. "I know I'm not supposed to say that, but..."

He just smiled. "You're welcome, Rain. Say it as often as you want."

Chapter Fifty-Four

The moment we got back to our suite, I told Aspen all about my little talk with Keir. She squealed with delight, pulling me down onto her bed, and then asked all the questions I wanted to talk about. Did he try to steal a kiss? No. Did he flirt? Yes. Did I like it?

Yeah, that was where I hesitated, because I did, but telling her that was hard. When I finally nodded, she threw her arms around me in a joyous hug. In that instant, all of my anxiety fled, and I finally got it. She was my best friend. One I happened to like kissing, who sometimes made me speechless like an idiot, and who I kept stealing glances at.

I liked a girl. I liked a boy. Both were ok, and there was a freedom to admitting it that I hadn't expected. That night, I fell asleep with Aspen's head on my shoulder and my arms wrapped around her. My fingers played with the line of her spine while I watched the soft glow of the plants in her room.

Jack was in my room, and every so often I could hear his feathers ruffle, but there was a peace to this. Ever since I'd been taken from my mother's home, I'd felt like I was simply passing through. A rubber bouncy ball, I'd thought, destined to eventually ping off to the darkest and most forgotten corners. Instead, I'd landed here.

For the first time in my life, I felt like I belonged. Truly belonged, not just tolerated. And to think, it was a school for the fae - for people who "didn't exist." I might not be a fairy princess or some long-lost whatever, but that was ok. Maybe I was the milkmaid or the dishwasher in this story. Either way, I was still a part of this fantasy, and I wanted to make sure I didn't let it slip away.

So, on Sunday, I met up with Wilder in the library to work on my Literature class. He went over the fae aspects of the stories I knew. Things like the magical animals in Snow White, or the divine power Joan of Arc was famous for - even though it was actually magic. However, Shakespeare's *A Midsummer Night's Dream* was going to be a big part of the exam. Since Titania and Oberon were featured in it, along with a few other fae things, I needed to read all of it again. This time, with a new perspective.

Studying with Wilder was strangely comfortable, though. I didn't know the guy that well, but he had a casual feeling about him, which made it so easy to relax. We talked books, from the ones I needed for my class to the ones I liked reading on my own. Those got compared to movies, and that ended up turning into a discussion about how hard it was to take a mental media to a visual one.

But unlike Torian, Wilder didn't want to talk about his time in Faerie. Those days had been dark, he'd said. His memories of that world weren't good ones, and screams had filled almost all of his nights as the Queen had hunted them down. He said his foster home had been so much nicer. Filled with iron, but still a lot less threatening than life in the Winter Court.

It was the only time he mentioned the Winter Court, but it made me realize something. This guy who was sitting beside me, talking so casually about a play by Shakespeare, had once been nobility of some kind. There was something rather surreal about that. Me, the nobody from middle-of-nowhere, Iowa, was being tutored by some fancy fae guy.

When we'd finally covered everything, and I was pretty sure I could pass this class, the pair of us called it a day. Like a true gentleman, Wilder walked me back to my suite, stopped in to make sure Aspen was good with her classes, then admitted he had to cram for his own exam tomorrow.

Then Aspen took over for biology. There would be no mitosis and meiosis on this test. However, there would be a discussion of magnetism and the magical nutritional values of earth plants and fae. Comparisons of chlorophyll to cyanophyll made my head spin, but I was keeping up. So long as this test was multiple choice - and the study guide said it would be - then I should survive.

I went to bed that night thinking about iron soil and the wildlings that had been called dwarves in Snow White. The balance between our world, the imbalance of Faerie, and the history that had caused it all. My dreams were crazy and jumbled, yet somehow, I managed to actually get some sleep.

The next morning, I woke to Jack pecking at my forehead. When I finally opened my eyes to wave him away, I realized my phone was blaring out an alarm. I managed to reach over and silence it, then realized I'd overslept by fifteen minutes!

Scrambling out of bed, I pulled on my uniform, tossed my hair into a ponytail, and went for the least amount of makeup I could tolerate. Today was not about looking pretty. It was all about passing my first test: math. Nothing else mattered but that.

I grabbed Aspen, finding her as much of a mess as I was, and helped gather her things. She was adorable in her half-awake confusion, though. Scrambling to make sure she had what she needed, Aspen reached out for a small potted plant and nearly lifted that to her lips. I was just barely in time to grab it before she tried to take a drink.

Putting the plant back where it belonged, I found her resin travel mug and pressed it into her hands. Sucking back a large gulp of whatever sugary drink she had this morning seemed to help, and Aspen cradled her cup the way I would a freshly brewed coffee.

"You have to make it through first period," I reminded her. "Then our math test."

"I have a test in first too," she admitted. "I was up all night. Maybe two hours of sleep?"

"Then you can nap through lunch," I told her. "Or if you hold off until after seventh period, I'll make sure it's quiet in here, and you can sleep yourself out." Wrapping my arms around her shoulders, I turned her for the door. "We got this, right?"

"Yay, midterms," she grumbled.

Instead of flying through the door to circle around our heads, Jack landed on Aspen's shoulder. The bird toyed with a short lock of her hair, offering his own brand of support. I could see her anxiety growing as we headed to the stairs, so I decided to walk her all the way to her class. When we reached the door, she paused to catch my hand.

"Good luck today," she told me, squeezing my fingers tenderly.

"You got this," I assured her. "Two classes down, right? Only five after that."

She nodded. "Now go, before you're late."

"Jack!" my bird croaked, nibbling at her hair one last time before moving to my shoulder.

I had to hurry to make it to Literature. Just as I reached the door, the bell rang and the teacher looked up. Lifting a brow, he flicked a finger for me to get to my desk as quickly as possible.

"Sorry," I mumbled.

"Up late studying, Rain?" Mr. Connors teased.

"You have no idea," I grumbled.

But the moment I sat down, something jiggled my desk. Magic. That made me look back to find Torian leaning forward. "Did Aspen make it to class?"

"Walked her there myself," I assured him. "Even made sure she didn't drink the plants." I lifted a hand. "Tell you later."

Then Mr. Connors started in on a semester recap. I almost sighed in relief, because he was going over so much of what was on the exam. The strange thing was I felt like I was actually keeping up. Shakespeare, Joan of Arc, and then he got to the fairytales.

"So, in all of the popular children's stories, there's a theme of animals suddenly becoming intelligent enough to help the young damsel in distress. Other times, it's to imprison her, like with Sleeping Beauty and the dragon. What assumptions can we make from what we've learned this year..." His eyes scanned the class and landed on me. "Rain?"

"Wildlings," I said softly, convinced I was wrong.

But Mr. Connors smiled. "Exactly. I actually bring this up because of your friend there. Jack, is it?"

"Jack!" the crow confirmed loudly, making a few people chuckle.

"As all of you can see, he appears to be a perfectly natural crow," Mr. Connors tried to explain.

But the bird had other ideas. "Jack! Jack-Jack-Jack-Jack!"

"He said appears," I whispered. "Hush. You're not the teacher."

Mr. Connors chuckled. "But I think he makes the point. While he looks like a normal crow, he has clearly bonded with Rain. In Faerie, this is considered an honor, and all wild things are meant to be respected. So, these fairytales written on Earth often have an element of that to them. From the helpful birds and mice to the dangers of briars and poisonous apples. Keep that in mind for your test tomorrow."

I leaned back in my chair and continued to listen, petting Jack's feathers. He was still sitting on my shoulder, and seemed somewhat insistent that he stick close. Probably because I was so tense about passing these tests. No one had said anything to me directly - either as a threat or reassurance - but that didn't make me any less worried.

Lately, it seemed like everyone had a story about someone who'd been expelled. Silver Oaks was elite, they said. The Institute had been created so fae could learn their magic in a safe place. The space was limited, so there was no reason to waste time on someone who wasn't interested in becoming a part of this new fae society we were being trained for - and I was the odd one out.

I could easily go back to a normal life. I didn't have magic to expose. I had no fae heritage. I just knew that if I didn't pass all of my classes this semester, I'd be out as fast as I got in. It only made sense. So when first period ended and I made my way to math for today's big test, my mind was spiraling towards a panic attack.

Harper fell in beside me halfway there. I braced for the worst just as Torian stepped up to flank her, pinning the girl between us. Her head whipped from me to him, a scowl taking over her face, and then she looked back at me.

"I'm filing a complaint about you cheating on your exams," she said.

"I haven't even taken one yet," I told her. "How exactly have I cheated if I haven't taken one?"

"Why else have you been secluded with all the pure-bloods? I know they're working up some magic to get you the answers."

"Oh, fuck off," I groaned. "I don't have time for your bullshit today, Harper. Shove your self-importance up your own ass."

And then I turned, angling for the hall that held my second-period classroom. Torian just chuckled, following my lead, and moved to meet up with our friends, who waited right by the corner. Aspen smiled at me and waved, then did the same to Torian, but she looked as tense as I felt.

"I'm going to fail math," she said as soon as I was close enough.

"You will not," Hawke told her, and it sounded like it wasn't the first time. Then he turned to me and offered a pair of Pixy Stix. "Make sure she eats one of these. The other is for you."

I took them both. "Force-feed the cute girl. Got it."

"Girls," Torian corrected. "One's for you, Rain."

I just caught Aspen's shoulder and turned her toward our class. "Bye, guys. Good luck on your own tests." Then I leaned toward Aspen. "We got this. We studied, we can mostly get the right answers, and we will pass, right?"

"I'm going to freeze," she whispered. "I hate math. The person who invented addition and subtraction should've been burned at the stake, because they started this cult. Now, we're all expected to follow it."

"Not a cult," I assured her. "It's just math."

She looked at me desperately as I steered us both into class. We broke off to walk down our respective rows, but she kept pace with me. Her face was a little more pale than usual, making it clear she was *really* worried about this. The moment she sat down, I held out both Pixy Stix to her.

"You need them. One for now, and one for halfway through," I said.

She looked at the offering, then up at me. "Hawke wanted you to have one."

"And I'm giving it to you. Re-gifting, Aspen. Doesn't make me appreciate his gift any less, but you clearly need it more." I tipped my head at the bird on my shoulder. "Besides, Jack has a good feeling about this."

He shook his head violently, making a lie of what I'd just said.

So I turned to glare at him. "Well, start! Have a little faith in us, Jack. We studied hard for this."

So he nodded. "Jack. Rain!" *Caw!*

Finally, a smile cracked across Aspen's face and she took both Pixy Stix. "I'll make it up to you, Rain."

"There's no debt," I assured her. "I'm just taking care of my best friend."

That turned her smile sweet, and a hint of color touched her cheeks. Yeah, I finally understood why guys said they liked it when I blushed. There was something so beautiful about that look on her. So vulnerable, and it hit me right in the heart. How could this girl be so sweet, so gentle, and yet so strong at the same time?

She was amazing, and she was *mine*.

My teeth found my lower lip and I flicked through my tablet, looking over my notes one last time as the teacher walked in. Everyone stilled, all eyes moved to the front, and she simply tapped her own tablet. Like a wave, the notification sounds began going off across the room. I looked down to see I had one file ready to open.

"You have the entire class time to finish. Begin when ready. The answers are multiple choice, and your grades will be posted on your tablet at the end of the week."

Taking a deep breath, I tapped to open it. I had this. I had to, because failing wasn't an option I could live with.

Chapter Fifty-Five

I made it through math, surprised at how many answers I actually knew. After that came biology. The next day, I had Literature and History of Faerie. Oddly, the first test felt a lot harder than the second. Then, on Wednesday, I was stuck with making a resin mold for Weapons-Crafting.

When the bell rang to end fifth period, I still wasn't done. So, with Tag's approval, I sent Jack out to fly and went back to keep working. I finished halfway through what was supposed to be my Self-Defense course, but it came out so much better than expected. Tag told me to put the whole thing at the back of the room, and she'd handle it from there.

So when I dragged myself into Self-Defense, everyone noticed. Bracken stopped mid-sentence and turned, his worried eyes looking me over. I'd known this was merely an explanation of what we should expect for our exam in here, so I hoped he wasn't too angry.

"Having trouble?" he asked.

"Um, my last test took longer than I expected. Sorry, Bracken."

He just nodded then sent me to my spot on the mats. For the rest of class, he discussed his scoring method, how we would be judged, and if we wanted to pair up early, then we should let him know by the start of class tomorrow. Fifteen minutes before the end of class, he released everyone to study, head to their next class, or relax with friends.

Then he walked right over to me. "Is everything ok? Jack showed up early, but he said not to look for you."

I groaned. "No, I had to make a mold in Weapons-Crafting, and I wanted to get it perfect so I wouldn't fail."

"It's only the midterms," he assured me.

"In classes that are nothing like the ones I had at my old school," I reminded him. "Half the time, I feel like I barely know what's going on, and what happens if I fail? We both know I'm only here on a technicality! I have to pass, and I'm so far behind, and I feel like I know all this stuff, but it's a jumble in my head, and - "

He caught my shoulder, clasping it hard enough to make me take a breath. "You're fine," he promised. "I saw you studying all weekend. Ivy said you were in the study hall almost every evening. There's no way you put that much effort in and won't at least pass, Rain."

"But what if I don't?" I asked him.

"Then we'll get you some tutors and catch you up."

I swallowed. "What if they kick me out? I don't want to go back to the real world. I..."

"Shh..." he breathed, dropping down to a knee beside me. "Rain, you have as much right to be here as anyone else."

"They're fae or faelings," I pointed out. "The few humans here are all related to the fae. Step-kids, right? Adopted?"

Bracken just ducked his head and huffed out a small laugh. "What do you think you are?"

I wasn't following him. "Liam's my caseworker. I know he said he's my uncle, but that's very much a technicality, and it's not exactly a secret. I mean, isn't he the caseworker for like half the school?"

"Listen to me," he said gently. "You are a foster child. Your foster father is Liam's brother. I am Liam's... we'll go with boyfriend. I am fae. I am pure fae, and I consider you family. That means you are related to fae as much as any adopted child. You've been exposed to our world now, and you have become an important part."

"Yeah?" I asked.

He nodded. "I promise. Besides, it's not like Liam and I can have kids of our own. The best we can do is spoil someone else's, and that's you, so relax. You don't have to prove your worth, Rain. You're here to learn, not be judged." He tilted his head to look me over. "What tests do you still have?"

"Yours," I admitted. "Self-Defense tomorrow and Offense on Friday."

"And that's it?" he asked.

I nodded. "I'm just waiting for grades on the rest of them."

"Those will come Friday," he told me. "Usually, they'll all hit just after the end of your last class." Then he lifted his head and waved someone over. "I also think you should declare a partner for both this exam and Offense."

Keir jogged over. "Yeah?"

"Would you pair with Rain for her next two exams?" Bracken asked.

Keir bobbed his head once. "Of course. I wasn't sure you'd allow that since I'm in the advanced section, though."

"This time, Keir, I'll be judging you on your ability to teach her, and hers on how to learn." Bracken rubbed my shoulder in encouragement. "And no stage fright. You know what you're doing, Rain. You just have to do it."

After that, he left us to practice. I wanted to drill everything, but Keir did a good job of focusing me. In the end, the whole thing was a letdown. On the day of our exam, Bracken didn't call anyone forward and make them put on a show. He simply meandered through the groups sparring and made a few faces.

Offense was even more subtle. Keir had me interrupting his casting while trying to drop him to the ground. I was laughing about him working so hard to actually conjure a spell when Bracken leaned in and whispered, "Pass," to me.

That was it! No stress. No display. No judgment. It was just like he'd said, and the best part was he didn't grade me any differently than he did anyone else. All of us were simply observed, Bracken noticed both our mistakes and our corrections, then he graded us on the entire sparring effort, not just one quick match.

But when we left the building at the end of the day, my tablet began going crazy. Keir's vibrated a moment later. Excitedly, he pulled it out and swiped at the screen, his feet pausing. I watched as his eyes scanned the screen, and then he let out a sigh of relief.

"I did it," he breathed. "As and Bs. Means I'm still eligible to be a TA. What about you?"

I lifted my tablet almost nervously and squinted my eyes hard as I opened the app. Then, sucking in a deep breath to brace, I opened first one eye, then the other. There, covering my tablet, was an entire page of my grades. A report card of sorts. Each class listed all of my homework and quiz scores in a row, but it was the number at the end that mattered most.

The midterm exam was the next to last, and the bold one in a box of its own was my semester average. Starting at the top with first period, I let my eyes run down them. B, C, B, A, A, B, A. Except for math, I'd not only passed, but I'd made *good* grades.

The whoop came out loudly, and I turned to throw my arms around Keir's neck, the tablet still in my hand. "I made As and Bs in everything but math. I got a C in that!"

His arms wrapped around my back and he lifted, hugging me hard. "That's my girl!"

Then we both paused. For a moment, I wasn't even sure I breathed. Keir was tall. He was hard, solid, and beautiful, and he was holding me so tightly. My feet were barely even touching the ground, and his face was right there. Those violet eyes met mine, and then he gently eased me back down.

"Sorry," he breathed.

"Are you sure Aspen won't be hurt?" I asked.

His brow furrowed for a moment. "Am I sure? No, but she's given me no reason to think otherwise. Why?"

"Because I almost kissed you," I said, the words barely coming out. "I wanted to, Keir, but I don't want to cheat on her, and - "

Just as I started to pull away, he caught me around the back, bent, and his mouth found mine. I relaxed into him, my lips parting, and he was right there. His kiss was hard, but not aggressive - amazingly masculine after kissing Aspen so much. His tongue explored my mouth, taking control, and I let him have it.

I liked this guy. Not just a little bit, either. I'd tried to like him as a friend, but he'd slowly worked his way into my confidence, and then more. I couldn't even say it was because he was beautiful - although he was that too - because it was *more*. I felt safe with him. Stable. Things I'd assumed I'd only ever feel with Aspen. Understanding and acceptance were all right there in his kiss, and I may have liked it too much.

"Congratulations," he said softly as he pulled away. "And now you can say *I* kissed *you*. Hopefully, that will help your adorable human guilt a little."

"What does this mean?" I asked.

He shrugged. "It means I kissed you, Rain. Nothing else has changed. I still like you. You still like Aspen. It only means I kissed you, and now I want to do it again." His eyes dropped to my lips, but he didn't try.

Instead, he draped his arm over my shoulder and turned me toward the school. I moved to press into his side, standing close enough I could've wrapped my arm around him, but I didn't. Not yet. Something about this felt serious, not like a fling I could throw away.

It felt like I did with Aspen. It felt real, fantastical, and impossible. It felt like my brain was being pulled in two, but in a good way. The sort of way that made me want to giggle, spin in circles, and scream it to the whole world. I'd kissed Keir. I was secretly dating Aspen. I'd passed all of my classes.

It was a fucking *good* day.

But when we reached the back door of the school, Jack was there waiting. He looked at Keir and began rattling in his annoyed way. There were a few wing flaps and a ton of feather shifting, too. The bird was agitated, and I couldn't imagine why.

"Is it the Hunt?" I asked.

That got a shake of his head in a clear no, but it didn't stop the complaining.

Keir just chuckled and crouched down. "I am not making her choose, Jack. I'm her friend. She's her friend. You're her friend. That's allowed, isn't it?"

Caw!

The sound was loud and pointed. Keir rocked back at the vehemence of it, but then he murmured. "So, if I screw up, you'll beat the shit out of me, right? Don't hurt your girl and all that?"

When Jack nodded his head, I had to bite back a laugh. "Is *that* your problem, Jack? You think I shouldn't be with Keir?"

He shook his head. So no.

"He thinks you're nervous around me," Keir explained. "Wild things have a sense for that. He wants to make it clear that if I get out of line, he'll put me back in my place. Considering he has a lot of friends, and they chased off the Hunt, I believe him. Jack will beat the shit out of me if I hurt you. I also don't intend to do that, so I think I'm ok."

Caw!

And then Jack flapped up to land on Keir's shoulder. I couldn't think of any better sign of approval. Pulling open the door, I let the pair of them enter first, but Keir pulled me against his side again once we were in the building. Then he steered me toward the dining hall, of all places.

"So, at the end of the semester, pretty much everyone meets in here to compare grades. Even the court. I have a feeling you'll want to brag, and I kinda want to be seen walking in with you."

"Sounds good to me," I agreed just as we pushed through the double doors.

And it seemed that "everyone" meant more people than I expected. I wondered why we hadn't simply used the back door, but when I saw people looking over, poking or smacking their friends to get their attention, then gesturing to us, I figured it out. Keir didn't lie. He wanted to be *seen* walking in with me, and he had been.

We didn't even make it halfway down the long room before Aspen saw us. "Rain!" she shouted, rushing over to hug me, not caring at all when she trapped Keir's arm under hers. "I passed math! I got a C!"

"Me too," I told her. "As and Bs for most. I passed everything, and I also got a C in math."

Aspen squealed loudly, bouncing in place with me and all but forcing Keir to work his arm out from between us. The movement, however, made Aspen remember his existence. She turned to him and threw her arms around his waist.

"You spent so much time helping her. You were kind and wonderful, and an honestly good guy." Then she looked up at his face. "Come sit with us?"

Keir's entire body heaved in surprise, as if he didn't know whether to laugh that off or hurry forward to accept it. "Really? Aspen, I'm not part of the court."

"No punching my brother, but you can at least socialize, right?" Then she grabbed my hand on one side, his on the other, and hauled us that way. "It's ok, I think you both belong."

Chapter Fifty-Six

The dining hall became a sort of party. People mingled about, calling out to their friends and complaining or bragging about their grades. In the corner, I saw a guy talking awkwardly to a girl. Probably trying to get a date for the Winter Solstice thing that was supposed to be such a big deal. Then there was the laughing about getting ready for it.

The mood was high, and there were smiles on most faces. I had a feeling those who wanted to cry because they didn't do well enough had gone to their dorms instead of hanging out here, though, so it made sense. Then Hawke and Wilder vanished, coming back with multiple plates of cake. It seemed the food staff were prepared for this. Even better, there was a slice for Keir, too.

He'd been accepted, and while it was subtle, a lot of people still noticed. Aspen claimed the chair on his other side, pinning him between us. Hawke claimed the other one beside me, leaving Torian straight across from us and Wilder beside Aspen. Even more shocking, the guys actually talked to each other. All of them!

But the fun couldn't last forever. Eventually, the night grew late, my bird had to be flown, and Aspen caught me in the atrium. When

Jack returned to land on my shoulder, we both agreed it was late enough to just head up. She sent off a text, then grabbed my arm. Linked like that, we headed for the elevator.

"So, I may have just left Keir with Torian," Aspen giggled. "Don't judge me."

I gasped. "That is not going to go well."

Aspen shrugged. "I know. I think it's funny. Tor's not used to anyone who won't kiss his ass. You don't. Keir doesn't. It's a new experience for him."

"Your brother is a self-absorbed prick at times," I told her.

"Mhm," she agreed, punching the button to take us to the fourth floor.

When we reached her room, Jack was off again. He had his food and water out waiting for him, and I was pretty sure while cake was tasty, that wasn't the same as nutritious. Letting out a relieved sigh, one filled with a week of nerves and anxiety, I flopped backwards onto her bed.

"You know, I'm glad you all like him," I breathed.

"Keir?" she asked.

I pointed toward the open bathroom door that led to my side of the suite. "Jack." Then I let my arm drop. "Speaking of Keir though, um... He kinda kissed me."

Her reaction was not at all what I expected. "Yeah?" she gasped, dropping down to sit by my hip. "Since you were still with him, I'm assuming he's not in shit for that?"

"But am *I*?" I asked, reaching out to take her hand. "I don't want to mess this thing up with you."

She leaned in and kissed me, shifting to brace a hand over my shoulder. "How many times do I have to say it's ok?"

"Just tell me again?" I begged. "This is me needing a lot of reassurance because you're my first girlfriend, and guys are just easier since I know what they expect, and I feel like I'm making a mess of it. Today's supposed to be a good day, so I'm over here terrified I've messed up."

"I've known you like Keir," she assured me. "I haven't missed that he likes you. I like knowing you have a guy out there, outside this room, who makes you happy. I really like how he makes you smile, and that you feel comfortable with him."

"But what about us?" I asked, watching her face for any sign she was picking her words too carefully.

She shifted to lie down against my shoulder. "I think you're the prettiest girl I've ever seen," she told me. "The first time I saw you in the atrium, I was completely entranced. You're like midnight, all cool and calm but filled with hidden secrets. I thought there was no way someone so perfect could even notice me, but you did. And the plants noticed you. There's a feeling that comes with being around you, like power but so different, and I couldn't stop thinking about it." She lifted her chin to look up at me. "I thought you were important, Rain. I never assumed you'd care about me."

"I do," I promised, curling into her. "Aspen, you really are my best friend, but so much more. I could spend hours here, all alone with you, and not miss anything else."

"Except Keir," she teased. "What I'm saying is we're fine." Then she stretched to kiss my lips. "I like it when you're happy. I don't like you worrying about this, but I'm happy for you. Keir's a good boyfriend."

"Boyfriend?" I gasped. "It was a kiss!"

She just giggled, squirming a little closer. "How does a guy kiss anyway?"

"Mm, hard," I told her. "All strong and powerful, even when they don't mean to. You kiss like velvet, and he kisses like steel."

"Blech," she mumbled, sticking her tongue out to make the point. "I like velvet then." But the smile would not leave her face. "So, how did it happen? Tell me everything!"

With a groan, I relaxed back into her pillow. "We'd just gotten out of the gym when our tablets both went off. Grades, you know? So he checked, and I was so nervous. I was sure all of this was too good to be true, and I'd end up failing out or something. Then, when

I saw how well I did?" I looked over at her. "And I've never made grades that good before!"

"I know," she gasped. "Me either, but I think it was all the studying. I mean, I normally don't care, because it's not like they'll kick me out, but I wanted to make sure you didn't feel weird about it."

"That..." I reached over and tickled her side. "Aspen, stop being so cute."

"Never!" she swore. "So? What next?"

"Well," I said, picking up my story again, "I was excited, so I threw my arms around his neck and hugged him. You know, kinda like you did to me when I came in the dining hall? And he hugged back, picking me almost off the ground. And his arms are so strong! Like, rocks, you know? It's kinda hot."

"He's pretty," she agreed. "But you can have all the rocks."

I just pushed at her playfully. "Do you want to hear this story or not?"

"Ok!" she promised. "I'll be good. Then what?"

"So I hugged him, and he hugged me, and it was like one of those body-crushing hugs, you know? Where like all the parts line up. No!" I gasped, realizing how that sounded. "I mean like pressing together." Then I groaned. "That's not any better, is it?"

"Not at all," she assured me, sliding her arm around my side. "So, you pressed up against that tree of a man. Then what?"

"I had like this urge to kiss him in my excitement," I said, grimacing to show I wasn't sure if I was crossing a line or not.

Her face lit up. "So you did?"

"No, actually. I told him that I wanted to, and I meant to step back, but *he* kissed *me*. He said this way I could tell you he did it. And he expected me to tell you."

"Aww," she crooned. "Ok, I like him even more now. That is so cute. But how was it? The kiss, I mean!"

I had to pause, because I didn't know. "Good" didn't seem to cover it. "Sexy" was all wrong. It hadn't been that kind of kiss.

"Powerful" worked, but that gave the wrong impression. Giving up, I decided to just ramble.

"Hot, gentle, different. I mean, different than you. Safe, I guess? I don't know, but I liked it. Like, I was breathing harder when he pulled away, and then I was feeling guilty, and - "

"Stop that," she told me. "No more guilt, Rain. I promise I would have no problem at all crawling on you with him." She flicked up both brows in a devious little look. "Besides, he gets it. He knows about us and he hasn't said a word. In fact, he's laughed it off, saying you wouldn't flirt back as much if you weren't into guys, and things like that. I like him, Rain. That's why I invited him to the court."

"What does that mean, anyway?" I asked. "I know it's a big deal, and I get that everyone wants the privilege, but I somehow got it, and I don't even know what the big deal is. I mean, just a popular crowd thing like with the jesters?"

"No," she assured me. "See, we don't have a family to fall back on. No parents who will come help us. The four of us were taught to believe in certain things, like supporting your people, so we made each other our people. Being a part of the court? It means we trust you. It doesn't mean we expect you to be fae, but for so long, it seemed like only we fae got it."

"So why wasn't Keir invited earlier?" I asked.

"Because he's a stubborn arrogant ass of a man," she teased. "Because he says what he thinks, and he's not scared of our power. That's a good thing, but the boys? They're so stupid sometimes. Torian expects Keir to acknowledge his power. Keir doesn't care. Wilder hates that Keir shows him up. Keir won't apologize for it - nor should he!"

"Like dogs," I realized, thinking back to what Bracken had said. "They all want to lead the pack, but they don't hate each other enough to fight for it, so they simply find their own territory."

Aspen laughed. "I suppose that's a good way of putting it. Wilder and Torian sorted out whose dick is bigger - or whatever guys do - and they get along. Hawke had no issue with it. He and Tor met in foster care, so it was easier. I don't have to toss out my dick because I'm a girl, and I'm not complaining about that, and now there's you."

"Me," I said, "the crazy human girl ruining your pretty little fae perfection."

This time, she was the one tickling me. "It is not like that!"

I stopped her by wrapping my arms around her back. "How is it you make me so happy all the time?"

She relaxed into me. "I don't know, but I feel the same. Last year, I was fighting all the time. I had to claw my place out of this school with everything I had, and since you've been here? I've never been this happy, Rain." She moved her hand to cup the side of my face. "It feels like you're the thing I've always been missing. I thought it was supposed to be finding my brother, but that only helped so much. Torian makes me feel like I'm not alone. Like there's someone to suffer through this with me. You?" Her icy eyes searched mine. "You remind me what it was like to be happy. That it's ok for me to actually *be* happy."

I pressed my face against the side of her neck. "I'm so glad you kissed me, Aspen," I whispered against the side of her throat, pausing to kiss her skin. "Every time I think this can't get better, you find a way to prove me wrong."

She sucked in a playful gasp. "Oh, because I helped you catch that hunk of a fae?" She giggled. "So, you didn't finish. Tell me more, Rain. Everything!"

"He said nothing has changed," I admitted. "We're still just friends, but he kissed me. Then, he was hugging me against him the whole way back to the school, and he kinda took the long way around so we'd come into the dining hall where everyone would see us."

"Oh, he's bragging," she gasped. "Next time, wrap your arm around him. You look really cute with him, you know. I mean, you're not short, but he's pretty tall. I can't wait to see you kiss him!"

"Aspen," I huffed. "You are not supposed to say that."

"But I want to say that," she told me, rolling halfway over my chest. "Welcome to living with the fae, Rain. We share. The fact that you care if I approve?" She slid her hand against mine, lacing our fingers together. "It makes me feel like I'm a part of that, and I like it more than I can explain. I give you my word that if I feel ignored, I will tell you, but I don't. I feel like behind these doors, you're mine. Out there, you can be his. It works, and this?" She leaned in to kiss my lips quickly. "That smile belongs there. I think he and I can make sure it stays."

"I do not deserve you," I whispered. "But if you kiss me again, I might stop caring."

"Always," she promised. "My girlfriend is getting herself a boyfriend."

Then she pushed my hand over my head and kissed me again. If this wasn't perfect, I couldn't imagine what was.

Chapter Fifty-Seven

The weekend became a flurry of activity. Half the students were going home for the winter holidays. I would've said Christmas, but most fae, it seemed, didn't actually celebrate that. The seasons were their holidays, not remembrances of human events. But packing meant finding the things they'd loaned out, stuff they'd need, and a general panic had spread across my entire floor.

I wasn't immune. So many little things were starting to build up. Most of them were good, but that didn't exactly help. There was this nagging thought in the back of my head, and I couldn't quite shake it. Aspen wasn't any better, although most of her anxiety was caused by people yelling up and down the hall in voices just a bit too shrill.

She dealt with it by calling Wilder over and taking her plants down to the atrium. There, she intended to plant them. I'd been invited to join her, but there was something else I had to do. Making an excuse was easy, and the trust Aspen gave me was wonderful. She joked about me going to see Keir, but I assured her that wasn't it. All week long, I'd been worried about getting kicked out, so now I had questions, and only one person could answer them.

Saturday evening, I headed over to the boys' side and rode the elevator up to the fourth floor. Not to see the guys from the court, though. I turned the opposite way and tapped on the floor chaperone's door. For a little too long, I stood there shuffling anxiously, hoping this wasn't going to be a big mistake.

Then I heard the door unlock and the latch released. It cracked open, and Liam quickly pulled it wide once he recognized me. "Hi, Rain. Come in."

"Hey," I said, stepping through.

Jack wobbled on my shoulder, but he was starting to get pretty good at riding along with me. Liam glanced at the bird and seemed to accept he'd become my constant companion. But as he gestured for me to head into the living room, he did a double take.

"Where'd you get the ring?" he asked.

I'd completely forgotten about the stupid thing. It wouldn't come off, it wasn't uncomfortable, and it hadn't caused any problems, so it had just become kinda normal.

"Um, Jack found it," I admitted, turning the corner to find Bracken sprawled across the couch.

He had a remote in his hand, his eyes on the TV, and he did not have on a shirt. I quickly glanced away, but Jack laughed in his own avian way. Bracken glanced over and hopped up, heading for the other room. Talk about awkward!

"Sorry," I mumbled.

"Brack, you're fine," Liam told him.

"I'm still going to put on a shirt," Bracken said. "Just glad I wasn't scratching my balls or something. Not the best impression from her teacher." He grabbed a shirt from the back of a chair and came back, smiling at me like he hoped I got the joke.

"Well, I actually didn't come to talk to a teacher," I admitted, turning to Liam. "I, uh, kinda needed my caseworker."

"Yep, let me put that hat on." Liam pantomimed changing imaginary hats. "Ok. What can I do for you, Lorraine?"

I stuck my tongue out at him. "Can I..." I gestured at a chair.

"Sit," he agreed, moving over to the spot beside where Bracken had been. "Is this a private matter? Bracken can go watch his K-drama in the bedroom."

"It's not a problem," Bracken assured me.

"No, it's actually about something you said," I told him as I took the chair. Jack quickly shifted to cling to the back, which allowed me to get even more comfortable. "See, everyone's packing to go home. I know you said I could stay here for the winter, but I'm guessing the Sparks are still my foster parents?"

"They are," Liam admitted. "Every month, the state gives them a check for your care. They're using it to feed the others a little better, so I don't see a problem with it, but there's no reason for you to stay there over the winter break."

I nodded. "What about over the summer? Can I stay here? I mean, summer school or something? With all these fosters, I was just hoping there might be some programs..."

Liam sighed. "Rain, it's two months."

"One week was enough to have them lock me in my room!" I insisted. "Maybe I could just stay with you? I don't mind sleeping on the couch, and I promise I won't hear anything."

Bracken snorted, having to turn away. "Where did you find her again?" He kept going, into their kitchen.

"John was adamant she was possessed," Liam said, leaning back. "Babe, come sit down. I'm not yelling across the house at you."

"Drinks," Bracken explained, and I heard the clanking of bottles. A moment later, he returned with a soda for me and a pair of beers in his other hand. "I'm going to guess you're not about to tell anyone we were drinking in front of students?" he teased.

"Never," I promised. "Just remember this when I need some secret of my own covered."

"Like Aspen?" Bracken asked.

My mouth hung open. "Who said that?"

He lifted a hand. "You did, Keir hinted, and I'm not stupid. Keir made a few comments, which made me curious. The fact that he's even trying to be nice to the court was the first hint. That he fought

Hawke for the right to wait for you after detention was another. Then he hesitated before calling Aspen your best friend."

"She is," I insisted.

"Uh-huh," Bracken said. "Rain, I can hear that lie. It's not a complete untruth, but that doesn't mean it's a complete truth either."

"And Bracken told me," Liam admitted. "So, are you dating Aspen Fox?"

"Yeah," I said. "Please don't make us change rooms."

"Left the teacher hat over there," Liam assured me. "This is my caseworker one, remember. I might have the counselor one ready if you need it, so spill."

Yeah, spill. There was so much, though, and I wasn't sure where to start! Rambling was the best I had. "So, I've never liked a girl before," I told him. "I wanted to talk to you, but Aspen said the rules would make one of us move. Probably me, since she's, well, her."

"And we want her close to the chaperone," Bracken agreed.

"Why?" I asked.

"Power management," Liam explained. "Rain, we've had magical accidents before, and with someone as powerful as Aspen? It's not a risk we want to take. So, yes. You would be the one to move - but so long as there's not a problem, I don't think it needs to be an official thing, does it?"

I pulled my legs up under me. "No, but, um..." This was the hard part. I really wanted to trust Liam, but I was used to not saying anything to *anyone*. Still, I needed advice, and he was kinda in the same situation. "So, that's kinda the thing. I mean, dating, you know?"

"Not at all," Liam said, turning to lean against Bracken so he was facing me a little more. "Still don't have on the teacher's hat, Rain."

So I just blurted it out. "I'm dating Aspen, and I really like her, but she thinks I should flirt with Keir, and he kissed me yesterday when we got our grades. She's happy about it, and they keep saying it's a fae thing, but I keep feeling like this is too good to be true. Since she's my first girlfriend, it's not like I'm doing so good at this. I don't even know how to show her how I feel, so what if I mess it up? What if I'm not what she wants? What if she gets tired of me trying so hard to figure all this out? I mean, I know you don't like girls so it probably doesn't make any sense to you, but I'm just worried because she is the whole reason I'm here, and - "

"Breathe!" Bracken snapped. "Holy shit, Rain. Breathe."

I pulled in a long, deep breath, but that torrent of verbal vomit had felt so damned good. All the thoughts in my head had finally been given a path to work themselves out, and these two men sat there, looking at me with a mixture of awe and amusement on their faces.

"I got this," Bracken told Liam before he got up and moved to my side. "Rain, it's a fae thing. More specifically, a Faerie thing. My own father was my mother's lover. There was no marriage, but there's also no shame in such things. Children are rare and should be treasured. Since you're surrounded by kids, you have no idea how many childless relationships there are. Taking lovers often was a way to have *some* kind of family, and it became habit."

"But..."

He lifted a finger, then knelt down before me. "One thing at a time. Love is love is love, Rain. Fae will move slower than the boys you're used to, so stop worrying about that part. The connection is mental, not physical. Don't get me wrong, we hook up too, but it's treated differently. Love is part of what Liam and I have. A marriage is something like a day job. A friendship, however, is love and trust combined. It's a connection that is deeper than flesh. To have lust with it? It only makes sense to act on it - and to share the wealth. So, if you have a girlfriend *and* a boyfriend, it's fine."

"That's what they both told me," I admitted. "But is this the kind of thing that will cause a wave of slut-shaming?"

He canted his head. "Unlikely, but I can't rule it out. The bigger issue is that you're aligning yourself with the most obvious users of Winter magic. Wilder and Aspen can't touch Summer magic like most others," he explained. "They also don't care if anyone else approves because they're strong enough to hold their own."

"But I'm not," I realized.

"Not magically," Bracken agreed. "But here's the thing, Rain. There's nothing wrong with Winter magic. Many of the fae who escaped came from the Summer Court, but that's because Winter nobility were killed. Their lovers, children, and distant relatives were all hunted down and killed. There aren't many left, and so the thinking became that it was because Winter magic was worse, or weaker, or inferior in some way."

"But it's not," I guessed.

"It's simply another season," Bracken assured me. "For the fae born on Earth, like many of the students here, it's a way to divide themselves. A simple manner to say they're better. A schism between our culture that was caused by the Mad Queen and carried over. None of that means it's inherently *true*."

"But it's a reason to come after us," I realized. "All of us? Even Torian and Hawke?"

"Even them," Bracken agreed. "Although, I think you have no problem with handling your bullies. I know Torian doesn't. Hawke has his own methods. Wilder and Aspen aren't weak, they aren't vulnerable, and they aren't trying to get approval for being what they are. But you? You're the odd one out in that group. Now, Liam and I are here to help. That doesn't mean tolerating the social dance of my kind will be easy, but you shouldn't refuse to do something simply because it might be hard."

My next question was almost too soft to hear. "And dating a girl?"

"That's not what you're really asking, is it?" Bracken asked.

"Kinda," I admitted.

"This one's mine," Liam said. "Give her space, Brack."

Bracken rocked back on his heels, and I closed my eyes, unsure if I wanted to die or not. Then again, I was the one who'd come here. I'd psyched myself up for this, told Aspen I had other plans, and I knew I needed to talk to someone. I couldn't very well talk to my girlfriend about *her,* and Liam was cool. Bracken was just as amazing. The whole teacher thing was weird, but this was a weird school, so I was just rolling with it.

"It's kinda hard to balance, right?" Liam asked. "You have this person with you, and most of the world thinks it's not what it is. You hang out, you laugh, and everyone assumes you're just friends. For me, they thought I'd found a fellow nerd. Some prep school prick, they'd joke, never realizing he was my boyfriend. I was too scared to say otherwise."

"And I can't because of the rules," I agreed.

Liam nodded. "But do you feel it? I mean, is she just a friend or do you feel that desire?"

"I feel it," I told him. "I know I'm not supposed to talk to you about sex, but you're kinda the only person I have..." I let the last word trail off.

"Talk to me about sex," Liam insisted. "Rain, I'm your uncle. Maybe not by blood, but I am currently your legal guardian. If you can't talk to me, then what adult can you talk to?"

I licked my lips to keep the dry mouth at bay, and nodded. "So, like, when I was with a guy, it was kinda intimidating, but mostly because I didn't really know. I mean, I knew what would happen, but not what it would be like. But with Aspen, I don't even know that. I know I want to. And I get the impression she does, but we kinda stop at kissing, and then we cuddle."

"Nothing wrong with that," he assured me.

I swallowed nervously. "But what if I do it and don't like it? What if she decides she doesn't like me? What if I'm... I dunno, like wrong? What if I'm confusing friendship for something else? Maybe I'm just lonely? She was the first person to be nice to me, and I know I owe her..."

"Does it feel like you're paying a debt?" he countered.

I shook my head. "It feels like everything is right when I'm around her. She makes me feel so alive. I want to beat the shit out of

Harper for giving Aspen crap. I want to hold her hand in the halls, and I just... I don't know what I'm doing, and all of this is perfect, and I'm so scared that I've just been given everything I've ever wanted and I'm going to mess it up! What if I ruin all of this?"

"Oh, Rain," he breathed, crossing the room to crouch before me and pull me up against him in the biggest hug. "No one is going to take this from you."

"It feels like I finally have a home," I said, the tears starting to well up in my eyes. "All my life, the moment I start to like things, I get moved again. I have tried *so hard,* Liam!" The first sniff broke out. "Don't you get it? I don't even do things and it still happens. No one wants me! No one has ever cared about anything other than the check they get for keeping me. I mean, one family did, but then they had to move, and now..."

Damn it, the tears were falling, so I pressed my face against his shoulder. "I know Silver Oaks can kick me out, and I know I'm not really supposed to be here, and I'm not magic. I'm not even special, except that Jack likes me. I'm just scared that if I mess up with Aspen, then this will go away too. She's all I have, and I don't know how to make this work, so I'm terrified I'm going to ruin it *all.*"

"Shh," he breathed, rubbing my back. "Oh, Rain, I will always fight for you, ok? I got you, sweetie."

"Jack..." my bird said softly, leaning in to nuzzle my hair. "Rain..."

"But you're not enough," I told Liam, reaching up to pet the back of Jack's head. "I'm not special, and I'm falling for the girl who got me into this school, and if I mess that up, I'm gone. I *know* I'm gone." I leaned back to wipe my eyes. "So what should I do, Liam?"

He caught the side of my face and used his thumb to wipe away the tears. "You should be a teenager, Rain. Fall in love. Fall out of love. If I have to, I will fight for you to stay here." He ducked his head to look me right in the eyes. "I give you my word. I can't make that binding, but I know you understand how important that promise is."

I nodded, sniffing again. "Yeah. It's magical when *they* do it."

"It's magical when we do too, sweetie - because we know the

importance of truth. If you like Aspen, then don't hold back. Don't try to play it safe this time. For once in your life, fall in love, get in trouble, and I'll do everything I can to smooth it all out."

"Hey," Bracken breathed, moving to squat beside Liam. "You faced the Hunt for us. I will use that if I have to, but you shouldn't have to worry about this."

"Not how it works for foster kids," Liam told him. "Home is a temporary thing at best, and also the biggest dream. It's not something they can find easily."

"That," I said, gesturing to Liam.

"You are one of my warriors," Bracken told me. "I want to put you in training to be a sentinel like Keir. Rain, sometimes being human makes you *more* special than the rest of us. As your teacher, I don't want to lose you." Then he reached over and wrapped his arm around Liam's shoulder. "And as your family, I don't either. You're a good kid. A brave one, and I don't think you have anything to worry about."

I nodded. "Even if I piss off Aspen because we don't work out and she wants me gone?"

Bracken slid his hand down the back of my head. "Believe it or not, I have a little sway over my niece. I will use it if I have to. She also owes me a favor, and I will burn it for you."

"Really?" I asked. "Wait, she's your niece?"

He nodded. "Not many people know that, but yes, our mothers were related. She also owes me."

"Brack..." Liam breathed. "That's not something you want to offer lightly."

"I'm not," he promised. "I meant it when I said I want her to be a sentinel. She knows nothing, Liam. Absolutely nothing, but she has the skill. She's learning, and she's almost keeping up with Keir. One day, if she keeps training, Rain will be great. I will fucking burn a favor for that, because the Hunt isn't stopping, and what else is Silver Oaks about than training my people how to survive your world? People like her? They're the answer."

"Like me?" I asked.

"Humans who can believe," Liam explained. "There aren't that many of us."

I just nodded. "So I'm freaking out for nothing?"

"No," Liam assured me. "You're freaking out because no one has stood with you before. We will. We're family, right?"

Damn, but I felt those tears welling up again. I just nodded, not wanting to risk crying. A family? That wasn't a word I'd ever expected to use. I hadn't even dared to hope for one. My plans had been to figure out how to take care of myself, but hearing him say that hit me right in the heart.

"One more favor, though?" I asked. "Can I hide up here until I stop blubbering so Aspen doesn't ask me what's wrong?"

Bracken mussed my hair and leaned back. "Like bad K-dramas? Liam wants to watch stupid human games."

"It's basketball," Liam corrected.

Bracken just looked at me like, "See what I mean?" then grinned. "If you stay, then it's two to one, and I'll even start it over from the beginning."

"I dunno..." I said. "Is there popcorn involved?"

"I'll get the caramel corn," Liam grumbled. "Fucking fae!"

Bracken just grinned at me, because that hadn't been directed at him. When he sat back on the couch and patted the spot beside him, I took it. Bracken started messing with the remote, staring at the TV, and asked, "So, you gonna tell me about this girlfriend you have?"

"She's perfect," I started, and then I didn't know where to stop. The whole time, Bracken listened. When Liam came back, he picked on me a little, but it was nice. It was comfortable. More than all of that, it was homey.

Chapter Fifty-Eight

Only a few people left that weekend. For the most part, everyone wanted to stick around for the Winter Solstice festival. On Monday, Aspen and I started getting ready early. She had a hot date with Wilder, and I had one with Keir. Evidently Torian and Hawke would be hanging out with us too.

From the sounds of it, there would be a large bonfire, a lot of hot drinks, and probably a few flasks filled with a little nectar as well. While we both picked out something warm and cute to wear, Aspen told me all about how the students last year had served warmed and spiced nectar, making it like mulled wine or something. Plus, the teachers wouldn't be there to stop us AP kids from drinking some of it.

Liam had mentioned the instructors had their own celebration. Most of our school staff - both teachers and everything else - lived in a community down the hill. I'd never seen it, but Aspen assured me that was intentional. None of them wanted us wandering around their homes, because teachers needed private time too, but it was still there. Tonight, the courtyard of their little townhouse-style complex would host their grown-up party.

Ours, however, would be a lot more fun. Not without rules, sadly. A few mentors would be wandering around the edge, making sure no one tried to kill themselves and that the minors mostly behaved ourselves. Aspen stressed the mostly part, making it clear that was her interpretation, not theirs, but I understood. No matter what school function it was, the teachers couldn't watch every dark corner and hidden spot. Add a combination of college students and magic, and it was a recipe for them to fail.

And for us to have too much fun.

So, by the time the sun set, the two of us looked as cute as we could. Lipstick wasn't an option. We'd kinda kissed it off each other when deciding what to wear. In the end, I had on her shirt, she had my sweater, and we both had a couple of layers under that. By the time our dates arrived, it was starting to feel a little warm in our suite.

Surprisingly, they showed up together. Wilder knocked at Aspen's door, and a second later, Keir tapped at mine. Since we were both in my room because of Jack, I opened my door. Wilder looked over, smiled, and then moved to Keir's side.

"So, you'll want coats," Wilder told us. "Going to be freezing out there, and I'm pretty sure it's snowing."

"It's trying," Keir said. "A few flakes falling, but don't plan for any snow angels."

"Then let's do this!" Aspen said, pushing my coat into my arms before pulling on her own.

There was a steady stream of people though the building, leading down and out the back. The four of us joined it. Aspen hung on Wilder's arm, but Keir wrapped his around me. That earned him a warning look from Wilder, so Aspen poked him in the side.

"Stop. They're cute," she hissed.

Wilder just rolled his eyes. "Yes, dear," he joked.

Which meant Wilder was merely being protective of his friend. They would've been a cute couple, though. She was so pale and delicate, where he was dark all over. Her head hit right at his shoulder, but he wasn't so broad or muscular as to make her seem frail. The guy looked like he'd been designed to complement her perfectly - the type of couple who would look good on a dance floor.

When we reached the doors, Jack slipped through, flying over the heads of the people before us. Someone squealed, shocked at the rustle of his feathers, but others laughed about it. It seemed my bird was starting to be expected around here, and I kinda liked that. Then we made it outside.

The snow was just enough to look like falling stars in the light coming off the building. The flakes were few and far between, and they certainly weren't piling up anywhere, but it was pretty. Letting Keir lead me, I looked up to watch it fall, taking in the back side of the Silver Oaks' main building. All that glass glowed with the lights from inside, and I kinda liked it.

But the crowd kept moving. The "line" of us was wide and spread out, more like a herd, and everyone else seemed to know where to go. It didn't take long before the glow of the school was lost and only the moonlit snow made it possible to see the ground. Still, we walked. Our breaths misted before our faces, and there was a dullness to the sound out here. It was as if even this small amount of snow was enough to muffle everything.

Then we crested a hill and I saw it all. Laid out in the low spot before us was everything I'd never realized I needed. When I'd thought of a "party," my mind had supplied images from human gatherings I'd snuck off to. This was nothing like those. This was a fae event.

A massive ring of trees had a fire in the middle of it. Glistening lights hung over groups in various colors. Magical ones. People danced in circles, not clumped up the way I'd expected. All of it was mystical, even dressed in some pretty normal clothes, and I had to pause for a moment to take it in.

"Rain?" Keir asked while Aspen and Wilder kept going.

"This is perfect," I breathed. "Is that a fairy ring?"

He chuckled, hugging me against his side so he could point. "The trees are. A very, very old ring. They grow around a place where much magic was once used, taking what they can from the ground. The fire is for warmth, nothing more."

"And all the lights," I said, not even ashamed of how I was gawking.

"People looking to meet up with their friends," he explained. "See the red glow over there? Those are the guys I normally hang out with. Blue, purple, and that white-striped one are all various college groups. Over there? The pink is the jester girls. The yellow is the guys. No, the color isn't significant. It's just what Harper chose to make sure she stood out, since no one else uses pink."

"Makes a strange sort of sense," I admitted.

"The court, however, won't use a light," he told me. "They never do." Then he got me walking again, following the path Aspen and Wilder had taken.

This whole section was out of view from the area around us. The depression was deep enough that the most anyone off-property would see was the glow of the fire - if that. I couldn't get over how they were doing all this out in the open, but I loved it. While Keir led me through the crowd of students, I saw so many people I knew laughing with their own friends, a few making out, and plenty of magic being tossed around.

In the middle of it all, we found the court. Torian stood before the massive fire with his arms spread. Aspen threw herself into them, hugging him hard. Wilder and Hawke moved to stand beside each other, so Keir aimed for the other side. As we got closer, I felt the warmth - more than the fire should've put off, if I was honest - but everything inside that ring of trees was actually rather pleasant.

"Who put up the barrier for the heat?" Keir asked.

Hawke jerked his chin up. "I did."

"That's a lot of power for the solstice," Keir pointed out.

Hawke chuckled. "Yep, I know."

"Where's the nectar?" Aspen asked.

"Oh, there's a whole slew tonight," Torian said, pointing out at the darkness. "Over there is a collection of actual alcohol. A couple of the older students brought it." Then he pointed another way. "The sparkling light? Yeah, that's a kettle of warmed nectar, and I'm pretty sure there's enough to go around."

"And the teachers?" I asked.

Torian crossed his arms and looked at me. "Seems Bracken and Liam offered to keep an eye on us tonight. It was going to be Ms. Rhodes and Ms. Hawthorne right up until Sunday. Then they suddenly changed their minds. You have any idea why, Rain?"

I sucked in a breath. "Um, I may have talked to Liam about being worried about getting kicked out."

"Why?" he asked.

"It was a long list," I assured him. "It started with being human and ended with my only special ability being that a crow likes me."

"Jack!" the bird in question called out as he swooped in.

I held my arm up, and he landed on it before bending to nibble at the fabric of my coat. It seemed to pass his inspection because he moved up my arm to my shoulder. There, he picked at my hair and then the knit cap I was wearing.

"Rain," he croaked.

"Yes, Jack," I said. "I'm wearing a hat so my ears don't get cold."

His response was simply to peck at it gently, feeling out the material. I just rolled my eyes and ignored him. Not getting a response, it didn't take long before he took off again, heading up to the trees above us to find himself a comfy little roost.

But in those few seconds, the guys had already moved on to something else. Torian had his phone out. Wilder and Hawke were heading for opposite sides of the fire. Keir stayed beside me, but he was also watching them. And then, as if it was some special ceremony, Torian offered the screen of his phone to Aspen.

"Let's get this party started!" she said, and then tapped it.

Music instantly began playing, but the sound came from everywhere. It was as if there was a sound system set up out here. My mouth dropped open and I looked around. Nope, I wasn't missing anything. That was definitely magically enhanced.

"Let's dance!" Aspen said, catching my hand to pull me outside the ring of trees. "Keir!"

He followed behind us, laughing like we were being cute. Ok, maybe we were, but there was a group of people quickly forming. Almost as if it was scripted, everyone began to move clockwise, dancing as they made a slow but steady circle around the outside of the trees.

"You," Aspen said, "will not dance yourself to death. You hear me, Rain?" she asked.

I caught her hand and spun her around. "Not tonight," I promised.

So she did the same thing back, but with a little push to keep me moving. That propelled me right into Keir. He caught my waist and spun us both, then sent me back to her. It was fun. There were no real steps, and the music worked with all the spinning, but it didn't last that long.

When the next song started, Hawke pulled me out of the line and pushed a plastic cup into my hands. "I have been ordered to keep an eye on you tonight," he said, steering me back toward the warmth inside the trees. "So, drink as much as you want, be as crazy as you intend, and know that if anyone tries anything, the court has your back. Otherwise, Aspen made it clear she'd hang my balls from my ears."

I snorted out a laugh. "Oh, I see. Scared of her, huh?"

"Tonight, I am," he assured me. "It's her season, Rain. I know that doesn't make sense to you, but it means she's the most powerful thing you can imagine tonight."

I lifted the glass and took a long drink, deciding I liked the sweetness even more this time. "Are you sure it has nothing to do with wanting to kiss me?"

His lips split into a devious little smile. "I never said it didn't."

"Which means it plays a part," I countered.

He just moved closer. "It plays a part. What happened to your pretty little Summer boy?"

"Keir?" I guessed.

Hawke nodded.

"Why, are you chasing him too?" I took another drink so I wouldn't smirk too much.

Hawke pointedly ran his eyes over me. "I'm starting to think I will never understand you."

"Aspen said I'm allowed to play. I'm playing tonight, Hawke. That's all it is. I passed my classes, I didn't get kicked out, I have the coolest uncle in the world, and a pretty kick-ass crow. My best friend makes me happy, and tonight is going to be a very good night."

"Then drink more, foundling, because the fun is just getting started," he said as Wilder appeared with a pair of cups.

Hawke took one and tilted it up, gulping back the contents. I lifted mine, matching him. With a laugh, Wilder did the same until all three of our glasses were empty. Just like Aspen had, the guys tossed theirs into the air and the things vanished, sent to some garbage bin somewhere. Then Wilder pointedly reached over and took mine, doing the same thing.

"And now she should dance like she's fae," he joked, grabbing me from behind by both shoulders to drive me back to the line. "Coming, Hawke?"

"Wouldn't miss this for the world," Hawke promised. "Even more fun knowing Keir's going to hate it."

"Exactly," Wilder agreed as we reached the line.

A line that was moving a lot faster, to music with more beat than the first song. Well, if that was how they wanted it, then I was more than willing to let them show off a little. Too bad for them, Keir was currently dancing with Aspen, and the pair seemed to be laughing like old friends. I had a funny feeling all of this was going to backfire on Hawke and Wilder.

Chapter Fifty-Nine

It didn't take long before the fae nectar began to have an effect. The world became a little blurry around the edges, and there was always another glass. The stuff was dangerous, though. Drinking it made me feel refreshed and ready to do a little more. It was like liquid energy with a dose of extra giggles.

At some point, Keir and Aspen joined us, and then the guys began twirling us girls between them. I tripped, was caught, and then spun on again. When Aspen and I met up in the middle, we forgot to care if anyone else was watching. We danced, hugged, laughed and more. Between all of that, there was always another glass of nectar.

When I started breathing too hard, Aspen shoved me out of line. The problem was that I staggered right into - of all people - Harper. With an annoyed huff, she shoved me back, but that was the wrong move. Aspen immediately surged into her face.

"Not in the mood tonight, Harper," she snarled.

Harper sneered at her. "You think you're so special? No one cares about you, Aspen."

"You do," I countered. "Clearly, you do. Otherwise, you wouldn't spend so much time making a big deal over just how much you hate us."

"Us?" she asked. "Saying this..." She wagged a finger between us. "...is a thing?"

"It's definitely a thing," I agreed. "Aspen is my best friend, which means I care about her, and I don't really like shallow little bitches picking on her."

From the corner of my eye, I saw Aspen's body relax slightly. She hadn't tried to stop me from saying we were together, but she'd braced for it. My words, however, walked that fine line of truth. I was starting to get pretty good at this.

"I guess you missed how Keir's been chasing her, huh?" Aspen asked. "Oh, how that must hurt. Never mind the rest. Without trying, Rain managed to get the one thing you never could: a place in the court."

With the intoxicating effects of the nectar coursing through me, I just couldn't help myself. I reached up and patted the side of Harper's face in the most annoying way possible. "Keep making yourself look desperate, though. It amuses us."

Then I grabbed Aspen's arm and we headed for the bonfire. The moment we turned away, both of us broke out into a fit of giggles. The shocked look on Harper's face when I'd patted her like that? It had been worth it! I just loved seeing a bully realize she had no power. That her friends had witnessed it all only made it better.

"I can't believe you did that again!" Aspen squealed, because it was the same move I'd done the last time Harper tried to give us shit.

I pressed my face against her shoulder, still laughing. "I'm blaming the drinks!"

"Oh, you can do that any time you want," she told me. "And go kiss Keir since you can't kiss me."

She gave me a little nudge, making it clear the guy in question was standing beside the fire, talking to some of his other friends. I turned back to Aspen with a playful and overly dramatic gasp, but she shooed me his way. Yep, that was all the encouragement I needed.

"Hey," I said as I caught Keir's waist, falling in beside him.

Without even thinking, he lifted his arm over my shoulders and pulled me against his side. "You look flushed," he teased. "Been having fun?"

"Dancing," I said. "Aspen won't let me have more than a few songs in a row, though. You seen Jack?"

Keir pointed up. "See him? No. Hear him? Often. He's been flitting between the trees, probably trying to keep warm."

But Fin couldn't handle being ignored. "So, is this a thing now?" he asked.

"Definitely a thing," Keir admitted. "Not sure what thing, but it's *a* thing. Why?"

Fin grinned mischievously. "Torian's not going to like that."

"I don't give a fuck what Torian likes," Keir assured him.

"Wait," I asked, looking between them. "Why does Torian's opinion matter?"

"You've been accepted by the court," Fin taunted. "That means you belong to him. He's the king, don't you know?"

I groaned. "That does not make me a possession, Fin. Not how that works."

"Cute little girl with no magic?" he countered. "Sure it does."

"No," Keir said, "it doesn't." Then he steered me away. "Pull your head out of your ass, Fin, and stop being a dick."

As we made our way around the fire, I just shook my head at the idiot. "Why is he your friend again?" I asked.

"Not the word I'd use," Keir assured me. "Suitemate, sure, but that's a favor for Bracken."

While that might be true for Fin, I was pretty sure some of the other guys were his friends, though. Not like it really mattered. In truth, it seemed as if he enjoyed hanging out with the court more - even *with* the crap he and Torian kept giving each other. Guy fun, or something. It had to be.

Although, when we made it to the other side of the fire, it wasn't Hawke and Wilder we ran into. Nope, a group of college girls all turned to smile at Keir just a bit too sweetly. One noticed me and her face turned cold, but the rest only tensed a little. A lovely brunette stepped up.

"Did the court stick you on babysitting duty?" she asked.

Keir gestured at her. "Rain, this is Cora. Cora, Rain."

Cora turned her eyes to me. "I'm an Enticer. You? Oh, that's right, you're a Legacy, aren't you?"

I sighed, her attempts to make herself look good a little too transparent. "Yeah, comes with being the human girl."

"And she's a friend to the wildlings," Keir countered before moving on again. When we were a few steps away, he sighed. "Sorry."

"Ex?" I asked.

His jaw clenched. "Yeah."

"Have you slept with every girl in this school?" I teased.

"Not *every* one," he insisted. "I mean, you, Aspen?"

"And?" I asked.

"I'm not that bad!" he groaned. "I've also known most of these girls for four years. You've been here a few months. Don't even try to compare."

I was laughing about that when I noticed something in the shadows outside the fire. Movement. That was what had caught my eye, but the flash of blonde hair made me keep looking. My eyes finally landed on Harper, but who was she trying to push around? Dark hair, olive skin... Was that *Torian?*

"Keir?" I asked.

"Yeah, I see it too," he agreed. "Leave it alone, Rain."

"She's pissed at him because I just made a fool of her," I said, pulling away. "Where are the guys?"

"I dunno," he admitted. "Go find them and I'll give Torian a little backup."

"Which is a recipe for disaster," I countered as I turned, taking a backward step toward Torian while still talking to Keir. "The last thing she needs are both her exes ganging up on her. You find the court. I'll give her a better target. Still have iron."

"Rain..." he tried, but I spun and headed that way.

The moment I left the circle of trees, I could hear Harper. "You ignored me for Aspen. That's why I was pissed. I gave you everything, Tor, so you owe me!"

"There is no debt," he told her. "There was never an agreement. I owe you nothing you haven't already enjoyed. The only reason people know you is because of me. The only reason they ever cared about you was because of me. I made you, Harper, and I've ignored you as much as I can." He stepped right into her face. "But keep pushing this and I can take it all away."

"You think being pure makes you special?" she snapped.

"No, but you do," he said, his voice devoid of emotion. "You hate being part human so much that you can't stop being angry. Never mind the power you have - "

"Enough to make you want me!" she insisted.

"I don't *want* power," he told her. "I already have it."

Which was when I reached them. Without slowing, I stepped right up to Torian's side and hooked my arm around his waist. The other went against his chest as I pressed up against him like a lover. As if he knew what I was doing, Torian turned to smile down at me.

"Get tired of playing with your little toy?" he asked, smugness wrapped all around the words.

"Were you *jealous*, Torian?" I teased, making it sound like he should have a reason to be.

Torian leaned a little closer, blatantly ignoring Harper. "Yes. I'm supposed to be the center of your attention."

"Her?" Harper asked. "You're hooking up with *her?*"

Torian laughed once. "You hate being part human so much, and you haven't yet figured out it's the most interesting thing about you," he told her.

And then he did the last thing I would have ever expected. The guy caught the side of my face - hard - and pressed his mouth to mine. There was no time to think. I'd come over here to convince Harper that Torian was taken. To give him an excuse to bow out gracefully. Instead, he was picking the kind of fight I liked, and that meant I had to play along.

So I kissed back. Oh, I had no idea how I was going to explain this to Aspen. As my tongue swirled against his, my hand fisting his coat to pull him even closer, I knew this was a bad idea, but holy shit. Torian could kiss! His arrogance and pride made him so confident, and there was nothing gentle at all about the way his mouth took control of mine.

But I didn't melt. I didn't swoon like he was probably used to. I took just as much as he was giving, and Harper could see it. She huffed with anger, then shoved. I wasn't shocked at all, but I still staggered. Tripping sideways wasn't exactly my best move.

Ignoring me, Torian spun to face her. "How dare you!" he snapped, the anger on his face forcing her to retreat before him. "Do not *ever* touch what is mine. Do *not* think you are better than me. Never put your hands on Rain *again!*"

"So is that it?" Harper asked as she backed away. "You're with the stupid human now? You're blowing me off for some bitch that can't even *touch* magic?"

She made it back into the open, but Torian didn't stop. The guy was livid, and I honestly had no idea what he'd do. I'd heard he was powerful, but this was not what I'd expected. I'd assumed magic. I'd imagined him flicking a finger and casting a spell. Right now, he looked like he was ready to order her execution - or carry it out himself.

Desperate to fix the mess I'd just made, I hurried to follow, but they'd already created one hell of a scene. Other students had noticed. People were starting to move closer. Some of them were Harper's friends, the jester girls who always stood beside her. Just as I got close enough to say something, Nevaeh lifted her hand and pushed.

A bright spark flared at the ends of her fingers, but Torian flicked his hand at her almost absentmindedly. A burst of white light went off like the flash on a camera, blinding me for a split second, and I wasn't the only one. A few people groaned, looking away, but it was already too late to prevent the spots before our eyes.

"How *dare* you?" Torian growled, his attention snapping over to her.

In all my life, I'd never seen anger like his. Not even on the day my mother had killed my father. Not even when I'd stood across from the Huntsman. This was the kind of fury that toppled worlds, and Torian wore it too easily. My heart stalled.

"Torian!" Bracken snapped, trying to diffuse the situation.

From the far side, I saw Liam hurrying toward us, which meant Bracken had to be somewhere near him. Scanning the crowd for them, I saw Aspen pushing through the bodies of people. Wilder was with her. On Torian's other side, I saw Keir and Hawke, but they couldn't get through. So many people were watching, oblivious to anything but the downfall of the jesters playing out right before them.

That meant stopping him was up to me.

"Know your place!" Torian yelled, and then he did something.

I reached for him, but the world slowed. Whiteness brightened. Not a light, but all the white already around us. The fat flakes of snow grew in their intensity. The dusting of it on the ground almost glowed. Every speck of white on the clothes of the people around us turned into so much more, and the air shimmered with it. This was the kind of power people kept talking about. The type that couldn't be stopped, and he'd just unleashed it all.

Nevaeh screamed as her body bent back and pale sparkles burst from her chest. Like glitter in the air, it floated for a moment before obeying Torian's command, forming tendrils that swirled back to him.

"Torian!" I screamed, not sure what he was doing, but I could tell it was bad.

People were gasping, stepping back, and horror took over the faces around us. All of them except Harper, who looked even more livid than she had a moment ago.

"Release her," she demanded.

And then she flung her hand out toward me. There was no pause to control her magic. No split second for me to react. Harper simply cast everything she had, and the green glow of it rushed at me faster than I could comprehend. I only had enough time to realize this was going to hurt.

Green slammed into me hard, her uncontrolled magic nothing more than an instinctual act of vengeance, and I was the target of her rage.

Chapter Sixty

Aspen's scream pierced the air as the wave of green slid into my body. My hair flew back and my cap was forced off, but I didn't move at all. It felt like a gust of air, nothing more - except for the surge inside me. For a split second, Aspen's voice was the only one splitting the night, and then everyone else joined in. The cacophony was intense, but I was still standing. For that single instant, I had no idea what was going on, but Harper didn't slow down at all.

"That's what you get!" she yelled at Torian. "You come after mine and I will come after yours!"

Then she threw her hand at him and green colored the air. Torian waved that off, causing the magic to splinter like shattered glass. Another flick of his fingers sent green back. It wasn't a glob or ball of it. The magic was just like a transparent glint to the air, barely even visible.

Then a guy at the side thrust his arm out at Torian. As if that was some kind of signal, all of the jesters attacked. Hawke was immediately at Torian's side, breaking up as much as he could, but the two of them couldn't stop it all. I saw a rainbow shield flash and shatter, proving Keir had just picked his side, and he was standing with the court. Then pale bursts began coming from the other side.

So much magic, the air sizzled with it. There was a scent too, like flowers and fresh snow, getting stronger with each brilliant flare of light. White and green were the most common, so Keir's iridescent and Hawke's flat grey magic stood out. I didn't know how I could help, but as fast as this had started, I knew I had to do something.

Over the chaos, I could hear Liam yelling. At the ring of trees, something was happening. Green flashes of light resolved into people appearing directly between the massive trunks. No, not people. Those were our teachers - all of them. Bracken rushed in, trying to stop the war that had just erupted between the students, but he was only one man. When one of the jester guys slung magic his way, I lost it.

A roar burst from my throat, and I slung both hands towards the ground before charging in. Shadows poured off me like smoke, pooling on the ground, but this was all Harper's fault. She'd started it. She would be the way to end it, and I had skills the others didn't - but the darkness kept growing. More blackness surged up from all the trees around us, but this time it had a voice. It cawed like a murder of crows, because they'd all just taken to the wing.

"Harper!" I screamed.

So the bitch turned and threw another conjuration at me. I braced, but one of Keir's shields exploded before me, taking the hit. From the corner of my eye, I saw him rushing my way, which meant I wasn't alone. I just wanted to stop this girl, to make her never able to attack anyone else again. Verbally, physically, or magically - I didn't care.

And the shadows obeyed.

"Rain!" Liam screamed, trying to get to me in the insanity. "Hold them, Rain. Just hold them, because we're coming!"

When he said that, it made me imagine the jesters all stuck in place. As if my wish were its command, the shadows obeyed. The moment the rolling fog reached their feet, it stuck. One guy tripped, falling face-first into the stuff. Others were screaming, trying to get away from it. The jesters kept fighting.

Green raced toward Aspen and she braced, but a rush of frost froze the spell mid-throw. Beside her, Wilder retaliated with an attack of his own. That was when the crows came, with Jack leading them all.

"Morrigan!" he screamed, diving right into the middle of so much thrown magic.

"Wildlings!" someone else cried out. It sounded like a girl, but I couldn't be sure.

I also couldn't stop. Everyone I looked at was targeted by the darkness. It rolled toward them like a wave, sucking at their legs and freezing them where they stood. It was enough of a distraction that each trapped jester stopped to fight against it instead of the court they'd been aiming for.

Slowly but surely, the odds were evening. Torian and Hawke had one side covered. Aspen and Wilder took the other, flanking the mob of jesters between them. While the faelings flailed and struggled to call magic, the court used it so easily. I'd never imagined anything like it, but I also couldn't slow down to watch. Liam needed me to somehow stop this.

The teachers finally reached us, trying desperately to catch and block spells before anyone was injured, but it didn't work. They couldn't halt the court, not without working together. I saw a pair grab Hawke, gesturing to shield his magic, but Torian simply turned and shoved them off with some invisible force.

"Do not attack us again!" he roared.

"Fuck you, Torian!" Harper called back. Then she turned and looked right at me.

"Morrigan!" Jack yelled again, and the entire flock of crows aimed for her. Harper didn't care. She stormed toward me, slinging both hands like she was throwing something. I heard Keir call out, but he wasn't quite beside me yet. The first one hit my shoulder, feeling warm as it passed into me and that feeling of invincibility grew.

I could do this.

I didn't even need to gesture. Whatever I wanted, the black fog did, so I sent it at her. I sent it at *all* of them. How dare they attack us? How dare they ruin tonight? Why did it always have to be them, thinking they were better than everyone else, and going so far out of their way to make everyone else miserable? I hated them. Most of all, I hated her.

"Hold them, Rain!" Liam begged. "Just hold, not anything else!"

"Shit," Keir gasped as he reached me. "Fuck!" And then he broke off again, aiming for Liam.

Because I was doing just fine. Harper, however, wasn't. She threw another spell, and again it did nothing. The look on her face was sheer panic. Again, then again, she hammered me with her magic. In the distance, I heard Liam yelling something. I heard Bracken. I heard Ms. Rhodes demanding we all stop, but none of it mattered.

"Just die!" Harper bellowed. "I fucking hate you, Rain. You ruined my life. You screwed up everything, so just fucking die already!"

"Shut the fuck up, you stupid piece of shit!" I yelled back.

And the shadows obeyed.

They raced toward her, ensnaring her legs even more, and kept going up. The tendrils of it looked as thick as water but vaporous. The color of them was so dark, it stood out even at night. Glancing to check on my friends, I saw the crows were evening the odds more than I'd expected. They dove at the jesters, flapped at anyone silly enough to get in their way, and completely avoided the court.

"Stop, Rain!" Ms. Rhodes yelled, hurrying toward me. "Stop it all."

But not even she was brave enough to wade into the pool of darkness moving with me as I marched straight toward Harper. The fog surged higher, pinning her arms to her sides, constricting her chest. The bitch had stopped casting, but only because she was bound now, trapped, and I didn't know what this stuff was. It was on my side, though, so I certainly wasn't complaining.

"Rain?" Ms. Rhodes called, worry in her voice. "Just hold them!"

Then someone grabbed my arm and yanked. I spun to find Keir right in front of me. "It's you," he said. "The Wild magic is from you. Stop it, Rain, before it kills someone!"

"I'm not magical!" I reminded him.

He just thrust his hand at the darkness rolling over the ground. "You kinda are, so stop it."

All I could do was shake my head. "How?" I begged.

"Focus," he said, looking right into my eyes. "Imagine what you want, see it as if it's a memory, and believe it will happen. That's control, Rain. Just believe it will *stop* and it will. Just make it hold them and nothing else. Remove the pool. We're scared of it. Hold the ones you have and let all the rest go."

His hands gripped my biceps too tightly. His eyes were dark, but the light of the fires glinted in them. The air smelled cold, like the heart of winter, and the calls of the crows were getting more distant. Pulling in a deep breath, I let my eyes close and imagined all of the jesters rooted in place by the shadows and the rest simply evaporating.

A breath rushed from Keir's lungs, sounding almost relieved. "That's it," he told me. "Just a little more."

And then I heard people start to move. Voices called out for people to go here or there, and all of them sounded like teachers. Opening my eyes, I found Keir right before me, and he was nodding proudly.

"Are you ok?" he asked.

"I'm fucking pissed," I admitted, turning back to find Harper bound with the shadows, her eyes wide in fear. "You stupid," I hissed, heading her way, "arrogant," and Keir followed, "stuck-up, self-centered, pompous little bitch! You tried to kill me? Over this?"

"Rain Brooks!" Ms. Rhodes snapped with a tone intended to stop me.

Oh, I didn't fucking care. I reached Harper and swung as hard as I could. My fist crashed into the side of her face and the shadows vanished one single second too late to allow her to balance. She cried out, falling right onto her ass, and I moved to stand over her.

"How many times have you attacked me?" I demanded. "And for what? Because you think I'm weaker than you, but I'm not. I never have been! I don't give a shit who you are, who you slept with, or what kind of magic you have. You tried to kill me!"

"I don't know why it didn't work," she whimpered, scrambling backwards.

I just followed, getting more pissed off because she acted like that should've been an excuse. "That doesn't make it better!" I screamed. "I never did a damned thing to you. I didn't ask for any of this, but you won't fucking leave me alone." She stopped, so I leaned in a little more. "Lucky for you, I. Am. Not. A. Bully."

Which was when Liam reached me, shoving a hand at my chest to push me back, but his complete attention was on Harper. "Get up," he told her.

"All of you!" Ms. Rhodes yelled, her voice carrying in an unnatural way. "And someone get rid of all the crows!"

"That would be Rain le Fae," Torian called out. "They're hers."

"Morrigan!" Jack declared one more time, and I watched all the color fade from the dean's face.

"Impossible," she breathed, turning toward me. "She'd have to go to Faerie for that."

"Or have the wildlings come here," Torian countered. "It's not the where, Ms. Rhodes. It's the what. Rain le Fae is clearly the Morrigan. She called Wild magic."

For a moment, I stood there staring at Ivy Rhodes, and she just stared back. The other teachers were securing the students, including both jesters and the court. The only thing that broke me from my stupor was Jack landing on my shoulder, the cold breeze from his wings enough to make me look away and squint my eyes.

"Jack. Rain. Morrigan!" he announced.

Ms. Rhodes just nodded. "Liam? Get her side of things and bring her to my office. Bracken? Make sure no one is injured. Treat them, if they are."

"Keir!" Bracken called out.

Keir just crossed his arms. "Don't make me choose."

"Check that she's not injured," Bracken told him.

"The rest of you!" Ms. Rhodes called out. "Go home. If you're injured or need help, find a teacher. If you know of someone who attacked another with magic, report it. Those who did? Take them to the office. We will *not* have this at Silver Oaks."

And those words made the pit of my stomach turn cold like I'd just swallowed ice. We were all going to be expelled. Harper's stupid obsession with pure-blood fae boys had just blown up in my face. Desperately, I turned to find Liam, but he was a few steps away, talking to a girl holding her wrist. Instead, Keir stood there.

"We're going to get expelled," I breathed.

"Was it worth it?" he asked.

I shook my head. "Not at all. I just didn't want her to come at Torian. I thought she'd yell, Keir! What if you can't graduate now?"

"Then it was worth it," he told me, leaning in just a bit. "Think about that, Rain. I still can't lie."

"Which part was worth it?" I asked.

His lips curled into a lopsided smile. "I finally figured out why you're so interesting to us. It's your shadow."

Again, I wiggled my head from side to side because that made exactly zero sense. "What?"

Keir gestured wide with one arm, indicating all the darkened land around us. "The darkness that was just here? The rolling shadows? It's yours. It's Wild magic. It marks you as the Morrigan. We thought you were normal, but we were mistaken. You, Rain, are magic."

Chapter Sixty-One

As soon as the insanity was sorted out, Liam led me back to the office. I walked silently beside him, convinced I was about to get in so much shit. I didn't even really know what had happened! One minute I was kissing Torian - which made Liam do a double take when I told him - and then all hell had broken loose. I didn't even know how I got the magic, and Jack was gone again, flying around with the other crows.

But the moment Liam opened the door to the school, a black streak shot through it to land on the other side. "Rain!" Jack croaked.

"Decided to come get expelled with me, Jack?" I asked, holding out my arm for him to come up to my shoulder.

While the bird launched himself up and got comfortable, Liam shook his head. "I'm not going to let them kick you out for defending yourself, Rain."

"I don't even know what happened!" I reminded him.

"Jack!" my crow informed me.

Usually, I could keep up with what he meant, but not this time. Still, no reason to put this off, and at least I wasn't getting kicked out on my own. Liam reached over to rub my free shoulder in support, and it was kinda nice. Even though I knew this was about to blow up, at least he would still be my caseworker - I hoped he would, anyway - and Keir said it was worth it. All of that meant something. I just wasn't sure what.

We walked into the main office to find Ivy Rhodes addressing a room full of students. "Each one of you will have an extra class next semester," she told them. "For eighth period, you will learn the repercussions of poorly-cast conjurations and enchantments, how to fix them, and the damage your actions could've caused. Do you hear me?"

"Yes, ma'am," a few of them breathed. Others just nodded sheepishly.

"Then get out of my office!" she demanded. "Back to your rooms, all of you, and I will have your doors enchanted before the night is over. Be glad I was having a good night." She lifted a finger. "And the fool who makes a joke about that will be going home before dawn."

Then she thrust her arm out towards the door, and the crowd began to move as fast as they could. Liam and I shifted to the side, quickly getting out of their way. Jack squawked, not liking the way I'd jostled him, and then he ducked his head into my hair as if he realized he shouldn't draw any attention.

"Your office," Ms. Rhodes told Liam. "I'll be in there in just a moment."

Liam pushed out a breath, then gestured for me to go first. I headed that way and took the chair before his desk. Liam moved to a padded seat at the side. Then, through the still-open door, I heard Ms. Rhodes' voice come back loud enough for me to understand every word.

"I don't give a damn who your mother is, Harper. You have proven you have no interest in working *with* fae society. We don't owe you a place here."

"What about the donations my family makes?" Harper shrieked.

"Too bad," Ms. Rhodes said. "Rules are rules, and you insist on learning that the hard way. The last time we were in here, I made it clear that if you ever attacked another student, you'd be gone. You did. You're gone."

"Fuck you!" Harper told her. "Maybe you're a pure-blood fae, but my mother was the Queen's handmaid."

"Your mother was no such thing!" Ms. Rhodes told her. "She laid out clothes and dusted the Queen's chambers. She never even saw the Mad Queen up close." There was a long pause. "Out of the kindness of my heart, I will give you the night here, but you had best believe your door will be locked. If you so much as cross into your suitemate's side, I will know. If you try anything else, you will be dealt with like any other threat against this school."

"I'll make you pay for this," Harper snapped.

Ms. Rhodes chuckled. "That's what they all say, child. I've been around long enough that I'm not scared of empty words from little girls high on their own self-importance. Now go to your room. Ms. Hawthorne is waiting to escort you the whole way."

"Fine!" Harper yelled.

There was a lot of banging, and then I saw the girl storm through the office, not even waiting for her escort. Ms. Hawthorne - a teacher I didn't know - seemed to not care too much, though. The woman was clearly fae, and she sauntered along after Harper like she wasn't worried about a single thing.

A moment later, the dean came out of her office and simply walked straight across to Liam's. Once she stepped inside, she let out a sigh and closed the door behind her. Seeing the chair open at Liam's desk, she took it, easing herself down with the grace of a queen.

"What happened out there tonight?" she asked me. "In your own words. I've already heard a few dozen versions, but I'm most interested in yours."

I glanced over to Liam, and he nodded at me. "The whole truth, Rain. You can't change history now, and I assure you we've seen it all."

So I pulled in a breath and just started. "It all kinda began when I bumped into Harper. I didn't mean to, but Aspen didn't want me to dance too hard. She's convinced that because I'm human, I'll kill myself trying to keep up with them. The court, I mean. So she shoved me out of line, I bumped into Harper, and then I didn't back down. I walked away - wait." I needed to be honest, and she'd already heard it all, so Harper had likely made me sound horrible. I needed all the details.

"You're fine," Ms. Rhodes assured me.

"I said something to her. Called her a bitch or something. I don't even remember, and then I patted her cheek. It was the nastiest thing I could think to do. But then I left, and we hung out, and I was with Keir. We walked around the fire, and I saw Harper shoving at Torian. Since I knew I was the reason she was in a bad mood - because I'd said some stuff - I felt like I needed to step in and help."

"Ok," she agreed. "But don't you think Torian Hunt can take care of himself? He isn't short on magic, you know."

"It's more that she's a girl, and she was already shoving at him, and he wasn't backing down, but that was it. I mean, what happened when she started hitting? So I kinda pulled the oldest trick in the book. See, Harper doesn't like how the court talks to me, and she wants - wanted - to get back with Torian. So I stepped into him like we were a couple. He kissed me, and then she shoved me, so he got mad and stormed at her. I'm not really sure what happened after that, but she threw something at me. Like, Bracken has been teaching me how to interrupt magic, but there was no moment of focus or planning. She just threw out her hand." I demonstrated the gesture.

"What is that?" Ms. Rhodes asked, pointing at my hand.

She meant the ring. Lifting my hand with the back to her, I let her see. "It's something Jack found in the atrium."

"May I?" she asked.

I nodded and stretched my arm out toward her. "It doesn't come off. I've tried, and Torian said it's an enchantment, but he didn't know for what."

She grabbed my fingers and leaned in, but the moment she traced the pattern in the ring, Jack began to caw at her, leaning in like he was ready to attack. Immediately, Ms. Rhodes lifted her hands and leaned back, making it clear to the bird that she'd stopped.

"Jack," he grumbled. "Rain. Morrigan."

"Evidently so," she agreed. "I just want to know how."

"I want to know *what*," I told her. "I didn't mean to attack anyone with anything, Ms. Rhodes. I honestly thought I was helping."

She patted the air. "Let's start with the ring. It is an enchantment, and the reason Torian couldn't identify it is because it's not one of ours." She tipped her head at Jack. "It's his. The marks on it are crows, which is proof so far as I care. That, Rain, is Wild magic on your finger, and it will not come off. It's the bond between the two of you, and it's how you controlled the Wild magic tonight."

"The black stuff?" I asked, just to make sure I was truly keeping up.

She nodded. "Joan had the same thing. Her ring was a little different, which is why I wanted to look, Jack." She paused to glance at my bird. "But it's close enough. It marks you as the Morrigan."

"What's a morrigan?" I asked.

"*The* Morrigan," she corrected. "It's always a human who enters the fae world. I'm not sure how you came into the power, unless it's because the gates are locked."

Caw!

Ms. Rhodes chuckled. "Which Jack seems to think is the case, I'm guessing. Rain, you are human. Completely human, but that doesn't mean you aren't special. Jack sees something in you, and the wildlings have their own rules. Just like the crowns of Summer and Winter focus the magic of the seasons, that ring focuses the Wild magic. According to what little I know, the Morrigan has no magic of their own, but their power lies in the magic they take in. You are immune to fae magic in many ways. Instead of being hurt by it, you are fueled. The agreement you have with the wildlings allows you to convert our power to theirs and wield it however you desire."

"So I'm magic?" I asked, hoping Keir was right.

"You are so magical, you can't even imagine," she agreed. "The Morrigan is a warrior who fights for balance. She - or he - is a protector of sorts. You can carry iron, are immune to our spells, and fae society considers you to be an equal to the monarchs of the seasons."

"Shit," I breathed.

Her stoic face cracked. "I think that about sums it up, yes."

"But how am I going to learn all of this if I'm expelled?" I asked.

"I will not let her be dismissed without a formal hearing," Liam said.

"Dismissed?" Ms. Rhodes gasped. "No! Oh, not at all. Rain, you stopped what could've been carnage out there. Torian, Aspen, Hawke, and Wilder killed no one. They blocked, subdued, and dispelled the magic thrown at them." Then she sighed. "Not that they're completely innocent, but considering the circumstances, I'm calling it a win."

"Are they being expelled?" I asked.

"No," she assured me. "From what I was told, the jesters attacked them. Yes, I do know the cute little names you all use among yourselves. Torian, however, will be punished for his attack on Nevaeh, but it was not a dangerous one. He showed great restraint, merely defending himself in an over-exuberant manner."

"When he pulled the white from her," I realized.

The dean's eyes narrowed as she looked at me. "Exactly. Also, Bracken has made it clear to me that he wants to train you as a sentinel. He said Keir has agreed to teach you. So, while the court does their own penance for this, I expect you to spend that time training in the gym."

"So I'm staying at Silver Oaks?" I asked, just because I needed her to say it very, very clearly.

"Rain le Fae, this is the only place that *can* train you. Yes, you are staying at Silver Oaks."

"My last name isn't le Fae," I mumbled.

"It is now," she told me. "Morgan le Fae, Joan le Fae, and now Rain le Fae. It is your title, no different than King or Queen." And then Ms. Rhodes bowed her head to me respectfully. "And it's my great honor to see another Morrigan in my lifetime. You don't realize it yet, but you might just be the hero the fae have been waiting for. A human warrior, chosen by wildlings, to stand before the strongest fae magic. You, Rain, are the balance of fae society."

"You belong here," Liam said. "I knew you did. Aspen felt it too. That's why she demanded you..." His voice trailed off as he quickly looked at Ms. Rhodes. "Ivy, I'm going to adopt her. If she's mine, then not even the state can take her from us."

"I don't have the power to alter state records," she told him. "I'm sorry, Liam. I simply can't conjure that much, that far away."

"No, but someone can," he told her. "Someone who owes me a debt, but I won't ask without your permission. I know this puts us into a very grey area..."

"Does she know?" Ms. Rhodes asked.

"She doesn't," Liam said. "Bracken and I already discussed this, and we were going to wait for summer to see if she'd be interested in us as parents, but this? I think we need to protect Rain so she can protect us."

"From what?" I asked. "Don't get me wrong, I like the idea, but..." I just gestured before me in confusion. "What's going on?"

Liam moved closer to squat beside me. "You want to be here, right?"

"More than you can imagine," I told him.

"Bracken and I want to be dads. We've discussed it a few times over the last month, but when you came over on Saturday, he told me he was sure. I have been for a while." He paused and swallowed. "Rain, we want to be your dads. We want to give you the home you deserve, and that means you'll be a part of fae society. One of those many adopted human kids who belongs here. This? It just proves how right we are. If you agree, I can make it happen. It won't be fast, but..." His eyes searched mine. "I want a family. You want a family.

Bracken wants a family. Now that you're the Morrigan, this will let us help you. To protect you! Say yes?"

I was already nodding. "Yes!" I gasped, throwing my arms around him. "Are you sure, Liam?"

"More than you can imagine, Rain," he promised. "No more bouncing. No more getting lost. No more being alone. This is where you belong."

"But don't change my name to Sparks!" I begged.

"Le Fae," he told me. "Lorraine le Fae. It has a damned good ring to it."

Epilogue
KEIR

I didn't get to talk to Rain again after the incident, so I sent her a text. It took a while, but she eventually let me know she wasn't getting expelled. Which made me relax, because if they kicked her out for that, screw this place. Screw my plans to follow in Bracken's footsteps. Screw *all* of this bullshit.

The next morning, an entire line of cars showed up to pick up students. Some of them were clearly going home for the winter holidays. Those kids had a suitcase at most. Then there were the ones with trunks and boxes full of their things. I saw Harper down there, along with two guys my age, one older girl, and a girl I thought had just started here this year.

Standing in the study hall, I wasn't the only one watching - or talking about it. The other guys were shocked that so many people had been expelled. Questions were asked - many mimicked my own thoughts - but there just weren't any answers. I had a feeling I knew where to find those, though.

An hour later, I was heading across the grass and into the gym. The steady clacking of a practice stick on wood proved I'd been right. Like me, Bracken always thought best when his body was in motion.

When I turned the corner and found him standing before the training dummy Rain usually used, I wasn't surprised at all.

"Same idea?" I asked, moving to get a pair of my own sticks.

"I'm going to be a dad," he said, pausing his routine to look back with a smile.

That made me stop in my tracks. "Uh... Do I want to know?"

Bracken laughed and waved me down. "Yes, you actually do. Liam and I have talked for a while about adopting. We never wanted a baby. Our lives just wouldn't make that possible. Not with our work here. He wanted an older child from the foster system, and -"

"Rain," I realized.

Bracken nodded. "Yeah. I just thought you should know."

"So, I suppose I shouldn't tell you about kissing her?" I teased, grabbing my sticks before heading around to the spot beside him.

"She already told me," he promised. "And about Aspen. Well, she told Liam, but I was there." The man looked down at the floor and smiled. "I'm going to be a dad."

"I have a feeling it'll be a while before she calls you that," I pointed out. "But I'm dying to know how much trouble she's in."

"Extra training," Bracken said. "Not because she's in trouble, but because of what she is. I was hoping you'd be willing to help her. The two of you seem to have an understanding, and not just that you want to get her naked."

"Please put her on birth control?" I asked.

The look Bracken gave me made it clear he wasn't amused. "Please don't ever tell me about it," he finally said. "But you have a point."

"And yeah, I'll train her. What happens next year, when she's in 'college?'"

"The bigger change will be once she's legally our daughter," he assured me. "Keir, the rules at this school are on paper, but rarely enforced. That's the only way we can make this place work. Because of the common age range magic shows itself, we needed to get both the tail end of high school and all the way up to early twenties in age. Fae power could show itself at any point in that range."

"Most of us start on the earlier side, though," I countered.

"Most of you who know you're fae," he said. "Plenty of the foster kids have no idea. If they gained access to magic out there in the real world? Our secret would be out. Humans would panic. This whole concept would collapse, and we'd lose the last safe place the fae have left."

"Yeah," I breathed. "But putting the Morrigan in college, Bracken? That's..."

"Our only way to train her," he finished for me. "But it means I'm going to need your help."

"With weapons, yeah," I agreed.

"With all of it," he corrected. "And I'm not talking next year. I'm talking next week, Keir. Harper is gone, but you aren't a fool. You've heard what people say about Aspen and Wilder. You know they're targeted because their magic is cold."

"Winter magic," I agreed. "Yeah, but - "

"And the Morrigan restores balance," he broke in. "Balance, Keir. She went right for them. The most powerful students this school has ever seen, and they were drawn to her the same way the crows were. Like moths to a flame."

"And they accepted her," I told him. "That's a big deal to her. The court fucking accepted her, Bracken, and Rain will stand up for them. As the Morrigan, that's going to be a whole mess."

"Not as much as you think," he assured me. Then the man chuckled. "She might even help, since we're not exactly set up for students who can snap their instructors like twigs."

"Speaking of that," I said, "How did Torian Hunt pull Winter magic out of that girl last night?"

"I can't say," Bracken told me.

"Because you've never heard of it either?" I asked.

He placed his training sticks on the dummy and moved to lean against the railing, facing me. "No. Because I gave my word. So did

Liam, Ivy, and a few others. I know how. I know it wasn't as dangerous as you think, and I'd prefer it if you made sure no one else thinks about it too much."

"What is going on?" I asked, setting my sticks to match his and then turning to face him. "Rain just tossed out Wild magic like she's spent her entire life using it. She's come along really well for a girl with no weapons training. The wildlings listen to her. Her, a human! And now this? Something's going on with Torian?"

"And Aspen," he said, offering nothing else.

"No, that's not good enough," I told him. "If you want me to train her, then you have to give me some idea of what I'm training her *for*. There are too many fucking secrets being kept, and she's not just a student to me, Bracken. I like that girl, and probably a lot more than I should."

"Then watch her back," he said. "Keir, she's *the Morrigan.* When they show up, things are never easy. How long has the Mad Queen locked us away from Faerie? We're stuck here, helpless, trying to survive the Hunt, and by sheer chance this girl is assumed to be a foundling?"

"Not sheer chance," I countered. "It all started because of a crow. Jack. He made sure she stood out. He pushed. He's a prince of the wildlings, possibly born here because they're locked out of Faerie too! She's the queen of the wildlings, right? That's how Morrigans get their power? Then why wouldn't they make sure she ends up where she needs to be?"

"Here," Bracken said, making me pause. "Not another community. Not bumping into some cute faeling guy or girl. Here. Maybe a hundred acres that way is the gate. The Hunt is coming more often."

"She says they're withering," I added.

Bracken just nodded. "Train her for everything, Keir. I want her to have a steel sword, too. I know you won't like it, and I don't fucking care."

"And then?" I asked.

He stepped closer and rested his hand on my shoulder. "Then

you watch her back. You can't block her magic, Keir. She won't need you to block the fae's. What she'll need is a partner who can protect himself, and that's you. Train her to fight with you, not against you."

"What's coming?" I asked, because he seemed a little too emphatic.

"Everything," he breathed. "I don't know how long we have, but..." He paused, searching my face. "That girl is about to be my daughter. I've been teaching teenagers long enough to know exactly what you think about her - "

"Bullshit," I told him. "Because if you think I just want to fuck her, then you don't know me well. She's figuring things out with Aspen, and I want to be her friend first. I want to keep her safe, Bracken. She has so much wonder in her eyes, and she just..."

"Feels fae," he finished for me. "Yeah, I know. She grew up with a wildling looking over her. Don't you get it? Jack didn't *just* find her. He's been there for most of her life! How often has he used his magic to keep her safe, to cause issues in one of her foster homes before she ended up paying for it? That girl has been bounced around more than you can imagine, but she's never been molested or abused. Not by a foster parent or a foster sibling. That's *magic*, Keir."

"Which is why I'm trying so damned hard to be her friend!" I snapped. "You know what Hawke said? She's never afraid. I don't think she knows how to be. That's never been an option she had to choose from. Rain always had to handle it, and she's figured out how. I want to give her the chance to lean on someone."

"You in love with her?" he asked.

I had to lick my lips, keeping my mouth from going dry. "It would be easy. I can't say no, though."

"Won't?" he asked, checking my meaning.

I shook my head. "Can't."

Bracken reached out and slapped my arm. "Treat her well and there will be no problems between us."

"And if she dies?" I asked. "Because if something's coming, that's always possible."

"Then we'll make sure we die first," he said, turning back to get his sticks. "I'm planning to have you teach her next semester."

"And after that?" I asked as I matched him, turning to face my training dummy. "Because she's not going to lose this power, you know. She's also not going to suddenly become straight."

"Trust me, I know." He flashed me a smile. "Like I said, the rules here are little more than glamours. I may have talked to Ivy about her situation with Aspen, too. She said that if Rain's fathers aren't opposed, then she won't see anything. Once she turns eighteen, it won't matter anymore, and her friendship with you has been a nice distraction."

I could feel my lips curling into a smile. "So does this mean you won't cut my balls off if she's in my room after curfew? You know, since it would keep up the distraction?"

"Keep dreaming," he told me. "Although, putting Finley with Aspen could solve *that* problem."

Which made me laugh unexpectedly. "Yeah, there's that." Because Aspen was powerful enough to break the guy's mind if she wanted. "Would almost be worth it to see him try his rapey shit on her."

"Still not worth it," Bracken countered. "I just need you to accept that Torian's not going to like this. None of this. He certainly won't approve of you pushing into his sister's relationship."

I glanced over and our eyes met. "She's Aspen's first."

"But not *only* Aspen's," Bracken said. "Oh, and I'm sure there will be more. She acts fae, after all. I'm just saying that while I'd rather not deal with any weddings, I'm not opposed to you as part of my family, Keir. Just don't fuck it up. Torian's involved now, and I know the two of you are like oil and water."

"We'll make it work," I assured him as I started my warmup routine. "I have a feeling Rain won't give us any other choice."

"No, she won't." Bracken just chuckled and slowly started his own training pattern. "I'm going to be the Morrigan's dad. My daughter is Rain le Fae." Another little laugh slipped out. "That is never going to get old."

"Congratulations, old man," I told him. "You deserve it. You and Liam are going to be great."

"So is Rain." The sticks clacked as he worked. "The kind of great stories are written about. We just have to make sure she can handle it."

"You have my word," I breathed.

The words were lost in the clatter of our workout, but that didn't matter. The rush of power still washed over me. When Bracken's pattern slowed, I knew he'd felt it too. That was my vow. I would do everything in my power to prepare her - or die trying.

But no matter what, she would never be alone again.

Books by A.H. Hadley

An Accidental Fairy Tale (Fantasy): *In Progress*

Mistaken Magic

Pixie Problems

Rebellious Royals

Harrowing Hunt

Wild Whimsy

Crows & Crowns

Rise of the Iliri (Epic Science-Fantasy): *Completed Series*

BloodLust

Instinctual

Defiance

Inseparable

Tenacity

Resilience

Dissent

Upheaval

Havoc

Risen

Hope

The Eidolon Chronicles (Paranormal): *In Progress*

Not A Vampire

Not A Ghost

Not A Succubus

The Wolf of Oberhame (Fantasy): *Completed Series*

When We Were Kings

When We Were Dancing

When We Were Crowned

About the Author

A.H. Hadley is the fantasy persona of the international best selling author Auryn Hadley. Known for rich plots and intricate world building, crossing over from romance to fantasy - and sometimes science fiction - only makes sense.

Biologist by education, horse person by choice, and an author because her muses simply won't shut up, A.H. Hadley merges her eclectic love of science and magic together to create books that will allow you to escape the doldrum of daily life. Currently living in Texas with her husband, four dogs, four cats, and a small herd of huge horses, A.H. Hadley is best known for writing strong women, intelligent men, and stories where the families we find are the ones that matter most.

For a complete list of books and to receive notices for new releases by A.H. Hadley, visit:

Amazon Author Page -
www.amazon.com/author/ahhadley

You can also join the fun on Discord -
https://discord.gg/Auryn-Kitty

Visit our Patreon site -
www.patreon.com/Auryn_Kitty

Facebook readers group -
www.facebook.com/groups/TheLiteraryArmy/

Merchandise is available from -

Etsy Shop (signed books) - The Book Muse -
www.etsy.com/shop/TheBookMuse

Threadless (clothes, etc) - The Book Muse -
https://thebookmuse.threadless.com/

Also visit any of the other sites below:

Books2Read Reading List -
https://books2read.com/rl/ahhadley

- amazon.com/author/ahhadley
- goodreads.com/ahhadley
- patreon.com/Auryn_Kitty
- facebook.com/AHHadley
- bookbub.com/authors/ahhadley